Black Sea Gods

✹ ✹ ✹

The Chronicle of Fu Xi Book I

Brian L. Braden

For Ryan.

Table of Contents

ACKNOWLEDGMENTS

My thanks to Amy Biddle and Katie French, my friends at *Underground Book Reviews*, as well as Kimberly Shursen for all your support from the beginning. Also, thanks to John Colarusso for his book *Nart Sagas From the Caucasus,* which partially inspired this story.

Prologue

"The only way back home is forward." – Aizarg of the Lo

***

Over a thousand lifetimes had passed since her forehead touched the earth. Her knees, which had long ago forgotten how to bend, ached on cold marble. Terror, shame and grief reacquainted themselves with the goddess's ancient spirit.

He emerged from the fountain in the guise of human flesh, but even still, the goddess couldn't behold his radiance without bursting into flame. She heard the water drip off his body and splash onto the glass-like floor. He lorded over her, bearing a terrible judgment.

"Nine have forgotten my name. Their temples are corrupted and their bastard children despoil what is mine. They are lost to me." His voice, stern but without malice, did not echo off the alabaster pillars of the Inner Temple like a mortal voice. "Are you lost to me, too, daughter?"

"No, Father." She gasped, trying to control her terror. "Forgive me!" Trembling, she reached out to touch his feet. He stepped back.

In the village far below they screamed her name, begging the Goddess of Tortoise Mountain to save them. Her beloved people were being slaughtered and devoured where they fell. She could save them with a thought.

"I beg you, let me protect my children!"

"They were my children before they were yours. If you truly loved them, you would have remembered that."

She pulled into a ball and moaned under the crushing truth. "Punish me instead. They are innocent."

"Punishment? Innocence?" He seemed to ponder the words. "You can save them, but only for a few days. That choice is yours. Save Nushen for but a short time and you condemn Fu Xi to share their doom. My heart is hardened, my judgment set."

She sensed her son drawing near.

If I had not sent Fu Xi away, the village would be safe.

The goddess tried to collect herself. "These strange people you ask Fu Xi to save, these Lo, are they more deserving of mercy than my people...of Fu Xi's people?"

"The righteousness of Nushen only thrives in the shadow of Tortoise Mountain."

The weight of her sins came crushing down upon her. "Do not make me choose. Take this burden from me," she moaned. "Everything I did, I did for love!"

"Everything I do, I also do for love." He gently touched her head and kissed her gray hair. She shuddered under the power of his touch. "Love is a tender curse, beloved daughter."

Fresh screams floated up the mountainside as the monsters began to feast on the women and children.

"Choose."

1. Aizarg Of The Lo

What shall I say of Aizarg of the Lo? I can say he was a fisherman, a father, a husband. Shall I say he was a good man? The wellspring of his goodness flowed from his people. No man loved more than Aizarg of the Lo, and in so doing, he earned the terrible favor of Heaven.

During those fateful days, Aizarg's worst nightmares took form. A humble fisherman witnessed the downfall of gods and men and, sustained by love, defied both to save his people.

In this mortal I found all I wanted to be. Shall I say Aizarg was my friend? I will forever call him my brother.

Aizarg of the Lo, you shall not be forgotten.

The Chronicle of Fu Xi

***

Aizarg lay on his warm sleeping mat, reluctant to rise, unable to go back to sleep. His eyes and ears told him all was as it should be, but his heart remained uneasy.

Something is missing, something is gone.

He reached over and caressed Atamoda's hip, savoring the way her curves rose and fell under his hand. He listened to his sons' gentle breathing across the hut. His hut's tranquility comforted him.

All is well. Aizarg pushed the unease from his mind.

Everything is fine, he reassured himself. *Get out of bed or Levidi will begin shouting for you and wake everyone.*

The Sammujad nomads eagerly traded skins and furs for dried fish. Aizarg covered his thatched floor with fox furs, preventing drafts from seeping up into the hut. He wondered if his father's spirit thought him decadent for such luxuries. Aizarg possessed a thankful heart and hoped *Psatina*, the Earth Mother, would see his humility and smile on him.

The Goddess Psatina didn't smile upon the lazy man though, as he summoned the courage to slip out from between the furs, careful not to wake Atamoda. His two boys slept soundly on their mat on the other side of the hut. A brass brazier sat in the center of the round room. Cool, moist air warmed over the smoldering brazier and then drifted up the hole in the center of the roof.

Aizarg grabbed his tunic and sandals, then wrapped enough dried fish for the day's journey into a wide leaf. He looked down at his wife's sleeping form, her round breast emerging from under the furs. Aizarg briefly entertained the idea of ravishing her before the boys woke. Then the thought of Levidi shouting from outside while he made love changed his mind.

Get up! There are fish begging to be caught! Levidi would yell until Aizarg poked his head out the door to shut him up.

Aizarg stooped through the low, skin-covered doorway to meet the day. The late fall sun remained only a promise in the southeast. Aizarg let the pre-dawn air fill his lungs and cool his skin, cleansing the fear from his soul. Fog and darkness covered everything. He couldn't hear water lapping against the stilts or the dock. *Sethagasi*, the sea goddess, slept this morning.

His people, the Lo, considered such mornings sacred, when the sky and the water became one and the sea goddess assured an abundant catch.

Aizarg's home, constructed of branches and logs from the surrounding marshes, was a typical Lo hut. A small wooden platform, wide enough for one person to walk, encircled the hut with an eight foot drop to the water. A ladder extended from the platform to a small dock, just large enough to tie his boat and dry his nets.

The Lo lived in villages dotting the northern shore of the Great Sea, sometimes called the Dark Sea by the savages of the steppe. Ten to fifteen stilted huts, constructed in the shallow waters just off shore, composed each village, or *arun-ki*. How far off shore depended on the old Lo saying: *Farther than the fleetest arrow, deeper than the tallest Scythian.*

Aizarg climbed down the ladder onto the dock.

He loved the familiar, fishy scent where the sea met the shore. His mother said places where worlds met, like the shore, were the most dangerous and sweetest places of all.

The boundaries between worlds are always magical, Aizarg, she once said. *These are the places you know you're alive!*

Perhaps that was why Aizarg enjoyed fishing close to shore the best, where the vibrant odor always filled his nostrils.

"Daddy!" Kol-ok's voice descended from the hut. His long black hair dangled as he hung upside down from the platform above. His face looked fuller as the blood rushed to his head, making his pouting lips more pleading. "Daddy, take me fishing!"

"Not today, little man. If I take you, there will be no room for all the fish I'll catch."

Disappointed but not dissuaded, Kol-ok pressed his father, "I'll sit on top of the fish!"

Aizarg feigned serious consideration of the boy's idea. "Yes...yes, that is a good idea. But who will go swimming with Bat-or today? And who will help his little brother guard the village? You are the son of the *sco-lo-ti*, with that comes great responsibility."

The boy withdrew, sulking, into the hut.

Aizarg smiled, remembering his youth and how badly he wanted to go fishing with his father. If he were just fishing the nearby shoreline, he would take his oldest. Today, however, he also hunted the marsh with Levidi. In the course of the day they would likely discuss things best only heard by men.

Next summer he'd teach Kol-ok how to build a boat, and then the boy's education would begin in earnest.

He will be a man before I know it. A pang of pride and sadness washed over him.

Tomorrow, he convinced himself. *Tomorrow I will take him fishing.*

Aizarg carefully folded his nets into the front of the boat as the horizon lightened to the southeast, ensuring each properly rigged to throw at the first sign of fish feeding near the surface.

Hopping back onto the dock, he reached underneath the hut and loosened several cords. From a storage cubby, he withdrew two long shafts. His light fishing spear, about three cubits in length, had an eyelet at one end for tying a rope, a wide leaf-shaped stone tip mounted at the other. He and Levidi planned to float up the mouths of a few of his favorite streams in search of big sturgeon and carp.

A thick bronze blade tipped the other, much longer and heavier, shaft. Too long to carry in the boat, he lashed his boar spear to the outside of the boat. Fresh pig would be a welcome addition to their stores of dried fish.

After securing the spears, he lifted a long, straight pole off the dock. He dropped it like a peg into a wooden block secured to the bottom of the boat. Next, he grabbed a large square reed mat and several ropes, his sail and rigging. The winds would come with the full sun, until then he'd use a small oar or the mast as a push pole.

The sun just breeched the horizon as he paddled away. His wake moved gracefully outward across the mirrored surface. Soon Levidi's boat pulled alongside him on the fresh water sea, the dawn a bloody smear across misty water.

2. The Black Tide

The Lo only needed two things to survive: fish and reeds. The reeds were the stuff from which they built their lives. It gave them fiber for their huts, boats, mats, clothes, and even subsistence when times were hard. If their villages were attacked, they fled to the vast reed beds to hide and survive.

The Lo believed the goddess Psatina made the world from reeds.

The Chronicle of Fu Xi

***

Aizarg's and Levidi's boats floated next to each other a stone's throw from shore. They faced opposite directions, casting their nets every few minutes. They let the nets settle, and then pulled them up with a drawstring rope. Each time, the nets came up empty. Using their masts as push poles, they moved a few yards up the shore, and then threw their nets again.

Unusually hazy and hot for late fall, sunlight reflected off the flat sea in lazy globs.

A calm sea invited insects to settle on the surface, which brought fish into the shallows. Today the insects were almost unbearable, but fish were nowhere to be found.

Between throws, Aizarg and Levidi quietly talked.

"Ood-i and his wife are arguing again," Levidi said.

"We hear them across the water," Aizarg said. "I don't think it's bad enough yet to send Atamoda to their hut, but we've discussed the possibility. Atamoda knows these things, so I leave it up to her."

"Good," Levidi said.

"Good? 'Good' as in I made a good decision? Or 'good' as in I defer to Atamoda in these matters?"

Levidi smiled. "Yes."

Aizarg huffed and sent his net spinning. Stone weights tied to the edges expanded the net to its full diameter just before it hit the water. Ripples spread across the surface. Aizarg waited patiently for the net to sink. His draw line didn't flinch, a sure sign of an empty net.

"We should fish in deeper water," Levidi commented.

Aizarg turned to Levidi with a grin. "Or shallower water."

Levidi smiled eagerly. "Of course!"

They pulled in their nets and unlashed the fishing spears from the sides of their boats. Aizarg knew this stretch of shore well. A marshland stream emptied into the sea around the next bend. The time for the giant sturgeon to spawn approached and this stream provided a perfect place to find them.

The tall reeds were a wall of lush green along the shore. They drifted closer to the spot where the thick grasses and water blended and became one.

They came within a spear's throw of the grasses, then turned parallel to the shore. Dragonflies and bees buzzed around them. An occasional horsefly landed on an arm or a leg then quickly departed, repelled by a thin layer of animal fat spread across their skins.

Aizarg led the way. He picked up his spear, tied a rope to the eyelet, and secured the other end to the boat's mast block. He gave the boat a big push with the pole, laid it down in the bottom, and coasted, looking for fish.

Levidi did the same.

"Why are Ood-i and his woman fighting?" Aizarg whispered.

"I don't know," Levidi replied. "But my sweet Alaya thinks Ood-i is sneaking into the Sammujad camps for drink and women."

Aizarg grunted. Atamoda told him something similar. It made sense to Aizarg. A distracted man, Ood-i's catches were small and his gear ill-kept. He didn't fish till the sun climbed high and often came home well before sunset.

The Lo were marked with a certain physical grace, a trait acknowledged even by the g'an dwellers. Ood-i didn't reflect those traits. As a boy, he was awkward and often the butt of jokes. This didn't improve as he grew to manhood. While tall like most Lo men, Ood-i was also wider and thicker than his kin. His shaggy beard and deep brow framed a meaty face and fleshy lips. Ood-i kept to himself, a solitary man even by Lo standards. His stutter didn't help matters. His father searched distant arun-ki for a bride, as none of the local girls wanted to be Ood-i's wife.

Aizarg made up his mind. Atamoda would have to pay a visit to Ood-i's hut. Discord in one hut often spread to the whole arun-ki, something a good sco-lo-ti could not abide.

"Alaya believes the source of the strife is Su-gár," Levidi added.

Once again Aizarg nodded. Ood-i and Ula's daughter, Su-gár, should have been married two summers ago. Ood-i approached several men, even some in other arun-ki, looking for a suitor but Ula, her mother, kept her home out of loneliness. A headstrong and stubborn woman like her mother, most acknowledged Su-gár as the most beautiful maiden in the arun-ki. He didn't blame Ood-i for seeking peace elsewhere. One hut is too small for two strong women.

"You know, Aizarg, if our people took more than one wife, like the Sammujad, our lives would be much easier. I'm sure Su-gár would make me an excellent second wife," Levidi said with a straight face.

"Yes, I'm sure you would like that. One woman beating you is not enough, eh?"

"Watch it!" Levidi growled.

Aizarg winked. "Any man who wants more than one wife admits he can't handle the first one. Have you ever wondered why the g'an dwellers are always making war? It's because they find no peace within their own tents; they're full of bickering women."

Levidi paused for a moment. "True...but we can always go fishing when our wives nag too much. They can only go look at their sheep."

"Their sheep look better than their women," Aizarg said.

Their laughter carried across the water.

Aizarg, leader of his people, often took counsel like this; in quiet moments, one man at a time.

A black shape slipped under the oily water. Aizarg squinted, trying to see below the sun's reflection.

Sturgeon!

A big fish, almost as long as the boat, moved parallel and just ahead of Aizarg's boat. Its long snout and armored body were clearly visible below the surface. Refraction and his angle made his throw problematic. He pointed to the fish, then signaled his friend to move to his right.

They approached the sandbar at the mouth of the stream. Aizarg slowly pressed the sturgeon forward as Levidi gave one big push with his pole, then laid it down. Once he skimmed past Aizarg, he'd be in the perfect position to attack the sturgeon's broadside. The fish would be forced to turn right toward open water or be trapped against the sandbar. Either way, Levidi would have a good throw.

Perched in the center of his boat, Levidi gracefully passed Aizarg and brought his arm back, spear at the ready.

The sturgeon continued its lazy swim toward the sand bar, unaware or uncaring of the two boats. Levidi hurled the spear. It sliced the water with barely a splash and completely penetrated the sturgeon's flank. Levidi yanked hard, snagging the fish.

The water erupted in a spray of blood and foam. Flint knife in hand, Aizarg leapt onto the thrashing fish. He grabbed it behind the jaws and plunged his knife into its soft underbelly.

Levidi leapt into the water and kept tension on the rope while Aizarg grappled with the beast, spear still attached. One wrong twist and the spear tip would gut Aizarg.

The fish slowed and then ceased struggling. Aizarg stood in the waist-deep water and hefted the sturgeon with a broad grin.

"You know, friend, you didn't have to jump in after it. My shot was clean."

"Of course," Aizarg winked. "And it would have dragged you until sunset."

With a grunt, Aizarg hoisted the sturgeon into Levidi's boat. The boat settled low under the monster's weight.

"I think we're going to need a bigger boat," Levidi said.

"I'm hungry," Aizarg said.

The men dragged their boats onto the sandbar at the mouth of the stream. They found a shade tree and sat down to their meal.

"The fish was poised to move upstream to lay her eggs. Soon there will be more," Levidi said, stuffing dried fish strips into his mouth. "We should come back in a few days."

Aizarg thought about Levidi's statement for a minute. Something struck him odd about this sturgeon. "It's a female, but no roe came out when I gutted it," he said.

Levidi considered this. "Hmm...true. That's odd. No matter, soon more of the fish will move upstream from the sea."

No sooner had Aizarg taken a bite of the smoked fish cake than he heard a grunt in the brush behind them. Both men looked at each other, quickly rewrapped their food, and ran back to the boats. They unlashed their heavy spears and hurried to the bushes.

They stopped at the edge of the thick foliage and listened to the soft grunts coming from the undergrowth.

"How many do you think?" Aizarg asked excitedly.

"Five, maybe six. At least one drift of sows and sucklings. If we're lucky, there's a boar sniffing around the sows."

Aizarg couldn't believe their luck. First, a sturgeon and now they were closing on a herd of pigs. Both men slipped into the reeds and moved uphill, away from the shore.

As the men vanished into the underbrush, shapes began to emerge from the reed beds and the stream. The fish slid noiselessly just under the surface and slipped past the beached boats. At first there were only a few, but in a matter of minutes dozens, then hundreds, filled the water.

Then there were thousands.

Great sturgeon, panfish, bass, catfish, and minnows swam side by side. Even crawfish scuttled across the sandy bottom under the black mass. The host moved silently under the water like a black tide. Not a tail thrashed the water, not one fin broke the surface. The bizarre school didn't dart or meander. They all moved with purpose in one direction...

...out to sea..

3. Fear

The Lo were not considered adept hunters by their land-dwelling, nomadic neighbors. This assessment was made out of ignorance. While the Lo seldom ventured beyond the coastal forests and marshes, they were excellent hunters in their element.

The Lo rarely left the marshes for the open steppe, and then only to nearby coastal trading camps. To them, the steppe, or g`an, was an alien place, dry and barren with no place to hide. There, they were vulnerable to hostile savages who possessed both horses and bows. Even their word for 'enemy' was a-g`an, or 'of the steppe.' So ingrained was the safety of the Great Sea in their blood, they didn't have a word for "fear." Instead, they used the phrase, 'I cannot smell the sea.'

The Chronicle of Fu Xi

***

Aizarg and Levidi stalked through the thickets, careful not to spook their prey. The terrain gradually sloped up and away from the marshy shore. Reeds gave way to small trees and grasses. Ahead, they heard the soft grunt of pigs.

Aizarg stopped as Levidi came up next to him.

"What's wrong?" Levidi asked.

"The pigs are moving away from the marsh. We're only a few dozen paces from the grasslands. Why is this herd moving there?"

"I don't know," Levidi sniffed the air. "The wind is light, but in our faces. If they're running from predators, they aren't coming from this direction."

"It's not a predator. They're not squealing warnings."

Levidi shrugged. "The wind is favorable, we should follow them."

The small fir and hardwood trees were now interspersed with steppe grasses. As the terrain opened up, they stepped more cautiously. If they stumbled upon a large boar it would take both of them to bring it down. A boar was as dangerous as a lion. Two boars were more dangerous than a pride of lions.

They emerged on the edge of a meadow covered in fescue and feather grass and caught glimpses of the open steppe just beyond the next row of trees. The men hunkered behind a thicket of briars and surveyed the field.

A big sow and half a dozen piglets milled about on the far side of the meadow, slightly beyond spear range.

"We'll have to make two trips to haul the meat back home!" Levidi couldn't contain his excitement.

Aizarg studied the pigs as unease rose in his mind.

"This is wrong," he said.

"Yes," Levidi agreed. "It will be difficult to swing around to the other side of the clearing without the beasts smelling us. If you go left, I'll go right. Drive them to me and I'll spear the big sow!"

"No, Levidi. I meant everything is wrong. Those piglets are too small for grazing. Look at the sow's teats, she should be in the swamp bottoms, suckling her piglets, not on the edge of the steppe where even a fox can steal her young."

"Are they being driven forward by our presence?"

"No. If so, they would try to move left or right and double back into the thickets. Pigs are smart. They're not agitated and the piglets aren't hovering close to their mother."

Levidi nodded at his friend's wisdom. They heard the brush rustle behind them.

They turned and faced a lion only a few paces away. Too late to run, they were trapped and now the prey. Both men crouched, too terrified to raise their spears.

Again, Aizarg sensed something wrong. The lion didn't crouch. Its eyes were unfocused and it panted lazily.

He's not attacking us.

The lion, one of the largest Aizarg had ever seen, strolled with a casual gait past them into the open field.

Moments later, several lionesses emerged from the thickets and trotted past. One brushed up against Aizarg, its short fur warm against his bare skin. He caught a whiff of its feral musk as a dozen or so cubs scurried from the brush chasing their mothers.

The pride sauntered out into the meadow with the pigs, which didn't even acknowledge the predators. Together, the drift and the pride turned and disappeared into the thin undergrowth on the other side of the meadow.

Aizarg slumped onto his bottom, trembling. Levidi knelt on both knees, leaning on his spear. Neither spoke for several minutes.

"What in the goddess's name just happened?" Levidi finally managed to speak.

"I don't know." Aizarg stood and looked around, wondering what might emerge from the thickets next. He scanned the meadow, then reached down and lifted Levidi by the arm.

"Stand up," he said.

Levidi stood and swayed, righting himself against Aizarg. He took deep, cleansing breaths to calm himself. Levidi turned back toward the shore when Aizarg grabbed his arm.

"No, not that way!"

"What do you mean? An evil has taken the beasts! We must consult the patesi-le."

Aizarg couldn't take his eyes off the other end of the meadow.

I am treading into the realm of gods and demons. Every instinct told him to flee, but the urge to see beyond the meadow overwhelmed his fear.

"Go back to the village if you wish. I will follow later." With that, Aizarg pressed into the meadow.

"The boats are this way!" Levidi tried not show his fear. He muttered something under his breath and ran after Aizarg, spear at the ready.

They emerged onto the grassy steppe. No longer shielded by the trees, the warm, dry breeze blew back Aizarg's long red hair. He didn't like the way it felt.

Fresh tracks scored the thick prairie thatch. They formed a wide trail in the black soil, leading over a hill before them.

"Turn around, Aizarg. Let's go back!" Levidi said between clenched teeth. "I no longer smell the sea."

Aizarg ignored him, eyes fixed on the hill. He said a prayer for protection and started to climb.

Levidi trudged up the hill after his friend.

Aizarg knelt at the summit, gazing over a gentle valley. Tears of awe streamed down his face. Levidi dropped his spear and fell to his knees beside him.

The bowl-shaped valley stretched north as far as the eye could see, with a stream cutting through the middle. The terrain sloped gently up away from the stream to the east and crested in low, rolling prairie hills. To the southwest, the stream entered thin forest and marshes.

From ridge to ridge, marsh to horizon, animals blanketed the entire valley so densely the men couldn't see the ground. There were more animals than Aizarg could count, more than he could imagine.

Great clouds of dust rose and drifted south from tens of thousands hooves and paws. Not a howl, bleat, or roar sounded in the valley, only the muted thunder of milling multitudes. Wolves lay down next to goats. Lions napped by wallowing pigs.

In the sky, clouds of birds wheeled and soared, casting dappled shadows over the entire valley. Darting here and there, smaller birds flew the lowest. Above them, the vultures drifted up and down on the currents of air. Above all, raptors kept watch on everything below.

The men didn't recognize all the animals. Some, like the giant monsters near the edge of the valley, were terrifyingly odd. They walked on all fours and had long noses with great horns growing out of their mouths.

The rising din of clicking and rustling suddenly drowned the distant sound of the milling animals. Levidi screamed and jumped up. Aizarg felt something move over his calf and scrambled to his feet. A sea of insects swarmed out from the marshes and flowed around the men through the tall grass toward the valley. The ground came alive as ants, centipedes, beetles and every imaginable creeping creature streamed into the valley.

Levidi danced about, trying vainly to avoid the swarming mass. Stunned, Aizarg stood motionless, letting the insects move over his feet.

A great buzz rose behind them. Both men turned to see a thick cloud of winged insects rise from the trees. The swarm ebbed and flowed like a living wave, blotting out the sun as it passed overhead.

Levidi looked down and saw a viper slither across his toes. He bolted back down the hill and Aizarg immediately followed.

"The world has gone mad!" Levidi screamed as they plunged into the brush.

4. The Tender Curse

It was Lo custom for the wife of the sco-lo-ti to serve as the village patesi-le, *the shaman. The relationship between earthly leader and spiritual leader represented the bond between* Psatina *and* Oeto-sy: *the earth and sky. They joined as one in their daughter* Sethagasi, *the Great Sea, who created the Lo. Man was the son of the Earth Mother, Woman the daughter of the Sky Father. The* li-ge *amulet, two teardrops, one black, one white, opposite and intertwined in a harmonious circle, represented the relationship between sky and earth, woman and man. The li-ge could only be worn by the sco-lo-ti and his patesi-le and symbolized their soul bond. The Lo said, "There is peace when the souls of man and woman flow together like water."*

The Chronicle of Fu Xi

***

Though he didn't want to, duty bound Aizarg to tell Atamoda about the Valley of the Beasts. As patesi-le, she prayed throughout the night on behalf of the village. In their hut, she knelt and chanted before a tiny altar, a rough wooden shelf which held a small brazier and several clay figurines, each representing a Lo god. Custom deemed it taboo to disturb her with earthly concerns while she prayed. Therefore, Alaya cared for their children while Aizarg met with the village men.

As the sun set, Levidi and Aizarg told their tale atop the *köy-lo-hely*, "the sacred meeting place of the people." This large open-air platform, the heart of the arun-ki, could easily accommodate fifty men. Four docks, each with its own ladder, surrounded the platform. A large, hammered bronze brazier stood on a tri-pod in the center of the platform.

The six elders sat closest to the brazier, the blazing light illuminating their deeply concerned faces. Elders were men who lived long enough to see all their sons take wives and were considered blessed. Though they had no formal power, a good sco-lo-ti valued their council. Behind them, the rest of the men sat in the shadows. Aizarg and Levidi finished their account.

"You've heard our tale. I seek your council," Aizarg held his hands out, palms up. "I have no knowledge of such things. As I speak, our patesi-le beseeches the spirits for guidance."

No one spoke until Atta, Levidi's grandfather, stood. The oldest man in the village at nearly fifty summers, his long gray hair held no trace of its original black and only a few teeth remained in his mouth. He still lived in his own hut, put his boat to sea every morning and came back with a respectable catch. Considered a source of good fortune, Atta sired more children than any man in village memory. When his second wife passed on to *heli-dar*, the afterlife, he took a third, who already bore him two healthy boys.

"Sco-lo-ti, I ask to be heard," he said, his voice deep and somber.

"Please." Relieved, Aizarg sat down in deference to the elder. Perhaps Atta, in his long years, had an answer to this mystery.

Atta furrowed his brow, ran his tongue around the inside his mouth, chasing the ghosts of his long lost teeth, and then spoke.

"My family, normally I say what happens on the g'an is not a concern to us."

Nods met his statement.

"However, this time things are different. What happens in the marsh *is* Lo business. What you saw today is magic, and only a god can wield magic this powerful. I am no patesi-le, but if the gods saw fit to drive the animals out of the marshes, it must mean they're offended. We've obviously done something wicked in their eyes." Atta waived his gnarled finger at the village men. "I think we have relied too much on hunting and not enough on fishing!"

Atta pointed an accusing finger at several of the younger men. "In my day, we Lo *fished!* Hunting was only used when absolutely necessary. Now the men of our arun-ki hunt all the time, like a bunch of Scythian horse lovers! I think Sethagasi is jealous. I wouldn't be surprised if she asked Psatina to send the animals away to force her children back to the sea!"

Atta sat to more murmurs and head-nodding, mostly from the elders.

Atta's words irritated Aizarg, who didn't think his generation hunted any more than his father's.

"I wish to speak," a hesitant voice came from the back of the platform.

Aizarg stood and saw Xva, his cousin and youngest man in the village. He completed the manhood ceremony last spring and his young bride expected a baby. As a man, he had a voice at the köy-lo-hely.

"Sco-lo-ti, I ask to be heard," he said.

"Speak." Aizarg did not sit this time.

Xva cleared his throat, paused and nervously looked around at the faces of the older men.

"This afternoon I fished alone in deep waters off the Silt Flats. I sought the white bass. A dark shadow moved under the water. At first I thought it only cloud shadow, but the sky was hazy and clear. It passed under my boat. They were fish, enormous schools of fish of all types, swimming straight out to sea! I have never witnessed such a sight. It moved under me from when the sun was high until it dipped halfway to the west."

Xva stopped, his lower lip trembling. "After it passed, I did not catch another fish."

"Why didn't you speak of this earlier?" Atta stood and challenged him.

"I...I didn't think anyone would believe me, but I heard Aizarg's tale and knew I should speak."

"You sought white bass where the Silt Flats meet the deep, eh?" Aizarg stroked his short, red beard. The white bass migrated to deeper water weeks ago. He suspected Xva didn't want to speak because he had no business in the Silt Flats, where giant swells crashed into the shallows. Aizarg knew Xva wasn't fishing, but instead wave riding with the older village boys.

Aizarg loved wave riding as a boy and hated giving it up when he became a man. As a young man, he, too, snuck out to the Silt Flats. He stopped after his father scolded him, saying men have to put food in their family's bowls and don't have time for such games.

Aizarg wasn't too concerned. He knew Xva was a good man. *I will have a quiet talk with my young cousin at a more appropriate time.*

Ood-i spoke up from the back, "W-When the sun crested noon, I c-c-caught no more f-fish."

"You probably didn't start fishing till the sun crested noon!" Levidi said. The men laughed, lifting some of the pall hanging over the gathering. Ood-i lowered his head and turned red.

Aizarg knew Levidi was probably right, but didn't approve of him publically shaming Ood-i. He hurried to get the attention off of Ood-i.

"Did anyone catch fish after the crest of the sun?" Aizarg asked. It soon became clear no one caught fish after high noon, but only Xva saw the fish migrate to the open sea.

Throughout the night, the men debated the meaning of the day's events. Occasionally, an elder or a younger man asked Aizarg a question about the Valley of the Beasts, but most of the questions centered on Xva's account.

Aizarg felt their fear. The men were concerned how long this would last, or if it would ever end. Without fish or game they would surely die. Each hut had several weeks of dried fish on hand, but hunger would grip the arun-ki within a month. The women could harvest wild grains and berries along the shore, but that would only last until the end of fall.

As Aizarg watched the men discuss the day's events he remembered his father's words...

A good sco-lo-ti speaks little and when he does, he speaks softly but firmly. He leads by example in every facet of his life. A Lo fisherman is a free spirit, he cannot be told what to do. He will die before he becomes a slave, for that is the fate of the a-g'an. He must be led by the spirits and his own inner light. A man's journey is his own, his sco-lo-ti and patesi-le are merely guides.

Aizarg closed his eyes and took a deep breath. *Father, how can I guide them when I am so confused?*

Aizarg raised his hands. "People, nothing we say here is of any consequence until the patesi-le emerges from her prayers. We should return to our huts and enjoy the company of our wives and children. When Oeto-sy rises in the east, perhaps Atamoda will bring us guidance from the gods."

The men voiced their agreement. Atta rose again.

"Sco-lo-ti, I offer one more course of action. I say we call a Council of Boats. Other arun-ki may have experienced the same phenomena, and a neighboring sco-lo-ti may have answers to the day's mysteries. Perhaps one of our fellow clans knows when the fish and animals will return."

Aizarg again stroked his beard and considered Atta's advice.

"Atta, I thank you for your wisdom. You are correct, we need to seek the counsel of our kin to the east and west. I, Sco-lo-ti of the Crane Arun-ki, call a Council of Boats for tomorrow evening. Xva..."

Xva snapped to his feet. "Yes, sco-lo-ti?"

"Gather two torches from each man and pole east until you come to the arun-ki of your uncle, Bla-la-te. Tell him of today's events and request he and his patesi-le attend our Council of Boats. Atta, will you do the same to the west and summon your cousin and his wife? Ask them to send boats to the next arun-ki, but no farther. I do not want to delay the Council waiting for distant clans to reply."

Both men nodded, then turned to leave. They suddenly stopped and backed up as someone climbed the ladder onto the platform.

Atamoda, clothed only in a loin cloth, normal attire for both Lo women and men, emerged into the firelight. She had swum from their hut. Her long black hair matted against her back and over her breasts. Her lovely brown eyes were red. Aizarg knew she'd been crying and struggled to compose herself.

The men rose for the holy woman.

She spoke in measured, formal tones. "Fishermen of the Lo, I, Atamoda, daughter of Kissar and wife of Aizarg, patesi-li of Psatina, seek private council with the sco-lo-ti." Her large brown eyes pleaded to Aizarg, *Please come home!*

They didn't speak during the short jaunt to the hut. She sat in front of his boat, head down as he poled to their dock. Behind them, the men's voices carried clearly across the water, confused about her sudden appearance.

She climbed the ladder to their hut as he tied off the boat. When he entered, she buried her face into his chest and sobbed.

"The gods are silent. They've abandoned us, Aizarg. We are alone!"

Aizarg's heart fell. His beloved Atamoda knew better than to make such an announcement before the men assembled upon the köy-lo-hely. She trembled in his arms, on the edge of complete panic.

"Tell no one until the Council of Boats," he whispered.

Intertwined in the furs, they held each other in the darkness until he finally heard her breathing slow and become regular.

As she slept, Aizarg stared through the roof's smoke hole, watching the stars come and go through the small opening. He thought of his youth, when he didn't have a care, beyond riding the giant waves beyond the Silt Flats.

As a boy, he accompanied his father and uncle on an overnight fishing expedition. There, he heard something he never forgot. Around a fire on the edge of the marshes, his father spoke to his uncle in a moment of confidence when he thought Aizarg asleep.

Around the hearth, the women folk say love and hate are sisters. Bah! Maybe for women! Men know better, especially a sco-lo-ti. Love is like the feeling one gets when away from the sea, when you can't smell it. The Sammujad call it 'fear.' I love my people. I love my family. The thought of losing them, seeing them hurt...(Aizarg heard his father's fist thump hollow on his chest)...that is what makes my heart sink like a stone, that is what makes me fear. I'm supposed to protect them. Love and fear...they are the same. Love is a tender curse.

For the first time, Aizarg understood what his father meant.

5. The Council of Boats

The Council of Boats served as a tribal summit and festival for the Lo Nation, which dwelt along the reed beds of the Great Sea's north shore.

From Aizarg's arun-ki, the reeds continued four days' voyage west. There, tall coastal grasses diminished into flat pebble beaches and the g'an transformed into low forested mountains. Three days voyage east, the gentle reeds suddenly ended in jagged cliffs. Where the reeds ended, so did the Lo world.

The Great Sea was the center of the universe. To leave her was to leave life itself. The farther one traveled from the Great Sea, the farther one drifted from all which was good.

The Chronicle of Fu Xi

***

Both Xva and Atta returned early and went directly to Aizarg's hut. In the night, they encountered torch-bearing messengers from other Lo settlements spreading the word of the fish exodus. News of the Council of Boats and the tale of the Valley of the Beasts rippled across the northern coast like a fire though the reeds. It quickly became understood Aizarg's arun-ki would host the hastily convened Council of Boats.

From the nearest reaches of the Lo universe, seven sco-lo-ti arrived by sunset. Most sco-lo-ti and their patesi-le were accompanied by villagers. Flotillas trailed behind the delegates' boats like ducklings.

The council would convene after sunset. Merriment often preceded a Council of Boats, but not this time. None of the usual laughter floated between the huts. Older children sat listlessly on docks, attuned to the dark mood. However, the crisis didn't prevent delegations from observing strict formality. Custom demanded they call on friends and relations prior to any council business. In accordance with this custom, the hosting sco-lo-ti and his wife didn't receive visitors. Aizarg and Atamoda prepared for the evening's events throughout the somber afternoon.

Aizarg leaned against the hut's entrance, watching little Bat-or play at the end of the dock. The child of four summers slapped the water with a long stick, giggled, and slapped it again.

Kol-ok crouched on the other side of the dock with a net, patiently looking for any fish lurking in the shadows under the log pylons. No fish swam under the dock today, or anywhere along the reeds. Usually watching his boys lightened his heart, but now it filled him with apprehension.

Atamoda doted on Kol-ok because he favored Aizarg down to his grey eyes and even temperament. He would grow tall and slender. Both quiet and contemplative, Kol-ok possessed the necessary traits of a future sco-lo-ti.

Stout little Bat-or possessed wide shoulders and his mother's large soulful eyes, though he had Aizarg's red hair.

"Stop hitting the water, Bat-or!" Kol-ok shouted. "You're scaring the fish!"

A scowl crossed Bat-or's dirty face as he crossed his chubby little forearms. He *harrumphed,* walked across the dock and urinated in the water in front of his brother.

Aizarg stifled a laugh.

"You little...!" Kol-ok pushed his brother into the water then leapt in after him. The boys grappled and splashed until their taunts and screams turned to laughter. Beyond his splashing children, he turned his attention to the fishermen trickling into the arun-ki.

Their boats skimmed across the sparkling water, crisp shadows in the brilliant sunset. He knew their nets were empty by how high they rode in the water.

Panic is only a few days away unless the fish return.

A warm, calloused hand clasped Aizarg's.

"Husband, your council garbs are laid out. The boys will play in the water until sunset," she whispered in his ear. A white marsh flower adorned her hair. "I need you."

I need you, too.

Aizarg pulled her close with one hand and slid the other under her long hair and lightly caressed the small of her back. With a sensuous arc of her neck she closed her eyes, turned and led him to their mat. She pulled him down and, to the distant music of their children's laughter, they momentarily forgot their fears.

Afterwards, they lay in each other's arms listening to the boys splash outside. Atamoda seemed to settle down since last night, but he still sensed her apprehension.

"Levidi thinks you need to talk with Ood-i and Ula," Aizarg said, trying to bring her mind back to life's more ordinary affairs.

"I *was* going to swim to their hut today, but with the Council tonight..." she said, trying to latch on to the topic.

"That is understandable," he said. "Levidi and Alaya believe the strife in Ood-i's hut has something to do with Su-gár still being unmarried," Aizarg pressed.

Atamoda looked up at him and smiled. "So Levidi is a patesi-le now? Has he given you his opinions on midwifing and raising children?"

"Levidi is an expert on all matters, just ask him."

She sighed and laid her head back down on Aizarg's chest. "In this, he may be right. Su-gár *should* be married by now. Perhaps this council will provide Ood-i an opportunity to find her a husband. I'll see if I can convince Ula to let her go."

Aizarg knew that sigh. It meant his wife wasn't telling him something. He opened his mouth to press the issue, but thought better of it. The sco-lo-ti pulled his patesi-le closer and watched the sun set through the hut's opening.

***

Atamoda sensed Aizarg begin to ask her something and was glad he remained silent. She didn't want to talk about Su-gár. She knew it wasn't Ula keeping Su-gár from marriage. Atamoda knew Su-gár had eyes for another man, one already spoken for. She didn't think Levidi knew this, and was certain Aizarg didn't. Men could be deaf to the ways of the heart. Atamoda vowed Su-gár would marry a man from another arun-ki, one far away, before the next full moon.

She ran her hands over her man's chest and listened to their children's laughter.

***

That evening, Atamoda watched Aizarg stand in the center of the ring of light. He raised his hands and the crowd hushed. In the central lagoon, boats tightly encircled the köy-lo-hely. They stretched well past the first few huts, packed close enough for people to easily step from boat to boat without danger of tipping. Each boat bore a torch, creating a sea of flickering light.

"I, Aizarg, sco-lo-ti of the Crane Arun-ki and husband of Atamoda, welcome my family to our Council of Boats," he shouted into the torch-lit darkness. The seven sco-lo-ti and their patesi-le sat cross legged in a circle around the large brazier, with Aizarg and Atamoda nearest to the roaring fire.

All the delegates, including Aizarg and Atamoda, were clad in ceremonial garb.

Aizarg wore long deerskin trousers and a loose shirt woven from silken marsh weed fibers and dyed with red berries. A headband of small, multi-colored shells in the shape of a wading crane declared his clan. Accustomed to wearing only a loin cloth, he found the garb stifling, but the formal attire announced his status as sco-lo-ti.

Atamoda dressed similarly, but her blouse was dyed robin's egg blue, the traditional color of patesi-le. She didn't wear a headband, but both she and Aizarg wore matching li-ge amulets.

Each delegation's garb displayed only slight variations denoting their clan. All wore the li-ge. Like Aizarg and Atamoda, the other sco-lo-ti/patesi-le delegations were spouses...except one.

Ba-lok and his grandmother, Setenay, represented the Minnow Clan. Ba-lok's wife, Kus-ge, watched from the surrounding boats. She couldn't ascend to village shaman until the preceding patesi-le died. Setenay's clear eyes and straight back told the world succession wouldn't happen any time soon.

A shrewd woman, her wisdom and kindness were renowned among all the Lo clans. Some elders called her the oldest person in the world. Old Atta called Setenay "the Grandmother of the Lo," and claimed her ancient when he was a boy. Legend says as a young maiden Setenay possessed stunning beauty. A Scythian chieftain spied her near the marshes and stole her away. So moved by Setenay's wisdom and grace, the horse lord released her. A renowned legend among the Lo, but Setenay never spoke of it.

Although little of Setenay's physical beauty remained, Atamoda marveled at the patesi-le's ageless spirit.

Relief swept over Atamoda when she saw Setenay arrive in Ba-lok's boat, for Ba-lok's beautiful wife was considered neither wise nor kind.

After formal introductions, Atamoda prayed to the gods and threw sacrificial fish into the fire, though she knew they were not listening. The futile act overwhelmed her with feelings of emptiness.

Bowls of spiced fish, meats, and wild grain cakes were placed before the delegates while Aizarg told the tale of the Valley of the Beasts. Gasps and murmurs from the delegates and crowd met his words.

Each sco-lo-ti gave an account of what his people had witnessed. Some spoke of the fish exodus, while others described silent marshes where insects no longer buzzed and chirped. Moans issued from the crowded boats with each new tale and the mood steadily grew more somber. The thin crescent moon climbed high over the waters before all the sco-lo-ti finished.

While the sco-lo-ti talked, Atamoda observed Setenay dwelling in the shadows behind Ba-lok. Then Setenay turned her full attention to Aizarg. Atamoda wondered why her mentor, the beloved woman who taught her the shaman arts, studied her husband so intently.

It frightened her.

A gentle touch on her shoulder brought her back to the business at hand.

"The sco-lo-ti sees with his eyes and touches with his hand," Aizarg said, while helping her stand. "The patesi-le sees with her heart and touches with her spirit. Now I ask our holy woman to speak."

Atamoda rose to lay her grim tidings before the council. Dreading her duty, she opened her mouth to speak.

"Atamoda, sit, dear child." Setenay stepped forward. "Let my old heart say what your young heart fears to speak." Relieved, Atamoda quickly sat down. Setenay leaned toward Atamoda and whispered, "Let me bear this burden." The sadness in the old woman's eyes shocked Atamoda.

Setenay walked around the fire, and then turned to face the council. Her softly weathered face suddenly grew hard.

The flickering fire cast deep shadows, transforming her ancient face into an image of doom.

"I will tell you what these omens mean, for Psatina has revealed her will to me." She lowered her gaze and sighed. "She has revealed her will like a scorned lover's slap across the cheek, a burst of pain and a lifetime of regret and sorrow."

She paused as the fire crackled.

"Sethagasi has called the creatures of the deep back to her womb. Psatina has summoned the animals of the g'an and Oeto-sy has hidden the birds from our sight. The creatures of the world reflect in flesh what the gods have done in spirit. The gods have turned their backs on us!" She shook her head and choked back a sob. "Oh, my family, and it is so much worse! The gods of the Great Sea have fled before the power of another god, a mysterious and silent god." She raised her hand over the crowd and shouted, "He intends to destroy the world!"

Horrified screams filled the lagoon. Several sco-lo-ti and patesi-le fell to their faces. Atamoda put her face in her hands.

Okta, the tall and lean sco-lo-ti of the Carp Arun-ki, challenged her. "Are you certain?"

"Slice off your arm and tell me if you are certain it is gone!" Setenay snapped. Setenay's pronouncement carried the weight of certainty, sealing the Lo's fate.

Atamoda watched helplessly as the council fell into chaos in a moment too terrible for words.

"No!" A voice rose above the chaos, though no one heard it above the wailing, save Atamoda. She looked up through her tears and saw Aizarg standing apart and tall. His teeth were clenched, his eyes clear and determined. Atamoda sensed that one small word, *no*, held power. It symbolized all the defiance Aizarg could muster against the power of fate.

It will have to do. She stood and wiped away her tears. *If he stands tall, so must I.* She moved behind him and touched his hand. Her presence seemed to give him strength.

"No!" he shouted louder. The word gathered strength. Several delegates stopped moaning and looked at him.

"NO!" he screamed at the top of his voice. The crowd's wailing fell to whimpering. "No! I do not accept this!"

Kus-ge called out from the crowd, "You must accept it, for it is Psatina's will!"

Aizarg brushed off Kus-ge's comment as that one word grew in power and gave birth to others.

"No!" Aizarg shouted. "I don't know the will of the Earth Mother. I only know *my* will! As long as there is breath in my lungs, as long as I have a boat under my feet and a good spear and the strength to throw it, *I have hope!* I will not lie down and die." He paused and stepped to the edge of the köy-lo-hely.

"If I have to sail to the very heart of Sethagasi's womb and drag the fish back, *I will!* If I have to walk into the Valley of the Beasts and slay every cursed animal there, I will do so before I see my sons starve! Do you hear me, Lo?"

The sobbing and crying tapered off as Aizarg finally had their full attention.

"Setenay." He gently placed his hands on her thin shoulders and asked, "Why has Psatina turned her back on us? How have we offended her and what must we do to turn away her terrible hand?"

Setenay shook her head. "I don't know, Aizarg, she is silent now, as silent and empty as the Great Sea and marshes. She gives no omens, no signs. Her heart is barren to me. I only know the end will come soon, though its form is unknown."

Aizarg walked around the circle, staring hard at each clan leader.

"Who among us committed so great a trespass as to deserve this? It was not my arun-ki! Ba-lok...was it your people? Okta...was it yours?

The sco-lo-ti responded together and loudly, *"No!"*

"If we are innocent, then why do we suffer? Do we deserve to watch our wives and children perish in agony?"

Another thunderous chorus rose from the crowd, giving more power to the word. *"No!"*

The council grew quiet. All eyes fell upon Aizarg.

"I do not know the spirit world, but I know the world of flesh and blood. We share this world with the people of the g'an." He pointed off into the darkness, to the shore and the steppe. "This crime against the gods may not be ours! If so, Psatina may want us, her blessed children, to put it right!"

He might be right, Atamoda thought.

Aizarg turned to Setenay. "Old mother, there *must* be a way."

The shaman smiled and caressed Aizarg's cheek, then turned away and addressed the council. "Aizarg speaks wisdom. This crime against the gods, whatever it may be, may not be ours. If the truth lies across the g'an, it is beyond my sight. Unfortunately, to walk the g'an is to die."

"Good mother, to do *nothing* is to die. I will walk the g'an. I only need to know where to go," Aizarg responded.

Okta rose to speak. "There are many reasons my clan does not touch the soil and chooses to remain in the womb of our Great Mother. My ancestors not only say 'to walk the g'an is to die,' but to walk the g'an *is to wage war!* Scythian horsemen attack all they see. Even the Sammujad will frown on a Lo party penetrating their grasslands. Your boar spears are no good beyond the reeds. The a-g'an will cut us down less than a day's walk north."

Ba-lok spoke, "And where will we go to inquire about this supposed crime against the gods? Who will we ask? What will we trade for information? We can spare no fish for barter. My arun-ki has only a month's supply of dried fish before our children's bellies growl."

Murmurs of agreement rippled across the water. No one wanted to trade away food.

Ba-lok continued, "There is no wisdom on the g'an. They are savages, no better than the animals gathered in the north! My people know this better than any of the Lo. We trade with Virag and his filthy Sammujad degenerates almost every day. To seek their council is to court fools. I say we stay upon the water, pray for forgiveness and forget Aizarg's foolishness."

Aizarg approached Ba-lok. "Foolishness? *Foolishness?* It is foolish to do nothing!"

Angry voices erupted behind torches.

"SILENCE!" Setenay's high pitched voice pierced the darkness. "My grandson is correct, action without purpose is foolishness," she said. "But Aizarg is also correct, prayer to a goddess who refuses to listen is futile."

Setenay glanced over to Aizarg again. Once again, Atamoda saw the same look in her eyes.

Why is she looking at my husband like that? Atamoda didn't like it. Setenay caught her gaze and Atamoda bowed her head.

"Aizarg, while not a woman, your insights into the spirit world are correct," Setenay continued. "I am not a man, but I ask you to respect my insights into the world of flesh and blood. A fisherman cannot blindly throw a spear into the water and hope he hits a fish. He needs a target, a shape below the murky surface. Am I right?"

The men grunted approvingly.

"Good, then perhaps I have a target for Aizarg's spear," Setenay's eyes narrowed. She pointed across the darkness to the northeast. "We must consult the *Narim*."

Atamoda hadn't heard that word since childhood. Her stomach tightened as she began to grasp the weight of Setenay's words.

"Good mother, please explain. I don't understand," Aizarg asked.

She walked to her place next to Ba-lok and patted him on the hand. "Grandson, it is your place to talk of such things."

Atamoda could tell Setenay knew better than let her shadow fall too far across the authority of her young sco-lo-ti. Only in his nineteenth summer, his father passed during the winter and he needed to make his own name among the Lo nation.

I do not fully trust him, but as long as his grandmother serves as patesi-le, his arun-ki will be well served.

He stiffly kissed her cheek. "Yes, beloved grandmother."

"My family!" Ba-lok began. "Under my father's leadership, a northern tribe called the *Hur-po*, the Men of the Yellow Metal, began trading with us. Like the Sammujad, they established an outpost not far from our shore camp."

Atamoda had never heard of the *Hur-po*, nor seen this 'yellow metal,' but Aizarg often traded with the Sammujad near their clan's shore camp. Perhaps they knew of them. Trading with the steppe dwellers, no matter how distasteful, was necessary.

Ba-lok continued, "Neither Sammujad nor Scythian, the Hur-po greatly desire our reed baskets and sacks for which they generously trade furs and bronze. They say they dwell on the eastern edge of g'an, where the dry grass meets the Adyghe Mountains."

"That's the edge of the world!" a voice called from behind the torches.

"Yes," Ba-lok said. "It is a place no Lo has ever seen. The Hur-po trade for baskets and sacks, then disappear across the g'an, only to return by the next full moon."

"They don't trade for fish?" Aizarg asked.

"Very seldom," Ba-lok reiterated. "They tell us they exchange the baskets and sacks for the yellow metal, dug from the earth near their village at the base of the Adyghe Mountains. They covet it and use it to decorate their bodies."

"Who digs this yellow metal from the ground?" Atamoda asked

"The Narim," Setenay interrupted, voice trembling in reverence.

Okta wrinkled his long face in disbelief. "The Narim are children's tales, and stories fathers tell their sons around the braziers when the cold wind howls and the sea breaks against the stilts."

"The Hur-po have seen the Narim for themselves," Setenay said. "The Scythians call the village of the Hur-po *Ghund-Ghund*, The Place of Mazes. It is within sight of where the last of the god-men dwell. There is no deception in the Hur-po's eyes when they speak of the Narim." She walked around the circle, addressing not only the sco-lo-ti, but those beyond the torches.

"The Narim are an ancient and powerful tribe of demi-gods. The Scythians call them the *Narts* and say they were once great heroes who ruled the entire g'an. They made a pact with an ancient god to give them long life. The Hur-po claim the Narim dwelling near their village are the last of their kind.

"They say food springs from the ground at the Narim's very command. They lay waste to entire forests, and then command the full moon to descend from heaven to gather the wood. If there is any hope of appeasing the gods, they will know. We must seek their counsel!"

"This is foolishness," Masok, the oldest of the seven sco-lo-ti, stood and shouted. "This place you speak of is *beyond* the g'an! It is at the edge of the world. If there is an answer to be found, it will be found here, upon the Great Mother's womb!"

Once again the council erupted into chaos.

Unnoticed by the men, Setenay stepped away from the hot center of the köy-lo-hely. In the flickering darkness on the edge of the platform, Setenay held council with each patesi-le, one at a time. She bent down to each and exchanged words. Each woman's eyes grew wide and then glanced at Atamoda. After a few seconds, each nodded, and then Setenay moved on to the next.

What is she doing? Atamoda wondered with dread. Finally, she approached Atamoda. Atamoda looked through the crowd at the other women, but no one met her eyes.

Orange firelight lit one side of Setenay's grizzled face, making her white hair look as red as Aizarg's.

She bears Aizarg's fate. She comes to take him away from me.

Setenay whispered in Atamoda's ear.

Atamoda grew pale and closed her eyes. After a moment, she nodded, and forced back the tears. Setenay's countenance softened and they embraced.

6. Uros

Bow your back only to retrieve your net and bend your knee only to steady your boat, but in the day of the Uros, all free men must bend to the will of the spear. – Lo Proverb.

The Chronicle of Fu Xi

***

Atamoda climbed down one of the ladders. Setenay didn't follow; she returned her attention to the Council. Atamoda walked from boat to boat towards her hut as their occupants held torches high and paid her no attention. Their eyes were riveted on the events taking place on the köy-lo-hely.

She almost reached her hut when she spotted Su-gár's lovely face, transfixed upon the center of the council and Aizarg. She recognized the adoration in Su-gár's eyes. Atamoda knew she should feel anger or at least jealousy. Instead, she felt a disconcerting emptiness.

At the end of the long line of boats, she hopped the remaining distance to her dock. Atamoda climbed the ladder and peeked into the hut. Kol-ok and Bat-or slept peacefully, oblivious to the events outside. She knew if Kol-ok were but a few seasons older, he'd be awake now, trying to grasp what transpired on the köy-lo-hely. She was thankful he was not.

Climbing back down the ladder, Atamoda fetched the object Setenay sent her for. She pulled the knots securing it to the wooden storage rack under the hut's floor where Aizarg stored his fishing and hunting gear. She grasped the object and slid it out. Much heavier than she imagined, Atamoda caressed its surface, in some places rough but in others smooth from repeated use. If she touched this object at any other time, it would be considered taboo. Now, it was holy.

I must be careful carrying it back, lest I fall in and lose it. That would be a terrible omen, indeed! Atamoda prepared to step to the nearest boat, but stopped. She gasped at the spectacle before her.

Across the water, hundreds of torches floated and bobbed, becoming more compressed towards the bright center. They merged into solid light around the köy-lo-hely. There Aizarg stood, in the center of his people, and above the lights. All the eyes of the Lo were upon him. She heard his voice, loud and confident above the fray. She never knew he had such a voice.

Who is this man? Where is my quiet, thoughtful Aizarg? Love, pride, and fear swelled in her heart. That was *her* man. As much as it hurt, she marveled at Setenay's wisdom.

"He will lead them," Setenay had whispered in her ear. "He will save our people."

Atamoda suddenly felt alone. She stood outside the circle of lights, separate and in darkness. A cold wind blew from behind her. She shivered, turned and saw only blackness. The emptiness returned and gripped her heart. She wanted to run back into the hut and embrace her children. She wanted to march across the boats and take her husband from the circle of light and scream...*You can't have him!*

When I carry this across the water, I lose him, probably forever. Atamoda struggled to keep her composure.

He is sco-lo-ti, I am patesi-le. She stepped across to the first boat, carrying the fate of her people.

No one paid attention to her as she made her way back. A few minutes later she set foot upon the köy-lo-hely, her heavy burden safely in her arms.

Heated debate raged around the brazier. No one noticed Setenay helping her up the ladder. Unseen behind the circle of chieftains, Setenay and Atamoda carried the object to Ba-lok. Setenay pulled Ba-lok away from the crowd and whispered into his ear. His eyes grew wide as he beheld the object.

"No!" he protested.

Setenay's eyes narrowed as she pitted her will against her grandson's.

Ba-lok shook his head in disbelief. "You truly believe we must do this?"

"It's the only way. You *will* do this."

Ba-lok regarded the object with awe, not because of what it was, but because of what it meant. Setenay pressed closer to her grandson. "The sco-lo-ti are paralyzed with fear. Look at them! You know my words are truth. All patesi-le are in agreement. It must be done and *you* must do it!"

Something flashed across Ba-lok's face. "Setenay, let it be me!"

Atamoda noticed the lustful look in Ba-lok's eyes as he regarded the object.

"No," Setenay said coldly. "You are not the one. It must be Aizarg. Now, step forward and speak the words I told you to say. Say the words with conviction, speak them like a sco-lo-ti!"

Around them, the bickering continued among the equals, despite Aizarg's best efforts to mediate. Reluctantly, Ba-lok stepped from the shadows and into the inner circle.

"LISTEN TO ME, MY FAMILY!"

The roar slowly died.

Gooseflesh rose on Atamoda's arms. *I hope he speaks the words correctly. So much is resting on him. He will have the honor of Nomination and perhaps that will satisfy his pride.*

"I, Ba-lok, son of Aie-lok, Sco-lo-ti of the Lo, speak these words...

"The a-g'an are in the marshes,
The women weep for the dead!
The shore camp burns,
The Time of the Spear has come!"

"Ba-lok, do not be a fool!" Masok shouted at the young sco-lo-ti, as if he spoke of things beyond his years. "We have not been attacked. This is a Council of Boats, not a Council of War."

"No," Ba-lok countered, obviously feeling the power of his role. "We *are* at war! We are at war with those who offended the gods and brought this curse down upon the world. Okta, you said to walk upon the g'an is to wage war. Well, then *we must wage war.*"

Setenay nodded approvingly from behind her grandson.

The crowd remained quiet. The Lo hadn't been to war in over a generation. In those days, when danger threatened the marshes, they did what Lo always do — melt into the reeds until the danger passed. This, however, was different.

Okta stepped forward. "Ba-lok's words are wise, though I hear his grandmother's voice on his tongue."

Ba-lok flinched.

"However," Okta continued. "This is the right path. I, Okta of the Carp Arun-ki, summon my spears."

One by one, the seven sco-lo-ti summoned their people's war spears, including Aizarg.

No one cheered. The Lo were not a warrior race and a War Council was an act of desperation.

The chieftains looked at one another with grim understanding about what happened next. Each sco-lo-ti leads his own arun-ki in peace, but a War Council requires a war chieftain, the *Uros,* to lead the nation. The sco-lo-ti who initiates the Summoning of Spears must also nominate a patesi-le, which cannot be his own, to choose the Uros.

Okta spoke again, "Ba-lok, who do you nominate for The Choosing?"

Ba-lok didn't hesitate. "I nominate Atamoda of the Crane for The Choosing!"

The crowd parted around a startled Aizarg. Atamoda slowly approached him, his boar spear held out in her trembling hands.

Crafted from heavy gopher wood, a hardwood native to the marshes, Aizarg's boar spear appeared much the same as every other man's hunting spear. Trembling, she bowed on one knee before him and held the spear over her head. Tears in her eyes, she spoke the ceremonial words in a quivering voice.

"Sco-lo-ti, the spears are summoned. I choose you, Aizarg, to lead them. Take the spear and become Uros of the Lo Nation until the Time of the Spear has passed."

Atamoda looked up at her stunned husband. The shock and uncertainty on his face were amplified in the ruddy firelight. She knew he didn't want this.

She bowed her head and stretched out the heavy spear.

She heard Setenay whisper to Aizarg, "This is not yours to choose or deny. You have been called. The time of the sco-lo-ti is past; the time of the Uros is upon you. Take the spear and lead us."

If he takes this, there is no going back. Aizarg could not relinquish the title until death or his patesi-le took the spear from his hand and spoke these words:

The marshes are quiet,
The dead are in the Deep.
The Lo can once again smell the Sea,
The Time of the Spear has past.

She looked from her husband's hesitant eyes and to each of the sco-lo-ti. All but one of them looked relieved this burden passed them by. Ba-lok barely masked his disappointment.

Aizarg and Atamoda looked at each other, seeing one another as husband and wife, not the sco-lo-ti and patesi-le. She wanted to throw the spear into the water and hold him. She wanted everything the way it was. Then she remembered her children sleeping across the water.

Her eyes pleaded as she mouthed, "Take it."

He seized the spear and called out in a strong voice that carried across the waters and high into the starry heavens, "I, Aizarg, Uros of the Lo Nation, shall find the edge of the world! I will see these Narim with my own eyes and set the world to rights!"

The crowd erupted with hope as the spear transformed into a magical symbol of power.

Each sco-lo-ti filed past and grasped the spear. They were now bound to follow his orders to the death. Men from the boats, led by Levidi, gathered to do the same. Soon, the men settled around the fire as the Council of Boats became a Council of War.

No one noticed Setenay's absence on the platform. She knelt in Atamoda's hut, holding the sobbing wife of the Uros.

7. The Reed And The Wood

The nomadic steppe tribes called the Lo many things: the Boatmen, Stilt Dwellers, and Marsh Men. Often, they referred to their southern neighbors as 'The Silent Ones.' Without silence, the Lo say, one cannot hear the gods. This saying goes hand-in-hand with the old Lo blessing: May You Live in Beautiful Solitude.

This means living a life of quiet introspection. The men often fished alone, spending hours or even days in solitary thought. Being alone and being lonely were two different and distinct concepts to the Lo.

When they sought each other's company they did so in small groups with soft voices. It naturally followed the Lo didn't beat drums or dance around fires like their g'an neighbors. In fact, they didn't dance at all. Music, however, saturated the Lo soul and filled their lives like the Great Sea herself.

Their wordless songs were composed of soft melodic humming. Often spontaneous, Lo music laid bare their innermost feelings. Low, soulful male voices blended with the natural chorus of frogs and crickets. Slowly, each man lent his voice and followed the originator's lead, sharing his joy or pain, until the melody spread throughout the entire arun-ki. This male harmonic foundation was called the halah, *or "wood." These deep harmonics pulsed far across the shore, permeating spellbound listeners miles away. Even at its crescendo, the halah never overpowered the surrounding natural sounds, but instead complimented them with an almost supernatural quality.*

The women added their voices like the songs of marsh birds at dawn. This is the ai, *the "reed." Whether one voice or many, the ai soared high above the halah while simultaneously dancing in and out of the male harmony and weaved both parts into a whole. The* ai-halah, *"the reed and the wood," was as much a foundation of Lo life as fishing. When the ai-halah floated upon the air it was said even the gods wept.*

The Chronicle of Fu Xi

***

Ba-lok and Kus-ge's passionate grunts and moans drifted across the lagoon as they coupled in the soft sand.

Ba-lok and Kus-ge emerged from the tall grass, away from the sleeping forms of their people huddled around smoking fires in the morning mist. Most of the delegations slept in the shore camp. They beached their boats and rafts on sandbars and sandy enclaves among the reeds.

Ba-lok and Kus-ge slipped into the still water and washed away the sand and sex from their bodies. She splashed water across his back where fingernails had dug bloody marks into his flesh.

He surveyed the pale image of Aizarg's arun-ki across the water. The fog surrounded it like a funeral blanket. He couldn't tell where the mist ended and the water began.

"It looks like our home," he whispered to no one but himself. His mind still dwelt on the events of the council. Kus-ge embraced him from behind.

"It should have been you," she whispered in his ear. "Your grandmother betrayed us."

"Hush, woman," he said without conviction.

"It's the truth," she pressed her body against his. "Atamoda is under her control and would have gladly chosen whomever the old witch instructed."

"I am his second. It is a great honor," he rebuked her without spirit.

"Yes," she rubbed his chest from behind and pressed her body harder against his. "And the second becomes the Uros should something unfortunate befall the first," she whispered.

Ba-lok said nothing.

It's too quiet. Neither crickets nor frogs sang in the marsh. Ba-lok shuddered at the thought of Aizarg and Levidi's tale of the Valley of the Beasts.

***

A lone figure stood among the sleeping forms in the shore camp and watched the embracing figures. Setenay's eyes narrowed, thinking of the plots Kus-ge might be hatching against her.

Kus-ge hailed from the Lost Arun-ki, the farthest Lo settlement to the east. Their marriage was arranged by Ba-lok's father over her objections. Shortly after Ba-lok returned with his new bride, her people mysteriously vanished, each hut burnt to the water line. No one knew why, but Setenay had her suspicions.

Kus-ge's people, the Gar Clan, spent too much time on land cavorting with the g'an dwellers. They became more of the earth than the water. It was also said they dabbled in mysterious Aryan magical arts. She suspected Kus-ge still prayed to the dark deities when she frequently stole away to the marshes at twilight.

Kus-ge possessed a musky beauty, with a body sweet as honey and almond eyes powerful enough to capture any man. She controlled Ba-lok from their first meeting.

She's poison brought among our people, Setenay thought as she watched Kus-ge embrace her grandson. *No good will come from her.*

Setenay dreaded the thought of Kus-ge becoming patesi-le. She knew her protests would only serve to drive Ba-lok into Kus-ge's arms.

"I am too old to counter the schemes of a ruthless witch," she muttered and turned to gather her things for the journey.

Setenay thought about the events of last night. Once the Council of Boats became a Council of War, decisions came in rapid succession. A scouting party, led by the Uros, would penetrate deep into the g'an seeking the Hur-po and subsequently the Narim.

They all agreed the party must be small enough not to raise alarm among the steppe dwellers, but only be composed of the strongest men, as not to invite attack. Several sco-lo-ti wanted to delay the expedition until they could fetch their strongest men, but Setenay vehemently disagreed.

"Time is short," she warned. "This I know, though I cannot say how. Our time is measured in days, not weeks."

Seven were chosen for the quest.

The party would assemble shortly after dawn at the shore camp. From there they would sail a day east to Ba-lok's arun-ki, then strike out over land along the trading paths and away from the marshes.

Okta, leader of the Carp Clan, represented his people. Slightly older than Aizarg, he had a reputation for even temperament and intelligence. He wouldn't allow any of his clan to accompany the quest. "I swore our peoples' spears, therefore I will endure the profanity of walking on solid ground," he told his delegation.

Ghalen, the handsome younger brother of Masok, represented the Turtle Clan. The tallest and strongest man present at the Council, no better spear arm was known among the Lo.

Setenay insisted she would accompany them as the *Isp*. Every Uros required a powerful patesi-le, or Isp. The War Council selected the Uros, but the role of Isp fell to the oldest and wisest patesi-le. If anyone had doubts Setenay could survive the journey, they held their tongue. She addressed their unspoken concerns.

"If the g'an is where I am to die, *so be it!* I possess more knowledge of Narim lore than anyone in the Lo nation. I also know the Scythians. Not to take me is foolishness."

Aizarg smiled as he put his arm around her. "If I have to carry you there and back, I will." She knew he had deep concerns about her ability to weather the trek, but she convinced him her wisdom and knowledge would prove advantageous.

Her grandson Ba-lok would serve as Aizarg's second, but Aizarg insisted Levidi be included.

***

Alaya lay naked on top of the furs, watching Levidi dart around the hut like a boy preparing for his first fishing trip. She carefully prepared his things late last night — bundles of dried fish, skins and his heavy garments. Still, he checked and rechecked everything.

He's forgotten I'm even here. His mind is somewhere else, maybe at the edge of the world.

Barely a woman, but with well-honed feminine instincts, Alaya understood her man. She felt his fear. The experience in the Valley of the Beasts shook him, though he wouldn't admit it. His friendship for Aizarg and honor overpowered any fears he harbored. No matter how badly she wanted him to stay, he'd be impossible to live with if he didn't go.

Levidi made repeated trips in and out of the hut, taking his things to the boat. When he returned, Alaya stood, clothed in her tunic.

"My spears are lashed and the bundles are loaded. I must go to the shore camp now," he said.

"You need to eat." She held out his breakfast, dried fish mixed with wild rice wrapped in a broad leaf.

"I'm not hungry, but I'll take it with me," he said.

"So be it, eat it later." She handed him the wrap.

Levidi absently kissed her cheek and turned to go. She grabbed his arm and pulled him back. She tried not to get angry. She wanted her husband's undivided attention.

"Kiss me!" she said. A broad, boyish grin and twinkling eyes replaced the brooding dark man who shared her hut and mat for the past two days.

There's my Levidi. Her heart almost broke as she fought back the tears.

"Do not be afraid, my little wren," he said as he pulled her close. "I'll be back soon enough, and with me will come the gods' favor." He touched her belly. "Everything will be as it was and as it should be."

They shared a long, deep kiss and then he slipped away. She didn't follow him out onto the platform.

Alaya knelt down and touched her belly where his hand caressed her. She'd been his bride for two years, but Atamoda's herbal tonics and Levidi's abundant libido were not enough to give them a child. Her mind told her if the gods were truly bent on destroying the Lo, maybe her barren womb was a blessing.

Her heart told her otherwise. She feared not having a child to remember him by, of their home growing cold as his memory died.

Alaya curled up on the cold mat and sobbed. She didn't want solitude; she wanted her husband.

As Levidi's boat slipped toward shore, Aizarg's fully loaded boat remained tied to his dock.

***

Aizarg woke after only a few hours of sleep to the smell of cooking food. Kol-ok nestled against his side and Bat-or lay sprawled across his chest. Careful not to wake them, he caressed each boy's cheek and softly ran his fingers through their hair. He heard Atamoda cooking over the brazier.

He wanted this moment to last forever. In the morning stillness, Aizarg said a prayer.

Psatina, if you've found my thoughts and actions in any way pleasing and deserving reward, then I ask only one thing. Let the afterlife be just like this moment, for this is all a man could hope for.

He glanced over at the curtain at the door. The sky lightened as daybreak, and his fate, approached. He closed his eyes, inhaled deeply, then gently moved Bat-or off his chest and placed him on the mat. Bat-or snuggled up next to his big brother. Aizarg covered both of them with a fur.

"Come, husband, sit next to me and eat." They both sat cross-legged near the fire in silence. He slowly chewed a simple meal of wild grain porridge and berries, his favorite.

Atamoda hadn't slept last night. She spent the early morning hours after the council preparing his gear and supplies for the journey and placing them in his boat. His boar spear, the new symbol of his power as Uros, leaned against the wall.

"Thank you, wife," he said as he finished his meal.

"Your heavy garments are over there, ready for you to wear."

He stood and changed into his winter clothes. Like the rest of the men in the expedition, he wore his heavy clothes, made to keep the wind off his skin when fishing the rough winter sea. The garments would be too warm for the early fall, but made them look more like g'an dwellers, at least from a distance.

"Wife, did you pack the extra rations of fish?"

"Yes, husband."

"Don't let the boys swim under the hut. I haven't cleared out the brush pile which drifted in from the last wind storm."

"Yes, husband."

"Kol-ok can use the raft by himself." Aizarg shook his head, unsure if it was a wise decision. "He's old enough, I suppose. He can take the refuse and dump it beyond the arun-ki, but he is not allowed to take it to the shore, and he is absolutely not allowed to let Bat-or ride with him."

He looked around, desperately trying to make sure he remembered everything.

She moved closer.

"It's fall, the storms will be coming soon. I should get back before the worst of the season, but if I don't, ensure the raft is tied securely every night..."

"Shush." She pressed her finger against his lips and ran her hand through his thick red hair. "It's all right, husband. You may be Uros, but this is still my hut. I will manage and Kol-ok is big enough to help me. It will be good for him. You need not worry, there are still plenty of men left here to help me if something goes wrong...and it won't."

He relaxed and smiled.

"I love you, wife."

"I love you, husband."

They held each other, neither wanting to let go. Finally, she gently pushed him away.

"Do not wake the children," she said. "They won't understand. I will tell them goodbye for you."

Aizarg grunted softly in agreement. Atamoda then placed something in his hand.

"Take this." It was her li-ge.

"No! You are the patesi-li, this is yours," he protested.

"You must be one and at peace, no matter how far apart we are. Take this and your spirit will be whole until we are together again."

"What about you?" he asked.

"I have your children. They carry a piece of your spirit. Be at peace. Go and save your people."

They embraced and kissed one more time, and then he turned to go.

There stood Kol-ok, trying to keep Aizarg's heavy spear from tipping over.

"I'm ready, father. Let me come with you!"

Aizarg knelt next to his oldest boy.

"Can you lift it?"

Kol-ok tried to heft the spear with both hands, but it fell. Aizarg caught it effortlessly with one hand before it slammed into the brazier.

"If you can't lift the spear, you can't come with me."

Kol-ok looked down, disappointed. "Are you going hunting?"

"Yes, I guess so. I'll be back in a few days."

Large tears welled at the edges of Kol-ok's eyes. "Gun-ar says all the fish are gone. Gun-ar says bad things are going to happen. Are they, Daddy?"

Gun-ar is like her mother. Aizarg tried not to get angry. *She talks too much about things she doesn't understand.*

Aizarg held his son's shoulders.

He's growing so much every day.

"The fish will come back and so will I. Watch over your mother and brother while I'm gone."

Kol-ok didn't look up as tears slid down his cheeks. "I don't want you to go," he whispered. The desperation in Kol-ok's eyes tore into Aizarg's soul.

He pulled Kol-ok close and picked him up. Aizarg had prepared for this moment all night, summoning all his strength and composure. Now, however, he found himself on the edge of tears. Atamoda moved to embrace them when they heard a scream outside.

Aizarg and Atamoda looked at each other and instantly knew where the scream came from.

"Ood-i's hut," they said together.

*   *   *

Ood-i absolutely refused to be omitted from the party. At the War Council he insisted he held the key to the expedition's success, though he wouldn't elaborate why.

"T-trust me, Uros," he said.

Aizarg adamantly refused his inclusion until Setenay mysteriously intervened and, without explanation, insisted Ood-i come along.

For the first time in many months, Ood-i's eyes were clear and his step purposeful. The sun just crested the eastern water, a dull orange ball hanging in the milky fog, when he stooped from under the skins covering his hut's entrance. His boat waited, boar spear tied to its side.

He hefted the heavy bag of dried fish over his wide shoulders as he gently shrugged off his wife's grasping hands.

"You're not taking it!" Ula screamed, trying to drag Ood-i back into the hut. "That's our food! We'll starve!" Ula cried hysterically, rage made more dramatic by her unkept hair.

"I t-told you before, each man must b-b-bring enough to b-barter with! There is enough left for you and Su-gár f-f-for several w-weeks. Now get back into the hut and l-leave me be!" Ood-i stuttered.

"Don't lie to me! You're taking our food to those whores in the trading camps. You'd rather be with them than us, dog!"

"I said get b-back into the hut, woman!" He pushed her back more forcibly and Ula fell to her knees.

"I hate you! I HATE YOU!" she screamed.

People watched the drama unfold from platforms and docks like unwelcome spirits in the morning mist. Ood-i looked around in shame at the staring faces across the water. He saw Aizarg paddling toward his hut with Atamoda riding in the front.

Su-gár knelt next to her mother and held her. Ula put her head in her daughter's lap and cried. Su-gár gave her father an icy stare. "Please go, Father. I will take care of her."

He knew Su-gár blamed him for everything.

Ood-i looked back at Aizarg and Atamoda. In another minute, they would be at his dock.

"Your m-mother will not listen to me, but maybe you will, daughter. I will say this quickly, for I don't wish Aizarg and Atamoda to hear m-my words. I see the same hatred in your eyes as y-your mother's. I don't know when it happened, b-but I've made one t-too many bad choices and now I am a lost man. I have spent time among the a'g-g-..." he squeezed his eyes shut, trying to force out the words, "...A-g'an. I've drank their wine and b-been with their wa-women."

Su-gár winced and turned away.

"I've b-brought shame to you and your mother. The old p-patesi-le said last night the world may be coming t-to an end. I think your mother's world ended a-a long t-time ago. I know you only stayed to comfort her. You both deserved better.

"If..." he whispered and ran his hands though his long, graying hair. "If in some way I c-can redeem myself, perhaps you will not think so harshly of your foolish old father."

Tears streamed down Su-gár's hot cheeks.

Aizarg docked and Atamoda hopped off the boat and made her way to the ladder. Atamoda didn't look at Ood-i as she knelt down next to Su-gár and Ula.

Aizarg called up to Ood-i, "Are you ready?"

Ood-i climbed down the ladder, gear slung over his shoulder. Without another word, he and Aizarg set off in their boats toward the shore camp.

***

As the fog dispersed and the sun rose higher over the eastern horizon, the party departed. Each man poled his own boat alone except for Ba-lok and Aizarg. Kus-ge rode with Ba-lok, and Setenay sat in the front of Aizarg's boat. Boats from Ba-lok's delegation surrounded the party and would accompany them until they reached their home.

The delegations from the other arun-ki stood on the shore. Later that morning they would depart for their homes, bearing news of the War Council.

Women gathering driftwood and wild grain stopped and waved as they passed. Children ran down the bank until the thick reeds slowed their passage. All of them knew the fate of their people rested with the seven.

Xva stood apart among the reeds, watching the party drift past. Aizarg met his gaze and nodded. He pleaded to go along, but Aizarg refused. Xva was too young and inexperienced. If Aizarg had a choice, Ba-lok would stay behind, too. This journey required experience and wisdom.

A deep undulating male voice carried across the water from the shore camp, quickly followed by another and another.

The voices sounded different to Aizarg, though he couldn't place why. Setenay turned and spoke to him.

"The halah sings alone this morning, without the voices of the marsh," she said grimly.

Yes, that's it. Without the underlying natural sounds, the male harmony sounded disjointed and out of tune. The men's voices were like a man trying to gain a foothold on a steep, muddy bank. It slipped and restarted, unable to find its footing.

It was a lost song for a lost people and Aizarg wished himself deaf rather than listen. Then a voice came from within the party, strong and loud. Aizarg looked back to see Ood-i standing tall in his boat. He poled forward and stared straight ahead with hard, purposeful eyes. His deep voice resonated clearly and without stutter. Aizarg rarely, if ever, heard Ood-i sing.

Aizarg didn't know why Ood-i chose this song to begin the journey of a war party, but felt the mood suddenly change. Aizarg smiled, as did everyone else. Aizarg added his voice, then Levidi, and then the rest of the men in the boats.

Setenay pursed her lips in a wry smile and nodded at this unexpected, but welcome omen.

In a matter of seconds, men from the shore camp and the arun-ki, still within sight behind them, latched on to Ood-i's voice. The familiar song, buoyed by the inner joy and renewal of the human soul, didn't rely on the sounds of nature to give it life and fullness.

It was the traditional Lo birth song.

From behind them, the *ai* began with a single voice. Levidi cocked his ear and smiled over to Aizarg.

That's Alaya. Aizarg smiled back.

Soon, the full chorus carried across the water. The ai-halah followed the party for many miles as they slowly made their way east.

8. Virag The Slaver

The steppe dwellers told a story of a powerful Scythian warrior whose heart was so black he was shunned by his people. In their fear, they overpowered him, took his horse, and cast him out. On foot, with only his long spear, he wandered into the marshes.

Along the shore he heard the haunting ai-halah. Enchanted, he stood immobilized. As tears streamed down his face, his black heart was washed clean by the music. In his rapture, he begged Psatina to make him forever one with the music.

The goddess Psatina's tears fell to the water, churning up the sandy soil around his feet. His toes turned to roots and his long spear became a stalk. To this day he stands as a cattail at the edge of the water, forever listening to the Song of the Lo.

The Chronicle of Fu Xi

***

They reached Ba-lok's shore camp by late afternoon and were surrounded by smiling faces eager for news. Gasps of

58

amazement met Ba-lok's announcement of the Council of War and Aizarg's appointment as Uros.

More supplies, mostly food for barter, were requisitioned as Ba-lok and Aizarg discussed the next stage of the journey. They could not agree whether they should rest for the night or press on to the Sammujad trading outpost beyond the marsh, a three hour walk to the northeast.

Aizarg didn't want the party to face the Sammujad at the trading camp exhausted, especially if Virag was present. The Lo may rule the water and the Scythians may rule the g'an, but Virag the Slaver held an iron fist over the Sammujad trading camps along the shore. They needed a guide to the Adyghe Mountains and he didn't want to negotiate, especially with the likes of Virag, until they were rested. Ba-lok, in what Aizarg thought youthful overconfidence, insisted they should forge ahead without a guide.

Levidi and Ood-i stood behind Aizarg, while the villagers slowly gathered behind Ba-lok. Aizarg quietly tried to reason with him, but Ba-lok, confident in familiar surroundings, didn't back down. His voice became louder and more agitated. Kus-ge emerged from the crowd, slid next to Ba-lok and touched him with a crooked smile on her lips.

Aizarg felt Ba-lok's conviction harden with Kus-ge's touch. Okta and Ghalen looked on with folded arms, obviously wondering how Aizarg would handle his first test of leadership.

Aizarg spoke coldly, "We'll press ahead to the trading camp, but we will secure a guide. Shoulder your bundles, we leave now. The Uros has spoken." He turned to gather his supplies and pull his boat onto shore.

Okta and Ghalen nodded at one another. Setenay didn't look at her grandson as she pushed by him with her bundle to follow Aizarg.

Aizarg whispered to Levidi, "Watch him."

"I understand," Levidi nodded.

Ood-i took the lead, his step quick and purposeful as if he already knew the way. Everyone else fell in behind him.

Aizarg looked back at Okta. The Sco-lo-ti of the Carp hesitated for a moment at the edge of the reeds. He looked back once to the sea, and then plowed ahead into the reeds with determination.

Aizarg knew it took great courage for one of the Carp Clan to walk the shore, let alone penetrate inland.

If he is afraid, he masks it well. Okta's wife, the clan's patesi-le, told him he would have to build a boat before he could depart the land as an act of purification.

In single file, they disappeared into the tall reeds and put the Great Sea behind them.

***

"Marsh men strolling upon the steppe are like fish flopping on the shore. Even a child can walk along and scoop them up." Virag the Slaver smacked his lips and talked around a mouthful of food. "If I give what you seek, it will only get you killed. Run back to the swamps, before a Scythian makes a bowl out of your skull."

Ba-lok lurched forward, ready to leap across the fire at the slaver, but Aizarg clutched his arm and held him fast. Aizarg gritted his teeth.

Ba-lok must control his passion or the Slaver will goad him into doing something rash. He would have preferred Levidi sitting next to him during these negotiations, but protocol and honor dictated he bring his second.

Yurts, round semi-permanent tents covered in animal hides, were erected haphazardly where the lush marsh met the dull brown steppe. Aizarg and Ba-lok negotiated with Virag in the largest yurt.

Virag laughed and spat a piece of gristle into the fire. He squatted before the flames in Sammujad fashion, as if ready to pass excrement. Aizarg thought he smelled like he already had. The entire camp reeked of offal.

Virag fished another piece of roasted horse meat from a wooden bowl. An outcast among the Sammujad, he was exiled to the marshes long ago. There he built a trading empire and set himself apart from the Sammujad. He commanded a small army of loyal warriors who enforced his will and brought him fresh stocks of slaves and trade goods. Many sco-lo-ti traded fish and cloth with Virag for bronze and pottery. He traveled the coast, moving from camp to camp.

Instead of wearing his hair and beard long, he plucked his body clean. He wore a loin cloth in Lo fashion, but kept a curved Scythian dagger tucked in its drawstring. A man without a people, he bought loyalty with flesh and goods. Some called Virag soulless. Aizarg disdained him, but like many sco-lo-ti, did business with Virag out of necessity.

Two Sammujad warriors stood motionless behind Virag. In the flickering shadows their bare chests shimmered with oil, as did their dark hair and long beards. Bronze swords hung loosely from their leather girdles. In their hands rested massive Sammujad spears called *sagar*. Their sagar were crossed low behind Virag, lest they slice open the yurt's roof. The thick, straight shafts were carved from a single piece of dark hardwood and tipped with iron, not bronze. The only known weapon capable of stopping a Scythian horse charge, the sagar's power kept the Sammujad clinging to some semblance of independence at the edges of Scythian territory.

Virag leaned back on a pile of blankets and pillows, belched and scratched himself. His hard eyes rested on the two men. Aizarg remembered the snake crawling over his foot in the Valley of the Beasts. He wanted to conclude his business with Virag as soon as possible.

"Let me try to understand what you two have told me," Virag mused, studying the dirt under his long yellow fingernails as if they held more fascination than these two men. "You want me to provide a guide to take your party to the Adyghe Mountains to find the Hur-po? For this you're willing to pay a handsome price in dried fish, furs, and blankets."

He pursed his lips and nodded as if mentally tallying the Lo offer. "Very handsome. I cannot hide my surprise at this strange turn of events. I've never known of marsh men wandering more than a spear's throw from the water. Well...*a few*." His smile turned dark. "But now they wear my brand on their flesh."

He waved his hand dismissively. "Excuse me, that was rude. Nevertheless, you tell me the world is coming to an end, and our salvation lies with the Hur-po...or these 'Narim' or whatever.

"Friends, the Hur-po are many, many days away. Trust me, they hold no secrets. As for these Narim; tales told by hags around the fire. If it is the gods' will the world must end, then what can mere mortals do to stop it? If I provided you a guide, I would surely lose some of my best customers and a guide to the Scythians. Therefore, there is no real profit in it. I cannot, in good conscience, do so."

He pushed the large wooden bowl full of meat towards the two men. "Enough. Eat and forget. I know you stilt dwellers don't keep slaves, but enjoy some of my stock this night. Enjoy my hospitality this evening. If you are bent on death, you may proceed east in the morning, but without my guide."

Virag's stubborn reluctance to even entertain the idea surprised Aizarg. When it came to Virag, everything was for sale. Aizarg assumed, for the right price, Virag would eagerly provide whatever Aizarg desired. However, Aizarg slowly realized the way to the Adyghe Mountains wasn't for sale and decided further negotiations might prove dangerous. Virag had sliced men open for the slightest offense.

Aizarg told Virag of Setenay's prophesy, but he did not tell the slaver about the Valley of the Beasts and the fish exodus. He didn't know why, but he felt divulging the omens might prove a mistake. He also made it clear to his men before they entered the trading camp that they were not to address him as Uros. The less Virag knew the better.

Aizarg delicately steered the conversation away from Virag's offer of women without offending him. He felt like a man perched precariously on a light boat in heavy seas. Err too far to either side and he would drown.

"Thank you, Virag, your hospitality is renowned." Aizarg nodded and took some meat with his right hand. "I'm sure your stock of women is of the finest quality. However, our business is pressing and we leave before daybreak, so we cannot exhaust ourselves on wine and women. If we cannot secure a guide, perhaps we can trade for bronze and sagar?"

Virag rolled his eyes and laughed scornfully.

"You Lo and your unfathomable custom of bedding only one woman is beyond me! However, business is business. Yes, I have bronze, and only the finest. Before you show me your fish, bring the rest of your men into my yurt. Virag will not be accused of being a poor host. However, your witch will stay outside."

Aizarg never intended for all his men to enter Virag's yurt, but now he didn't have a choice. Several slave women and children filed in with bowls of steaming meat, porridges of wild grains and nuts. Wine skins appeared and were passed around. Aizarg took a token drink then handed it to Ba-lok, who took several generous swigs.

Aizarg shot him a warning glance. He leaned over and whispered to Ba-lok, "A drunk second is no good to the first."

Ba-lok met his eye and took another swig.

Aizarg shook his head and turned his attention to the slaves.

Poor souls.

The serving women were nude, thin creatures with dead eyes. Each bore scars on their backs from Virag's whips, the skin around their necks rubbed raw from his collars. Some of their faces were disfigured from beatings, with twisted noses and toothless mouths. Most were small, dark Sammujad wenches, but a few were obviously Lo. This infuriated him, but there wasn't anything he could do about it. Lo youth were instilled not to wander too far from shore, but some never listened. They were lost to their people forever.

Occasionally, Virag slapped one hard on the thigh or back for being too slow and laughed in wicked glee. In the firelight, he looked like a demon.

A guard fetched the rest of the men into the yurt. Each bowed to their host and settled cross-legged across the fire from Virag.

Aizarg met each man's eyes as they filed in. He knew what they were thinking, as they'd dealt with Virag before. They wanted to conclude these matters and be on their way. Ba-lok, on the other hand, ate heartily. To Aizarg's relief, Levidi sat at his other side. Aizarg quietly informed them of the night's events, but he had to choose his words carefully. He could not appear to be whispering, as that would offend their host.

Ood-i didn't enter the yurt. Okta caught Aizarg's quizzical expression and shrugged his shoulders.

Virag intently studied each of them while tapping his right index finger against his cheek. He remained silent for several minutes.

"Seven...my men reported seven of you. I count three sco-lo-ti of the Lo Nation, two strong spears, and the witch outside. That leaves one unaccounted for. I will be offended if he does not avail himself to my hospitality...," he trailed off.

Anger boiled in Aizarg's chest. He imagined Ood-i enjoying women and wine somewhere in the trading camp. If so, he'd send him home immediately, quest or no quest. He couldn't suffer such a liability on the open steppe.

Virag leaned forward and continued with an astonished expression. "You seek a guide and Sammujad weapons. Aizarg, my mind and my gut do not agree with each other. When this happens, I always trust my gut. Do you know what my gut tells me now?"

"What, friend?" Aizarg said flatly.

"It tells me you are a war party! Or, at the very least, a scouting party. But my mind says this cannot be. The Lo idea of war is hiding in the mud. Yet, here in my yurt three Lo sco-lo-ti ask for guides and heavy spears for an expedition deep into foreign lands. I am truly intrigued."

"You know our intentions, Virag. We only seek the way and means to turn the wrath of the gods."

"Perhaps. Men go to war for many reasons...riches, glory, women. But men like you, Aizarg, only go to war for one reason," Virag grunted, leaned back on the blankets, and took a deep swig of wild berry wine. "Fear."

Virag studied the fire with a distant gaze. "Men only fear if they think they have something to lose. Something they love. *Ahhh*, and men love so much! Even if you take away all he has, a man will fear for his life. Men are only truly free when they no longer live in fear."

Virag's nostrils flared with simmering rage. He motioned to the yurt wall behind Aizarg's party. "Do you see that, Aizarg?"

Aizarg and his men turned and saw a sagar hanging from the wall, a weathered human skull tied to the end. Aizarg looked back at Virag and nodded.

"My father was burned alive in front of my mother and me for supposedly offending the chieftain. My mother was impaled, alive mind you, on the chieftain's sagar while I was forced to watch. As a warning to wandering Scythian raiders, he erected the spear with her still struggling body outside the village and tied me to it. I was only in my sixth summer.

"She struggled for life for two more days. She couldn't scream or moan, but I felt every wiggle of the spear. When she finally died, they dragged her body to the distant marshes and dumped it, spear still attached. They left me for dead next to her, where I stayed until the stink and thirst drove me away."

Aizarg and his men exchanged glances, worried where this tale might be leading. Virag didn't look at his guests, his eyes were focused beyond them.

"Weak and near death, I wandered until I found myself drinking deeply on my belly at the shore of the Great Sea. I don't remember passing out, but I do remember waking up." His eyes lightened and a faint smile touched his face. "There, on the shore, I heard the ai-halah for the first time. I thought it was my mother's spirit calling for vengeance."

Virag's voice trailed off. Aizarg thought he saw a deep sadness in Virag's eyes. For a moment, Aizarg felt pity.

Virag's beady eyes came back into focus and he looked around. A sinister grin crossed his face. "When the music faded, little Virag didn't turn into a cattail," he cackled. "Instead, I returned to my mother and struggled for hours to pull the heavy spear from her stinking corpse. Eventually, I had to break her jaw open with a stone. I returned to the marsh to hunt and fill my belly. I lived. Do not doubt I loved my mother, though she was the last human I can honestly say that about."

Virag's dark mood charged the room with potential danger. Aizarg desperately tried to think of a way to get his men out. Virag leaned forward as if sensing Aizarg's building apprehension. "That skull you see tied to the sagar's tip…" He pointed behind them. "That is the skull of the chieftain who killed my family. He begged for his life before I impaled him with it. He learned too late what I am trying to tell you now — our lives are not truly ours. Love nothing, even your own life. Cut the bonds which bind you and make them your slaves. Once you make peace with this fact and lose your fear of death, life can be enjoyed to the fullest."

He leaned back and shook his finger at Aizarg. "Yes, this is the reason. I smell the stink of fear upon you and your men. Well, not all your men. Your young buck there…" he motioned to Ba-lok. "…is too young and full of piss to be afraid." He sneered and waived a dismissive hand at Ba-lok. "Heed my words. If what you say is true, and all we know is coming to an end, then the will of one man cannot stop it. Let go, Aizarg. Just let go…"

A pall settled over the party like thick smoke. Aizarg didn't know what to say. The slaves moved toward the walls and away from their master's sight.

Virag took a swig of wine. "So where is this seventh man? Why does he offend me by not joining me in my yurt?"

As if on demand, Ood-i emerged though the flap.

Virag's eyes lit up and he leapt up toward Ood-i.

"Ood-i!" The darkness and rage instantly evaporated.

Ood-i held out his arms and embraced Virag. Aizarg and Levidi looked at each other in stunned amazement.

"It's good to see you, old friend!" Virag beamed.

"And you!" Ood-i responded with a large smile. These men apparently had real affection for one another, though Aizarg couldn't fathom why.

"Finally, someone who knows how to enjoy themselves. Come, Ood-i, sit next to me, you old dog!" Virag offered Ood-i his finest blankets and pillows.

Virag the Snake vanished, replaced by Virag the Jolly. He clapped twice and another warrior entered the tent and bent before his master.

"Send in more wine...and the good stuff, not this dog piss. And get these serving hags out of here. I want the beautiful women. Ood-i is here, it's time to celebrate!"

The hulking warrior nodded and hurried off. Levidi shrugged, shook his head at Aizarg, and mouthed, "*I don't know.*"

Already halfway into a wine skin, Ood-i paid no attention to the quest party.

"Ood-i, you sorry old bag of dung, why didn't you come in with your party?"

Ood-i wiped his mouth with the back of his arm and belched, "B-Because I was in the tall grass taking a sh-shit! I am now pluh-pleased to inform you your t-trading camp smells much b-better."

Virag exploded in laughter and slapped Ood-i across the back.

Fresh wine skins appeared and were passed around. Ghalen and Okta couldn't help but smile. Ba-lok guzzled the wine and passed the skin to Levidi, who took a generous swig.

Levidi passed it to Aizarg and said, "If the world is truly going to end, this isn't a bad way to end it, eh?"

Aizarg wasn't pleased. Now Ood-i's presence guaranteed the proceedings would drag on into the night. He took a small sip as Virag watched him out of the corner of his eye.

Aizarg's eyes widened at the unexpected richness of the berry wine. The Lo weren't known for drinking. He'd have to be careful and measure his portions. He didn't want to get drunk and end up at Virag's mercy.

A line of slave women filed into the yurt. They bore wooden trays of meat, fish, and blocks of goat cheese. These weren't the pale shadows who served the men earlier. Instead, these were vibrant women and girls, well fed without marks on their skin. They even had most of their teeth. They wore collars and just enough clothing to fire the imagination.

Two young boys of no more than eight summers entered and sat down in the corner with a reed flute and a drum to add to the merriment. Ba-lok ran his hand over the thigh of a plump black-haired girl. She giggled and cast off his hand as she moved among the men with a tray of meat.

Aizarg tapped Levidi and nodded to Ba-lok, who slowly swayed under the wine's growing influence. Levidi scowled and slowed his drinking. Aizarg also eyed Ghalen and Okta with growing disappointment as their eyes glazed and their smiles dulled.

Then it occurred to Aizarg that Okta didn't know better. He'd never been in a trading camp and had no dealings with the a-g'an. *I wish I could have left him outside, too.*

Aizarg studied the women. He spotted two Scythian women by their long legs, olive skin and graceful curves. They had a fire in their eyes, a fire meant to burn men's soul.

Even their women are dangerous.

He needed to get his men out of the slaver's power, but minute by minute they fell deeper under Virag's spell. As the night wore on, only Aizarg and Levidi remained sober. Aizarg's heart sank and he watched his fellow sco-lo-ti wallow in a pile of flesh and laughter.

Ood-i and Virag bellowed, grasped each other's shoulders and ignored the rest of the party. Aizarg wasn't sure what they were talking about over the noise, but apparently they were old friends. Aizarg knew Ood-i routinely snuck away to partake in the pleasures of the trading camps, but he had no idea he'd built such a close relationship with no less than Virag himself. As sco-lo-ti, Aizarg felt in some way he had failed Ood-i and his family.

Now Ood-i failed him, too.

Ood-i's eyes suddenly grew sober. Aizarg followed his gaze to the yurt's entrance. There stood a small, slender woman holding open the flap. She wore the collar and skimpy rags of a pleasure slave, but somehow stood apart from the other women.

Her gray and piercing eyes were unlike anything Aizarg had ever seen. Her straight brown hair fell well past her buttocks in sharp contrast to her pale, perfect skin.

Ood-i and the gray-eyed girl locked eyes. She lightly stepped over the intertwined bodies rolling on the floor like twisted branches on the shore. Levidi and Aizarg followed her with their eyes, transfixed as she approached Ood-i.

Virag smiled as if privy to an inside joke.

She slid onto Ood-i's lap and wrapped her arm behind his neck. He wrapped his arms around her and they kissed. It wasn't the embrace of lustful passion.

This is love, Aizarg thought

"You are a lucky dog, Ood-i," Virag said. "Two days ago I was offered a generous price for her...two goats and one stone of tin."

Just for a moment, Aizarg saw panic cross Ood-i's face.

"That was a very good p-price," Ood-i commented nonchalantly. "Why d-didn't you accept it?"

"I did," Virag said.

"I don't understand? Then wha-why is she still here?"

"The damn fool's goats ran off before we spit on the deal. Then his sheep ran off, too!" Virag slapped his knee and laughed. "He went chasing his herd off to the east and I haven't seen him since!"

Ood-i played with the woman's hair and fondled her breast. "She is fine stock. I've enjoyed her m-many times. Two goats and one pound of tin? You are a c-cunning merchant, Virag. Let me ask you, a-a g'an d-dweller...how many d-days will two goats feed a man and his family?"

Where is the drunken fool going with this? Aizarg wondered. He didn't like being a spectator to his people's fate. Virag would have to get up to relieve himself soon, maybe then he could get Ood-i and most of his men out of the yurt.

Virag leaned in and stroked his bald head.

"One goat, if properly cut and dried, will feed four warriors for one cycle of the moon. If it feeds a man and his yurt, perhaps a little longer...snot nose brats eat more than you'd think. So, two goats, is about two months."

Ood-i considered this, then continued, "And a stone of t-tin is no good to the smelter without a stone of cu-cu-copper, eh?"

Ba-lok stood up with the plump brunette in hand and stumbled out of the yurt. Aizarg watched them go with growing anger.

This is getting out of control.

Virag's eyes lit up. "Yes, tin needs copper," he responded.

"If she is worth t-two months of food and half an unfinished spear head, then wa-would you sell her to me for two heavy bags of dried fish and a f-finished bronze spear tip?"

"Is a man of the Lo buying a slave?" said a stunned Virag.

"*Ood-i!*" Aizarg whispered harshly. Ood-i wouldn't look at him.

Virag snapped up a hand towards Aizarg.

"This is my business in my yurt, sco-lo-ti! It is between me and this man, you have no right to interfere."

Ood-i smelled her hair and looked up at Virag. "If the world is going to end, I wish to d-die with this woman in my arms."

"She is valuable to me. Goat meat puts fat on the ribs, fish doesn't."

"Smoked fish will not spoil as fast as g-goat meat. My spear tip is ready to be mounted."

"Yes, I'm sure it is!" Aizarg heard Levidi hiss under his breath. "Three bags."

"Two bags and t-two spear tips, I have no more."

Virag studied his friend. Ghalen and Okta managed to pull themselves up from the women and focus on the events unfolding before them, too stunned to react beyond slack jaws.

Ood-i committed sacrilege, an obscenity and affront to the Lo and their gods. *Maybe we deserve our fate.*

Okta and Ghalen suddenly became aware of Ood-i's actions. Okta looked at the woman in his arms and pulled away, ashamed.

"I know you care for this slave, Ood-i," Virag continued. "I know you will give much more for her. However, I will sell her to you for two heavy bags of fish and two spear tips. The pleasure of seeing a Lo man civilize himself is something I cannot put a price on. Also, your sco-lo-ti fumes like a smoldering fire. I've felt the heat of his rage since you stepped inside. Ood-i, my friend, I wouldn't doubt he kills you when you leave my yurt. I find the prospect of what might follow tonight's events...intriguing."

The thought of killing Ood-i occurred to Aizarg, though he was angrier at himself for bringing him.

"Do we have a da-deal or not?" Ood-i pressed.

Virag spit on his right palm and extended it to Ood-i. Ood-i did the same. They clasped hands and it was done.

Ood-i departed and quickly returned with the merchandise and handed it over to Virag.

"That's all the fish he brought," Levidi whispered to Aizarg.

"I know," Aizarg muttered.

Ood-i placed his arm around the woman's waist. She melted into him, eager to be at his side. She seemed relieved.

"Virag, please don't think me rude for wanting to take her away and enjoy her now."

"Of course not, go! I will conclude my business with your...*leader*," Virag chuckled. "Her beauty appears to agree with your stutter."

Then, like the autumn wind, Virag's mood suddenly blew cold. "The rest of you, go as well. My generosity is not unlimited. This feast is over unless you pay for more. Aizarg, if you have further business with me, stay."

Ood-i finally met Aizarg's stare as he left. Aizarg could not find shame in Ood-i's eyes.

Aizarg pondered this for a moment as the yurt emptied of men and slaves. Now he sat cross-legged across the fire from Virag, who now slumped on his pillows. With one finger on his lips he considered Aizarg for what seemed an eternity.

"So, do you still wish to barter for spears?"

"Yes."

"Three bags of fish and four blankets per spear."

"We cannot pay such a price!"

"You are desperate men," he said with speed and conviction. "Desperate men will pay any price. If the world is going to end, as you say, then my price is small."

"Two bags and two blankets."

Virag waived his finger. "No bartering. My price is final. Wander onto the steppe with your boar spears and the Scythians will cut you down. If they see you carrying heavy sager they'll assume you know how to use them and think twice. If you carry less than four sager, they'll see it as weakness. If they press the attack, the sagar might buy you a few minutes of life."

Aizarg mentally tallied the party's supplies. If he paid Virag's price it would take all the goods they brought to barter with and cut deeply into their own stocks of food. They wouldn't have enough food to complete the quest.

He knew Virag was right. Without the sagar they would likely perish on the g'an, especially without a guide.

"Deal. We'll exchange goods at dawn when we can inspect them. Then we can spit over the bargain. If I don't like the quality of the spears, the deal is off. You have the same right regarding the food and blankets, of course."

"Of course." Virag smiled.

Aizarg rose and turned to go.

"You feel betrayed, don't you, Aizarg?"

Aizarg stopped, but didn't turn around.

"Don't be too harsh on him. Desperate men do desperate things, *don't they?*" Virag sank down into his pillows and laughed.

Aizarg stepped out of the yurt and into the soft night air. He took a deep breath, trying to purge the stink of Virag's yurt from his lungs.

***

Aizarg marched through the small trading camp, past dying camp fires and yurts where people slept, tightly wrapped in blankets. His jaw tightened as he spotted his camp fire at the edge of the settlement. Shadows moved around it.

"He's coming," he heard Okta say.

The image of Okta, sco-lo-ti of the Lo, rolling on the dirty yurt floor with a Sammujad whore filled his mind and heart with renewed rage.

He spotted Ood-i sitting next to the fire, the gray-eyed slave kneeling before him. Setenay stood next to him, her hand on his shoulder.

Levidi ran out to meet him. "Listen, Aizarg! You must listen!"

Aizarg pushed him away. Levidi tried to grab Aizarg's arm, but Aizarg shrugged him off. He again tried to get between Aizarg and Ood-i. "Uros, please, it's not what you think..."

Aizarg pushed him into the dirt and kept going. Ood-i tried to stand and say something, but Aizarg tackled him before he could react. In seconds, Aizarg had Ood-i pinned to the ground, punching him. It took all the men to pull him off. The gray-eyed woman leaned over Ood-i's bleeding face, screaming.

Aizarg pulled away from the men, but didn't attack Ood-i again.

Aizarg pointed and shouted, "We haven't taken our first step onto the g'an and you've put all of us in danger! Your recklessness costs us almost all our food. At daybreak, Virag will come and exchange four spears for twelve bags of food and twelve blankets because your...*your stupidity* left me no bargaining room!"

He turned and looked at the men. Ba-lok, bleary-eyed, swayed back and forth in front of the fire. The plump slave girl was nowhere to be seen.

"And you...you *sco-lo-ti!* I am ashamed to call you that word. You rolled in that filth like pigs. It doesn't matter if we find the Hur-po or the Narim. The gods are right to destroy us. We are no better than the a-g'an for all our pretenses."

Setenay touched his arm.

"Are you finished?" she said sternly.

His anger shriveled under her gaze.

"Good. Now perhaps the Uros will listen for a few moments and stop acting like an ass. From what I've heard, there's been more than enough bad behavior this evening. Aizarg, the only one failing this evening is you.

"Don't look like a hurt little boy," she scolded. "What did you think would happen when you took your men into the tent of a slave trader? You are brave and smart, my dear

Aizarg, but every Lo woman knows you don't stroll into a fox den without getting bit. You strolled into a fox den and he bit you. All of you!"

She extended a bony finger to all the men around the fire. They hung their heads low, unable to meet her gaze. She poked Aizarg in the chest.

"Now, either you can learn from this or not. Your rage will only get us killed."

She was right, and that revelation made him angrier still.

"I shouldn't have lost control. It was unbefitting, but..."

"But what?" she eyed him, arms crossed.

"But my men didn't control themselves and it cost us dearly."

"True. Especially this one," she kicked Ba-lok. He fell over and passed out.

"However, from what I gather, some of your men acted admirably. Brilliantly."

Aizarg looked back at Levidi and nodded, proud of his friend. "Yes, true."

Levidi shook his head and pointed back to the fire.

Confused, Aizarg turned back to Setenay. She stared at him quizzically and patted his cheek.

"Aizarg...I'm not talking about Levidi, but I'm sure he performed well in that viper pit. No, I'm talking about Ood-i."

Aizarg took a step back. Maybe she didn't hear the real story of what transpired in Virag's yurt. Maybe Ood-i came back and lied to her.

"He bought a slave!"

The gray-eyed woman wiped Ood-i's bleeding lip with a rag as he looked up at Aizarg. "I am suh-s-sorry muh-my Uros. There was no ta-time to explain." Ood-i grimaced and fought to control his stutter. "Whu-When w-we entered the t-trading camp at dusk, I realized Virag was puh-present when I saw his standard in front of his yurt. Then I saw her. I had to act quh-quickly."

"I don't understand," Aizarg said.

"Child, come here," Setenay summoned the gray-eyed girl to come forward.

Demurely, she approached Aizarg and knelt before him.

Setenay gently lifted her by the arm. "Rise child, it's not our custom. Tell him your name."

She stood and spoke. "I am Sarah of the Hur-po. I know the place you seek and can lead you there."

9. Sarah

"The old Uros once told me that some souls burn so brightly they are like campfires on a dark shore, calling the lost fisherman home."

The Chronicle of Fu Xi

***

While they were in Virag's yurt, Setenay had been busy preparing the camp. She had gathered reeds from the nearby marsh and skillfully bundled them into tightly wound 'logs'. These bundles would burn longer and slower than loose reeds simply thrown on the fire. A Lo woman could easily bundle enough reeds for a night's fire in only a few minutes. Reed fires burned hotter and with less smoke than a driftwood fire. The men's bundles were also arranged with care, each of their mats unrolled to form a circle around the fire.

Setenay and Sarah would sleep outside the circle, away from the fire. Lo custom gave men the closest places to the fire. It was said among Lo women, *Take care of the man who takes care of you, and you will never be lonely or hungry.*

The tired men kissed Setenay on the cheek and thanked her for preparing the camp. Except for Ood-i, they eagerly fell upon their mats, ready to put the night's events behind them.

Ood-i hesitantly approached his Uros. Aizarg shook his head and firmly clasped Ood-i's shoulder. "There is nothing to say, friend. Get some sleep. Tomorrow, we'll talk as friends do. You will speak of those things you've been hiding here," he tapped Ood-i's chest over his heart, "and I will listen. I am sorry I failed you."

Ood-i smiled weakly as an expression of relief washed over his face. "Thank you, sco-sco-..." He couldn't finish and turned to his mat, alone. It wasn't lost on Aizarg that Ood-i tried to call him *sco-lo-ti*, and not *Uros*. The word felt soothing, like a healing balm.

Setenay smiled at the exchange as she covered her intoxicated grandson with a flaxen blanket. She stepped over Levidi and Ghalen to her mat, and then prepared a place for Sarah to sleep next to her.

Sarah moved to help Setenay but Aizarg took her firmly by the arm. "I need to speak with you." He pulled her toward the far edge of the firelight, where they sat down on a log.

The rest of the group paid them no heed and settled in for the night.

"We should be thankful we didn't shame ourselves further this evening," Okta said, his words dripping with regret. His eyes were far away as he stared up at the stars, his hands behind his head. "I want to wash myself off."

"Speak for yourself!" Ghalen mumbled. "I am the only unmarried man here. It's too bad *I* had to leave the yurt. I wonder where that plump, black-haired wench ran off to."

"Hush!" Setenay screeched and threw a pebble at Ghalen.

"Ow!" Ghalen smirked and rubbed his cheek in mock pain. "Come on, old woman! It will be cold tonight. Why would you deny a man a companion to warm his mat? I seem to remember you are no longer a married woman." He winked, opened his blanket, and patted his mat. "Why don't you come over here and keep me company?"

The rest of the men snickered.

Setenay knelt on her mat, folded her arms, and turned up her nose. "I am too much woman for a man like you. Besides, I would exhaust you to the point you would be useless. We need your spear arm strong and ready for the difficult journey ahead."

The drunken men erupted into laughter. Ghalen smiled and rolled over. "You are breaking my heart, holy woman."

"You're lucky that's all I'm breaking!" Setenay said with a mock scowl.

Aizarg grinned at the playful banter between possibly the oldest woman in the world and Ghalen, who many considered the most eligible bachelor in the Lo nation. Sarah giggled next to him.

Her laughter took him by surprise. It carried an unexpected sweetness, an innocence he didn't expect. Aizarg looked down at the little woman sitting next him.

"Why do you laugh, girl?" Aizarg tried to sound stern.

"That man, Ghalen, had better watch out!" She pointed and covered her smile, whispering while trying not to laugh. "He's taunting a lioness! Even I can still see the fire in the old woman's eyes. He might wake up and really find her in his bed."

Aizarg looked up and frowned, considering her words. For a split second an unwelcome image filled his mind before he could push it aside, an image of the ancient patesi-li naked and mounting a shocked Ghalen.

And he laughed. Aizarg didn't just laugh, he doubled over and howled. Tears streamed down his cheeks as the pressure and anxiety of the last three days erupted in a spasm of uncontrollable laughter. Every time he tried to force the absurd image out of his mind, it came back with increased clarity.

Sarah's child-like laughter bubbled over too, and that only fed Aizarg's laughter. With the exception of passed out Ba-lok, the rest of the party sat up and considered the pair as if they had lost their minds.

Aizarg's laughter quickly spread to the rest of the party. The cleansing laughter floated through the slaver's camp and drifted into the marshes.

***

The fire died down to red embers as they waited for the rest of the party to fall asleep. Aizarg needed to talk to Sarah alone, without distractions. He felt it important to find out what lay ahead of them, to digest and sort out any new revelations she might provide.

Like a good slave, Sarah sat with eyes downcast and arms folded in her lap, patiently waiting for Aizarg to speak. He sensed her anxiety.

Aizarg dearly wished for Atamoda's presence. He desperately needed her now. Part of him wanted to wake Setenay, but knew the old woman needed sleep.

From time to time Sarah shivered, still dressed in the thin slave garb.

"You are cold. I will get something to warm you," Aizarg whispered.

She looked up at him in the starlight. "Thank you." A special beauty came through in her eyes, even in the darkness. It spoke of tenderness and trust, two attributes he felt certain should not have survived the slaver pens. A familiar, unexpected, feeling took root in his heart.

I understand how Ood-i fell in love with her.

Aizarg quickly looked away, stood up, and went to his mat. As he rummaged through his bundle for an extra blanket, his hand struck something hard. He pulled out Atamoda's li-ge amulet and stared at it. He took a deep breath and then slowly exhaled.

How do I begin with this woman-child? What would Atamoda do?

Without thinking, he placed the amulet around his neck, and then pulled out the extra blanket. He sat back down next to her, but didn't give her the blanket.

"Lean over," he said flatly.

"What?" she responded, confused.

"Do as I said, girl. Bend over and pull your hair up away from your neck."

Unsure, the slave girl closed her eyes and complied.

"Bend over farther," he said and pushed her head down until it fell almost between her legs, exposing the entire sweep of her backside to him.

That's when he saw the mark seared on her thigh. It was Virag's brand, a burn scar in the shape of a circle with a spearhead cutting though the middle.

Aizarg clenched his teeth to control his anger. He placed his fingers under her slave collar until it almost choked her.

"Please, no..." she begged, fighting back the tears while in the power of this stranger.

Aizarg ignored her and pulled the bronze knife from his belt. With one clean slice, he cut the collar from her neck.

"You can sit up now," he said.

She sat up, astonished, and rubbed her neck.

He held the heavy leather collar away from his face, pinching it with two fingers. It curled to retain its former shape as if clinging to a foul memory. The outside of the collar felt rough, the inside worn smooth with sweat and misery. He examined the place where it had been fused around her neck with brass rivets.

Aizarg imagined the young girl's terror as she knelt in a smoky, filthy yurt while one of Virag's henchmen permanently riveted the collar around her neck. Aizarg could almost hear her screams as the monsters seared her flesh.

"The fire is dying," he said, dangling it in front of her. "Throw something on it to keep it burning."

"I...I thought you were going to..." She started to cry.

"As long as you are among my people, you will never have to fear that possibility again. Now, burn this abomination or I will."

She took the collar as if in a trance. Sarah stood and slowly walked to the fire. There, she remained for several minutes, examining the collar in the dull red light.

He expected her to cry, or otherwise show some form of emotion. She didn't.

She cast it into the embers. A shower of sparks flew up around it, but it didn't burn. Instead, it smoldered with an evil, oily smoke.

Aizarg somberly looked on as Sarah calmly threw bundles of reeds and scavenged wood onto the fire until the flames danced high and completely consumed the collar.

Flames silhouetted Sarah's slight body, arms tightly wrapped around her shoulders. She showed no reaction to her new freedom.

Aizarg came up behind her and placed the blanket around her small shoulders. He finally saw her face, graced by a faint smile. She looked like someone lost in pleasant memory until he saw a single tear slide down her right cheek.

Aizarg didn't know what to say in the face of her tranquility. "Are you well, child? I thought you would be happy. Your reaction seems a bit...subdued."

"Oh, I am Uros, I am!" Her face lightened. "I am also thankful, and not only to you, but to the one who promised me I would one day be free."

"Did Ood-i promise you that?"

"No, not Ood-i. Since I was sold into slavery, I prayed every night to the spirits of my ancestors for deliverance." She looked back at the fire. "But they were mute. Then, one night, a beautiful spirit of mist and swirling wind came to me in a dream. She looked through me with fiery eyes like blue stars. The spirit made three promises, the first of which was I would be freed by my lover's king."

The hair stood up on Aizarg's forearms. He held up his palm. "Please! Tell me no more. These are matters for the patesi-li. Setenay will share words with you, not I. Then she will tell me what is proper for my ears."

She looked confused, but nodded. "As you wish."

He took her delicate fingers into his large, calloused hand and led her back to the log.

"We do not abide slavery, it is abominable to us and the goddess. I hereby deem what Ood-i paid as a ransom for your freedom, not a price for your flesh. It is something we often do to free our lost daughters from the slaver's whip. You are a free woman." Aizarg patted her knee like a father.

She smiled and closed her eyes like someone suddenly released from intense pain. "Thank you, dear Uros!"

"*Ah, ah, ah!!*" He held up a finger and cautioned her. "Don't get too excited. This is a debt you must repay my people. You must lead us to the Narim."

She frowned. "But Uros, I was going to do that, anyway."

"I know, but now you are bound to do so, and you are also bound to follow my rules. And my first rule is you must never again share a mat with Ood-i. He is married, and by Lo tradition cannot sleep with another woman. It is forbidden."

The joy ebbed from her face. Her shoulders sagged and her face dropped. "Yes, Uros. I swear to it."

"Also, I do not want to know what happened between you and Ood-i. Setenay will also take care of these matters, as such affairs are better left to patesi-le and not men. I have more pressing questions which need answering."

She nodded. "I will help in any way I can."

"First, can you really lead us back to your homeland?" Aizarg asked.

He saw determination in her face as she spoke her next words, "Oh, certainly, Uros! I can recall every step, every hill, every stream between here and Hur-ar. I have a memory as sharp as your knife. Besides, the way is still fresh in my mind, as Virag has made the journey several times since he bought me."

"Hur-ar?" Aizarg asked.

"Hur-ar is the home of the Hur-po. It lies at the foot of the Adyghe Mountains and the realm of the Narim."

"So, these Narim, they are real?" he asked.

"Oh, yes, Uros! They are as real as you are."

"How far is Hur-ar and the Narim?"

She spoke in hushed tones, glancing over at Virag's yurt as if he would burst forth any second and drive a spear through her heart. "The way to Hur-ar is a closely guarded secret. It's two or three days to the east. We must follow a hidden depression between two hilly ridges. This path will lead us almost the entire way there."

"Two or three days!" he gasped. "We were told it's at the edge of the world. We thought it was at least a seven day walk."

She cocked her head and stared at him as if he were a child. "I've heard your people are isolated upon the waters, like children who've never left the womb. The world is much, much bigger than you think, Uros."

"How big?" Aizarg's eyes were wide in wonder.

She shrugged. "Virag's caravans have trekked around the outskirts of the steppe. The ice wastes to the north are at least a two-week journey." Her face darkened. "The Aryans in the east are probably the most accurate about where the world ends. They say the world ends where the Scythians begin."

"This is probably true," Aizarg said grimly. "How does Virag get past them?"

"Virag pays them off in food, iron and..." she winced. "...other things. In return, they let his caravans pass unmolested. The way to Hur-ar is his most lucrative trade route. My people possess great wealth. He would sooner see the world end than divulge its location.

Something didn't make sense to Aizarg.

"Keeping this trade route a secret was so important to Virag he wouldn't provide us a guide. Why, then, did he sell you to us?"

She frowned and looked at Aizarg quizzically. "Isn't it obvious, Uros?"

"No, child, it isn't."

She laughed like a bubbling stream on a spring day. Sarah leapt at Aizarg and tightly hugged his neck. "You are so much like Ood-i! Are all the Lo so wonderfully ignorant?"

Aizarg couldn't help but embrace her in return. "Well, *tell me!*"

"It's because I am just a woman, and a stupid slave girl at that. In Virag's black heart, he could never fathom I could lead you back to Hur-ar."

Aizarg considered her words. None of the a-g'an valued their women as equals like the Lo. He, nor any Lo man, would ever off-handedly underestimate a woman.

"Well," Aizarg laughed. "Let's keep your splendid intelligence a secret until we are far from Virag's camp, shall we?"

***

Sarah slept snuggled next to Setenay for warmth as the fire faded to glowing embers. Aizarg sat alone on the log, his boar spear on his lap. His chin rested on his fist as he leaned over, deep in thought. Sleep eluded him as his mind raced from trouble to trouble.

Sarah's tale of the spirit with fiery eyes filled his mind.

He pondered this and many other things when he heard someone move next to the fire. He looked down to see Ghalen rise from his mat.

"It's a little cool this evening," Ghalen said, rubbing his arms. "You need to sleep, Uros."

Aizarg nodded, but said nothing as Ghalen threw the last of the bundles on the fire. The bundles quickly leapt into flame atop the hot coal bed. Glowing embers drifted high into the starry sky.

Ghalen smiled and rubbed his hands together. "A good fire!" Aizarg saw Ghalen's breath in the firelight.

Ghalen turned to lay back down when he saw Setenay and Sarah snuggled under the blanket in the cold shadows. He put his hands on his hips and sighed. He looked up at Aizarg with a twinkle in his eye and winked. "I *did* offer to keep her warm tonight."

Ghalen then slid his mat closer to the fire. He turned, bent on one knee, and gently lifted the old woman in his arms. She didn't wake, but instead snuggled into his chest. With the utmost care, he swiveled and slowly set her down on his mat. With equal tenderness, he lifted Sarah and placed her next to Setenay and covered them with both his blanket and their own blanket.

Without another look back at Aizarg, Ghalen flopped on Setenay's bare mat beyond the inner fire circle and almost instantly began snoring.

10. Death Slaves

"To walk the g'an is to wage war. To walk the g'an is to die." —
Lo Proverb.

The Chronicle of Fu Xi

***

At dawn they struck camp. Aizarg concluded his business
with Virag while making sure he kept Ood-i and Sarah out of
the Slaver's sight. They waited back at the campsite until
Virag returned to the comfort of his yurt.

Aizarg laid out the trade goods in front of Virag's yurt
and signaled the slaver's henchmen he was ready to conduct
business. Virag emerged from his yurt with furs tightly
wrapped around his shoulders, squinting against the rising
sun as if he found it offensive. He made cursory inspection
of the goods and muttered, "They'll suffice."

Two of Virag's warriors brought forward the heavy
spears and laid them before Aizarg. Aizarg and Virag spit
into their palms and grasped forearms.

"Good luck, mud dweller. The next time I trade with Scythians I'll be sure to look for your skulls tied to their horses." With that, he gave the sun another disapproving glance then returned to the warmth of his yurt.

Ghalen and Okta retrieved the sagar as Levidi went to fetch Ood-i and Sarah. In single file, with Aizarg and Sarah leading the way, the band trudged onto the open steppe. Except for Sarah, everyone kept looking over their shoulder at the marshes. A fog swirled in front of the trees and soon all traces of the lush vegetation and reeds vanished. The sun rose over the dry steppe.

Aizarg, Uros of the Lo Nation, led a scouting party beyond the realm of the Great Sea and into the g'an.

***

By mid-morning they found themselves many miles east of Virag's trading outpost. With a wary eye, the men marched with spears pointed high as a warning to strangers. Setenay kept pace in their midst, showing no indications of fatigue.

The sky, a paler shade of blue than over the Great Sea, faded to dingy brown on the horizon. The morning breeze stirred the grass like waves on the water.

Ghalen and Levidi walked a few paces ahead with little Sarah in between. Barefoot and dressed in one of Aizarg's extra flaxen tunics, she hurried to keep up with the men's long strides. It covered her slight body like a robe. She reminded Aizarg of a child dressed in her father's clothes.

It pleased Aizarg that Ghalen and Levidi were here. His pleasure at having his best friend along was obvious. Ghalen, however, was as close to a true warrior as the Lo could muster. He stood almost half a head taller than Aizarg, and a full head taller than Levidi. While the other men carried their unwieldy sagar pressed against their shoulders with both hands, Ghalen carried it comfortably in one hand. The heavy bundle and boar spear on his back didn't appear to burden him. He strolled easily, head high and long sandy hair blowing in the breeze as if this were a hunting expedition along the shore.

The other men were sullen, each alone with their thoughts and fears. Some men were more alone than others. Ood-i shuffled along, slightly removed on the group's left flank. He hadn't spoken since they left the camp.

Aizarg never thought highly of Ood-i, but no one did. Now Aizarg's feelings for Ood-i turned more to thoughts of pity. *He is a Lo brother, from my own arun-ki, and I don't even know him..*

On the opposite flank from Ood-i, Ba-lok stumbled along, pale and bleary-eyed. Suddenly, he dropped his sagar and bolted to the tall grass, where he fell on all fours and vomited. He arched his back and croaked until his stomach had nothing left to expel. The stink of bile mixed with sour wine filled the air.

The reek of Virag's yurt still follows us.

Aizarg looked away, not wanting to see his lieutenant humbled so. Setenay shook her head. Levidi picked up Ba-lok's sagar and waited until he finished.

Ghalen laughed in his easy manner, grabbed Ba-lok by the arm and pulled him up. Ghalen and Ba-lok were almost the same age, but Ghalen, even with his light-hearted spirit, appeared much older.

"Ba-lok, when this is all said and done, please remind me to visit your clan more often," Ghalen bellowed as he dusted Ba-lok off. "You, my friend, know how to enjoy yourself!"

Ba-lok shook Ghalen off, snatched his spear from Levidi and stomped away.

The group resumed their trek as Okta came alongside Aizarg.

"The sco-lo-ti of the Minnow Clan has some growing up to do," Okta said dryly.

Aizarg nodded. He had serious doubts about Ba-lok's ability to control himself. He also had doubts about Okta, as well. Aizarg couldn't easily shrug off the older man's loss of judgment last night.

"He is young," Aizarg said. "The duties of a sco-lo-ti have been thrust upon him at an early age. The burdens of our time are heavy enough for any man, let alone one so young."

"I will try to share your optimism," Okta said in the same dry tone.

Okta was Aizarg's distant cousin, but many said the two sco-lo-ti looked more like brothers. Aizarg acknowledged the physical similarities, though Atamoda often told him the older sco-lo-ti had a bigger nose, more gray hair, and wasn't nearly as handsome as Aizarg. He enjoyed it when his wife said such things. He suspected Okta had a darker, moodier personality than his own. He did, however, acknowledge Okta's intelligence and renown as an effective leader. Aizarg hoped last night was just a passing indiscretion.

"This girl, she leads us into low-ground." Okta motioned to the small rolling hills rising on both sides of them. They were in a shallow indentation, a depression, between the two ridges about a hundred paces wide. It stretched east as far as they could see.

"She said it's the route Virag follows to Hur-ar," Aizarg responded.

"I am uncomfortable being at the bottom." Okta took something out of his waist pouch and put it in his mouth. "I am uneasy being unable to see the horizon. We are ripe for ambush from the ridges above. If we walked on the crest of either the northern or southern ridge, we could see approaching a-g'an. Let us follow this route, but from above."

Aizarg thought this sound advice. He clicked loudly twice with his tongue to get Ghalen's attention. Ghalen looked back and Aizarg pointed to the top of the northern ridge. Aizarg extended his hand out, palm down and motioned away from his chest. Ghalen nodded.

Ghalen turned north and started up the gentle slope. The group followed, but Sarah hurried back to Aizarg.

"Uros," she said with urgency. "We must stay in the low land!"

"We are blind to an ambush. We can still follow Virag's route, but from above."

The group stopped and gathered around Sarah and Aizarg.

"Uros, you are wiser in such things than I," Sarah said, visibly apprehensive. "But Virag was adamant that his caravans always stayed in the low ground. He didn't even put scouts on the ridges."

Ba-lok spoke up. "Does the Uros listen to a sco-lo-ti or a slave wench?"

Sarah shot Ba-lok a scornful look. Setenay folded her arms but remained silent.

"I think the girl means well," Okta spoke softly from behind Aizarg. "But down here, our sagar are useless. The Scythians can rain arrows down on us from above."

Aizarg stroked his beard and considered his options.

"Uros," Ghalen spoke. "On the ridge, any Scythian horsemen will have to charge uphill. We can also fall back behind the ridge if necessary. This might shield us from some of their arrows."

Levidi nodded. "It sounds reasonable to me, Aizarg."

"It's plainly common sense," Ba-lok agreed and narrowed his eyes at Sarah. "I don't know why the Uros even hesitates."

Only Ood-i and Setenay had not offered their opinions. Aizarg expected Setenay to remain quiet on a matter well within the realm of flesh, suitable for an Uros and his men to decide.

"Well, Ood-i, what do you have to say before I make a decision?"

Ood-i looked over at Sarah and then back to Aizarg.

"Sarah would not c-council us to remain in the low country if she didn't have a g-good reason. I trust her."

Sarah and Ood-i smiled at each other.

"Hah!" Ba-lok laughed. "I would expect as much!"

It was choice between the advice of a former slave girl or every man in the party except her lover. Something gnawed at Aizarg, a piece of critical information he felt missing. Her words cast a shadow of wisdom, but he couldn't give the faint specter enough form to override the advice of his men.

"We walk the ridges."

***

The men's spirits rose as they crested the ridge and pressed east.

"Look how the ground gently rises and falls. The hills look like waves frozen in place," Levidi remarked, looking out across the endless expanse of rolling grasslands. The grin on Levidi's face reminded Aizarg of an excited boy taking his first boat ride beyond sight of the arun-ki.

"Perhaps the whole world was once a sea," Setenay remarked at the view spread before them. "Maybe Psatina transformed this part of the sea into soil as a home for the a-g'an out of pity."

When put in that way, the g'an is almost beautiful.

They marched along the crest until the sun arced toward the horizon and their lengthening shadows preceded them. The Lo seemed to liven up as the day wore on.

Sarah walked close behind Aizarg, looking left and right as if she expected a line of Scythian raiders to emerge from behind a hill at any moment.

"Come here, girl. Walk next to me." Aizarg motioned her forward. She wore an expression of relief on her face, as if being closer to him would protect her.

He suddenly remembered when Kol-ok was much younger, when Bat-or still slept in Atamoda's belly. Aizarg took him for his first walk deep into the marsh. Every sound frightened the boy, though he tried to hide it from his father. The boy walked so close to Aizarg it was difficult not to trip

92

over him. Aizarg reached down and took the boy's hand and Kol-ok's fear melted.

As Sarah walked next to him, Aizarg resisted the urge to hold her hand.

"As I told you last night, you are a free woman. When we reach Hur-ar, your debt will be paid and you may remain with your people."

"They will not take me back," she said, finally looking down. "My father permitted a favored wife to sell me into slavery. Under Hur law, it is his right. If you return me, he will simply sell me again."

Aizarg halted and considered her. "Are your people savages?" He raised his voice. "How can a man sell another human, let alone his own flesh?"

"My people are worse than savages," she said darkly. "They think of themselves as civilized, superior to all. The Hur are haughty and wicked."

Aizarg shook his head and continued east. "I shudder at the thought of a father betraying his daughter to the slaver's whip. I pity you, poor Sarah."

An iron gray sky forming in the north slowly banished the pale blue sky. The leading edges of the thin clouds burned fiery orange and red in the sinking sun.

Aizarg often wondered if the clouds were really on fire, but the prospect didn't concern him upon the Great Sea. Now, however, they traveled across endless expanses of dry grass.

Will they burn the grass if they dip too low? He saw no evidence of recent prairie fires, so he supposed such things didn't happen.

"May I stay with your people?" Sarah whispered, interrupting his thoughts.

He frowned as he considered her plea.

"Ood-i is married," he said after a long pause. "We do not take more than one wife, nor do we tolerate concubines. If you live among us, it will certainly cause strife. I cannot bring an element of discord into my village."

"Ood-i has vowed to no longer bed me. He said as much before you and Setenay this morning. I, too, made that vow."

"It's not that simple." Aizarg briefly thought about the warmth he witnessed between Sarah and Ood-i earlier. "Do you deny Ood-i loves you?"

"I do not," she replied softly.

"Do you deny your love for him?"

"I do not."

Aizarg sighed. "The ways of the heart are a mystery to me, but even I know you two will eventually find your way back into each other's arms. Ood-i is a good man, albeit a weak one. You will live in scorn, isolated from the village women even if you keep your vow."

Aizarg caught Ood-i's wary eye. "No, Sarah, you cannot live in my arun-ki. Even though I sympathize with your plight, my people must come first."

She kept her head down and continued to walk next to Aizarg, trying to keep up with his long strides. Finally, she spoke in a calm and clear voice, but Aizarg couldn't mistake the deep sadness riding on every syllable.

"Uros, then I ask you release me within sight of my homeland. I will find my own way in the wilderness."

"Sarah, I admire you're spirit, but you will surely die alone."

Sarah stopped. Her face burned with determination. "I would rather die alone and free than live another day as a slave."

Aizarg didn't show any response and resumed walking. Thoughts of Kol-ok and Ba-tor filled his mind.

"Sarah?" Aizarg finally spoke again.

"Yes, Uros?"

"We will not abandon you. I will consult Setenay and ponder your dilemma further."

Sarah smiled and nodded. Her pace quickened.

"Sarah, something has been gnawing at my mind since we left the low ground. You said Virag paid off the Scythians, but how?"

Sarah shrugged. "Before Virag forms a caravan and embarks on a journey, he always sends a runner to bring the Scythian chief to his trading camp. Shortly thereafter, the horde descends upon the camp and remains for a day or two, enjoying Virag's 'hospitality.'" She spat out the last word.

"Once the Scythians are sated with wine, women and treasure, they let us proceed. Virag orders the yurts to be disassembled and, along with his trade goods, packed on the backs of his slaves. Even the pleasure slaves must bear heavy burdens for the journey. We walk along this deep depression for several days, and then make camp in the shadow of the Adyghe Mountains. However, the Scythians always emerge from the steppe and meet us just west of Hur-ar to extract another tribute before the return journey."

"Do the Hur-po pay the Scythian's a tribute as well?" Aizarg asked.

"No!" she said adamantly. "They will not come within sight of the Black Fortress! Hur-ar and its people are protected in its shadow."

"The 'Black Fortress?' Is that the dwelling of the Narim?"

Sarah nodded.

"*Fortress*..." Aizarg frowned. "I do not know that word."

"It means 'the place that is strong in god,'" she said.

"What does it look like?" he asked.

Sarah looked toward the distant east and spoke, her voice barely audible above the wind. "It is a mountain within a mountain."

Aizarg shook his head in frustration. "Every description of these Narim is more like a riddle than truth! It confounds me. I don't understand, as I have never seen a mountain, though I've heard tales they are mounds of dirt much larger than hills." He pointed to the rolling terrain. "How much larger are mountains than these hills? Twice as big? Four times? Tell me."

She looked up at him again and covered her mouth, trying not to let the Uros see her smile. Her nervousness and fear were gone, replaced by girlish delight.

"Do not make sport of me." Aizarg didn't know if he felt anger or amusement at her reaction. Maybe he felt a little of both.

She bit her lip to keep from smiling.

"Forgive me, Uros, I was not trying to be rude. Please, give me a moment to consider your question." Her face became very serious and then her eyes showed a spark of inspiration.

"When I was a child I heard tales of the Great Sea, but could not imagine it from others' descriptions. Only when I finally beheld the mighty waters with my own eyes, I truly understood what those tales actually meant. I also came to understand there are some wonders too glorious for the crude sounds uttered by mortal lips."

She sighed. "These mountains escape mere words. They are beautiful, and the only thing I miss about my homeland." She waved her hand across the rolling prairie. "Compared to them, these hills are like puddles left on the shore by a passing wave."

She had the ghost of a strange accent on her lips and her words were refined. *She doesn't speak like a common slave girl. She speaks like a patesi-le.*

Aizarg chewed on her words as a small commotion stirred at the front of the column where Levidi and Ghalen engaged in a lively debate.

"You don't throw it, you idiot!" Levidi scowled. "You plant the back of the shaft in the dirt and let the charging horse impale himself on it! If you weren't so busy chasing women around the lagoon, you'd know these things."

Aizarg smiled. *Levidi, always the expert on all matters.*

"So, my short friend," Ghalen smirked. "Do you say 'please' when you ask the horse to impale himself, or do you just order him to jump on your spear-tip?"

The rest of the group laughed.

"No! No, you...you..." Levidi sputtered and pointed to his spear tip, flustered with Ghalen. "No! The horses, they are running so fast they can't stop."

Ghalen thoughtfully put his finger to his lips. "Yes, I can see that. It must be easy to surprise a Scythian and his horse out here." He swept his arm over the vast, open expanse.

"I don't know!" Levidi said defensively. "Maybe the Sammujad hide in the grass, and then jump up at the last minute."

"Or maybe they just throw the damn spear!" Ghalen laughed.

"It's too big to throw," Levidi shot back. "It's too heavy, and too long."

"Maybe too long for *you* to throw, but not me," Ghalen said as he signaled for the party to halt. He shrugged off the bundle and boar spear and hefted the great sagar in his right hand. Ghalen tossed it up and down in his palm to get the feel for its balance point. Though very thick, especially at the base, the long shaft flexed slightly as he tossed it.

"Wait." Levidi held up his hand and dropped his sagar. He pulled the much shorter boar spear from his back and dropped his bundle. "If you cannot throw a sagar farther than I can throw a boar spear, then it's not worth throwing. Agreed?"

Ghalen grinned. "Let's take it further...if I can throw a sagar farther than you can toss a boar spear, you must carry my bundle for the rest of the journey. If I can't, I carry yours. Agreed?"

Levidi hefted his boar spear with a confident grin. "Agreed!"

Aizarg knew of few spearmen as good as Levidi, but in an equal throw he would not wager against Ghalen. Even with Ghalen's mighty arm, this was no contest. While the boar spear had a heavy iron tip and cross piece, the sagar weighed twice as much. Aizarg believed the difference too great, even for the likes of Ghalen.

The group backed up and gave the men room. Levidi shook out his limbs, hoisted the spear on his shoulder, and faced downhill toward the depression. Ghalen raised his hand. "One moment."

He reached down and picked up a few twigs of dry grass. He crushed the stalks, raised the pieces over his head, and let them fall.

"The wind blows that way." Ghalen pointed east along the ridge's gentle spine in the direction they were walking. "I suggest you throw with the wind to your back. It might help your chances."

Levidi scowled at Ghalen. He cocked his arm and prepared for a running throw.

"STOP!" Ghalen raised his hand. "Throw from a *standing* position. That will keep the competition fair and will *also* better your chances."

Levidi lowered the spear and crinkled his face. "I see. Your concern for fair play and my welfare is admirable."

Ghalen bowed low and spread his arms.

Levidi placed most of his weight on his back leg. His eyes narrowed and his brow lowered in concentration. He fully extended his left arm up at about a forty-five degree angle. His left palm faced down and flat, as if telling the other arm where he wanted the spear to go. His right arm cocked back and his bicep bunched into a tightly wound ball of captive energy.

Levidi hesitated for only a breath, and then sprung forward. All his weight instantly shifted to his left foot. His left arm fell, and in a blur, his right arm revolved over his head. With a sharp grunt, all his bodily energy transferred through his right arm into the spear.

A collective 'ahhh!' rose from the group.

The spear sailed through the air with just a hint of wobble. It arced, nosed down, and firmly planted itself into the thick soil with a solid, satisfying *shoop* all the way to the iron cross piece.

Satisfied with an excellent throw, Levidi grinned. The spear landed just shy of where the ridge sloped away into a small saddle, easily forty paces away. The men slapped their chests in approval and Aizarg beamed with pride.

"That throw would have easily killed a boar," Aizarg said to Sarah.

"Ghalen," Okta said. "That was Levidi's own spear. He's been familiar with its feel and weight since becoming a man. You've only carried that sagar for a day and have never thrown it. I think you wagered in haste."

The smile vanished from Ghalen's face as he gauged the distance to Levidi's boar spear.

Ghalen bowed his head to Levidi. "That was an excellent throw. You are truly a great spearman," he said with all seriousness.

Once again, he lightly tossed the sagar up and down in his right palm. As he did so, he worked his grip farther back down the shaft until two-thirds of the spear lay ahead of his hand. Ghalen tightened his grip and hardened his face. He relaxed and rested the sagar on his shoulder. His throwing arm, long and lean, didn't bunch up like Levidi's. At first, Ghalen took a similar throwing stance as Levidi, but he lifted his front foot completely off the ground. He slightly bent his forward knee and pointed his toes down.

Whereas Levidi lunged forward, Ghalen's throw was a picture of fluid grace. His throw didn't start in his arm as much as it began with his back leg. Ghalen dropped his forward leg as the energy traveled forward through his body like a wave. He bent forward like the tall grass blowing around his feet and exhaled on the release without grunt or strain. The giant spear cleanly sliced through the air without the slightest trace of wobble. To Aizarg, it almost looked as if it accelerated after it departed Ghalen's hand, as if propelled by some unseen force. The sagar looked like it belonged in the air.

Even Levidi gasped.

A few seconds later, the spear gradually nosed toward the earth, slid out of the air, and disappeared behind the slope. A muffled crunch, like broken pottery, emitted beyond from where the sagar landed, easily twenty paces beyond Levidi's boar spear.

A cheer went up as Levidi shook his head in disbelief. Everyone gathered around Ghalen to congratulate him. Everyone, that is, except Aizarg.

He walked towards the slope.

Ghalen called after him, "Uros! Pace off the spears, I want to know how far they went!"

Aizarg ignored him. Something about the sound when Ghalen's sagar landed wasn't right. He passed Levidi's spear and came to where the slope fell away.

Dread filled the pit in his stomach. He tightened his grip on his boar spear. Ghalen's sagar was buried deep into a weathered human skull. Tufts of tall brown grass grew around the skull and in between a dismembered skeleton. The arm and leg bones, carefully arranged in a spread-eagle pattern, were pulled away from the rib cage and pelvis. A single Scythian arrow, fletches dyed red and black, protruded from the center of the rib cage.

Ghalen's spear shattered the skull, but Aizarg saw the entire skull cap above the eyes was cleanly sawed off. To the left of Ghalen's spear, another sagar extended from the head of the skeleton. In contrast to Ghalen's smooth, dark spear, this one was broken in two, weathered gray, and starting to split.

Aizarg spotted more broken sagar poking above the grass every few dozen paces along the ridge, with ribs and arrows protruding at the base of each spear. The grisly pickets stretched as far as he could see.

The rest of the group came up behind him. Sarah inhaled, put her hands over her eyes and buried her face in Aizarg's chest. The only sound was that of the wind whipping at their backs.

Setenay stepped forward with her hands behind her back and lips pursed in an expression of utmost seriousness. She walked in front of the first few skeletons.

"This is foul magic!" Ba-lok hissed. "Aizarg, we must leave this place!" Ba-lok turned to leave, but Aizarg barred his way with an arm across his chest.

"Wait." Aizarg pointed to Setenay strolling along the ridge, looking down on the bones as if she were inspecting the daily catch laid across the dock. "Your grandmother will be the judge of what this means. We will not leave until I hear her council."

"Look!" Okta shouted, pointing to the opposite ridge. There, highlighted against the sky, were the thin, but unmistakable silhouettes of broken sagar sticking straight up at regular intervals.

Setenay looked up and across the expanse to the far ridge. She squinted against the bright orange sunset. The harsh light emphasized the deep lines in her craggy face as the ever present wind blew back her stiff, silver hair.

"Hhhmph," she scowled, and returned to calmly inspecting the bones at her feet.

"What does this mean?" Levidi whispered to Aizarg.

"It means the Scythians let the dead guard the trail to Hur-ar," Setenay spoke up.

"I don't understand," Aizarg said.

"The Scythian witches enslave the spirits of the conquered dead to guard important places, like their burial mounds. These slain Sammujad are now Scythian death slaves."

Aizarg noticed how Setenay showed no fear in the face of the evil before them. This was her element, the realm of spirits. The men, however, were visibly afraid. While Aizarg tried not to show it, the terror he felt at the Valley of the Beasts stirred fresh in his heart.

"We should leave *now!*" Okta said with urgency.

Yes, we should leave, but where do we go?

"Uros, we should abandon the ridge and low ground altogether. If we follow the rising sun we should surely find these mountains." Okta stood with the rest, united.

The other men grunted in approval.

Setenay shook her head and opened her mouth to speak, but Sarah spoke first.

"Uros, I think we need to follow the depression," she said softly, now looking at the skeleton like Setenay did, her earlier fear seemingly gone.

"Aizarg!" Okta could not conceal the panic in his voice. "The low ground is clearly death!" He pointed his spear to the bones for emphasis.

"Go on, child," Setenay said to Sarah.

Setenay knows something.

Sarah hesitated, looking between Setenay and Okta.

"Speak," Aizarg said.

"Look at the eyes of the skulls. They look inward, toward the depression below. Their feet point to the low ground. If we sent someone to the opposite ridge, I believe they will also be arranged pointed inward. I think they're here to keep those below away from the surrounding steppe."

The men looked at each other.

Setenay looked sideways at Sarah, almost suspiciously. "How do you know this, child?"

Sarah shook her head and squinted as if focusing at something beyond the bones, something only she could see. "I just do, but why I cannot say."

Setenay smiled broadly, exposing her blackened teeth to the sunset. "Yes, child! The damned have but one purpose, to confine those traveling below. The broken sagar symbolize the broken earthly power of the defeated Scythian enemy. Their spears are only good in the spirit world, to torment and curse any that stray from this depression."

"It means we've reached the edge of the world." Aizarg nodded in understanding. "Beyond these deathly totems we enter Scythian territory." He pointed downhill. "It means we are all going back down there for the rest of our journey."

"Do we have anything to fear from them?" Okta asked.

Setenay shrugged. "It depends on what enchantments the Scythian witches chained around their captive souls. If we stay to the low ground, we might escape their torment." She eyed Ghalen's sagar and the shattered skull. "However, the spirits do not smile upon a despoiled totem."

"Old mother," Aizarg spoke up. "Is there anything you can do to protect us, perhaps a charm you can invoke?"

Setenay shook her head and turned her back on the bones. With a look of deep concern and her hands still clasped behind her back, she started downhill. "The magic here is like a hornets' nest in the dead of winter. What rage lies inside is hidden to me. If we let it be, perhaps we might pass without being stung."

Setenay abruptly stopped and looked back at the setting sun dipping below the slate-gray clouds, as if she suddenly remembered something. Her eyes were wide and unfocused. "It is a cold sunset," she said absently to no one in particular. Then her eyes came back into focus and she turned back downhill. "No," she said, not turning around. "I doubt you men have anything to fear from the dead."

Resigned to their fate, they started downhill, following Setenay into the cool, blue shadows.

While Aizarg didn't fathom all of Setenay's words, he now understood the source of the undefined fear he experienced since they left the low ground. The Scythians' message was clear: *Stray beyond the ridges and die.*

He looked at the rolling grassland with new eyes. In the darkening overcast, the rolling hills looked even more like waves. He wasn't the only one who saw the similarity.

"We are now trapped between these frozen waves," Okta said. He spat out some black juice onto the ground. "May they not crush us."

He's chewing mud weed. Mud weed grew in shallow, calm water. Patesi-le often recommended chewing it to calm the nerves or sooth tender gums. Too much of it stained the teeth and left one's breathe foul.

Gloom settled across the party as the wind turned cold and shifted out of the north. The gray clouds finally covered them like an iron blanket, their fiery edges now extinguished.

Ba-lok spoke. "If caravans think they'll die if they leave the depression, then perhaps the Scythians won't patrol here as often."

"Perhaps you're right."

Perhaps he is starting to think instead of simply reacting to situations.

"I agree," Okta said. "I think our young sco-lo-ti is correct. The broken sagar speak of crushed Sammujad power, so perhaps these foul totems will repel wandering Sammujad as well."

Ba-lok let a smile of self-satisfaction escape at Okta and Aizarg's praise.

"If the Scythians are confident in their control over this caravan route and not expecting Virag any time soon, we might pass unnoticed. The depression might be as safe as any stretch of the g'an," Aizarg said. "We should stay in this fold of earth. It's the best chance we have. We'll continue on for a little while longer, then make a cold camp. I don't want to chance a fire being spied by unfriendly eyes."

Aizarg looked over at Sarah. "I will not doubt you again."

Setenay came alongside Sarah and wrapped an arm around her shoulder. "Let us women step out of earshot from these men and talk."

"These didn't help those poor souls up there." Levidi shook his sagar and nodded up at the ridges. They could clearly see broken sagar above them, lining the ridges on either side.

Ghalen laughed and shoved his bundle and boar spear into Levidi's chest. "Those 'poor souls' should have learned how to properly throw their spears!"

11. Fu Xi, The God Of Names

'Home' represents all a man can hope to attain in his earthly life. Home is more than a shelter against wind. It is the fertile soil from which memories bloom, where today becomes yesterday and one can see beyond the dust from which they are formed.

Only within her home's embrace can a woman tend the hearth and nurture without fear. Home is where a wife can love without reservation. For without love, a man cannot dream. In dreams we find hope.

Hope gives mortals a fleeting glimpse of eternity's endless landscape. Forever's promise is the foundation of faith. Without faith, men cannot find their way to God.

This is what made the Lo different from the rest of wretched humanity. Home was an alien concept to the nomadic brute, whose savage heart sees the past as the ashes of a cold camp and the future as the next hunt. The sheltered marshes of the Great Sea gave the Lo a home and fostered their gentle spirit. They lived and died with a true understanding of faith, hope and love.

Love of home was the bond I shared with Aizarg. In my heart, I believe this is why we both gained Heaven's favor.

The Chronicle of Fu Xi

***

He sat tall on the black stallion's back; one hand on the reins, one hand on his hip. The gray mare slowly followed behind, head down, and content under her burden. Late afternoon sunlight poured between towering cedars. Dust motes drifted through the shafts of light in the otherwise still forest. The narrow trail wound along the rim of a cool, deep glen which dropped off to his left. To his right the terrain sloped up through an evergreen forest, where occasionally he caught glimpses of bright cliffs between the dark trees.

Pulled low over his eyes, his wide conical hat hid a square jaw firmly set in concentration. Fu Xi contemplated great and important thoughts only the God of Names could ponder.

"Hhorrssse," he let the word slowly roll around his mouth and trickle out, trying to get a feel for the alien syllable. *"Horse!"* he said it very quickly this time, as if the word would sound better if he spit it out. He shook his head. No matter how he said it, the word was crude. He didn't like what the men of Wu called these beasts, these 'horses.' Like the rest of their guttural tongue, the word sounded as if spat, not spoken.

No, the word 'horse' will not do.

Fu Xi brought the gift of language to many dark places where savages could previously only point and grunt. He'd grown accustomed to making up words for the new things he encountered in the wide, empty world. He knew the root of any name must lie in its inner nature, its spirit. During the long journey home he often pondered the inherent nature of these beasts. He concluded that 'horse' utterly failed to capture their spirit and resolved to invent a new word for these magnificent creatures.

They are large and powerful and fast, like the wind and water made one. These two traits were obvious, but Fu Xi considered their more subtle attributes.

They are graceful, especially when they run. Ahh, yes, strong, do not forget strong. I have never seen such strength.

These creatures deserved their own name, a name which captured the spirits of wind and water as well as encompassing grace, beauty and strength.

It was easier to bestow names to the sun and moon than these creatures.

Fu Xi stretched, yawned and fondly looked back at the gray mare plodding along. Then he considered the black horse beneath him.

"You," he poked at the animal and pointed back at the gray horse, "are not as sweet as she is."

The black horse neighed in response.

Fu Xi reached into a bag laid over the horse's back and pulled out a handful of crab apples. He leaned over and offered them under the horse's snout. The animal quickly gobbled them up and then tried to bite his hand.

"Hmph!" Fu Xi snapped his hand away and sat straight up. "That's what I get for being nice! I guess I won't be sharing my apples with you. Too bad. You should see the apples my mother grows in her garden." He held out a hand as if weighing a heavy object in his open palm. "They are big and juicy. My mouth waters just thinking about them."

He leaned down and whispered into the horse's ear. "I ride you only because you are proud and strong, and I respect that. Don't assume I like you, because I don't. However, I look good riding you and such things are important."

Something gently nudged him from behind. The gray horse pushed at the sack of crab apples. Fu Xi let go of the reins, grabbed a handful of apples, and offered them to her. She ate out of his hand as he rubbed her neck.

He'd gotten to know these horses very well since they departed the edge of the world last winter. Fu Xi often talked to them as they trekked westward down lonely, treacherous paths. Each had its own personality. The black one was temperamental and proud, the gray one sweet and affectionate. Both proved themselves loyal.

"No, I do not like 'horse,' but I cannot name either of you properly yet. Perhaps my mother can help in this matter. Until then, I shall have to continue to call you by your temporary names: Heise and Huise." *Black and Gray.*

Fu Xi gazed up through the golden leaves of the familiar forest. Many of the older oaks had not changed, but new saplings sprung forth on the dappled forest floor. Old friends were now mushroom covered logs, rotting in the shadows.

The sunset is approaching. The Honey Lotus Bridge is very close. I am almost home.

Memories of a thousand past homecomings drifted though his mind, a happy blur of warmth and love.

***

Sunrise is a time for beginnings, high noon for mortal toils, and at sunset we lay our labors aside and rest in the company of those we love. Perhaps that is why I always returned to Nushen at sunset. It wasn't something I necessarily planned, it merely came naturally.

The villagers knew this, too. At dusk the children always played on the pebble lane at the west end of the village, hoping to be the first to glimpse Lord Fu Xi emerge from the forest.

As I stepped from the forest onto the pebble lane, the children swarmed around me and shouted, "Lord Fu Xi has returned!" The older children showered me with hugs and kisses as the younger ones kept their distance. They had only heard tales of Fu Xi the Wanderer, The God of Names, the Immortal Son of the Goddess Nuwa.

"Where have you been, Fu Xi? What have you seen? What did you bring us?" the children cried. In my pack I always carried exotic treats or strange wonders to show them. I would never come home without something for my beloved children. The little ones quickly lost their fear as they watched their older brothers and sisters crowd around my legs.

The Chronicle of Fu Xi

***

Peeking through the high branches, Fu Xi glimpsed Tortoise Mountain rising steeply in the distance. His mother's temple, its alabaster pillars carved out of the living rock, gleamed in the late afternoon sun.

The snowpack is almost gone, he thought surprised. Tortoise Mountain's snowpack never came this close to melting away.

The Silver Stairs rose out of the tree line and vanished between the alabaster pillars. His mother called them the Silver Stairs because the white rock shimmered gloriously in the morning sun.

Perhaps they are glorious in the dawn, but in the sunset they look like what they really are: long, steep and narrow. He groaned and started to laugh.

"We've travelled since the end of last winter's snows." He patted Heise. "You've carried me across mountains and deserts. Now, I only regret you cannot carry me up the Silver Stairs."

For countless centuries, Fu Xi walked from one end of the Cin to the other and never thought twice of it. Now that he found these wonderful creatures he could not imagine ever walking again.

"No, friends, you are too big to climb the Silver Stairs. You'll have to stay in the village. The acolytes will take good care of you. By day you'll graze in pastures of soft clover. By night you will sleep within the confines of the convent, where I shall build you a stable. You two are my favorite things in all the world and only the best shall do!" Fu Xi laughed, feeling the joy of his homecoming.

Then he paused, pursed his lips and rubbed his beardless chin, thinking he might have spoken rashly. "Well, except maybe for women. Yes, you are the dearest things in my heart except for women. It's not as if I can share a bed with you."

Heise neighed and shivered slightly.

"My sentiments exactly!" Fu Xi laughed heartily.

Fu Xi removed his wide, conical hat and let his thick black hair tumble over his broad shoulders. His sparkling eyes and smooth, bold features were that of a man barely out of his teens. His spirits rose with every glimpse of Tortoise Mountain, soothing the woes of an ancient life and a long journey. On rare days like this, eternal life and eternal youth were the same.

***

Behind the children, the villagers came running, the fields and rice paddies forgotten in their rush to welcome me home.

I never grew accustomed to the changes. Like a splash of cold mountain water, there was no way to brace myself for it. Boys were now young men, sweet maidens were now mothers, and mothers were now old women. Absent smiles were freshly carved stones in the burial ground, but there would be time for mourning later.

At midnight on the first full moon after my return, long after the wine and merriment were over, I would walk through the stone garden and remember. Sometimes Mother joined me, arm in arm, and spoke of how my friends lived and died in my long absence.

At each grave stone, Mother recalled a name and story. Here was an old man who passed in his sleep, a young bride who died in childbirth, or a stillborn baby. In the moonlight, away from the eyes of sleeping mortals, my tears ran freely. Mother never cried, though I often heard sadness in her voice.

I once asked her why she never cried.

"The day when the gods finally weep for the woes of mortals, the world will drown in our tears."

The Chronicle of Fu Xi

***

Fu Xi carried many woes. He had witnessed dark and mysterious things since the last time he saw Tortoise Mountain. The icelands were retreating. Vultures and maggots ignored the dead and black demons stirred in the streams and rivers. The previous night the stars fell from the sky in sheets of dazzling light. What would she tell him of these signs and omens? What would she tell him about the men of Wu?

He sorely needed his mother's council, but his troubles could wait a little while longer. The happiness of the present demanded his full attention. Fu Xi rode in silence for a spell longer, savoring all the expectations of his imminent homecoming.

"Yes, the peasant daughters of Nushen are the fairest in the land. Ahh, they are so well-fed and beautiful."

Fu Xi frowned for a moment and patted his horse.

"You know, of course, I cannot consider the pleasures of soft flesh without the delights of rice wine. Please, do not be offended, but you are definitely my favorite thing in the world except for women and rice wine."

Suddenly, he remembered the women of the Palace of Wu and a cold wave of shame interrupted his happiness.

Fu Xi gazed upon the temple longingly and sighed. "Perhaps I shall sleep upon my own bed tonight." He thought about the silken bed roll, stuffed with the softest wool, sitting next to the family dinner table. He wondered if his mother had already unrolled it.

Of course it is unrolled. She always prepared for him.

"Perhaps I am too hasty." He smiled, his good mood reasserting itself. "You are my favorite thing in the world except for women, wine and a good night's sleep."

Fu Xi readjusted his numb bottom, ready to stretch his legs. Only a thin, roughhewn blanket separated him from the animal. He guided the beast with a simple harness and bit of iron, wood and rope.

The bridle is adequate, but perhaps some type of leather seat strapped to the horse's back might be in order. His mother taught him the skill of leather craft and he, in turn, introduced it across Cin. He would put it to good use fashioning some manner of cushion.

The trail widened as he rounded a bend. Up ahead, a small stone bridge arched over a defile, at the bottom of which ran a stream. Usually, it was almost dry this time of year. However, now it bubbled vibrant and full.

As Fu Xi crossed over, he suspiciously eyed the water. No black shapes slithered through it. He breathed a sigh of relief that his mother's realm hadn't been defiled. The stone bridge marked the boundary of his mother's domain. Nushen, *the Village of the Goddess,* lay about a half a mile beyond.

I'm home.

***

The gong sounded from the heart of the sanctuary, announcing my return. The convent's gates flew open and the acolytes rushed out of the compound. The Holy Mothers could only smile and get out of the way. From the youngest acolyte of six summers to those on the cusp of womanhood, the girls were usually dressed in their white cotton work clothes.

When I returned there was no ceremony or pomp. On those glorious days the acolytes could be children again. Like small white flowers in a summer field, they intermixed with the jubilant crowd of peasants surrounding me.

Drums and flutes joined with laughter as I let the crowd carry me into the convent courtyard.

The Chronicle of Fu Xi

***

Smells, more than the sights of home, warmed his heart and filled his spirit with nostalgia. Fu Xi took a deep breath and closed his eyes, letting the familiar scents fill him. Heavy foundations of musky earth and moss supported the crisp, airy scents of falling leaves and honeysuckle. He knew these would give way to the warm odors of harvest fields, jasmine, and the cooking fires of Nushen. It wasn't just the smells that made this forest unique in all of Cin, it was its gentleness. Other forests were dangerous. Nuwa, the Goddess of Tortoise Mountain, protected this one and all who dwelt here were safe from harm.

Excitement stirred in his chest, and for a fleeting moment, Fu Xi wanted to spur the horses into a gallop and race into Nushen.

On second thought, perhaps not.

He laughed softly as he remembered the first village he travelled through on his journey home. They fled in terror when they saw him approaching on horseback, thinking him a two-headed monster. He quickly learned the wisdom of dismounting and walking the horses whenever he approached a settlement.

No, I will go slowly and savor the moment.

Judging by the colorful leaves, harvest was underway. The acolytes, under the watchful eyes of the Holy Mothers, would be busy pouring freshly reaped grain into the granaries. The village courtyard would be packed with large pots of rice waiting to be placed in the cellar storehouse under the kitchens. In the cool of the evening there would be music in the air and rice paper lanterns hanging over the courtyard.

Fu Xi always preferred the Harvest Festival to spring's Offering Festival. Food, drink and light-hearted celebration marked the Harvest Festival. Offering Festival's somber purpose tended to put a damper on things.

Fu Xi always spent the first few months home catching up on village gossip. The Holy Mothers and his friend Tiejiang would fill him in on everything he'd missed.

Tiejiang will be getting along in years. Is he too old for blacksmithing? Fu Xi didn't want to consider the possibility Tiejiang might have passed into the stone garden.

Fu Xi knew he'd been gone several years, though how many he wasn't sure. Time was like water added to the painter's brush — too much and the pigment of life becomes pale and diluted. Time slowed even more so in the Palace of Wu.

Fu Xi thought again of what he witnessed in that land across the Sunrise Sea, a place he once thought of as the edge of the world. He knew better now. The world was much bigger than he ever dreamed, far grander than the land of Cin. Now home was more precious than ever.

She sends me abroad more often, as if she wants me away from Nushen. Maybe this time I can stay. There are enough names in the world and my soul is no longer restless.

Heise suddenly stopped and pranced nervously. Huise whinnied and pulled against the rope.

"Whoa..." Fu Xi pulled back on the reins and halted the horses. He sat high and looked about.

Sometimes mother allows predators into her forest when the deer become too numerous. It's likely a bear or a wolf, though I do not remember them hunting so close to the Honey Lotus Bridge.

When Nuwa permitted predators into her domain, she always lingered nearby to protect the village, but Fu Xi didn't sense her spirit.

He'd come to trust his horses' instincts and pulled the lance from the pack tied to the Heise's flank.

"Well, my friends, if it's a wolf or tiger, I'll wager I can spear it."

A whiff of smoke assaulted his senses. It wasn't the wood smoke of a cooking fire or a smoldering forest, but the acrid stench of hate, of something aflame which had no business burning. Objects fashioned by the hand of man were being destroyed for no other purpose except a blood lust.

Disbelief seized him. Those smells, so common beyond these sheltered lands, were impossible in the goddess's dominion.

He quickly dismounted and led the horses into the trees; all the while carefully looking about to make sure he wasn't being watched. Fu Xi loosely tied the horses to a tree. If they needed to escape they could pull free with one tug. If danger truly existed up ahead, he didn't want to endanger them.

Patting Heise's nose, he whispered to the horses, "Be still, be silent. I will return for you. If danger comes, run and I will find you."

He returned the lance, a tool for slaying animals, to Heise's pack. Fu Xi needed a weapon to kill men...or monsters.

He pulled a lanyard and opened the heavier pack on Huise's back. Fu Xi half-expected to see the familiar leather-wrapped hilt of his trusty bronze sword. That blade, however, lay broken on a distant shore. He drew the Red Sword from his pack.

Fu Xi hadn't removed the precious gift during the entire journey home. The slender, slightly curved orichalcum blade felt good in his hand. The blood-colored metal gleamed dully in the cool shadows. He lightly flicked his wrist to and fro as the light blade cut the air with a metallic whoosh.

He put his hat on top of Huise's pack, which also held the Red Armor. For a moment he considered donning the armor, but chose the speed and stealth afforded by his soft wool trousers and loose cotton tunic.

He turned and peered into the dimming forest. The reek permeated the windless air like an invisible fog, an abomination assaulting his boreal sanctuary.

Fu Xi knew Nushen had been violated, though by what he did not know.

Until I fully grasp the scope of this threat I will avoid the road and cut through the forest to the village.

The youthful twinkle in his eye vanished. The God of Names raced into the forest, sword in hand, toward his home.

***

As always, we eventually found our way under the willow tree in the courtyard. My friends crowded around me. Above us, festival lanterns softly glowed as fireflies blinked amongst the willow's branches. Hugs, tears, and laughter pressed upon me from all sides. A cup of rice wine appeared in one hand and a sweet cake in the other. I was home and, for now, my restless soul content.

If the gentle reader of these words wonders why the script is less than graceful or the ink might smear across the parchment, I humbly seek your forgiveness. My strong hand trembles and my keen eyes mist. Each memory is a sweet cut, fresh and cruel. I must put down my brush and listen to the desert wind, for these words fill me with unbearable pain.

Nushen will forever be my home.

The Chronicle of Fu Xi

12. The Beast And The Black River

Beware, oh Children of the Sea.

Death is the sudden chill in a warm summer current. It is the rotten smell along a lonely shore. It is the slime that unexpectedly slips through the toes on a sandy bottom, or black ice on a cloudy winter day.

Mothers, watch your children as they play on the dock. Fathers, tread the deep with vigilance. For the water demon rises from the depths to steal your next breath. - Chant of the Patesi-le

The Chronicle of Fu Xi

***

"Wuh-What is it?" Ood-i jabbed the hairy mass of dead flesh with his spear. His spear barely penetrated the shaggy, dark brown hide.

"A giant, of course," Ba-lok said with smug certainty.

"It is huge, but it doesn't look like the giants in the stories of my youth," Ghalen said.

"I've seen something like this before," Aizarg muttered as he circled the hulking corpse. "Only it was somewhat different."

"Yes, I remember now," Levidi said. "There were several of them in the Valley of the Beasts, only they weren't as hairy."

At first, Aizarg had thought it a pile of sticks and brush coated with dead grass and mud. Only when they neared the bank of the swollen river did they realize they gazed upon a dead beast of breathtaking size. Its four legs, which still lay in the water, were like tree trunks. The rest of the beast lay on its side on the grassy bank. What Aizarg thought were dry sticks protruding from the pile were instead two large horns curled back into each other with a long, snakelike nose curled on the ground between them. Even on its side, the creature loomed over the party. In life it would have been twice as high as a man and might have weighed more than fifty horses.

"I wager it drowned far upstream," Ghalen said. "I do not know what manner of creature this is, but it's been dead for some time. The eyes are gone and its belly is burst." He wrinkled his nose at the putrid smell.

"It must have been a muh-magnificent creature in life," Ood-i said. "Imagine trying t-to hunt such an animal!"

Setenay poked it with her stick. She sniffed at the carcass and looked to the sky with a wary eye.

"Sarah?" Aizarg asked. "Do you know what this thing is called?"

Sarah faced the river. She wrapped her arms tightly around her shoulders as if cold, though the late morning sun shone pleasantly warm.

"Sarah?" Aizarg repeated.

She turned around as if snapped out of a trance.

"What is wrong, child?" Setenay asked.

Sarah ignored the dead creature and looked out across the swift river. "This river...every time I made this journey it was only a delicate stream, barely knee high and only a few paces across."

Aizarg came alongside her and looked across the water. The ridges on both sides were sliced open by the river, exposing sheer cliffs of rich black soil. The river cut through cliffs in the ridge to the north, flowed wide and swift across the shallow valley for about a mile, and then disappeared through another set of cliffs in the ridge to the south. A low roaring sound filled the air and seemed to emanate from both sets of cliffs, though Aizarg could not detect the source.

Aizarg surveyed the immediate area of the river. The soggy grass outside the banks bent over in the direction of the current, as if recently under water. Clumps of dead grass, flotsam and sticks formed a high water mark several dozen yards away from the bank, which continued to expand away from the river as he looked toward the southern cliffs.

"This river was even bigger a few days ago," Aizarg commented, pressing his sandaled foot into the squishy ground. "This whole area was covered in water."

"Why wouldn't it just run along the low ground we've been traveling through instead of cutting though the high ridge?" Ba-lok said.

"Because, young sco-lo-ti, that means the ground we've been traveling on has been slowly going downhill, and on the other side of this river it must go back up hill," Aizarg jabbed the ground with the dull end of his spear. "Water spirits eat soft clay like this easily. When enough water backed up against the southern ridge and could not easily flow through the small pass, the spirits simply made a bigger hole in the ridge. I suspect the water backed up on the other side of the northern ridge until the spirits opened those cliffs. The water gushed through and flooded this low land, and then ate away at the southern ridge."

"Hmm. Perhaps," Ba-lok said, almost dismissively. "Or this river has always been here and Sarah is lost."

"I know where we are!" Sarah snapped back at Ba-lok. "The river is larger."

"Stop it!" Aizarg commanded and scolded Ba-lok. "Even a child could not get lost following the low ground. The path is clear. I believe her. The question before us now is how to cross."

"Uros," Okta said. "The river's current is as swift as I've ever seen. It will push us significantly downstream as we swim across. If we enter here, there is a chance we could get swept beyond the southern cliffs and to points beyond. We don't know what lies on the other side of the ridge, and there may be no place to pull ourselves out of the water. I suggest we cross as close as we can to the northern ridge, giving us the whole expanse between the ridges to gain the opposite shore."

"An excellent idea, sco-lo-ti," Aizarg nodded. He turned north along the shore and the others followed.

The northern ridge rose only about a quarter mile from the dead beast. Aizarg could smell the freshly exposed dirt of the soft cliffs as they approached. The grassy shore rose to a sharp, crumbling embankment and then transformed into cliffs with no shore. Shreds of grass overhung the top of the cliffs, as if the ground was ripped out from underneath its roots. The water boiled and roared as it rushed over ragged exposed boulders between the two cliffs. As it moved away from the cliffs it settled down, but still moved rapidly.

Aizarg stopped where the flat shore gave way to the embankment.

"Have you ever seen water churn and boil like that?" Levidi asked Aizarg, raising his voice to make it heard above the water.

"Never."

This was the dull roar he'd heard while standing next to the dead beast. All the rivers and estuaries in the marshes were slow and lazy. Their bottoms were sandy and giant rocks of this magnitude were unthinkable. Here, the water washed away the hill and exposed the very bones of the earth.

Aizarg and the men silently considered the river. Setenay walked as far up the embankment as she could and examined the cliffs.

Aizarg didn't like this river; it had a wicked look to it. Sticks and small logs quickly drifted by. Downstream of the rapids, silt completely blackened the water. Eddies and swirls formed and reformed in the dark water, testifying to back currents lurking just below the water.

Eddies and back currents indicate deep water. This wild river has many secrets. Aizarg looked back downstream at the dead animal. *If this river killed that giant, we must give it proper respect.*

Aizarg pointed to his immediate right, where the white water settled down to flat water. "This is a good place to cross," Aizarg shouted above the roar of the rushing waters to his left, trying to exude confidence. "We have a long stretch of flat shoreline on the eastern side to make a landing, though I think it will only push us downstream perhaps halfway to the dead giant. Everyone, prepare to swim."

The men and Setenay quickly stripped off their winter clothing until they wore loin cloths. They stuffed their heavy garb into their oiled skin packs.

"Ahh...that feels so much better!" Levidi stretched with a big smile on his face, obviously feeling more comfortable in his normal attire. "It's going to feel good to take a swim, even in that muddy water. I'm as filthy as a Scythian."

"Sarah?" Ood-i remarked. "Why aren't you in your loincloth? You have to p-put your clothes in a pack to keep them dry."

Sarah stood facing the group, her arms folded and shoulders stooped. Her lip trembled as tears formed at the edge of her eyes.

"I don't know how to swim," she whispered.

The group looked at one another, bewildered.

I neglected to consider she is a-g'an. Many of them do not know how to swim.

Aizarg lifted her chin. "Do not fear. Lo learn to swim before we walk. One of us will carry you across on our back."

She looked up at him again with a weak, but trusting smile. The same fondness stirred in his heart that bubbled up in front of the fire in Virag's camp two days ago. Her inner strength, courage, and intelligence touched something deep inside and he couldn't stop thinking of her plight. Since yesterday evening, a bold idea formed in his mind. He would have to discuss it further with Setenay and Okta before he could act on it.

After a few minutes of conversation, they agreed Okta would carry Sarah across. His people where acknowledged as the best swimmers among the Lo. Ba-lok would carry his grandmother and the extra gear and weapons would be divided equally between the other men.

"I will carry Setenay if you wish, Ba-lok," Ghalen offered.

"I can take care of my own flesh and blood!" Ba-lok shot back.

Ghalen raised both hands and backed up. "I was only trying to be helpful."

Setenay came between them. "It was very kind of you to offer your assistance to the sco-lo-ti of the Minnow Clan, Ghalen." Setenay grimaced at Ba-lok and spoke between gritted teeth. "I'm sure he knows how to *politely* decline your offer like a good sco-lo-ti should." She emphasized the word *sco-lo-ti* each time.

Ghalen nodded and turned away.

Sarah stripped to her loin cloth and stood almost naked next to the men. She arranged her long hair to cover her breasts. Aizarg sensed Sarah's discomfort at being unclothed around the men. He didn't understand her modesty, as she probably wore little more in Virag's yurt.

Setenay must have sensed it too, as she touched Sarah's arm and spoke softly to her. "I understand the a-g'an cover themselves, especially their women, unless they intend to couple. We do not." Setenay proudly motioned to her ancient body as if she were still a maiden. Her dilapidated breasts hung almost to her waist and her leathery skin sagged in loose folds over protruding ribs. She stood without shame in front of the men as if she were fully clothed.

Aizarg tried to reassure Sarah. "Lo women stir men's passions with more than just the sight of their naked flesh. When a Lo boy begins to notice women and his excitement is apparent to all, he is ready for the Rights of Passage. When he returns from the Rights, the mere sight of a breast or curve of a hip will not cause him to become aroused. He is a man, in control of his passions."

Setenay cackled and slapped her knee. "Only a dead man is in control of his passion! But the Uros is mostly correct, just the sight of flesh does not stir the Lo loins as it does the a-g'an savage." Setenay considered Ba-lok and continued dryly, "Unless wine is involved."

Her smile returned as she turned back to Sarah and wagged her finger. "Ahhh, but when a Lo girl returns from her Rights of Passage, she will have learned to not only capture a man's body, but his spirit as well. This is truly how a wife keeps her man's flesh and soul satisfied over the long years."

Sarah seemed to relax. "I am alright. I am ready to cross the river."

The men removed ropes from their packs and bound their sagar and boar spears tightly together, forming three narrow rafts of two to three spears each. Aizarg, Ghalen and Ood-i collected the extra gear and packed it into bundles. Then they firmly bound the bundles to the thick base of the spear rafts. They tied a rope to their waists with a slip knot, so it could be easily disconnected in case of trouble. Finally, they securely attached the ropes, about two yards in length, to the pointed end of the spear rafts. This would allow the bundles to streamline in the current and reduce the likelihood of snagging.

"We will proceed one at a time. I will go first," Aizarg said, contemplating the river.

Where does all this water come from?

Something caught his eye. Something took shape in the muddy water about mid-stream. It rose and bobbed for a moment and then melted back into the stream. Then his eyes caught another object, and then another.

"I see them, too," Okta whispered, "Are they sticks or logs?"

"No," Aizarg said. "They are flat and have odd shapes and seem to blend in with the water.

"Setenay, are those shapes lurking in the angry water spirits?" Aizarg asked.

Setenay shook her head. "The spirits of water and earth departed with the gods. If this river is angry, it's because it is soulless, and all things soulless are malignant and cannot be appeased. We should cross quickly."

Aizarg took a step into the stream and instantly recoiled.

"What is wrong?" Sarah asked.

"I have never felt anything so cold!"

With an expression of deep concern, Setenay put her foot in the water and suddenly turned ashen. She stood there for what seemed like an eternity, her eyes wide and darting back and forth over the water's surface as if she were watching something. Her lips were moving, but she uttered not a sound. She stepped out of the water, pursed her lips, and put her hands behind her back as if weighing something in her mind.

"The river is cold because it is soulless. It will seek to replace its departed spirits with new ones. That's probably what happened to that beast. When we immerse ourselves in it, the river will try to devour us."

They jumped as a large chunk of the earthen cliff splashed into the water to their left.

"It heard me," she said solemnly. "No one enter the river until I say so."

She put her feet back into the river and gasped, eyes wide and breathing shallow. She stood motionless for several long moments, gazing upon the black water.

"What is she doing?" Sarah said.

"I think she is talking to the river," Aizarg whispered.

Suddenly, a massive section of the cliff gave way and crashed into the river, burying many of the rocks.

Setenay jumped back. For a few seconds, a large black island of dry earth stood in the middle of the river between the cliffs, rising several feet above the water.

In a few seconds, the banks fell away into the water. Within minutes the island narrowed and dissolved completely into the swift waters.

Setenay turned back to the group, her eyes wide with fear. Her expression frightened Aizarg.

"What happened?" Aizarg held Setenay's arm.

She hesitated and looked back at the river. "Nothing," she mumbled.

"What did it tell you?" Okta said. "Will it let us pass?"

"I..." she stammered. "It..." She took a deep breath and collected herself.

Aizarg sensed her hiding something. "What does it mean?" Setenay looked up into Aizarg's eyes as if about to say something, but then held her tongue.

They encircled Setenay, waiting for her to answer.

With a stern expression of resolve, she looked at each of the men. "This river is empty and barren, it is filled with only cold rage. If we enter its body it will give us battle, for its intention is to kill us. We can defeat this black river by gaining the other shore. Swim like Lo men, don't look back, and we will persevere."

The roaring river taunted them. With grim resolve, Aizarg turned to the shore and shouldered his bundle.

"So be it. If the river wants battle, I will give it battle. I will go first, followed by Ood-i, then Okta with Sarah. Ghalen, you will enter with Okta in case he needs help. Balok and Setenay will enter next, with Levidi as their escort.

Do not enter the water until the previous group is safely on the other shore, am I clear?"

Everyone nodded.

Once again, Aizarg entered the stream. The cold cut into his leg muscles until he couldn't feel the grassy bottom. Even the Great Sea in the dead of winter did not approach this level of freezing. He moved deeper into the stream, taking shallow, rapid breaths and trying to get used to the water, but his legs didn't acclimate. Instead, they started to numb. The current tugged hard at his legs. He could feel the river trying to pull him down and rob him of his life.

He took one look back at his people and tried to give them a reassuring smile. They gave him shouts of encouragement, except for Setenay. She resumed her silent chanting.

Aizarg was a powerful swimmer, but this river gave him pause.

Our first enemy along the journey is water, the one thing we love and hold dear. He took a deep breath. *If I don't start swimming now, I never will.*

He dropped his bundle and dove into the water.

The river assaulted him. The cold gripped his chest and attacked his arms, quickly numbing them. Every time he came up for air, he saw the opposite bank shift farther south. Now the swim didn't look like a short dash, but instead an agonizing distance swim. Aizarg no longer felt his arms and legs, but he kept swimming.

His bundle quickly floated downstream. The rope tightened and then jerked against his waist. The bundle acted as a sea anchor, further dragging him along with the current.

Something slammed into his left side. It hit with enough force it should have hurt, but he only felt the pressure. He looked up and saw a large black limb float by, twigs and sticks protruding from it like skeletal hands trying to snare him. He pushed it aside and resumed swimming when he saw it heading for his bundle. If it snared the rope or bundle, it could drag him downstream and drown him. He gave the rope a quick jerk downward and the limb floated over and safely past his bundle.

Treading water, he looked back and saw the party well upstream. Aizarg turned to swim again when his left hand struck something hard.

It almost felt like it bit me.

Aizarg pulled back and shook his hand. He saw nothing. He reached out again and touched something smooth and flat. It felt like a rock with the added sensation of cold that clearly registered through his numb hands. After a few seconds he realized what it was.

A large chunk of ice floated by, its smooth top flush with the water's surface.

These were the strange shapes I saw floating in the water.

Ice might form in thin crusts in the shadows along the shore of the Great Sea in the dead of winter. For Aizarg, ice of this magnitude, like the dead beast along the shore, defied imagination. He didn't have time to marvel at the massive chunks of ice, he had to keep swimming.

With his jaw chattering, he kept pushing himself. He felt himself starting to warm. Part of him welcomed the sensation and part of him felt the black river wrenching his soul from his body.

His vision began to fade.

He thought he felt something touch his leg, but he couldn't be sure.

Perhaps it is the grassy bottom. Then he felt pressure just like an icy hand. Terrified, he jerked his leg back and the pressure abated. For a fleeting second a thought crossed his dimming consciousness.

I might not make it.

Then his foot bumped the soft, grassy bottom. He didn't know how, but he found his rubbery legs and stood. As Aizarg staggered forward, it seemed that the current suddenly grew stronger, as if the river raged at his escape.

Aizarg stumbled from the water and the illusion of warmth vanished. He shivered so hard he had difficulty seeing. He pulled against the rope and, with great exertion, dragged the bundle out of the water. Adrenaline ebbed and left him weak. Aizarg trembled at the realization the river almost defeated him.

The sun began to warm his shoulders and the sensation gave him comfort. He wanted to fall to the ground and let the sun work its magic, but he knew he could not let the others see him fail.

Aizarg looked back across the river. To his amazement, he had drifted a few yards past the dead beast, more than halfway to the southern cliffs.

Thank you, Okta! If he had started next to the carcass he would have surely been swept past the southern cliffs and into the unknown.

He untied the rope from his waist, shouldered the bundle, and walked upstream. The river's spell faded with each step and Aizarg's limbs began to warm. Soon, he ran. As he neared the shore opposite the party, he waved to let them know he was all right. They waved back and Ood-i started forward with his bundle.

"Wait!" Aizarg shouted and held up his hand to motion Ood-i to stop. Ood-i halted in acknowledgement.

Aizarg unwrapped his bundle and placed it in the grass away from the water. He coiled up the rest of the rope and tied a wide loop on the end. He had enough to throw about a third of the way into the stream.

Suddenly angry at himself, Aizarg knew he should have strung several ropes together and carried one end across with him. Even with nothing to secure the ends to, two men could have anchored the rope while the rest of the party pulled themselves across. Then they could have simply pulled the last man to the other side and retrieved the rope.

Pride in his people's mastery of water kept him from thinking of such a practical idea. That pride almost cost him his life and Aizarg feared what the rest of the party now faced.

With rope firmly in hand, Aizarg braced for Ood-i's crossing. He raised his hand and shouted, "Come across and be careful! The river is swift and full of debris!"

Ood-i cupped his hand over his ear and shook his head.

"COME!" Aizarg shouted and prayed for the best.

Aizarg saw Ood-i gasp and stiffen when he entered the river. He cringed, for what he knew Ood-i felt. Without further hesitation, Ood-i threw his bundle into the rushing stream and dove in.

"That is a Lo man, indeed!" Aizarg whispered with a smile.

With powerful strokes and large splashes, Ood-i didn't swim as much as he attacked the water. Unlike Aizarg's graceful style, Ood-i punched his way through the river. Instantly, the current dragged him south. Aizarg trotted along the shore, rope at the ready and fully prepared to reenter the water should his friend need help.

Oblivious to everything except his next stroke, Ood-i ignored the limbs, logs and chunks of ice bobbing and sliding around him.

To Aizarg's amazement Ood-i neared the shore several dozen yards upstream from where Aizarg did, pulled himself up on all fours and crawled out of the water. Aizarg reentered the water up to his ankles and pulled Ood-i up. He began to shiver all over again.

Ood-i's lips were blue.

"I...I th...th...think my t...testicles have shriveled all the way into my throat!" Ood-i stuttered between gulps of air.

Aizarg laughed and untied Ood-i's bundle. "Come, keep walking and you'll feel better. We have to be ready to help the others."

Aizarg shouldered Ood-i's bundle and the two men walked back upstream.

Aizarg laid out Ood-i's bundle next to his and added Ood-i's rope to his section.

"Uros," Ood-i stammered, looking back at the water. "It almost felt like something t-tried to suck me down into the depths. For a few moments I wasn't sure..."

Aizarg interrupted, "Put that aside and concentrate on bringing our friends across. Hold one end and wrap it firmly around your waist. You are the anchor man. If someone gets in trouble, I will enter the water with the other end and you will pull us to safety."

Aizarg signaled for the next group.

With trepidation, Aizarg watched Okta and Sarah approach the water. Ghalen stood next to them on their downstream side.

Good, Ghalen will be there in case she falls off.

He saw Okta and Setenay reassuring her again, and then Okta leaned down. Sarah put her arms around his neck. A knot formed in Aizarg's belly.

He has to pull himself and her extra weight through the river. Okta volunteered eagerly to carry her.

He's glad to enter the water again, no matter how cold.

He saw Sarah close her eyes and Okta gently slipped into the river.

Sarah screamed in agony at the shock of the water's icy slap, but she held on. Her weight forced Okta into a breast stroke, further slowing him down. Aizarg saw the strain on Okta's face as he battled the river and fought to keep Sarah's head above the water.

If Ghalen struggled against the cold, Aizarg could not tell. He kept this head above the water with a side stroke a few feet downstream of Okta and Sarah

"All right, Ood-i, let's move downstream with them," Aizarg said and started briskly walking.

Once again, branches and logs floated past the swimmers. He heard Ghalen's voice getting louder, shouting directions to Okta about oncoming dangers and offering words of encouragement. "Slow down, there's a log about to pass ahead of you...Speed up and it will pass behind you...You're doing great, Sarah, you are almost to the shore!" Each time,

Ghalen expertly dodged the logs as they passed Okta and Sarah.

Sarah slowly turned white with cold and terror, but Ghalen's voice seemed to give her strength.

Ghalen has the strength of a lion and the heart of a sco-lo-ti. At every turn he proves himself. Aizarg wished Ghalen, a natural leader, was sco-lo-ti in the Turtle Clan, and not his older brother Masok.

"Uros!" Ood-i tapped Aizarg on the shoulder and pointed upstream. Ba-lok and Setenay were entering the water with Levidi off to the side, just as Ghalen had done with Okta and Sarah.

"Why are they getting in?" Aizarg said, bewildered. "I gave specific instructions!"

Okta and Sarah were two-thirds across the river as they approached the point opposite the carcass. Ghalen concentrated on Okta, who began to struggle.

Aizarg spied a stealthy shape materialize in the muddy water and then vanish just upstream of Okta.

Ice!

Aizarg didn't have time to shout a warning before the table-like triangle briefly reappeared behind Sarah's feet, water spilling over its smooth, flat top. Aizarg didn't have time to breathe a sigh of relief before the ice block resurfaced to the right of Ghalen, whose head ducked briefly underwater between breaths.

The ice slammed with full force into Ghalen's skull. He instantly became still and vanished beneath the water.

"*Ghalen!*" Sarah and Aizarg screamed in unison. Okta kept looking ahead, struggling for the next stroke and oblivious to Ghalen's dilemma.

"Pull me back in when I get him!" Aizarg shouted to Ood-i. He quickly tied the rope around his waist and plunged into the water. Immediately, the icy river attacked him. Aizarg swam as fast as he could, but the water robbed his strength faster this time.

"Okta, save Ghalen!" Aizarg heard Sarah scream when he came up for air, but Okta kept swimming forward, his eyes beginning to glaze.

Aizarg came up for air again where he thought Ghalen might be, but saw nothing.

The giant's carcass sped by and the southern cliffs loomed ahead.

"I see him!" Sarah screamed to Aizarg. Perched on Okta's back, she had a slightly better view than Aizarg. Oblivious to Ghalen's peril, Okta carried her farther away.

"Where?" Aizarg screamed.

"To your left, I can see his back!" A large log floated by Sarah and Okta, barely missing them.

"I can't see him!" Aizarg grew desperate.

"To your *left!*" she repeated.

Aizarg spun about, still unable to locate Ghalen.

Then Sarah did something Aizarg did not expect. She let go of Okta's neck and dove for the log. She didn't make it and slipped below the filthy water.

"SARAH!" he screamed.

Then her small hand emerged from the water and grabbed black bark. She pulled herself up, trying not to let the log roll back on top of her. Sputtering and gagging, she didn't hesitate a second before she starting kicking her feet. Sarah's desperate, uncoordinated splashes were adequate enough to propel her toward a point a few yards to Aizarg's left front.

Aizarg heard the muted roar grow louder and looked to his left. They were seconds from entering the rapids in the shadow of the southern cliffs. That's when he saw an island of white skin and a shoulder blade briefly bob out of the water. He lunged toward it and caught Ghalen by the hair and, with all his remaining strength, grabbed a hold of the log Sarah rode.

Suddenly, the rope around his waist tightened and water rushed over the back of his head. He strained to keep one arm around the log and the other hand on Ghalen. For a few seconds he felt hard rocks bump against his thighs, but then the bottom smoothed and wisps of smooth grass caressed his back.

Ood-i dragged Ghalen from the water while Aizarg helped Sarah. Aizarg turned to see Okta laid out on the grassy bank, exhausted and taking heaving gulps of air. He laid Sarah next to him and attended to Ghalen.

Ood-i knelt over Ghalen, gently slapping his face trying to get him to respond. A gash arced over Ghalen's left eye and fresh blood began to cake the left side of his face and matt his wet hair. The gash looked odd to Aizarg. It looked less like a cut and more like a double claw mark.

"His wound will heal," Ood-i said. "But he has water in his lungs. Help me t-turn him over."

Aizarg assisted Ood-i and then stood back, knowing exactly what Ood-i was about to do.

Every Lo learned this skill at a very young age, because even children of the Great Sea could drown. Ood-i positioned Ghalen's head to one side and straddled his back. Ood-i put his big, meaty hands over each side of Ghalen's upper back and pushed forward. After a few strong thrusts, Ghalen croaked and vomited out a few good bites of the river.

Ood-i turned him over. "He'll be fine!" Ood-i chuckled and stood. "I remember having to do that more than once when my little Su-gar fell off the d-dock as a b-baby."

Ghalen groaned and pulled himself on his elbows, squinting against the sun. "What happened?"

"The river almost took you," Aizarg said, examining Ghalen's head. "We'll have Setenay take a look at that..."

Setenay!

Aizarg shot up and looked back up river. To his relief he saw the figures of Levidi, Setenay and Ba-lok walking along the shore towards them.

Sarah pulled herself up and rolled over to Okta. "Are you okay, Okta?"

He raised his hand and nodded. "Yes, I just need a few moments to recover my strength."

Ghalen put his hand to his head and looked at the blood. "Who pulled me out?"

Aizarg smiled over to Sarah. "You owe this girl your life. Without her bravery I would not have been able to find you."

Sarah smiled under Aizarg's praise.

"Ood-i," Ghalen said weakly, lying back down with his hand over his wound.

"Yes, Ghalen," Ood-i leaned in, listening intently.

"I think your girlfriend must like me," Ghalen grinned.

Ood-i sat up with a scowl and threw the wet rope at Ghalen. "Bah! That's the last time I pull your sorry hide out of the wuh-water. Next time, learn how to swim before you cross such little streams!"

Aizarg began to laugh, followed by Ghalen and Sarah. As hard as he tried, Ood-i couldn't suppress a smile and soon joined them.

"They've all gone insane," Ba-lok said as they walked up.

Levidi and Ba-lok looked no worse for wear, and, surprisingly, neither did Setenay.

Aizarg stood and confronted Ba-lok. "I told you to wait until Okta and his group crossed. Why did you disobey me?"

"Do not blame me, Uros, speak to my grandmother. She insisted we cross when we did. She wouldn't accept no for an answer."

Puzzled, Aizarg looked to Setenay.

"I had my reasons. That is all I will say," she said.

"So be it. The matter is closed. I am thankful you made it. Ba-lok, how was the crossing?"

Ba-lok shrugged and motioned to his grandmother, "Easy, I had another pair of kicking legs."

Aizarg looked back at Setenay.

"I am Lo. In my day, I could outswim any of you," she said with all seriousness.

Aizarg looked back to Setenay but she wouldn't meet his eye. He sensed she wasn't telling him something, but decided not to press the issue.

Levidi brushed past Aizarg and whispered, "I dread the day I have to enter that cursed river again!" Levidi quickly untied his bundle and pulled his heavy garments out of his pack. "I can't believe I'm saying this, but I can't wait to don these winter clothes. I'm freezing!"

Aizarg turned to ask Ghalen and found him already changing into his heavy garments. Only the blood drying on Ghalen's smiling face spoke of his recent struggle.

Under the warm afternoon sun and light breeze, they were all dry in a few minutes, dressed and ready to continue the journey.

Levidi shouldered his and Ghalen's packs and looked back over the river.

"Aizarg," he said, where only his friend could hear. "I miss home. The thought of the Black River standing between us and everything we love somehow fills me with sadness."

Aizarg shielded his eyes against the western sun and looked back down the long valley from whence they came.

He felt it, too, the sensation of suddenly being cut off and isolated, as if they just passed a point of no return. He placed his hand over Atamoda's li-ge and pictured her and his boys waiting for him on the dock.

Aizarg clasped his friend's shoulder. "Our purpose will guide us, our friendship will support us, the memory of our homes and families will sustain us. No river, no matter how black and foul, can wash this goodness from our souls."

A sly grin lit Levidi's face, "You sound just like Atamoda!"

Aizarg gazed to the distant horizon with a warm smile. "Yes, I suppose. As long as she is in my heart, I am home. Hold true to Alaya's love and you will never be far from home, either."

The two old friends walked side by side as the rest of the group filed in behind them across the grassy steppe. They recounted the excitement of the river crossing as the wind blew warm from the southwest and a few puffy clouds raced across the pale blue sky.

***

Setenay lingered a few moments at the bank. She had carried a very different recollection of the events along the Black River.

Dozens of flat yellow eyes stared back at her from the depths. Wispy humanoid shapes darted to and fro, suspended and yet separate from the muddy water, so many they slithered over each other like spawning eels. Setenay shuddered as she considered how fortunate they were to escape relatively unscathed.

She wasn't entirely truthful when she told Aizarg this river was soulless. Hordes of demons, not water spirits, possessed it.

Setenay knew such demons existed in all bodies of water, as water possesses the power of life and death. She'd never seen so many schooling at once, and so brazenly in the shallow water and open sunlight.

Like marsh locusts without birds to eat them, the demons have spawned to fill the void left by the absent water spirits. The elements are out of balance.

Setenay elected not to tell the rest of the group about the water demons, thinking it best to let them believe only floating ice and freezing water assaulted them. They had no choice but to cross the river, so she had no reason to frighten them.

The patesi-le knows when to speak the truth to the blind, and when to simply lead them to safety.

Without her protective chants, Aizarg and Ood-i would have surely died within seconds of entering the cursed river. However, as both men drifted downstream and neared the opposite shore, her incantations lost power and demons darted at the men like hungry catfish. By then, however, the men's natural strength sufficed to ward off the demonic assaults.

When Okta and Sarah entered the water, the black horde attacked them like a murder of crows descending upon a crust of bread. The demonic onslaught caught Setenay unprepared. They shattered her protective spell and lunged not for Okta, but Sarah.

At that moment Sarah screamed, perhaps sensing the blackness ripping at her soul. To Setenay's surprise, instead of dragging Okta and Sarah into the depths, the water demons were hurled back and fled to the bottom as leaves scattered before the wind. Setenay immediately turned to Ba-lok and ordered him to take her into the water. The demons also parted from Setenay's path, but not with the same fear as they parted for Sarah. When Sarah lunged into the water to save Ghalen, her powerful aura scattered the demons yet again.

"Grandmother!" Ba-lok called out. She snapped out of her trance and turned to see them all looking at her, waiting.

"I'm coming," she said, and turned once again to the water.

Setenay looked down on the shadows slithering over each other in the shallows. She waved her hand over the water and the demons scattered like minnows away from a rock thrown off a dock. Suddenly, large chunks of the northern and southern cliffs broke free and crashed into the water.

A chill went down her spine. She pondered the moments when she had her feet in the water before Aizarg's crossing. She knew Aizarg recognized the fear in her eyes, grateful he didn't press for an explanation. The demons' presence didn't shake her spirit, it's what they told her.

With her feet in the water, she communed with them, ever mindful of their deceptive nature.

Let us pass, hell spawn, for I am a witch of great power!

We do not doubt your power, they hissed in unison in her mind. *Enter the water. Join with us and we will make you more powerful still!*

Save your lies, she reached out with her thoughts. *Part before my power and speak truth. Why do you gather here in great numbers?*

You might defeat us this day, Lo bitch, but your days are short. Be fearful, for the springs of the deep have cracked open and we are free from the Abyss. Behold, for we shall devour all the earth.

Another chunk of the northern ridge fell under the onslaught of the river. Setenay turned and followed her grandson and the rest of the party to the east.

13. The Children Of Fu Xi

Even immortals have a beginning, an earthly springtime of life where the heart rules the mind. In my youthful pride, I tried to bring enlightenment to the Ice Men, the dwellers of the north. In form and manner they were so much like the Tall Men. I was certain I could light their path.

Mother didn't try to stop me, but she gave me no encouragement, no advice or new craft for my quest.

"They are monsters," she warned.

"They are men."

"A pebble and a seed may look the same upon the ground, but only one will yield fruit," Mother said.

"Are they not worthy of Grace? Is there no hope for them? Why is this breed of man treated so differently from any other?"

"I will speak no more of this," she said. "Search your soul for the reasons why you do this. Is it for their welfare or for your pride?"

Without her blessing I traveled into the icelands. Millennia ago those wastes were not so distant. They covered the mountains and kissed the deep forests. I returned with only bitterness as my reward.

The Chronicle of Fu Xi.

139

***

Fu Xi saw the lifeless body before he emerged from the forest. Like the bars of a cage, the black trees framed the grisly scene beyond the shadowed woodland. The terraced fields fell away from the south side of the compound and sloped down to the forest edge. The body, an unnatural mound amongst the stubble of the harvested fields, rested halfway between the trees and the south compound wall.

Fu Xi saw no purpose lingering in the forest, no reason to hide. He abandoned the forest twilight for the fading warmth of the harvest sunset.

The ancient village perched high along the spine of a gentle ridge which fell off to terraced fields on its north and south slopes. In autumn, the south slope caught most of the sun. This is where Fu Xi now strode, sword extended low and ready.

The convent's southeast wall, its whitewashed clay reflecting the brilliant sunset, crested the hill about a hundred yards away. The graceful arch of the sanctuary roof rose above the outer wall. Both the wall and the roof were covered in red terracotta tiles shaped like carp scales.

About a dozen thatched huts stretched along the main road beyond the convent's west gate. From this perspective, Fu Xi could only see the back of the huts. A small corral, where the villagers kept their pigs and goats, nestled behind each hut. The bamboo fences were shattered, the livestock gone. Tendrils of smoke rose over the huts. Farther west, beyond the dwellings, Nushen's main road vanished into the forest. That is where he would have normally entered the village.

Out of sight to his right, hidden behind the convent, a path led downhill from the compound's east gate toward Tortoise Mountain.

Fu Xi approached the corpse. The dry crunch of his sandals on the stubble sounded unnaturally loud in the still air. The open field afforded ample room to fight, and he hoped the enemy would reveal itself.

Finally, Fu Xi stood over the child's dead body. He slowed his breathing and blinked back the tears.

Fu Xi did not recognize the boy, perhaps ten summers old. Born in his absence, the child provided Fu Xi a gauge of the years gone by. He lifted the child's torn peasant garb with the edge of his sword and instantly knew what horror befell his beloved village.

His mother once told him the fruits of pride are slow to ripen and always bitter.

"I understand now, Mother," he whispered.

***

I never referred to them as 'unfinished men', my mother's disdainful term. Nor did I use the wretched names bestowed upon them by the Tall Men, like 'troll.' I called them 'Ice Men,' because they roamed the glacial northlands. In them I thought I found my true purpose, to bring them into the light of civilization.

I returned to the cave after several days of scouting the glacier. I sent the Ice Men east to hunt reindeer without me. They needed to master their new spears, to gain confidence in their own skills without their god looking over their shoulders.

Two days previous, I spied a herd of mammoths on the central glacier and hurried back to the cave to tell my children. A small band of nomadic Tall Men tracked this herd, as well as another clan of Ice Men.

The Tall Men hunted a big female mammoth with a wounded leg, hoping to separate her from the main herd. The Ice Men followed the Tall Men like starving jackals, just out of sight and undetected. Only armed with sharpened sticks, this scraggly band aspired to glean leftover meat.

The Tall Men did not concern to me. I wanted my clan, armed with their new spears and improved skills, to get to the female mammoth first. The Tall Men had plenty of other game in their warm lowlands; the glaciers were for my people. As for the other Ice Men clan, my goal was to combine the two groups. Getting the two dominant males to cooperate, however, would be a daunting task.

The mammoths were still several miles south. If my clan wanted fresh meat, they would have to hurry. I also wanted to keep them away from the Tall Men, knowing the encounter between the two races would result in battle.

Snow blew thick out of the gray sky when I reached the mouth of the cave.

The Chronicle of Fu Xi

***

The child's head tilted back, his face frozen in a grimace of agony. His wide eyes were dry and beginning to shrivel. His face had started to pull back and decompose.

This happened about three days ago. But how?

The child's arms and legs were gone, ripped off his body while they held him down. He bled out, but not before several of the attackers gnawed on his stumps. The boy wasn't dragged off, which told Fu Xi the child likely died first in the attack, when the creatures' hunger and bloodlust was raw and fresh.

Fu Xi closed his eyes, took several cleansing breaths, and clenched and unclenched his jaw. His imagination ran wild with visions of what the child suffered. He opened his eyes and looked to the sky.

No vultures. No flies. The strange curse has infected Nushen, too.

He examined the ground around the body. Dried blood stained the stalk stubble, now flattened by dozens of heavy bare feet.

Ice Men.

Dozens of tracks emerged from the forest to the southeast, indicating a large clan probably led by a powerful dominant male. Fu Xi knew they were probably driven south by hunger.

A stick and a leather ball lay several paces downhill from the body. *The boy played in the field. He watched them rush out of the forest and didn't sense the danger until it was too late. They butchered him on the spot.*

Why should he have been afraid? Nushen had never suffered an attack since the dawn of time.

The tracks led into the village.

They are still here, still feeding. Perhaps the Holy Mothers closed the gates before the Ice Men overwhelmed them.

The silence blanketing the village told him otherwise. He looked up the mountain at his mother's temple.

Where is she?

He slowly rolled his neck around, listening to each joint pop and letting the sound calm him. The lessons of the Olmec war masters, the men who taught him the ways of the White and Red Swords, came back to him. He never thought he'd have to employ their skills within the confines of his own village.

He flicked the sword twice, turned, and reentered the forest. Without a sound, he made his way west and then north inside the tree line. Fu Xi climbed the embankment and emerged from the darkening woods onto the road leading into the village. He would not steal into his village like a thief. He would enter Nushen the way he did after every journey. The last of the sun warmed his back as he followed his long shadow home.

***

A fresh snow drift quickly formed at the mouth of the cave and began to cover fresh tracks leading up to the entrance. I recognized them as the footprints of the clan males. They had dragged something heavy and bloody into the cave.

I was pleased the men had a successful hunt.

Several months previous I discovered this clan of seven males and two females in this very cave, huddled together and starving. They would be my first attempt to bring the Ice Men out of darkness, as I had done with the Tall Men of the south centuries ago.

Naturally, they feared me at first. The clan accepted me as their leader when I subdued their dominant male. They worshipped me as a god when I taught them the art of fire.

At the cave's entrance a roaring fire defied the north wind, but oddly, without a lookout huddled over it. I climbed up to the ledge at the cave's entrance, which overlooked the ice fields in the valley below. Several blazing fires burned throughout the cave, creating a trail of light leading deep into the bowels of the earth. I removed my heavy furs and shook off the snow.

The main chamber was curiously empty.

The Chronicle of Fu Xi

***

The red dirt trail widened and became a neatly manicured lane covered with white crushed pebbles. It stretched about eighty yards to the first huts that flanked either side of the road. Only a blackened heap remained of the second hut on the left, home of Zuchanshi, the midwife. Several huts on the north side of the lane were also burned to the ground. A small fire smoldered in the center of the road in front of Tiejiang's hut. Fu Xi looked beyond the fire toward the convent.

The convent's ornate cedar gates were askew, as if one of the young acolytes had innocently forgotten to close them in her rush to supper. The last of Fu Xi's hope vanished. He tightened his grip on his sword.

Something caught his eye. The Ice Man emerged from a hut and walked toward the fire with a distinctive side-to-side sway. The creature had all the traits of the Ice Men: barrel chest, stooped shoulders, short stocky legs, sloped forehead and bold lower jaw. It was naked, covered only with a light mat of curly black hair. Unaware, it squatted next to the fire with its back to Fu Xi. The Ice Man picked up something Fu Xi had taken for a piece of wood. Fu Xi recognized it as an arm when the creature took a large bite out of it.

Suddenly, the creature stopped gnawing on the arm and grunted. It arched its back and passed excrement in the middle of the well-manicured lane. When it finished, it promptly returned to its feast.

Fu Xi could take no more. Wrath boiled in his chest as he slashed the sword through the air to get the monster's attention.

It dropped the arm and spun around, stepping in its own filth. Dried blood, ashes and grime streaked the creature's body. Its belly distended in grim testimony to recent feasts. It pulled back its lips and snarled a warning, revealing strong yellow teeth; teeth made for crushing and ripping, but incapable of speech.

The monster howled and raised its thickly muscled arms, trying to appear as large and fearsome as possible.

Fu Xi made no move to attack. He waited patiently for the rest of the monsters to emerge in response to the warning cry.

And come they did.

Dozens stumbled from the huts and out of the shadows. They didn't wear their usual heavy animal skins. The warm Valley of Nushen was a far cry from the northlands. Some carried spears; thick, gnarled sticks with crude flint tips.

The sight of the flint spears filled Fu Xi with shame. He taught the Ice Men that deadly craft long ago.

***

The men's furs were laid next to the central fire to dry and their spears leaned against the wall. The blood-streaked flint tips and shafts further testified to the hunt's success. I mused as to what kind of animal they had slain. It was probably a reindeer, a week's worth of meat at best. It was imperative I lead them to the mammoths if they wanted to eat through the long winter.

I hefted one of the spears. Like fire, they learned this craft quickly. A crude, but effective flint tip wedged into a notched wooden shaft and secured with raw sinews. The sinews were not toughened by boiling, like those of the Tall Men's spears, therefore not as strong. I hadn't taught the Ice Men the art of pottery yet, so they could not boil water. It could take several generations before they managed that craft. Thus far, I'd been unable to teach them to throw their spears. I supposed it was due to their bulky shoulders and thick necks. However, an Ice Man was significantly stronger than a Tall Man and could bring down a woolly rhino with a single, well-placed thrust.

I heard noises and suspected the clan was butchering the kill deep in the cave. It was imperative that they keep as much of the smell of blood inside the cave as possible not to attract wolves or bears.

I walked toward the back of the cave, curious about what game my children had secured for their meal.

The Chronicle of Fu Xi

***

Fu Xi stood relaxed with his legs slightly apart, both hands on the hilt of his sword like a cane. His eyes narrowed as he counted the horde and calculated his attack.

The Ice Men lined up across the narrow road and slowly approached. They shrieked and barked like a pack of hyenas confronting a lion, baring their teeth and shaking their weapons. Fu Xi had his back to the sun, forcing them to squint. They advanced half the distance before they hesitated.

They are uncertain why I don't retreat in the face of overwhelming numbers.

The one Fu Xi waited for finally pushed his way to the front. The largest Ice Man slapped the smaller ones to the side. The pack leader's greasy black hair tumbled over his shoulders and back. He communicated to his horde with animal-like snorts, barks and grunts.

They sound like Olmecs. That thought further stirred Fu Xi's rage.

The leader pushed the two nearest Ice Men toward Fu Xi. One had a spear, the other didn't.

The leader wants to test me before he commits to battle.

The spearman attacked first, running headlong at Fu Xi, shaft outstretched. The unarmed one followed closely in his wake.

Fu Xi waited patiently until the first charging Ice Man almost reached him. At the last second, he pivoted left and flashed his sword up to the right. The creature's momentum carried it past Fu Xi as its spear fell to the ground in three clean parts.

In a blur, Fu Xi spun into the path of the second Ice Man. Its head thudded onto the gravel and rolled into the grass. The creature's body stopped and stood for a few seconds before it crumpled to the ground.

Bewildered, the first Ice Man examined the shaft stump still in his hands and then considered the head of its compatriot lying in the grass. That's when it noticed a thin red line along its abdomen, just below its hairy belly button. Dumfounded, it reached down and touched a single drop of blood trickling from the line. The line quickly thickened and entrails suddenly tumbled to the creature's feet. It shrieked and fell to its knees, trying to gather its innards from the dust.

Fu Xi calmly examined the sword. Perfectly clean except for a sliver of blood on the leading edge, the orichalcum seemed eager for the taste of vengeance.

The lion slowly approached the hyenas.

The creatures bumped into one another as they fell back. Their leader howled, trying to frighten Fu Xi and stir his pack's courage, but the cries of the Ice Man thrashing on the ground overwhelmed him.

I once called them my children.

Fu Xi exploded into their ranks, a whirlwind of righteous fury. They swarmed him, but Fu Xi remained a blur, effortlessly eluding their clumsy grasps. Not a single hand touched his garment. Clubs and spears met only air and metal.

The leader fell first, his right leg cleanly severed below the hip. One after another, the Ice Men crumpled until the pebbles glistened with blood. Limbs and intestines littered the ground, but not one Ice Man died immediately. Fu Xi wanted them to suffer for hours in immobilized agony.

Fu Xi hardened his heart. This day there would be no mercy.

After only a few moments, the remaining handful broke off and fled into the darkening forest. Breathing relaxed and forehead dry, Fu Xi ceased his attack with legs slightly apart and bent, red sword extended in mid-swing. Not a drop of blood found its way onto his garment.

The dying Ice Men surrounded him like an ant mound. Fu Xi leapt over the quivering bodies and calmly pursued the survivors into the trees. Ice Men were at home in the wide open expanses of the glaciers and tundra. The closed-in forest only added to their panic as they crashed through the undergrowth.

Twilight faded to a moonless night as Fu Xi patiently hunted them down, leaving each slowly dying amongst the ferns.

Eventually, Fu Xi emerged from the forest near the western road where the battle began. The great expanse of the Milky Way unfurled overhead in the moonless sky. Disembodied wails and agonized moans floated through the darkness, replacing the absent sounds of crickets and frogs.

Fu Xi suddenly tensed as a shadow emerged from the forest onto the road. He crouched and brought up his sword. The shadow moved again, followed by a lighter shadow. He relaxed and made his way up the embankment onto the road.

"Didn't I tell you to wait?" he gently chided the horses. As if sensing Fu Xi's pain, Heise and Huise surrounded him and tenderly nuzzled his face. He wrapped his arms around each of their necks and buried his head into Huise's flank.

I cannot cry. That will come later. I must find any survivors.

He patted them and whispered, "Do not follow me again. Wait here until I am certain it is safe." He removed a torch and his tinder kit from the pack on Huise's back. In a few minutes, the flickering torch led his way. Fu Xi stepped around the dying Ice Men and into Tiejiang's hut.

***

I made my way past the furs and pine boughs where the clan slept. I didn't sleep among them in the main chamber. Instead, I slumbered under the sheltered overhang at the cave's mouth. It was important I avoided over-familiarity with these mortals whom I considered my new children. One reason was dogged persistence of the two mature females, especially the red-headed one, to mate with me. I, being the son of a goddess and a Tall Man, could not bring myself to find them desirable, especially in the near emaciated state I found them in.

However, after only a few months with their new spears, the clan finally had enough food. The women were better nourished and pregnant, though with whose child, I wasn't sure. The Ice Men coupled like dogs whenever the fancy struck them, but the females gravitated toward the strongest males. I did not judge them too harshly, as the first wild clans of Tall Men I taught were much the same.

I named the oldest female 'Peacock', as she was almost pretty and especially proud of her long red hair. The clan leader I called 'Broad Back', due to his immense shoulders. The youngest man I called 'Morning Star'. He had sensitive hazel eyes under his tangled brown hair and deep brow.

Morning Star joined me at the mouth of the cave each morning, where we silently watched the sun crest the eastern mountains. In him I rested my hope for the race of Ice Men.

I never knew what they called each other. Other than crude grunts and primitive hand signals, the Ice Men were apparently devoid of speech. I tried, and failed, to teach them the language of the Tall Men. I needed to believe they had the capacity for speech, but the longer I lived among them, the more doubts plagued my mind. Without the gift of speech, men cannot define their humanity. Without a sense of humanity, there can be no compassion.

The Chronicle of Fu Xi

***

Grain, pottery, iron tools, glassware, looms, and other treasures were cast aside by the Ice Men as junk. These were the treasures Fu Xi lovingly labored for centuries to teach mortals. The torch cast ruddy light upon shards of broken pottery interspersed among torn bodies. Suddenly, he caught Tiejiang's vacant eyes staring at him from the shadows.

He dropped the torch and fell to his knees. He cradled Tiejiang's head between his knees and stroked the dead man's gray hair.

For what seemed like an eternity, he knelt over his friend's body. "How did you grow so old?" Fu Xi laughed between tears. "Was I gone so long?" When Fu Xi bid farewell many years ago, Tiejiang was a man in his prime.

"I'm sorry...I'm sorry..." he whispered over and over as he rocked back and forth. He couldn't bring himself to look down at the blacksmith's violated body. A small hand lay across Tiejiang's butchered abdomen. Fu Xi reached out and touched the dead child's head.

He could have stayed there all night stewing in his grief, but the thought of possible survivors somewhere in the village stirred him. A full oil lamp hung from a peg next to the bloody sleeping mats. Fu Xi stood and lit the wax wick with the torch. The lamp glowed to life, providing a brighter and steadier light than the torch. Fu Xi shook the torch to extinguish it. He held the lamp high and turned to leave the hut.

Fu Xi stumbled throughout the village, finding only carnage. His grief and anger were rekindled with each new grisly discovery. Eventually, he found his way to the convent. He pushed the gates open wider and stepped into the courtyard. Fu Xi clenched his eyes shut and swayed back and forth, assaulted by an image beyond his worst nightmare.

The remains of the acolytes were piled under the ancient willow tree in the courtyard. The grim heap of gnawed limbs and gutted torsos were still clothed in bloody tatters of their white robes.

They were practicing for the Offering Festival.

When he opened his eyes, he could not bring himself to look upon the sacrilege. He numbly gazed up at the paper lanterns hanging limply, dark and lifeless, from the willow tree.

My world has come to an end.

He looked up at the silhouette of Tortoise Mountain against the brilliant stars. He threw his head back and screamed, "MOTHER!" His anguish echoed off the cliffs above.

Fu Xi's sword clattered to the cobblestones as he fell to his knees. He set the lantern down, leaned his head forward to the ground and sobbed, pounding his fists against the stones.

"Why?"

***

I strolled along a small ledge on the right side of the main chamber into the dim recesses of the cave. As I walked, I reached out and caressed my proudest accomplishment with the Ice Men thus far, the one that gave me hope they may one day speak.

Not long after their cave was illuminated with firelight, I noticed Morning Star scratching crude images on the walls with sharpened bones. I seized the opportunity and spent hours teaching him how to mix plants, roots and different clays to form various pigments.

After several weeks, Morning Star had adorned the cave walls with bears, bison, and mammoths. The beautiful black, red, and ochre paintings struck a chord in my soul. I may have shown Morning Star how to mix the colors, but the artistic mastery belonged solely to him.

One night, I made my way to the back of the cave and found Morning Star curled up under a bison fur, sound asleep. His fingers and face were streaked with pigment. I tenderly stepped over the young man, careful not to wake him. There, on the wall was my image; an immense godlike figure in crisp blacks and reds. I was robed with my broadsword held high. Seven small, black figures danced at my feet, hands held high and heads craned back in adoration.

If being worshipped was necessary to establish a civilization among this race, so be it. Was this so different than the altars to my mother among the Tall Men? If Mother could see Morning Star's astonishing art, she would be forced to reconsider her opinion of the Ice Men. I believed there was nobility below their savage veneer. I determined to mold it, just as I'd done with the Tall Men. I would prove Mother wrong.

As I walked to the back of the cave on that snowy night, I once again passed by Morning Star's painting. Then, something I never noticed in the painting caught my eye. At first I thought it might be a trick of light or the texture of the rock. I paused and looked closer.

Behind my image was a shadow. Perhaps it was soot from a torch, I thought. Shape and shade drew my eye in, forming an image much larger than I originally suspected. I stepped back and scanned the cave wall from where it curved at the roof to where it met the dirt floor.

Looming over my image and the seven dancing figures was an immense shadow, almost like a watermark, in the vague form of a serpent. Serpents were strangers to the glaciers and unknown to the Ice Men.

Armed with this new perspective, it appeared the seven dancing figures, their heads craned back, were actually worshipping the black serpent. I shook my head and tried to refocus. No, I thought, the dark image couldn't be a serpent.

The Chronicle of Fu Xi

***

Somewhere in the darkness he heard a faint wail. Fu Xi sat up, wiped his tears, and strained to hear the sound. It came again, this time louder and stronger, from somewhere inside the convent.

A baby!

He snapped to his feet, sword and lantern in hand.

The convent was composed of two low slung buildings against the north and south outer walls, and the high-roofed sanctuary against the east wall. The sanctuary housed the Celestial Gate, also called the East Gate. It led downhill to the foot of Tortoise Mountain and the Silver Stairs.

The baby's cries didn't come from the sanctuary or the living quarters in the south building. It emanated from the north building, which housed the kitchens, granaries, and food storage.

Fu Xi held the lantern high and rushed into the archway leading to the open kitchens. On the floor, a dead Ice Man lay sprawled with a bronze kitchen knife protruding from its chest.

Someone fought back!

His elation withered when he spotted a body splayed on one of the long tables. He recognized dear old Tiro, the cook. Thick and strong as a water buffalo, Tiro seemed to spring from her mother's womb old and cranky. If anyone would have instinctively fought back against the Ice Man, it would have been her. They crushed her head, but otherwise left her uneaten.

Why eat an old strap of leather like Tiro with so many young, tender morsels about?

The infant's cry rose out of the darkness again, this time stronger.

The root cellar.

Fu Xi dashed toward the rear of the main kitchen, beyond the gaping hearth. An archway opened to a small room behind the mud brick chimney. Split firewood sat neatly stacked to the rafters against the far wall and a wooden stairwell descended into the darkness to his left.

Fu Xi held up the lantern over the stairwell. "It is I, Fu Xi. The Ice Men are dead. Come up, it is safe now."

From the blackness below, the baby wailed again. Fu Xi heard a shushing sound as a small shadow materialized at the bottom of the stairwell. Fu Xi took two steps down, lantern out and sword ready.

His heart sank. The dingy light fell upon a naked Ice Man child, a boy of perhaps three. The boy on the bottom step considered Fu Xi without fear, his thick brown hair a wild mess. Other than his thick brow and sloped forehead, he looked like a Tall Man child of the same age. It wasn't until puberty that noticeable differences manifested between the graceful Tall Man and the squat Ice Man.

An arm shot out from the darkness and pulled the boy into the shadows.

The infant cried again, louder this time. Fu Xi descended to the bottom.

I should have expected this. Ice Men are cave dwellers. The cellar is a natural place for the pack's females to take refuge with their young.

Two females crouched against the earthen wall between two pots of rice. One mature female, perhaps sixteen summers, had long red hair and hazel eyes and bore an uncanny resemblance to Peacock, now dead thousands of years. She held the newborn against her full breasts with one arm and pointed a sharpened stick toward Fu Xi with the other. The baby tried to latch onto her breast, frustrated with her uncooperative mother.

With budding breasts, the other female stood on the cusp of childbearing. She held the boy tightly against her. All of them were naked and covered in grime. The terror in their eyes filled Fu Xi's heart with pity. He lowered his sword and scanned the room.

That's when he saw the shattered femurs on the cellar floor.

The Ice Men brought the marrow to their females.

His vision swam.

***

I convinced myself it had to be a trick of light and continued deeper into the cave. The shadow was a natural stain upon the rock. It was always there, I must have missed it before.

The Ice Men were learning as fast as I could have hoped. When summer came, they would migrate north. I still didn't know how different clans interacted, but I assumed they would submit to the power of the strongest male. It was my hope Broad Back would defeat any challengers and draw other clans into his brood. In that way, I hoped my clan would share their new skills with other Ice Men.

Firelight gave birth to giant shadows dancing across the cave's roof, like one of Morning Star's paintings come to life. Grunts and thuds echoed from ahead. I heard the ripping of flesh and breaking of bones. The clansmen were feasting on their kill. I took a deep breath and steeled myself for the bloody scene.

I attempted to introduce the skill of cooking to the Ice Men, but they would have none of it. I prepared my meals in front of them, roasting all my meat on an open spit. I offered them cooked food. They only sniffed and poked at it, turning up their noses as if it were offal. There was something disconcerting about the way they tore at their kills with animal-like zeal. I was also shocked by how much meat they could eat. The average clan male easily consumed twice the meat of a Tall Man. And they only ate meat.

After a kill, they always reserved the finest haunches for their god. My stomach rumbled at the thought of roasting a tender backstrap over the fire.

I also taught them the art of butchering with a flint knife, as opposed to simply ripping the dead animal apart with their powerful hands and teeth. They were usually good about using the knife in my presence but, judging from the sounds coming from the back of the cave, I suspected they resorted to their familiar savagery in my absence.

At that moment, I recall smiling in self-satisfaction and thinking I couldn't expect miracles in seven months.

I crested the small rise where the cave dropped off into a shallow pit at the back wall. My children squatted in a circle around the pit. They turned with bloody smiles as their god approached.

Seeking my approval, Broad Back beamed at me and held up the piece of meat he was gnawing on. Morning Star had his head buried in a torso, blood and gore matting his hair against his forehead.

My mind caught up with what my eyes beheld and my smile evaporated. The forms of the dead animals seemed odd. Why were there bloody strips of tanned leather and polished beads strewn across the cave floor? Then I saw the unmistakable shape of a human foot, ripped off above the ankle, in front of Peacock.

Naked, she squatted over a pile of flesh. Her belly was starting to show with the baby inside her. She smiled up at me, strings of flesh stuck in her teeth and blood smearing her enlarged breasts and swollen belly. She held a human femur, broken in two in the middle. She was sucking out the rich, fatty marrow.

As the horror of what I witnessed dawned on me, my first stunned thought was how natural it was for them to give the rich marrow to the expecting females.

They saw my rage and their smiles vanished. I knew at that moment they didn't see the Tall Men as human, worthy of compassion. I was also angry at myself. I should have foreseen this possibility, though the thought they would eat something so much like themselves came dangerously close to violating the natural law of the soul.

I had to make them stop and burn into their simple minds that Tall Men had souls and were fellow beings favored by the Emperor of Heaven.

I drew my sword and screamed, "Stop!" As my voice thundered through the cave, they dropped their meat and scampered against the far wall. They cowered behind Broad Back and whimpered, terrified and confused about how they had incurred the wrath of their god.

Now I saw the severed human heads against the back cave wall. I recognized these people as the Tall Men who were stalking the mammoths on the glacier. Broad Back and his men must have picked up the trail of the Tall Men after I departed to the west, though how they beat me back to the cave was a mystery. Blinded by the snow, we must have just missed each other out on the glacier. The sight of the pile of bodies sickened me. How was I going to communicate to them eating the Tall Men was wrong?

The torso Morning Star feasted on caught my eye. It was short and thick. I blinked and looked again.

I looked closer at several of the other bodies. Two were Tall Men, two were not.

They were Ice Men from the clan on the glacier.

I stumbled back. The warm cave now felt oppressive. I felt confined, overwhelmed, and unable to breathe. I turned and fled. As I passed Morning Star's painting, the shadow loomed over me. It was now darker and unmistakably that of a black dragon.

I fled into the storm, never to return to the frozen lands of the Ice Men.

The Chronicle of Fu Xi

***

The sword barely stirred the air before the cellar fell silent. He fled the convent and stumbled out the Celestial Gate toward Tortoise Mountain. The path sloped down and ended at the Offering Temple.

The Offering Temple, nothing more than a graceful archway, stood at the base of the Silver Stairs. The top of the archway had three red-tile spires. At the threshold of the Offering Temple the pebble pathway split around a central dais. Beyond the dais, the pebbles gave way to carved limestone and the Silver Stairs began. Just off the path to the right of the archway he saw the sacred Tree of Immortality outlined against the stars. A few yards beyond the archway, the limestone path crossed over a small arch-like bridge spanning a grotto, at the bottom of which a stream separated Tortoise Mountain from the village. The Silver Stairs ascended up the steep mountainside, illuminated by a sparse necklace of torches.

Fu Xi examined the Offering Temple. Withered flowers were scattered over seven empty candle holders carved into the jade dais. He picked up a dry lotus flower and crumbled it in his palm.

Something stood in the pathway just beyond the temple. He crossed under the archway, a realm forbidden to all mortals save the chosen acolyte and the husband of the goddess.

Two pillars of salt stood in the middle of the grotto bridge, each in the shape of an Ice Man, spear in hand, running up the stairs. A fresh white lotus flower lay at their feet.

She was here. Fu Xi's mother protected her own temple, but abandoned the village. Unable to fathom the mystery laid before him, he sheathed his sword and raced up the Silver Stairs.

***

The word 'Ice Man' will no longer cross my lips or flow from my brush. Human in form only, these unfinished men are devoid of compassion. I, the God of Names, have no name for these monstrosities and my words only serve to remind me of my failure. From henceforth, I shall use the names bestowed upon these creatures by mortals: goblin, troll, or ogre. Hunt these monsters until they are no more.

The Chronicle of Fu Xi

14. The Scythian

They first appeared in the time of Aizarg's great-great grandfather. Fishermen caught glimpses of ghostlike apparitions watching from the shore. More than one sco-lo-ti dismissed such tales until refugees from the eastern g'an pressed into the shore camps, begging the Lo to take them in. They brought terrifying stories of attacks by two-headed monsters. Then the tribes of the western g'an flooded into the marshes, desperate for sanctuary.

The marshes slowed the invaders, but didn't stop them. They drove the Lo from the shore camps and far into the marshes. The hordes stopped at the water's edge and that is when the Lo established the arun-ki, the stilted villages upon the sea. The Lo proved too difficult to conquer and the enemy turned away from the Great Sea. The Lo endured the invaders' onslaught, but the Sammujad never fully recovered and were forced to the outer reaches of the grasslands.

Many of the refugees were adopted by the Lo, quickly abandoning the brutal ways of the g'an for the gentle life of the sea. Ood-i and Levidi, darker and stockier than men like Ghalen and Aizarg, were descendants of those refugees. In those black days a Lo proverb was born - In the face of darkness, mercy.

In time, the Lo and the tribes of the g'an learned the invaders were men, not monsters. They rode creatures new to the g'an — horses. However, the original name stuck — "Scythia," the blended ones.

The Scythian invaders brought two new realities to the world of the Lo: the horse and the bow. Only the Great Sea offered haven from both.

The Chronicle of Fu Xi

***

As the day warmed, talk of the icy black river slowly died. Occasionally, they stopped to rest and eat dried fish, but only for a few minutes. The sun started its slow descent at their backs as they trudged onward, always keeping to the low ground.

Levidi looked back at Aizarg, who trailed behind with Setenay and Okta in quiet conversation.

Aizarg did all the talking. Setenay listened with concern. She held her walking stick with both hands behind her back and stared hard at the ground ahead of her. Occasionally, she nodded or shook her head. Okta appeared unconcerned.

Levidi couldn't hear them and wondered what they were discussing, but stayed out of the conversation.

If the Uros wants my council he will ask for it.

He wanted to walk with his friend, to get Aizarg to loosen up. He could see the weight on Aizarg's shoulders, especially since the river crossing. Levidi knew heavy burdens fell on Aizarg in his new role as Uros, responsibilities far beyond those of a common village sco-lo-ti. Levidi shuddered at the thought of having that much responsibility.

My duty is to serve the Uros. I will help him any way I can.

Levidi's eyes bore into Ba-lok's back, now only a small silhouette far up the draw.

He has no business being a Second to the Uros. In fact, he has no business being a sco-lo-ti.

160

Levidi rubbed his aching left thigh, unaccustomed to marching long distances. He wanted to complain (something Alaya told him he *was* accustomed to), but he knew better.

Aizarg needs a dependable friend. Ba-Lok is unreliable. I will have to be Aizarg's Second, if not in name, then in spirit. A good Second does not complain. I will not complain.

He needed something to take his mind off his aching legs, so he struck up a conversation.

"The terrain is changing," he said to Sarah and Ghalen. "It appears to go uphill in every direction."

"So it is, at least ahead of us," Ghalen commented. "Are you tired, Levidi? If so, I can take my pack. Perhaps it is too heavy?"

"It is not too heavy! That's not what I am saying."

Sarah, walking between the two men, stifled a giggle.

"I apologize, for I did not mean to offend. What is it you are trying to say, friend?" Ghalen continued with a look of mock concern.

Levidi huffed, "All I am saying is the terrain appears to be changing. It feels steeper, though I see no hill ahead of us. And there are rocks poking out of the ground here and there. I cannot pull them out. When we stopped to eat earlier, I tried to dig one up and it kept getting bigger."

"We are climbing higher as we near the Adyghe Mountains, though it is difficult to tell because it is so gradual," Sarah said, pointing ahead of them. "Soon, perhaps by nightfall, we will begin to see the occasional scrub oak on the ridges to our north and south. The ridges on either side will grow narrower and steeper. As I told the Uros, by tomorrow afternoon we will come to a place where this low ground terminates in a canyon, closed in on three sides. We will climb the eastern rim and there overlook the Hur Valley."

"What I really wanted to know is when does it go back downhill? My legs are killing me and I believe Ghalen put rocks in his pack."

Levidi winked at Sarah and Ghalen gave a hearty laugh.

"*Aizarg!*" Ba-lok's alarmed cry came from far ahead. Ghalen and Levidi set off at a full run, spears at the ready.

In a few minutes the party found itself standing in amazement alongside Ba-lok and Ood-i.

The grasslands were ripped open and trampled from north to south in a swath so wide they couldn't see the other side. Endless tracts of exposed roots and clods of dry earth were turned up to the sun and wind.

"Is this what you saw near the Valley of the Beasts?" Okta asked in awe.

"Yes," Aizarg responded. "Though the tracks leading to the Valley of the Beasts from the marshes were not on this scale."

Ghalen bent down and clenched a handful of the torn ground. A good hunter, perhaps as good as Aizarg, Levidi trusted Ghalen's tracking skills. He was pleased Ghalen accompanied the party, even if he did lose a bet to him.

If there is one man among us who might give the Scythians a good fight, it's Ghalen.

Ghalen let the dirt slip between his fingers. "The earth is dry, but the tracks are deep and sharp. This happened maybe two days ago. I recognize some of these tracks, but others are strange."

Levidi didn't like the smell of the exposed dirt. He had once seen a band of Sammujad bury one of their dead on the edge of the marsh and the memory made him shudder. The musty odor of the disturbed soil reminded him of that Sammujad grave all those years ago. The Lo surrendered their dead in the Great Sea, but the a-g'an buried them in the ground, a custom Levidi couldn't fathom.

One buries refuse and excrement in the soil, not the body of a cherished one.

Setenay poked the earth with her walking stick. "How many animals did this?"

"All of them," Ghalen said dryly.

"Come," Aizarg said. "We must cross." He stepped out onto the broken ground.

Levidi stepped out onto the shattered soil behind his friend. The group followed. Tendrils of dust floated around their feet as they trekked east.

Levidi felt thankful for one outcome of the perilous river crossing — he was no longer dirty. Sweat and grime still permeated his clothes, but didn't coat his skin.

Fools and animals let themselves get filthy. It won't take long walking over this ground before we're all filthy again.

Sarah and Ghalen strode well ahead of the group as Ood-i brought up the rear. Aizarg quietly spoke of what was to come.

"We'll camp tonight on the open grasslands. Tomorrow we'll follow the low ground until, according to Sarah, we will encounter three distinct hills she calls The Canyon. Beyond that is a place Sarah's people call the Dead Forest. It lies on the western shore of the Hur River and within sight of the mountains and Hur-ar."

"Why do they call it the 'Dead Forest'?" Levidi asked. He didn't like the sound of this place. Anything with the word 'dead' in its name couldn't be good.

"The Narim destroyed it long ago."

"Did they burn it?"

"No, they took it."

"*Took it?* How does one *take* a forest?"

"They cut it down."

Levidi frowned. He couldn't imagine this. Stone and brass hand axes were good for breaking up driftwood or small marsh scrub, but quickly dulled when confronted with any sizable tree. Beach salvage composed the bulk of the Lo's usable wood.

"How did they transport the wood to their mountain?" Ghalen asked.

Aizarg appeared to struggle, as if unable to find the right words. He shook his head. "I will sound foolish if I try to repeat Sarah's words. Sarah says the Narim possess craft and powers unknown to us."

Ba-lok, walking closely behind Aizarg, rolled his eyes.

Levidi gave Ba-lok a sharp look. "Do you have a problem with what the Uros says?"

Ba-lok matched his stare. "I only council caution, we are putting too much faith in the hands of one little girl."

Levidi knew Ba-lok came from a line of great sco-lo-ti, including Setenay's late husband.

Ba-lok possesses the blood of great men and a legend such as Setenay, but he shows few of their virtues. He is an arrogant brat that chafes at Aizarg's wise leadership.

Levidi harrumphed and set his gaze forward.

If I had grown up in the Minnow Clan, my friends and I would have quickly set young Ba-lok straight.

It wasn't uncommon for the young boys of an arun-ki to 'humble' a sco-lo-ti's son with a good drubbing if he grew arrogant with his father's power.

Setenay finally spoke, "Do not underestimate this young woman. She is not a firefly, a random light in the marshes that darts to and fro in the darkness for children to chase. She is a torch, leading us with purpose, though this purpose is not her own."

Levidi almost opened his mouth to ask her what purpose, but thought better of it, sharing the fear of the supernatural instilled into all Lo men. The rest of the men remained quiet. Setenay's words put the issue to rest and gave Levidi something else to think about other than his dislike of Ba-lok or his aching legs.

Ghalen and Sarah ran back, breathlessly signaling for everyone to get down.

"Scythians!" Ghalen said in a low voice.

Levidi tightened the grip on his sagar and took a deep breath.

***

Aizarg dreaded this moment with their first step beyond the marshes. He hoped they could avoid the horseman, but deep in his heart he knew they would likely cross paths with the Scythians sooner or later.

The rest of the party lay flat in the tall grass while the Uros and the two sco-lo-ti crawled forward on their bellies until they came to the tracks.

"Yes, those are Scythian horse tracks." Aizarg examined the disturbed ground and flattened grass.

"How are you so sure?" Okta asked. "This ground is covered with all sorts of tracks."

"Look at the hoof prints," Ba-lok said. "They have a double edge not seen with wild horses. The Scythians forge pads of bronze and attach them to their horses' feet with iron pegs to make them more fearsome."

"I've never heard of such a thing," Okta said as he chewed on a wad of mud weed.

"It's true," Aizarg said, poking the dirt around one of the tracks. "When wild horses come into the marshes looking for water, they follow game trails. When Scythians come looking for blood and slaves, they often don't follow the trails. This allows a good hunter an opportunity to compare the tracks."

Aizarg grimaced. The tracks spoke to him, but he had a difficult time believing what they said.

He stood up and brushed himself off.

"Uros, get down!" Okta pleaded.

"Okta, take another close look at the tracks and tell me what they say to you," Aizarg said respectfully to the sco-lo-ti, knowing Okta was out of his element, but he wanted to nurture in him the necessary tracking skills to survive.

Okta cocked his head, intensely studying the ragged indentations. Ba-lok crawled closer to the tracks, trying to discern what Aizarg hinted at.

"They are in full gallop!" Ba-lok said in a loud, proud voice.

Aizarg smiled, but wished Ba-lok would have given Okta a chance to figure it out. "Yes, my Second. What else can you tell me?"

Sometimes I want to praise him, other times I want to strike him. Aizarg suddenly wondered what kind of man Kol-ok would grow to be.

Okta looked over Ba-lok's shoulder as the young sco-lo-ti muttered to himself in concentration. "The tracks don't cut very deep. There are perhaps ten to fifteen horses, they are scattered and..." Ba-lok's eyes grew wide. "They're riderless!" he blurted.

"Yes, Ba-lok. These animals are stampeding and riderless. Where are these tracks headed?" Aizarg already knew the answer.

Okta stood as his eyes followed the tracks up the southern rise until they disappeared over the ridge. "They go to where the other animals went, to the Valley of the Beasts."

Aizarg signaled the rest of the party to come forward.

"This is a sign from the goddess," Levidi said cheerfully. "Without their horses, the Scythians are less of a threat!"

"I see, Levidi. And what else does the goddess have to say today?" Setenay shot Levidi a look as if he were a child who spoke out of turn.

Levidi smiled sheepishly and shrugged.

She turned to Aizarg. "Heed my council, Uros. Are the horseless Scythians less of a threat? The answer is yes and no."

"How so?" Aizarg asked.

Setenay continued, "They will move slower, of course. That is good. But whatever power has drawn the animals to the Valley of the Beasts has also broken the Scythians' powerful spell over their horses. The Scythians will be frightened and therefore unpredictable."

"Frightened, unpredictable, and still armed with powerful bows," Ghalen added. "And, I suspect, chasing their horses, which means they'll be coming from that direction." He pointed toward the north. "Uros, I recommend we get moving and quickly."

"Yes," Aizarg nodded. "They'll see our tracks, but hopefully they'll be preoccupied with finding their animals and continue south."

"I know they'll be cha-chasing these animals," said Ood-i, standing in waist-high grass several paces to the east. They quickly gathered around him.

Sarah gasped when she saw what lay at Ood-i's feet and buried her head into his chest. He gently put an arm around her.

Aizarg studied the dead Scythian. He'd experienced several close calls with their warriors during his life, but this was the nearest he'd come to one.

The warrior's rigid body arched back slightly. His shaven head twisted and grossly cocked to the side, swollen tongue protruding from broken jaw. Vacant eyes stared wide from a tattooed face, now bloated and purple. A frayed leather strap wrapped around his bare foot spoke of how he died and of a soft-soled, high leather boots lost somewhere along his grisly journey. Deerskin trousers, richly beaded with fearsome geometric patterns, were shredded and bunched around his waist. A gash along his shin exposed bright white bone on the warrior's other leg. The Scythian's red *cherkesska*, a coat with a tight fitting torso and flaring below the waist, twisted around his neck like a gruesome scarf.

"Poor soul," Setenay said. "He was young. The goddess only knows how long his horse dragged him before he died."

"Poor soul?" Ba-lok frowned at his grandmother. "I doubt this man ever uttered the words 'poor soul' in his entire, miserable life."

"He was important," Setenay continued, ignoring her grandson. "Look at his face, only Scythians who've led men in battle bear tattoos on their face. His coat is red, signifying what they call 'blood power,' the right to slay one of their own at will and without repercussion. It's a privilege reserved only for chieftains and princes. I'll wager many of the skulls tied to his horse were from his own people. He was likely feared and respected."

"I hope it was one of those skull tethers which snared his leg," Ba-lok said and spit on the body.

"Do not disrespect the dead!" Setenay snapped. She steadied herself against her stick and bent down to examine the body more closely. She turned pale, closed her eyes and took a deep breath.

"Setenay, are you all right?" Ghalen asked.

"I am fine. Even the old are sickened by a tragic death."

"We must go," Aizarg said.

As they turned to leave, Aizarg looked back. Sarah knelt next to the Scythian's body, digging with her hands.

"Sarah!" he called. "Come!"

She didn't look up.

"What's she doing?" Levidi asked.

Aizarg walked back and knelt next to her.

Sarah tore into the prairie soil until her fingers bled. Her tears fell into the shallow hole.

"We do not have time for this. The Scythians may crest the northern ridge any moment. We cannot bury him," he said softly.

"I must."

The rest of the party encircled them.

"Leave him!" Ba-lok sneered. "The savage got what he deserved."

"NO!" Sarah jumped up and pushed Ba-lok back with unexpected force.

Setenay interjected herself between them, shushing Sarah.

"It's all right, child. Tell me, why do you feel the need to bury the Scythian?"

Sarah looked down at the body with a mix of emotions Aizarg did not understand.

"I know him." She closed her eyes and composed herself. "He was Tuma, a Scythian prince. He was the son of Sawseruquo, the chieftain Virag bribed for passage. He..." she paused and choked back a sob. "In the darkness, where others were savage, he was gentle."

Ood-i winced and turned away.

"Son of Sawseruquo..." Setenay whispered so low Aizarg barely heard her. She closed her eyes and turned away from the group.

"This thing must be done," Sarah said with conviction. "I feel it in my blood!" She looked frustrated, trying to find the right words. "I pity him."

"Sarah, he might have shown you kindness when not under the eyes of his people. But if he were alive, he wouldn't think twice about killing or enslaving you," Ghalen said, taking her by the elbow and trying to coax her away. He glanced again over his shoulder at the northern ridge. "Pity will kill us on the g'an."

Sarah pulled away and pointed down at the dead man. "He showed *me* pity! Ood-i showed me pity! Maybe the gods turned their back on us because we don't show enough pity. It's not my place to judge this man worthy or unworthy. It's only my place to show mercy."

Sarah broke down, sobbing into Setenay's shoulder. The old woman embraced her and stroked her hair.

"Aizarg, talk some sense into this woman," Ba-lok said with contempt. His tone set Aizarg's blood boiling.

"All of you!" Setenay interrupted before Aizarg could respond. "Quickly, gather stones and rocks. Ghalen, straighten the Scythian's limbs and garments the best you can."

Setenay shushed Sarah. She moved the girl's hair out of her eyes and wiped away her tears.

"Sarah," Setenay whispered. "Scythians don't bury their dead; they cover them in mounds they call *zhaqas*. We can at least fashion some poor version of this to honor the..." She paused for a moment, transfixed on the body. "...the stranger."

Sarah nodded, fighting a fresh wave of tears. "Thank you, Setenay."

Ba-lok shook his head in disbelief. "Grandmother, this is a *Scythian!* Have you forgotten they kidnapped you? Ghalen, how many of your clan's women and children have vanished from the marshes? Uros, how many of your men have died under their arrows? Are you prepared for the quest to fail, for us to die under a blanket of arrows to honor one who would take our skulls if he could draw one more breath?"

"Grandson, do not lecture me on my own past!" Setenay's low voice carried power. She turned to Aizarg. "Uros, follow her light."

Follow her light.

Setenay's last words evoked an almost physical reaction in Aizarg. Suddenly, he felt a wave of urgency and purpose.

"Gather stones. Make it quick," Aizarg said with finality.

Ba-lok's disbelief rapidly turned to outright anger. "Have you all taken leave of your senses?"

Aizarg moved to confront Ba-lok, but Levidi moved between them.

"I grow tired of your continual disrespect toward the Uros!" Levidi hissed between clenched teeth. "He has given a command. You are bound to follow it."

Aizarg had never seen Levidi so upset.

"Out of my way!" Ba-lok shoved Levidi backwards. Before Aizarg could intervene, Levidi dropped his packs and spear and tackled Ba-lok.

Sarah screamed as the two men punched and grappled on the ground in a cloud of dust, occasionally bumping up against the dead body.

Ghalen and Okta jumped back out of the way, but made no move to separate the two men. Ghalen grinned every time Levidi landed a good punch.

Aizarg knew he had to immediately assert control, but Setenay gently pressed her stick into his chest.

In a calm, almost formal tone, she whispered where only Aizarg could hear. "Uros, your Isp humbly begs for permission to resolve this situation. One seeks the approval of his best friend, while the other..." she sighed. "Well, the other just needs to grow up. It would be most unfortunate if the Uros had to broker a peace between the two, for it is an unwinnable task."

Aizarg stepped back and motioned Setenay forward. "Proceed."

What would I do without her?

Setenay calmly stepped forward as the men rolled and tore at each other. She cocked her head sideways as if pondering who might actually win the fight. Then, with the quickness and efficiency of someone who had delivered countless spankings and mild beatings to generations of Lo children, Setenay proceeded to whack both men with her stick.

Aizarg cringed with each strike to the men's backs and thighs. A few sharp blows even landed on heads and faces.

The men yelled "Ouch!" and "Stop it!" as they quickly separated and scrambled away from the stick-wielding woman. At first Setenay struck with dispassion, but as the men ran away, her face filled with rage. She darted after them, swinging her stick wildly.

"Why are you running, brave men? Fight me!"

Ba-lok, who obviously suffered Setenay's beatings more than once in his life, moved quicker than Levidi and suffered fewer blows.

Ghalen, standing next to the dead body, began to laugh at the sight. Setenay, eyes full of wrath, suddenly came at him with the stick.

"Do you want a taste of this, too?" she yelled.

Ghalen held up both hands and backed up, "No, old mother!"

"Good! Then behave yourself!"

She lowered her stick and looked at each man except Aizarg with blistering scorn.

"Now, can you all act like Lo men, the men our people and your Uros need during this desperate hour? What would we do if one of you were seriously hurt? Leave you here? Would you leave us with one less spear against the Scythians due to your senseless bickering?"

The men hung their heads in shame.

She walked to Levidi. Face streaked with dirt and blood, he bent over with his hands on his knees trying to catch his breath. Levidi put his hand to his face and examined the blood on his fingers.

"Setenay, you broke my lip!"

"I'm sorry, Levidi," she said tenderly. She held his chin and moved his head to one side, examining his lip. "Does it hurt?"

"Yes, it does," he sulked.

She slapped him hard across the cheek.

"Agghh!" he shrieked. "Why did you hit me?"

"To take your mind off your lip," she said calmly. "Listen to me carefully, you are *not* the Second, so stop acting like it. Am I clear?"

"Yes, old mother," Levidi said softly.

She reached up and gently straightened his hair and rubbed his cheek. Her voice turned soft with kindness and affection. "You must serve Aizarg as your Uros, not like a childhood comrade."

"Yes, old mother," Levidi said once again.

Setenay turned and walked up to Ba-lok. "Listen, *sco-lo-ti!*" She took a breath. Her words were quiet but stern. "Sarah is the reason we're still alive. She's the key to finding the Narim. It is no accident she's with us. The Uros sets our course. You serve the Uros. You pledged your spear, the highest oath a man can make. If you did so with anything less than your full heart, it will be a curse upon our quest."

Ba-lok, also covered with dirt and bloody scratches, looked coldly at his grandmother through a rapidly swelling right eye.

"I will serve my Uros, with my heart and with my life, if need be. But I will not bury a Scythian dog!" He turned to Aizarg. "I will do something useful and stand watch on the ridge while the rest of you play in the dirt."

Ba-lok picked up his pack and sagar and stomped off.

Setenay's eyes followed him with sadness. Aizarg felt her pain. She loved her grandson as much as he loved his children. For all her power and wisdom, she couldn't control his heart.

"Let us quickly finish our business and depart. There is still enough daylight to cover a good distance," Aizarg said. He knew wounds were opened today which might never heal. He needed to keep the group moving.

Ood-i and Sarah wandered about, looking for stones, and were soon joined by the rest.

Occasionally Aizarg looked to the north and saw Ba-lok standing motionless, his back to the low ground.

Ba-lok's small, solitary silhouette reminded Aizarg of the broken sagar which lined the ridges the day before.

The wind picked up from the north as each of them brought stones to Sarah. She didn't cry or show any emotion as she quickly arranged the rocks with care until the body vanished under them.

When she finished, they stood around the pile for several long moments. No one spoke a word until Aizarg grabbed his boar spear and turned to leave.

Sarah touched his arm and whispered, "I'm sorry I caused discord among your people."

"You opened no wound that wasn't already festering."

"Excuse me, child, but I need the ear of the Uros." Setenay stepped up next to Aizarg, took his arm and pulled him back from the main group. "Walk with me, Aizarg."

"I take it you want my ear and my ear alone, my Isp?"

"Tell me, what have you noticed since we left Virag's camp?"

"I don't know what you mean."

"How many insects crawled across your mat last night? How many flies have you swatted away from your face? Do you see any birds in the clear, blue sky? The beast by the river should have been covered with flies and vultures. The Scythian should have been a feast for the same."

Aizarg didn't respond.

"Do you not feel it, Uros?"

"Feel what?"

"It is as if the world is holding its breath, waiting for something. I sense the hand of a strange god, one more powerful than the earth or sea or sky."

She looked back over her shoulder toward the setting sun.

"Our time is running out." She gazed up at Aizarg. "I thought about your idea, the one you told me and Okta about before we found the tracks."

Aizarg raised his eyebrow, "Yes? And...?"

"We should do it tonight, when we make camp. I see no reason to wait."

Aizarg smiled. "What convinced you?"

Setenay looked to the north and watched Ba-lok on the ridge. He walked alone just below the crest, parallel but separated from the group.

"In the face of darkness, mercy," she whispered. She laid her head against Aizarg's arm while they walked. "I want to tell you something I've never spoken to anyone, Uros, even my late husband."

Aizarg cocked his head. "Yes?"

"Let me tell you of a Scythian prince and a Lo maiden..."

15. The Two Dragons

At midnight we stood arm and arm under the unblinking gaze of the Threshold Dragon, about to begin our long journey down the Silver Stairs. It would be dawn before we reached the Offering Temple. It was the first Offering Festival and Nushen was only an isolated convent carved out of the untamed forest. My immortal flesh was still that of a young boy and my dead father's ashes were still warm on his funeral pyre atop Tortoise Mountain.

"Why are we going to the village, Mother?" I asked, looking down at the Silver Stairs glowing in the full moon. Far below, the convent's lanterns twinkled on the other side of the grotto bridge.

She placed her shaking, wrinkled hand on my shoulder. "It is spring, the time of renewal. My children below will offer up their most treasured harvest so that I may be born anew."

I pondered her words. "Will they renew my father as well?"

"Your father is dead," she said flatly. "His body is gone and his spirit dwells forever with our Celestial Emperor."

"Will I die, too?"

A smile lit her wizened face like the way the sun kisses the east, welcome and warm after the dark night.

"Beloved son, you shall grow to become a shepherd of men and live as long as the earth abides. I will teach you many wondrous things, and in turn, you shall instruct the Tall Men. With the light of truth you shall drive evil from this fallen world. The Emperor of Heaven would sooner curse the world before death corrupts your flesh."

Her words didn't soothe my grief, but they gave me hope. She took my hand.

"Please help an old woman down all these stairs. Dawn's bitter duty will be here soon."

The Chronicle of Fu Xi

***

Fu Xi bounded up the Silver Stairs, the red sword tucked in his sash. Fury gave fire to his flesh and he didn't pause at the platforms.

Before reaching the top, his lantern died. He cast it off the mountain and kept running. Fu Xi didn't need light to find his way. Each of the 12,342 stairs and nineteen switchbacks were etched in his mind. He climbed higher until the air became thin and cold. Faint white strips, icy survivors of last year's snowpack, clung to the mountain, waiting for winter's salvation.

Fu Xi once asked his mother who built her temple on top of Tortoise Mountain.

"My three realms were born of fire," she replied. "Brought forth like water from a spring, they radiated into being like ripples across a lake."

The First Realm began with the first limestone step beyond the Offering Temple and encompassed all of Tortoise Mountain. The dome-shaped mountain stretched twenty-one miles in diameter and almost perfectly circular. A deep, cold river flowed from the far north and split into two streams surrounding the mountain in a moat-like canyon.

The canyon cliffs rose hundreds of feet, forming an impregnable fortress. Nushen's grotto bridge presented the only way to cross over to the mountain. The two branches rejoined under the grotto bridge and flowed into the forest.

A deep coniferous forest blanketed the mountain above the cliffs, summoning an image of a giant turtle rising from the earth. No trees grew within a hundred yards of the Silver Stairs as they zigzagged up the mountainside. At each switchback, a small platform was cut from the rock.

A silver torch, about the height of a man, and looking as if it had been formed by rolling a sheet of rice paper into a tight cone, imbedded into the rock on each platform. They could not be extinguished by the mightiest wind or heaviest rain. Next to each silver torch sat a small stone bench.

Chest heaving, Fu Xi stood between the last two torches flanking the top of the Silver Stairs. Beyond lay the temple's entrance and threshold to the Second Realm, a broad, smooth platform supporting seven giant pillars.

The alabaster pillars were so glossy they almost glowed in the starlight. The colonnade supported a stone entablature of living rock shaped into a giant dragon. The Threshold Dragon, the sacred symbol of the Goddess Nuwa, looked as if writhing from the living rock. Fu Xi never encountered a flesh and blood dragon such as this throughout his many travels.

Long and wingless like a snake, it possessed a face similar to a lion's. Its short legs were armed with menacing three-toed claws. Covered in gilded scales, the dragon stretched the entire length of the temple and then doubled back on itself. Its head loomed over the center of the colonnade as it peered straight down the Silver Stairs with fiery eyes that outshone the silver torches.

Fu Xi walked under the dragon's stare and stepped between the center pillars into the Second Realm of Nuwa. Far below at the base of the mountain, the glittering string of silver torches slowly extinguished one by one.

***

I cannot easily recall each time I accompanied my mother down the Silver Stairs. Can one remember the details of every spring or every harvest of their lives? I will therefore tell the tale of the final Offering Ceremony which transpired many decades before my journey to Wu.

The preceding winter, a thin tendril of white smoke rose from Tortoise Mountain, announcing the mortal husband of the Goddess Nuwa had died. The village hummed with activity, as the goddess would chose an acolyte in the spring.

In the weeks preceding the Offering Festival, the Elder Mother carefully selected seven candidates. Those girls not chosen had to watch the proceedings with the villagers. It was a bittersweet moment for those in their eleventh year of life, the final year of eligibility as an acolyte. Never again could they wear the white silk robes. Husbands, babies, and common lives were now their fate.

On the spring equinox, the seven blessed Acolytes of Nuwa, virgins all, filed down from the convent in the cool darkness. Tortoise Mountain was a shadow against the lightening east. The acolytes dressed in long, white silk robes and carried white candles. The children fully understood the implications of being chosen by Nuwa, but their solemn, tender faces betrayed nothing.

The Chronicle of Fu Xi

***

In Nushen, he sometimes found time's unrelenting flow uncomfortable. The Second Realm, which his mother called the Place of Perfect Sorrows, separated the physical world from Nuwa's inner dwelling. When he crossed this membrane the fury of earthly change ceased.

He stepped from the limestone colonnade to a polished granite foyer as wide as the outer threshold. About seven paces inside the foyer stood another set of alabaster pillars, identical to the outer structures, and beyond that a sunken peristyle courtyard. Fu Xi rushed several paces into the courtyard, intent on confronting his mother.

"Your sword," her voice reverberated from deep in the temple.

Fu Xi halted, his fury checked by the power in her voice. He sighed, pulled the red sword from his sash and approached a table against one of the foyer pillars. The small black lacquered table contrasted perfectly against the alabaster. On top of the table sat a crystal rack in the image of a carp arching out of the water, supported on its pectoral fins and tail. A deep groove carved into its back matched his old bronze blade. Fu Xi knew the smaller, lighter orichalcum sword would slide out of the groove. He placed the sword on the table next to the holder and stepped away.

"All things have their place," her voice echoed again.

Fu Xi frowned and placed the orichalcum sword in the groove on the carp's back, expecting it to fall out and clatter to the table. The two pieces fit as one, like art purposely formed whole from the craftsman's hand.

How did she know? Alas, one more mystery he may never understand. Impatient for answers, Fu Xi's anger simmered as he turned to enter the inner sanctuary.

"Is this how you enter my house, child?" the disembodied voice came again.

Fu Xi stopped and saw two pairs of simple wicker sandals against the pillar opposite the sword, one pair large and the other small. Both pairs' soles were worn and rubbed, comfortably molded from years of use.

Heng still lives if his sandals sit next to hers.

Fu Xi sighed and took off his wooden sandals, much larger than the other two pairs, and placed them against the pillar.

"Purify yourself," she called from the depths of the temple.

***

Along the hill and on each side of the path the villagers waited silently in the dark. Everyone looked on in anticipation. No torches or lanterns were allowed except the acolytes' candles.

An Offering Ceremony came but once in a lifetime.

The old hoped they'd live to see this day. The young would speak of it the rest of their lives.

The acolytes filed past the Offering Temple and placed their candles in the jade dais. Two Holy Mothers stood on either side of the dais, holding large paper fans decorated with the goddess's symbol: the wingless, three-toed spirit dragon encircling a white lotus flower. Their duty was to shield the candles from the wind. It would be an ill omen should any girl's candle extinguish before the ceremony was complete.

One by one, the girls approached the sacred peach tree, where the elder Holy Mother waited in her unadorned black silk robe. The children's hair piled high on their heads and held in place by ornate ivory pins. The robe wrapped tightly around their small bodies and held in place by a pure white sash. Their long sleeves flared outward at their wrists and their small, delicate feet were bound in silk slippers. In each sash was tucked a folded paper fan, also adorned with the goddess symbol.

As they approached the Elder Mother, they removed their fans and spread them demurely in front of their faces. In turn, each bowed by slightly bending her knees and nodding her head. The Elder Mother returned the greeting and motioned to the tree.

One at a time, the acolytes plucked a peach. The sacred Tree of Immortality only bore fruit in the years of the white smoke, and then the little tree produced exactly seven peaches. The peaches sprung ripe from blossoms seven days before the ceremony. They hung low and heavy on the small branches. Any impure mortal unwise enough to touch one would instantly die. The tainted fruit would wither and fall from the tree and be replaced by a new blossom in a day.

Holding the peach in their right hands and the fan in the other, the acolytes stood side by side along the pebble lane, oldest to youngest, from the Offering Temple. The sun was only moments away from cresting over the temple as all eyes were on the Silver Stairs.

The Chronicle of Fu Xi

***

Here, Fu Xi felt his immortality. Here, Fu Xi felt his spirit grow in power. Part of him wanted to defy her and storm the Inner Realm, but the wiser part knew better.

He stepped past the pillars and down into the courtyard. Seven pillars, each with its own silver torch, lined the expansive courtyard. Above, the courtyard opened to the night, but neither snow nor rain ever fell on the temple.

In the center of the courtyard, a polished granite fountain seven feet across rose out of the floor. Steaming water gently flowed over its smooth sides, giving them a glass-like texture, and into four shallow canals cut into the floor. The canals formed a cross with the raised fountain in the center. At about three feet across, each canal ran along a cardinal direction until it vanished into a hole in the rock in the courtyard's edge. A round island, upon which grew a small peach tree, rose in the fountain's center. The Eternal Tree, sister of the Immortality Tree in the village, retained only a few brown leaves on its bare, black limbs.

The tree may never be renewed.

To his right, on the east side of the fountain, stood the Altar Rock, a raw piece of granite protruding about four feet above the polished floor like an island. Several small steps carved into its side led to the rock's polished slab top. The fountain's eastern canal flowed under the rock and emerged on the other side.

He once asked his mother why she called the Second Realm the Place of Perfect Sorrows, but she never answered.

***

We stood arm in arm on the last platform above the grotto bridge. From here, the villagers were shadowy forms along the hill below us. I could hear murmurs. Their excitement was palpable.

The seven acolytes were already in a line, waiting for us.

Mother's frail arm gently locked in mine, she grasped her cane in her other hand. Usually, we waited here in silence for the sun, but this morning she spoke.

"I assume you will return to the village tonight for the festival?" she said dryly.

I raised an eyebrow at the unexpected conversation.

"Of course."

She poked at my formal robes. "I also assume you positioned a change of clothes at Tiejiang's hut?"

"Yes, Mother."

She shook her head, doing a poor job of masking her disgust.

"Another night of drinking and carousing with mortals, eh? I should forbid it, but I suppose there is a price for your familiarity with them."

I patted Mother's hand and winked. "It's a steep price, but one I'm willing to pay."

She turned away and scowled. "You are more of Nushen than of Tortoise Mountain," she sighed.

A thought simultaneously crossed my mind and my lips. "Then let me marry one of them. Let me raise a family and be one of them."

She didn't say anything for several long moments, and then spoke. "They revere me, but they love you. It is your father's gentle spirit that has earned that love."

"You are permitted the love of a husband," I blurted. "Why do you deny me a wife?"

Mother's eyes narrowed, but she didn't look up at me. "I picture the maidens of Nushen competing for your hand. I see the young men sulking at the thought of a god stealing their sweethearts." She paused and looked beyond the eastern horizon. "I see your children and their children. They will be giants among men. Your father's gentleness would be diluted in their bloodline, but your power will not. Nushen is not enough for such men. The world is not enough for such men." It was her gaze to the east that still haunts me. Perhaps she was looking to Wu and thinking of my next quest. "Anyway, you are too young to get married...and too innocent." She shook her head and tugged on my arm. "Son, please help an old woman down all these stairs. Dawn's bitter duty is upon us."

The Chronicle of Fu Xi

***

Fu Xi stood on the fountain's lip, let his clothing fall to the floor and slipped into the comfortably hot water, which welled up from the heart of the mountain through holes cut in the stone.

He sank to his chin and his long black hair floated around him. Fu Xi closed his eyes, submerged below the water and stayed there until his lungs burned. He slowly rose above the surface and let the used air slip between his teeth in a slow hiss. His breathing eased. He relaxed his body until his fingertips floated independent of any mental control.

This wasn't a bath as much as purification. Without scrubbing or washing, the waters lifted not only the dirt from his skin, but the turmoil from his soul.

He opened his eyes.

Through the Eternal Tree's barren limbs, the Milky Way slowly flowed across the sky. Nuwa told him the fountain's water represented time flowing from Heaven to the four corners of the world.

While calm and centered, peace still eluded Fu Xi. His rage and anguish were only numbed.

Fu Xi stepped out of the fountain to discover his clothes were gone, replaced by a neatly folded homespun wool towel and a golden silk robe. A pair of wicker sandals sat next to them. As he dried off, he found an ivory comb placed in the folds of the towel. He ran it though his long black hair until it was straight. Fu Xi tied his hair into a top knot and placed the comb through it. He donned the robe and sandals and placed the towel around his neck. He took a deep breath, exhaled and felt ready to confront his mother, to make her answer for abandoning the people of Nushen.

He stepped around the fountain, his sandals lightly clopping on the floor. That is when he spotted a set of wet footprints emerging from the fountain towards the Inner Realm.

Those are recent and too big to be either Mother's or Heng's. The evening's mysteries deepened.

Fu Xi followed the footprints and climbed the steps on the opposite side of the courtyard from whence he entered. He passed through the seven pillars and into her inner sanctum, the Third Realm of Nuwa.

***

Mother always appeared exactly when the sun crested over Tortoise Mountain. Gasps rose from the crowd as the equinox dawn silhouetted their deity's small form. For many in the crowd, it was the first time they'd ever beheld the goddess. I sometimes wondered if they were disappointed, though I doubt it. I was too familiar with her, accustomed to her power and grace. I could not see her through their eyes.

She was dressed in a white silk robe similar to the ones the virgins wore, except with a red sash and a golden spirit dragon emblazoned across the front. Her mortal body was shriveled and frail, with pure gray hair and deep lines etched into her soft face. Nuwa's eyes betrayed the power of her divine nature.

I think this is when I loved her the most, when her ancient spirit and old body were most aligned. That's when she most felt like my mother. I think she liked herself that way, too. She used to say an old body felt like worn leather, soft and comfortable.

Arm in arm, we walked down the Silver Stairs. I was dressed in a black robe and white sash, emblazoned with a mirror image of the same golden spirit dragon on mother's robe.

As we crossed the grotto bridge, the villagers bowed low. She departed my side, stepped across the temple threshold and onto the pebble walkway. Nuwa raised her hands and called her people to rise.

"Stand, children, and rejoice in the renewal of the world."

She never raised her voice, but her voice carried an otherworldly power and delicate strength. I cannot adequately describe it, for it floated with the airy lightness of a butterfly in flight that could instantly turn hard and cut with the strength of diamonds and fire. Only years later would I describe it as the voice of orichalcum.

She rarely smiled. More often than not, her expression was haughty. In front of her mortal servants, Nuwa was as firm as the mountains, as cold and powerful as the wind across a winter glacier. During the Offering Ceremony, I thought I detected a hint of entitlement in her expression, a trace of pride.

She approached the elder Holy Mother, who gracefully bent at the waist and kissed Mother's hand. "Great Goddess, bringer of the dawn and guardian of life, I humbly present seven empty vessels. We honor you and pray we may please your perfect grace."

Mother leaned over and kissed the Elder Mother's forehead.

With a stern countenance, Mother slowly stepped from girl to girl and examined each in turn, as if they were wares in the market. The acolytes were instructed to look the goddess in the eye so she could test their souls. They trembled and tried to be brave. I pitied them. They were beginning to understand the true nature of the sacrifice they were about to make.

The Chronicle of Fu Xi

***

Beyond the polished granite pillars a pebble pathway wound through a scene of idyllic peasant life. A split log fence lined the path and led to a small cottage, much like those in the village below. To either side of the path, empty fields lay dormant under autumn's midnight frost. In the distance, a shadowed outline of a pine forest encircled the fields. Though he could not see it in the darkness, Fu Xi knew towering cliffs jutted high above the forest in every direction, boldly pronouncing the summit of Tortoise Mountain was a crater.

The split rail fence surrounded the hut to form a small compound. A handful of goats slept in the fields under the starlight at the edge of the forest. To his right, a small bamboo barn stood at the edge of the trees. A stone draw well stood like a guardian only a few paces outside the hut's door. He ducked under its long draw-pole as he approached the house.

The oil-skin windows glowed warmly from an inviting light within. Larger than a common villager's, the hut still maintained the simple one-room style he taught the mortals for generations. Under the tranquil starlight, everything appeared as it should be, perfect and at peace.

Fu Xi's wet hair steamed in the chilly air. His golden silk robe, out of place against the pastoral scene, did little to keep out the cold.

The bamboo door opened before Fu Xi could reach for the wooden lever. His mother's small, hunched silhouette stood in the doorway. She clutched a bamboo cane in one hand and the door in the other. He almost gasped.

Physically, both in age and dress, she looked as he expected. She wore a homespun cotton blouse and trousers. A few gray tendrils fell across her face, like any other old peasant woman who had been performing chores all day. Her gray hair piled up in a bun and held by plain wooden pins. However, he saw no haughtiness in her face. During his entire existence, she took his measure with each glance, but now she couldn't meet his eyes.

She looked mortal.

Nuwa glanced away and slowly hobbled into the hut.

"Welcome home, favored son. I have prepared tea. Heng has been anxious to see you. Come, sit and talk with him while I prepare something to eat."

The fight evaporated from Fu Xi's spirit. He walked around her and into the hut. He removed his sandals, placed them against the wall next to the door, and bowed low to his mother.

"Thank you, honored mother. It is good to be home."

While similar, several notable differences existed between their home and a peasant hut. In contrast to mud brick, a sturdier baked brick hearth stood against the left wall. Also, neatly joined cedar planks covered with fiber mats, not dirt, composed the floor. Whereas peasants took their meals from a central bowl on the floor, a low pine table sat against the far wall with three wool cushions placed around it.

Two simple bed rolls, linen sleeves stuffed with soft wool, were rolled up by the table. A third roll, this one of silk, sat rolled against the wall.

She hasn't prepared my sleeping mat.

Against the right wall, an old man lay on a low, cushioned couch. Like Fu Xi's robe and silken bed roll, the luxurious couch, carved of rich mahogany and covered in plush silk cushions, existed in marked contrast to the rest of the simple hut. Unlike his mother's peasant garb, the old man wore a blue silk robe.

Nuwa walked toward the hearth where a brass pot hung over the fire. Fu Xi sat down cross-legged on the floor next to the sleeping old man.

A pang of sadness stabbed Fu Xi's heart as he saw how time had ravaged his old friend. Heng's hands, once strong and broad, were now bony and covered in liver spots. His beard and hair, once as black and full as the midnight sky, were now thin and wispy. Heng labored under slow and raspy breaths.

Fu Xi remembered how his own father looked near the end.

"He is sleeping, mother. I do not have the heart to wake him."

Nuwa approached, leaned over her husband, roughly shook him and shouted, "Wake up, Heng! Fu Xi is here."

Heng's eyes fluttered open and rapidly darted left and right as if confused. Slowly, they came into focus and rested on Fu Xi. After a moment, recognition and a toothless smile graced the old man's face.

"Fu Xi! How are you, old boy? Your mother and I have been expecting you. She said you would be home today."

Fu Xi took Heng's palsied hand and softly patted it. "It is good to see you, too," Fu Xi spoke softly.

"Eh?" Heng said and held his hand to his ear.

"I said IT'S GOOD TO SEE YOU," Fu Xi said loudly and slowly.

Heng's pale, glassy eyes couldn't quite focus and teared at the edges. Fu Xi knew his mother's husband hovered on the edge of death.

"I tried to stay up until you came home, but I knew you would be too busy celebrating in the village. I wish I could have been there, under the willow tree in the convent when you came home. I miss those days." Heng's eyes went somewhere else. "Did you see Tiejiang? How is my grandnephew and his children?"

Fu Xi struggled to maintain control and looked back at his mother. She hunched over the tea pot across the room and would not look at him.

"Yes, I saw everyone," Fu Xi smiled the best he could. "We all danced under the willow tree, under the lanterns. They all miss you and send their love."

"Did you say you danced, eh? Ahh, that is good. I miss them, too. It's been a long time since your mother and I went down the Silver Stairs," Heng continued. "My knees are not what they used to be, you know."

Heng's eyelids began to droop and his voice trailed off. "I want to hear about your journey, but I'm afraid you will have to tell me all about it in the morning. I am weary. I hope you found some dragons...I so want to hear about the dragons..." Heng's eyes closed as he drifted off to sleep.

Fu Xi stroked Heng's hair and whispered, "Sleep, old friend. We can talk in the morning."

Fu Xi stood and turned. His mother knelt on a cushion by the table, a white ceramic cup of steaming tea in front of her. A paper lantern hung above the table, casting a dim light that highlighted the deep lines on his mother's face.

Fu Xi knelt on the cushion opposite her. Before him sat a steaming cup and a wooden bowl full of rice mixed with bean sprouts and strips of goat meat. Two wooden chopsticks sat next to the bowl.

"You journey has been long. Eat, and then we will talk," she said.

***

Leaning heavily on her cane, Nuwa paced up and down the line of acolytes. The Elder Mother tried not to show her trepidation that her selections may not please the goddess.

Finally, Nuwa stopped in front of the smallest and youngest of the seven acolytes, a girl of about eight. I saw the child gasp under the goddess's stare, knowing what lay ahead of her before the sun set that day.

It didn't surprise me Mother chose her. She had full cheeks and a complexion like the finest ivory. Her eyes were bright and intelligent. She would grow to be a strong, beautiful woman. Mother would choose nothing less than the finest, of course.

Excited murmurs issued from the crowd when Mother took the peach from the child's hand. She took one small bite and handed the little girl the rest.

Then the goddess spoke the ceremonial words, "Your life is my life. Your blood shall be my blood. Your flesh shall be my flesh."

On cue, the child ate the peach and finished every bite. Self-consciously, she wiped the juice from her mouth with the back of her hand, took a deep breath and spoke, "Your spirit is my spirit." She paused, overwhelmed by the moment. When she continued, her voice quivered and cracked. "My blood shall be your blood. My flesh shall be your flesh." With those words, the child placed the peach pit in Nuwa's hand.

The crowd erupted in cheers. Nuwa's face was softer now, content. She turned to the first acolyte in line and placed the peach pit in her hand.

The crowd cheered again. This girl would become the next Holy Mother, a guardian of the Temple of Nuwa and the gateway to Tortoise Mountain. This girl was older than the acolyte chosen for the Offering Ceremony and in her last year of eligibility. Taller and thinner, she had a long face and narrow hips. She bowed to the goddess. She would spend the rest of her life a virgin, dedicated to the service of the goddess.

I once asked Mother what criteria she used to make her selection, but she never answered. When I asked her what criteria she used to select the next Holy Mother, her answer came swiftly and accompanied by a rare smirk.

"The ugliest, of course."

Mother turned and handed me her cane. She raised her hands over the villagers, who fell silent and dropped to their knees.

"Blessed are all of you, oh Children of Nushen! In the bloom of spring's promise, the cycle of life shall renew. Go, and be at peace."

Under the watchful eye of the Holy Mothers, the remaining virgins turned and strolled in single file to the convent's East Gate. There, they would carry their peaches to the sanctuary and cast them into the fire.

I took one of Mother's arms while the acolyte supported the other arm. A Holy Mother took the cane from me. It would be stored in the Sanctuary until the goddess asked for it again, perhaps a lifetime from now.

The villagers drifted away, some singing. The Goddess Nuwa would make another Offering and the world would be renewed. Tonight, they would rejoice.

I would return to the village that evening. It wasn't a celebration unless Lord Fu Xi presided. I had my eye on a few beautiful maidens and there would be drink.

Everyone knew I would get drunk, though the villagers never knew that I needed to get drunk. For the villagers, the ceremony was over. For Mother, this child, and myself, the Offering Ceremony had just begun.

I caught my mother looking over her shoulder at the dissipating crowd. Her old eyes lingered upon Heng, one of the boys in the village on the edge of manhood. I knew she had already laid her plans.

The Chronicle of Fu Xi

***

Fu Xi slowly finished his meal while his mother quietly sipped her tea.

She finally spoke. "Tell me of your journey."

Fu Xi stopped in mid-sip and looked up at his mother. He clenched his jaw, not wanting to hear his mother wax and wane. The peace of the fountain faded and the raw images of Nushen began to burn through his calm.

"You sent me to find dragons. I failed. Now you know of my journey." His voice was as sharp as his red sword. "Tell me of Nushen."

She didn't react to his tone. Nuwa took another sip of her tea. "Your anger will accomplish nothing."

"You are correct, anger is futile. How mortal of me."

Nuwa's eyes bore into her son across the table. "The fruits of truth cannot be found in the briar patch of rage. Anger has never tainted my Inner Realm and I will not permit it now."

Fu Xi challenged his mother's stare. "Was it your rage that permitted the Ice Men to slaughter your children?"

"No, but it was rage that led you to slaughter women and children in that cellar."

"It's not the same!" Fu Xi shouted.

"SILENCE!" she snapped. The earth trembled and the lantern swayed from side to side, casting Nuwa's face in alternating shadow and light. In each shadow, her eyes faintly glowed with a blue light.

She drew a deep breath and closed her eyes. Fu Xi saw the turmoil on her face and it frightened him. He'd never witnessed pain on her face, even when his father died. Nuwa flexed her hand over and over.

"Clear your mind, son, and speak to me with respect. My wrath is not one even the great Fu Xi would care to witness."

Fu Xi reached up and steadied the lantern. "Please forgive me, dear mother. My heart is torn with pain."

"My grief is every bit as deep as yours."

"Mother..." Fu Xi leaned in. "What happened?"

Nuwa picked up the tea cup with a trembling hand. "Son, why did you journey to the Unfinished Men all those years ago?"

In typical fashion, she answered a question with a question. He needed direct answers. "Mother, I simply want to know..."

"No." She held up a finger. "Answer me. Why did you go to the northlands centuries ago?"

If he wanted answers, it would be on Nuwa's terms.

***

It was almost sunset when we reached the Threshold Dragon. As was required in the ancient ceremonial etiquette, the girl did her best to support Mother. But, as usual, I ended up supporting the goddess up the mountain. It would have been easier if Mother just let me carry her, but Nuwa wouldn't hear of such things. She insisted she ascend the mountain with her own strength.

The little girl's awe renewed with each new switchback. She gazed in wonder over the lush valley far below.

"The world is so big," she blurted. I enjoyed seeing my familiar home anew through the eyes of a child. In this way, I learned to love my home all over again.

I also wanted to remember what this little girl's eyes looked like, to burn their image into my mind before they disappeared forever. She had so little time to see through them.

I knew this little girl's name was Lian, but we could not call her by her name. That part of the ceremony Mother and I always honored.

As we approached the last switchback, Mother sat down on the stone bench next to the silver torch.

"Let me rest a few moments and enjoy the sunset," she said.

Lian walked to the base of the final flight of stairs and looked up at the seven giant pillars. She pointed up to the Threshold Dragon. "Lord Fu Xi, is that a real dragon?"

I knelt down beside her. "Yes and no. That is a spirit dragon. It represents the power of creation bestowed in the Goddess Nuwa. It serves as a guardian of the goddess's realm and carries her prayers to her father, the Emperor of Heaven."

She frowned and paused for a moment. "Are there real dragons?"

"*Yes,*" *I said with all seriousness and sat down on the stairs. "Once, dragons of flesh and blood filled the world.*"

"*It looks so fierce. It frightens me,*" *Lian said and scooted closer to me. I picked her up and put her on my lap.*

"*They had to be fierce! For dragons were created to battle giants.*"

Lian's eyes grew wide. "Giants are real, too?"

"*In the most ancient of days, the spirits of Chaos and Creation were incarnate as flesh; powerful giants that roamed the world. Like the fires of a volcano, these giants were magnificent and terrible. They swam through the seas and flew through the air. The earth trembled when they walked. Their roars were like the thunder of a thousand storms.*"

"*Lord Fu Xi, did you see these giants?*" *she said, amazed.*

"*No, but the goddess did. She also told me in those days the giants always fought and there was no peace. Sometimes, the powers of Creation held sway too long and the world faded and became icy and sterile. When Chaos reigned, all was fire and ash. The Emperor of Heaven formed the race of dragons out of both flesh and spirit to subdue Chaos and Creation and bring them into balance.*"

I looked at her out of the corner of my eye, feigning a scolding look. "Didn't the Holy Mothers teach you about this?"

She held her hand up to her mouth and whispered, "Maybe. I can't remember."

I winked and tousled her hair. She gave me a delightful smile under her hand, like the sun behind a puffy afternoon cloud. It was times like this I panged for a family. Holding this child was another reminder of the price of my immortality.

"*That's all right. I will refresh your memory.*" *I pointed up to the Threshold Dragon. "The Emperor made dragons out of both Creation and Chaos, so that they might do battle with the giants, but that was not enough. These forces only gave them raw power, but not Grace. He knew the dragon needed more...*"

Lian's eyes grew wide. "I remember this! Holy Mother Jia taught us the Seven Virtues of the Dragon!" Lian crawled off my lap and stood in front me with her hands behind her back. She bit her lower lip, screwed her face up in concentration, and began to recite, "The Seven Virtues of the Dragon are...For their armor, the Emperor of Heaven dipped their scales in the Lake of Righteousness. In their eyes, He kindled the Light of Wisdom. He sharpened their claws on the Rock of Justice and honed their teeth on the Anvil of Fortitude. He fashioned their wings from the Silk of Faith and Gossamer of Hope. The greatest gift of all, He bestowed the Gift of Truth, a flaming sword with which to smite the enemies of Heaven."

"Very good! Very good!" I clapped, genuinely pleased.

She beamed and crawled back on my lap.

"Holy Mother Jia taught you well. Did she also teach you about the Two Dragons?"

Lian looked up at me, confused. "No, Lord Fu Xi."

The Chronicle of Fu Xi

***

They never talked of the Ice Men after he returned from the icelands. She never asked and he never offered. The pain still burned so he buried it, seeking diversion in other journeys, other quests.

Fu Xi gazed into his tea cup and fiddled with a chopstick. "I thought I could teach them as I had done with the Tall Men."

"Do you recall how I counseled against it?"

"Yes, Mother. And I went anyway."

"Before that ill-fated journey and since, have you ever undertaken a quest that I had not sent you on?"

"No, Mother. I have submitted myself to your wisdom and guidance. I am your humble servant."

She suddenly threw her head back and laughed. Fu Xi's eyes grew wide in surprise.

"Dear Fu Xi, there is nothing humble about you." Large teardrops formed and rolled down her cheeks. "However, you are humble enough to gain Heaven's favor, and for that I am eternally thankful."

The tears turned to sobs as she buried her head in her hands and leaned over the table. Lightning flashed outside, followed by peals of thunder.

Since the day he emerged from her womb, he never witnessed his mother cry, let alone laugh. Astonished, he walked on his knees around the table and held her in his arms. He had never had to console her, even after the passing of her husbands. Now, he didn't know what else to do. She surrendered to her son's embrace.

The thunder became sharper and closer. Rain began to pound on the roof.

"I heard their screams!" she moaned into his shoulder. "I could not save them."

The wind began to howl. Fu Xi looked around at the shuddering hut. He didn't know what he feared most, the hut flying apart or the sight of the once proud goddess in tears. He pulled away and stroked her wet cheek.

"Shhh...shhh...Mother, it's all right. It's all right. Please." He lifted the tea cup to her lips. She took a sip and calmed down. The rain and the wind ceased.

"Why couldn't you save them?" he pressed.

She looked upon him with such sweet sadness Fu Xi thought his heart would break. "By the command of the Celestial Emperor himself."

Fu Xi felt as if his heart stopped. He couldn't speak as his mother continued.

"You went to the northlands because of your pride, didn't you? No good can come from pride, especially the pride of a god.

"I allowed the Ice Men into my valley. I had no choice."

Fu Xi recoiled and shook his head.

Nuwa's face darkened. "They paid the price for *my* sin."

Fu Xi found his voice. "What sin? You are Nuwa, Celestial Goddess of the West. You are perfect!"

She shook her head, tears threatening to break through again "*You*, my son, are my sin. The price of forgiveness is always blood."

***

"I will have a talk with Holy Mother Jia if she isn't teaching you children about the Two Dragons." I stroked my chin with a very serious expression.

"Oh, she did! She did, Lord Fu Xi! Please, do not scold her. She is a very good teacher. But, please, tell me again."

I knew Lian was stalling, but I wanted to put her at ease.

"Yes, I know Mother Jia is a good teacher, but I will tell you again. The Celestial Emperor bestowed his earthly children, both dragons and Tall Men, with the Spirit and the Flesh. These are the Two Dragons. The Flesh is our earthly shell and the Spirit is our soul..."

"Man is the Flesh and Spirit is the woman," Lian blurted out.

"I thought you didn't know about this," I chided.

Lian looked up at the Threshold Dragon and then at Mother resting on the bench. *"I'm sorry. Please, go on, Lord Fu Xi."*

"When we abide in the Seven Virtues, the Two Dragons are in balance," I continued. *"That is when we are happiest and at peace; with ourselves, with one another, and with the Emperor of Heaven. Balance is harmony. When they are out of balance, there is only strife and conflict. There is not only the balance within each of us, but the balance in the world around us.*

"Mother calls dragons the First Race. Before Tall Men walked the earth, dragons were the beloved children of the Emperor of Heaven. 'Bring the world into balance. Tame it that I might plant a garden and bring forth other children into the world,' he told the dragons. Armed with the powers of Spirit and Flesh and the Seven Virtues, they subdued the giants of Chaos and Creation and their powerful spirits sank into the earth and became fire, rock and ice. Throughout the world, the Two Dragons were brought into balance."

"Where did the dragons go?" Lian asked.

"I don't know," I said with a hint of sadness. *"I have not seen one in many years."*

"Are the Two Dragons still in balance, Lord Fu Xi?" she asked.

Before I could answer, the wind suddenly rose behind us, cold and strong. I turned and saw Mother standing behind us, the setting sun

196

blazing around her. Her robes fluttered in the wind like beating wings and her gray hair caught the sunlight like a golden mane.

In times like this, the gulf between us became clear. I am an earthly creature bestowed with eternal life. Mother was a goddess cloaked in borrowed flesh. She pressed through the thin membrane separating this world from the next, occasionally giving me a glimpse of what lay beyond.

Lian wrapped her arms around my neck and buried herself against my chest. Nuwa's voice rose above the wind, deep and resounding against the mountainside.

"After the dragons defeated the giants, the Emperor of Heaven did as he promised. He planted his garden, the Place of Perfect Happiness, at the center of the four rivers. In it, he created a new race. He didn't bestow upon them any of the virtues he granted the First Race. He gave them only one gift, a piece of his living spirit — the gift of Love. The dragons understood this was the most precious gift of all and mourned for what they could not have. Without love, all of their gifts were hollow. The dragons retreated to the remote places of the world and wept.

"Then, Lu Xi Fu, the Corruptor, made a bargain with the dragons. 'Lend me your form, that I might go to the Place of Perfect Happiness and bring back the gift of Love and once again you will be the most favored of Heaven.' The dragons agreed and granted the Deceiver the shape of the Black Spirit Dragon. He entered The Place of Perfect Happiness and deceived the new race into eating from the Tree of Knowledge. In doing so, Lu Xi Fu brought both races bitter anguish. Lu Xi Fu laughed and kept the form of the Black Dragon as his own."

The wind died and Mother's robes settled. She seemed to hunch and shrink as the sun disappeared behind a wisp of cloud.

"Since that dark day," she continued with her old voice, "the world has been out of balance. Men possess Love without Virtue, and the dragon Virtue without Love. The Two Dragons, the Spirit and the Flesh, are in conflict and the world is at war with itself."

Lian relaxed and looked at me as if she needed me to confirm what the goddess had just spoken.

"The goddess and I must bring the world into balance," I said and gently put her off my lap. "This time, however, we do so through the race

of men. We must lead them on the road to redemption, and in turn, bring the Two Dragons into balance. Only then may we hope to gain our Heavenly Emperor's favor. You, child, have an honored role to play."

Lian looked up at the Threshold Dragon and then to me. She whispered, hoping Mother wouldn't hear her. "Lord Fu Xi, I am afraid."

"Come, child," Nuwa said without her usual coldness. "I am rested. Let us finish our journey. The only way home is forward and we have but only a little way to go."

Under the dragon's gaze, we held Lian's hands and slowly climbed the last stretch of Silver Stairs.

The Chronicle of Fu Xi

***

"I don't understand. How can I be a 'sin'? I am your faithful and obedient son." Fu Xi searched his mother's eyes for understanding.

"You are an obedient son." Nuwa's soft voice accompanied a resigned expression. "The sin was mine, but its costs will be paid for by mortal generations to come...and by you. The nature of this sin has been laid before you; you only need to open your eyes."

"The lateness of the hour and the stench of blood in my nostrils have made me weary of your riddles, Mother!"

"No riddles. You carry many questions for me from distant lands. Tell me of your journey, and in the telling, you will find your answers." She paused for a moment. "This quest was unlike any other, wasn't it?"

Fu Xi stood and turned his back to her.

"In the past, you always sent me into the world to enlighten the Tall Men. This time, you sent me to find dragons. That alone made this journey different."

"And in this you were unsuccessful?"

"The mountains and glaciers are empty, the roar of the mighty bulls are gone. The glitter of gossamer wings no longer graces the sunset. The First Race is extinct."

Nuwa raised an eyebrow, but said nothing.

He turned and narrowed his eyes on his mother. "You knew that before you sent me east, didn't you?"

"If you found no dragons, then what kept you away all these years?" She looked out the dark oil-skin window. "Dawn is still far away. Tell me of your journey, Fu Xi, and I will give you the answers you seek."

As he spoke Fu Xi paced restlessly, occasionally ducking his head under the low rafters. His words started slowly and then burst forth like a confession.

"I discovered a changing world. Things I once thought as timeless and enduring as the mountains and...and..." he frowned and then pointed to Nuwa,"...as *you*, are transforming at such a pace even mortals can mark the differences."

***

Mother stood in front of the Altar Rock and held her hand out to Lian. Lian pressed against me and gripped my forefinger with her tiny hand.

"Come," Mother's voice echoed flatly off the mirrored granite. "It is time."

Lian was on the verge of tears. No amount of practice or repetitive lessons from the Holy Mothers could prepare one so young for this moment.

I did what I always did during the Offering. I tried to give the young acolyte courage. I knelt next to her and placed one hand on her chest.

"You were chosen," I spoke tenderly. "The courage has always been within you. Nuwa looked into your soul and saw it. Through your sacrifice, the Two Dragons will find balance and the world shall be new again."

Lian wiped away her tears and turned toward Mother and the Altar Rock. She stopped when she saw the crimson gleam of the Offering Blade in mother's hand. Its handle was shaped like a golden spirit dragon, which twisted a third of the way down the blood red blade.

Lian gasped, turned around and threw her arms around my neck. It was all real now, substantial and horrifying. She squeezed me with the desperation of one bound by duty to grim fate. My heart ached for her, like all the chosen acolytes stretching back to the beginning of time.

She pulled away and looked intently at me, fully aware these were her last few moments. "Fu Xi, I have a secret," she whispered. "Had I not been chosen, I wanted to grow up and marry you."

I embraced her and held her tight. Moved by the innocent confession, I fought back the tears.

She released me and turned away. Mother pointed the dagger at the top step on the Altar Rock and motioned for Lian to come forward and take her place.

My role completed, I was relegated to mere spectator. I wanted to close my eyes and turn away. Thousands of years and a thousand Offerings didn't make this moment any easier. I took my place next to the sacred fountain. The Eternal Tree wilted and the last of its leaves fell into the water. It was time.

The acolyte and the Offering dutifully took their places upon the rock.

Lian squeezed her eyes tightly. I held my breath, afraid she would lose her courage and flee the chamber.

She didn't. Like all the acolytes before, she opened her eyes and nodded to Mother.

"I am ready," Lian said.

Mother nodded and calmly looked up at the tree, then to me and spoke the final words, "Let the spirit and the flesh be parted."

I flinched as the knife plunged into the heart of the Offering. I heard the tip of the red blade strike the granite underneath and prayed it didn't get lodged in the rock.

Lian gasped, released the blade, and stepped back off the step. A stream of blood from the Offering boldly splattered her face and robe.

"Remove the blade and remain on the step," I whispered sternly. The cut was properly delivered, but the blade could not remain in

Mother's shell. Shaking, Lian pulled the knife out of Mother's shell with both hands. It slid out effortlessly.

That was the last time I ever saw Lian's eyes.

Mother arched back on the slab and exhaled. She didn't cry out, but then, she never cried out. She turned her head and looked at me with a final glimmer of lucidity. The divine spark intensified and then faded. The presence of the goddess fled the mortal body.

For only a moment I saw the eyes of the little girl I escorted up the Silver Stairs decades earlier. Her name was Mei, and now she looked back at me with her own eyes. I stepped forward, leaned down and kissed her forehead.

"Blessed be she who gives her life in love," I whispered.

The old woman, who as a child had given her body to be Nuwa's shell, tenderly smiled up at me as a thin stream of blood tricked out of her mouth. Her eyes unfocused and then glazed over as a death rattle sounded in her chest.

Mei's blood streamed down the slab and dripped into the eastern canal under the Altar Rock. It ran against the current and quickly spread to the three other canals. The water welling up from the fountain turned red. Before my eyes, the small tree stretched and filled with life. Brittle brown boughs lighted and lifted with vigor. Peach blossoms exploded against a deep green curtain of shoots and sprouts.

A light mist formed over and drifted towards the fountain. It danced and wandered just above the surface, the blood vanishing in its wake. At the fountain, it began to swirl and take a human form. The gentle vortex silently drifted toward Lian and enveloped her. Within the mist, I heard the Offering Blade clatter to the floor. The mist seeped into Lian's body and vanished.

She stood on the first step and leaned against the slab with her eyes closed. Her eyes fluttered open and she looked about, slightly disoriented, until her gaze rested on me.

"The spirit and the flesh are one." The childlike voice carried the ancient tone of the goddess. Lian was gone, replaced by the Goddess Nuwa.

She stepped down, still moving like an old woman. It would be many days before Mother remembered how to be young again.

"Carry Mei's body outside, that we might honor her."

I gently picked up Mei's body and carried it to a tranquil meadow in the crater forest. On a granite outcropping similar to the Altar Rock, we cremated her. It was where I cremated my father and all of mother's mortal husbands. In the twilight, we prayed to the Emperor of Heaven to accept Mei's soul into Paradise.

The white smoke glowed in the starry darkness and carried high above Tortoise Mountain. It told all in Nushen the Offering Ceremony was complete and the Goddess of Tortoise Mountain had taken a new shell.

Across the land of Cin, she was known by many names: Xi Wangmu, the Queen of the West, and Yaochi Jinmu, among others. She preferred the name Nuwa, but I simply called her Mother. Today, she sacrificed herself that the world may be forgiven and renewed for another lifetime.

The Chronicle of Fu Xi

16. Heart Of The Dragon

"A father's duty is to sternly forge his sons into men, but with daughters he may dote and give unselfish love. This is the way the goddess intended." – Lo Proverb.

The Chronicle of Fu Xi

***

They still hadn't reached the end of the trampled ground when they established camp on the leeward slope of the northern ridge.

Setenay sat on the slope with her blanket wrapped around her thin shoulders. She could see the difference in the landscape. Though trampled, the grass was shorter and tougher than the long, slender stalks on the other side of the Black River. Dusty gray sand littered with stones and pebbles replaced the soft, black soil whence they came. Small trees, forever bent by the wind, held vigil atop the ridges like twisted, tortured spirits.

Here, even the trees bend in pain. The farther we journey from Sethagasi's womb, the more inhospitable the world becomes.

Setenay didn't want to show it in front of the men, but the journey was taking its toll. Each step sent flashes of jagged pain up her shins and back. She couldn't seem to shake the Black River's icy grip. Her thin blood begged for warm sunshine and a blazing fire.

At her age, Setenay had reached accommodation with her body. Being old meant always being in some degree of pain. She knew most of these aches would subside after a few days of rest, but the new twinges and tugging pressures in her chest concerned her.

Levidi collapsed on the ground and lay with his head on his bundles. "I've never seen so much animal dung in my life. I'm filthy again!"

Ghalen stretched out on the ground to expose as much of his body to the setting sun as he could. He put his hands behind his head and closed his eyes. "I know of a cool stream a day's walk to the west," he said. "I'm sure you could wash off there."

"If I get any filthier I *will* get back into that cursed river!" Levidi folded his arms and scowled.

"We need to make a fire," Ba-lok said as he walked up behind the group. "Ghalen, gather wood."

Setenay cringed on the inside. *He's not learning his lessons.*

Ghalen sat up and spoke calmly, "First, I don't take orders from you. Second, just *where* in the goddess's name do you expect to find any wood out here?"

Ba-lok folded his arms and stared defiantly at the Ghalen. "I am Second to the Uros. I am a sco-lo-ti."

Ghalen lay back again and returned his hands under his head. "The Second to the Uros? Impressive, but not impressive enough to snap your fingers and produce reeds or cords of wood. Oh, and you are not *my* sco-lo-ti."

Ba-lok turned deep red. "We can burn bundles of grass!"

Ghalen laughed. "These thin blades of scrub are not like thick marsh reeds. You just can't bundle them and throw them on a fire." Ghalen pointed back over his head to one of the few trees lining the ridge. "These pitiful excuses for trees might provide a twig or two at best. And I suppose you'll volunteer to gather grass all night? That will be fine by me. I'll sleep and you can scurry about like a little boy in shore camp, throwing handfuls of grass into the fire."

"Enough, both of you," Aizarg interjected.

Setenay scowled and picked up her stick. Ghalen and Ba-lok saw her and grew quiet.

Aizarg put his hand on Ba-lok's shoulder. "I appreciate your intentions, but I don't think we can make a fire tonight."

Aizarg is in need of council, too. Though, I cannot provide it. He is still the sco-lo-ti, but he needs to become the Uros.

Setenay thought of the dead Scythian. *Such men lead with authority and force. Such men are feared. The men love and respect Aizarg, but they do not fear him.*

Sadness swept over her at the memory of the dead prince's bloated face. *His name was Tuma.*

She knew the meaning of that name..."Half-breed."

A shiver went up her spine.

Perhaps it would be best if they feared Aizarg. Fate will either forge Aizarg into the man he needs to be or we will all perish.

Setenay glanced at Sarah, who wandered downhill from the camp. Sarah turned her head from side to side, scanning the ground, then she stooped, and picked up an object. She carried it a few paces, dropped it, and then repeated the process over and over.

What is she doing?

As the sun dipped to the horizon, the men debated what to do next.

"Are we prepared to travel for days without a fire?" Okta said. "The nights will only grow colder."

"We'll be all right," Aizarg said. "We endure cold winds on the sea for days without complaint."

Setenay would not get involved, though her old bones secretly yearned for a fire.

"Bed down and try to stay warm," Aizarg said.

"Where is Sarah?" said Ba-lok, looking around.

"I smell smoke," Levidi said, surprised.

They found her on her hands and knees in the middle of a circle cleared of grass. She gently blew on embers struggling for life at the base of a small pile of dry grass. A stack of dried animal dung and a small pouch of flint chips sat next to her.

"Didn't you hear the Uros, woman?" Ba-lok demanded. "No fires tonight."

She ignored him and continued to blow on the grass. Ba-lok moved to stop her, but Aizarg held him back.

The embers below the grass suddenly sprang to life and started to consume the pile. She took a chip of dried animal dung and held it to the flames. The chip slowly caught fire and released a dull orange flame and thick oily smoke. As the waste began to heat, the smoke lightened and the flame brightened to yellow. She added a few more chips and the fire flared to life.

"Sarah!" Setenay said in amazement.

She smiled up at Setenay. "This is common knowledge to those who dwell beyond the marsh. I suppose it's understandable the Lo wouldn't know about this kind of fire craft."

Setenay smiled. "I forgot about this craft of making fire. I haven't seen it used..." she saw the Scythian's face again. "...Since I was about your age, Sarah." She felt a little embarrassed she'd forgotten such a practical skill.

"This is a pleasant surprise," Aizarg commented with a grin. "Why didn't you speak of this earlier?"

"I thought it easier to show you than try to explain it," Sarah said with a self-conscious smile, as if she were afraid she'd done something wrong.

She knows when to speak the truth to the blind, and when to simply lead them to safety.

"Also, I had to wait until sunset," Sarah continued. "That's when the wind usually settles. Grass fires are terrible things; they can travel far and kill many. We'll have to be careful in the morning and cover the embers with lots of dirt."

Ghalen nodded. "During dry seasons, the marshes burn as well."

"Another reason I waited until dark is the smoke can be seen for a day's journey in every direction. My people say only the dead make daytime fires upon the g'an."

No one spoke. They gathered around the fire started by a little slave girl who knew more about the world they found themselves in than any of them. In this moment Setenay realized how lucky they'd been so far. They survived negotiations with Virag the Terrible not because of Aizarg's leadership, but because of the fruits of Ood-i's indiscretions. The effect Sarah had on the water demons still mystified her. And now they had a fire because of this intelligent, crafty former slave.

She looked at Aizarg, who stared at the fire, eyes unfocused and lost in his own thoughts. Setenay touched the small of his back and whispered, "Perhaps the gods haven't completely abandoned us. She certainly is a blessing, isn't she? Maybe it's time to do that thing you discussed with me and Okta."

Aizarg's eyes refocused and he smiled broadly down on Setenay. He turned to Ba-lok. "Take the first watch."

Ba-lok frowned, grabbed his pack, and went up the ridge. Setenay and Aizarg agreed Ba-lok should not be present for what was about to transpire. Setenay wanted no disparaging remarks to spoil what should be a joyous and solemn event.

Everyone else moved their belongings down next to the fire and unrolled their mats and blankets.

"Old mother," Ghalen said as he put her pack next to his mat. "You will sleep next to the fire tonight. I am going to put your mat next to mine, but don't get any ideas."

She smiled, reached up and patted Ghalen's cheek. "You are safe tonight; am I?"

Ghalen kissed her on her forehead. "Dear woman, I am only mortal, but I will do my best to control myself."

Everyone ate, and settled close to the fire, their eyes grew heavy. Aizarg, Okta, and Setenay looked at one another and nodded.

Aizarg stood. "Sarah, stand next to me."

Confused, she did so. With a wry smile, Aizarg took her by the hand.

Setenay stood and instantly wished she hadn't sat down. Her thighs and calves ached in protest.

It's not the köy-lo-hely, but it will do.

Okta remained cross-legged on his mat with a wide grin, while the rest of the party looked on.

Setenay spoke, "The Lo are a compassionate race. We did not abandon the refugees during the Scythian scourge in my grandmother's time, and we will not abandon you now, Sarah.

"However, we cannot have a daughter of the g'an among us, tempting a husband to further adultery. I know your heart, child, and I know dear Ood-i's, too. If you came to live with us, I know both of you will genuinely strive to keep your vows, but the seeds are already planted for your failure."

Ood-i leaned forward. "Setenay, w-what is this all about?"

The patesi-le held up her finger, "Patience, hear us out."

"Therefore," she continued, "there is only one path open to us. Sarah, do you want to live among the Lo for the rest of your life?"

A spark of hope lit Sarah's eyes.

"Yes!" she said breathlessly.

Aizarg spoke to Sarah, "You will stay with us, in my arun-ki, until you are properly trained in the ways of our people. Then the day will come when you will be married off to a man from another arun-ki. I promise he will love and cherish you, but this is the condition you must accept to stay. Do you accept it?"

Sarah looked back at Ood-i. Tears rolled into his beard as he nodded once. She turned and nodded to Aizarg.

"I accept."

Okta stood and spoke to Sarah, "When the time comes to marry, you will travel to my arun-ki. There, several young men will compete for your affections. Usually, these are arranged, but Aizarg thought it important you choose. It is a bit unorthodox, but we believe it is imperative you love the man you marry without reservation."

Setenay saw Ood-i's shoulders sag.

"Child, give me your hand." Setenay took Sarah's hand and placed it in Aizarg's.

"Aizarg, will you accept Sarah of the Hur-po as your daughter? Will you take her into your hut as if she were of your flesh?"

Aizarg placed his large hands over her shoulders. Tears welled in Sarah's eyes.

"I will take Sarah into my home as if she were born of my wife's flesh. She will be loved and cherished as a gift from the goddess herself until the day we are returned to the goddess's womb...*if* she will have me as her father. Sarah, will you?"

Sarah leapt at Aizarg, wrapping her arms around his neck with sobs of joy. He picked her up in a big bear hug.

Setenay wiped the mist from her eyes and looked at the smiles of joy ringing the fire. Even Ood-i looked happy, though she sensed sadness below the surface.

Setenay continued, "There is a ceremony appropriate for this occasion, handed down from patesi-le to patesi-le for generations. It is long and I am tired. Aizarg, Sarah is now your daughter. I'm sure you'll do a fine job explaining it to Atamoda when we get home. Good luck.

"Sarah, you are no longer of the Hur-po. You are a Lo woman now. Your new mother, Atamoda, will be in charge of your education."

Sarah struggled to speak through the tears, "I will not let her down."

"Be a good person, true to what is right, and you won't," Setenay caressed her cheek and then turned to the men.

"As in those terrible days of old, we find hope in times of trouble," Setenay said with finality. "From darkness, mercy."

"From darkness, mercy," they all repeated.

With a yawn, Setenay rubbed her palms together and held them up to the fire. "Let's get some sleep."

Levidi spoke up. "Imagine, a patesi-le having her own pick of any man she wants in an arun-ki full of eligible men. That's something I've never heard of."

Setenay, Aizarg, and Okta's heads all turned at once toward Levidi, mouths agape.

"What?" Levidi said, hands out in supplication. Setenay, Aizarg, and Okta looked at each other in amazement.

Levidi burst out laughing and rolled over backwards, holding his gut. "Oh, my goodness! You didn't think about that, did you?"

Sarah searched each of their faces. "I don't understand."

"Young woman," Okta smiled from ear to ear. "You are now the daughter of a sco-lo-ti. No...*Uros* of the Lo people. Your adoptive mother is a patesi-le. By tradition, you must become a patesi-le, a holy woman, of the Lo people. We may have to search far wider than my arun-ki for a husband. By tradition, a patesi-le marries the son of a sco-lo-ti. If you must know, I do have unmarried sons."

Setenay blew out a long sigh between her teeth. She and Aizarg discussed many facets of this arrangement. What they didn't consider were the implications of the sco-lo-ti and a patesi-le adopting a girl. The law was clear, Sarah must be become a patesi-le.

You old witch, how could you overlook that one, small detail?

She exhaled between puffed cheeks. "I'm getting old."

Aizarg looked at Setenay, "Can we do that?"

Setenay shook her head and waved dismissively. "She can turn shit into fire. I guess that's a good start for any patesi-le. How this affects her eligible pool of suitors is an issue for another day. I'm going to sleep."

Levidi still laughed, rolling on the ground as Setenay walked by. She kicked him in the side, which made him laugh even harder.

***

Aizarg threw a few more chips into the fire and then sat down with Sarah in the grass.

"Soon we will look upon Hur-ar. You have told me some things about it, but I have more questions about what to expect once we arrive. How long will it take us to travel from the Canyon to Hur-ar?"

She took a deep breath. "Only a few hours. Once we descend into the Hur Valley, we can quickly cross the Hur River at the Bridge of Kupar. The Dead Forest lies on both sides of the river. A road cuts through the middle and leads directly to the bridge and all the way to the city."

"Bridge? What is a bridge? You didn't mention that," Aizarg said.

"It is a giant structure spanning the river by which we can cross. The Narim built it long ago when they took the Dead Forest. They also built the road. The road and Bridge of Kupar have existed for well over a hundred years. The Kings of Hur-ar have kept both in good repair."

"I greatly look forward to seeing this 'bridge'." Aizarg wanted to finally behold all the wonders Sarah had spoken of over the last two days. "Is this 'Kupar' one of the Narim?"

"Kupar was the type of tree which used to grow in the Dead Forest. The bridge and the Black Fortress are made of kupar wood, which is very hard. Once the Narim took all the wood, not a single sapling returned to the banks of the Hur River. Where there was once a great forest, now only grasslands and stumps remain."

The shadow returned to her face and she turned away.

"What is wrong?"

Sarah shook her head and bit her lower lip. "Forgive me, father, but I have a confession."

"Go on."

"When we left Virag's camp, I fully expected we would be dead before sunset. I know I should have had more faith, but you are Lo, and Lo have no business on the steppe. I assumed we would flee to the marshes or be cut down at the first sight of Scythians. I never thought we'd actually get this close to Hur-ar."

Aizarg laughed. "I will not fault you for common sense. I'm surprised to be here myself."

"Hur-ar offers dangers every bit as deadly as the Scythians. You and your people are wholly unprepared for them. The Hur-po are snakes, deceitful and evil. In many ways, I was better off with Virag."

Aizarg pursed his lips and stared straight ahead. "Go on."

"The Kupar Bridge is guarded by the King's warriors. They wear bronze armor and carry swords and bows. You and your men are no match. Virag had to pay bribes and tribute at the bridge and the city gates before they would let him enter the bazaar. We have no gold and no trade.

"Even if we gain passage into the city, the Black Gate lies all the way against the mountain, up the Cliff Road. We have to pass through the entire city, with all its cutthroats and foulness. The thought of you and your...*our* beautiful people having to endure such evil fills me with dread. I vowed I would die before I returned to that place. I am afraid for you!"

Aizarg lifted her chin. "Do not fear. Something has guided us to this point, of which you've played no small part. We must have faith. My wife..." he paused and chuckled softly, "...*your mother*, says the future is fog upon the water. Look for the stars, feel for the bottom, and call upon the goddess for help. A man makes the decisions he thinks best and poles forward. You can't reach the shore by sitting in place, hoping for a friendly tide which may never come.

"Tell me everything about Hur-ar and the Black Fortress so we can both get some sleep."

She spoke while Aizarg occasionally nodded or asked a question on some detail. Sometimes he shook his head in disgust.

"You've given me much to think about, daughter."

Sarah looked up at him, as large tears welled up and slid down her cheeks. She dropped her head into her hands and began sobbing.

He put an arm around her and tried to console her.

"What is wrong, daughter?" Aizarg couldn't fathom why she cried.

Now I will have two emotional women in my home. He suddenly thought of Ood-i and all the strife he had to endure with both Ula and Su-gar in his hut.

My hut is not large enough for two strong women, two patesi-le. Perhaps I should have thought of this earlier. He took a deep breath. *I wonder what else I have failed to consider on this quest.*

He gently rubbed and patted Sarah's back as if she were a child. "Speak to me."

Her sobs became even louder. Several heads popped up off their mats and looked at them quizzically. Setenay's was not one of them.

"Daughter, now sit up and speak to me."

Sarah straightened, her face wet with tears. "I love the way that word sounds, rolling off your tongue...*daughter*. It drips with the love I never knew among my own people. This moment is an answered prayer."

Aizarg put his arm around her and gave her a little squeeze.

"I hope you find happiness and peace among us."

"Father," her voice suddenly changed to a hushed tone. "Tonight, the spirit's second promise was fulfilled. She told me one day I would know a family's love."

"I see. I know I should not ask this, but since you are both my daughter and will one day be a patesi-le, I suppose it's all right." He paused and looked over at Setenay, who snored loudly.

Perhaps I should wake her for this.

213

He collected his thoughts and asked anyway. "Did this swirling spirit you speak of foretell the fate of our quest or our people?"

"No, Father, but the spirit said I would see Hur-ar again and..." she looked at her hands in her lap and paused.

"And what?"

"The swirling spirit with fiery eyes said after I found a family, she would descend from the Heart of the Dragon and carry me to Paradise."

I should have woken Setenay. He felt like a boy swimming in water much too deep and swift. The current began to carry him away, but still, he kept swimming.

"What is the 'Heart of the Dragon?'"

Sarah pointed to the darkening sky. "There, in the northern sky, do you see the star that does not move? We call that the Heart of the Dragon. The long constellation surrounding it, which rotates around the star throughout the night, is called The Dragon."

Aizarg squinted. "We call that the Home Star, as it will always lead us to shore. I think I see this constellation you call The Dragon. We call it the Marsh Snake. Is a dragon a kind of snake?"

"No, Father. A dragon is a creature of terrible power. It can fly and vomit fire. Legend says a mighty dragon drove the Narim from their homeland before they settled in the Hur Valley."

Aizarg wanted to change the subject, to swim back to familiar waters. He winked at her and gave her another squeeze. "The spirit likely speaks of a day many summers from now, when you are as old and wise as dear Setenay. You will have a long, happy life."

A faint smile touched the corner of her mouth, but the shadow never fully left her face. "Perhaps."

"Enough," he said. "I need to ponder these revelations. Go to sleep now."

Before she settled onto her mat next to Setenay, Sarah threw several more dung chips onto the fire. Soon, she fell asleep.

Aizarg lay on his back and considered everything Sarah said. His mind raced, trying to formulate a plan to get them to the Narim. He watched the Marsh Snake slowly revolve around the Home Star.

What did she call it, the Dragon?

Aizarg's eyes grew heavy and he fell asleep.

***

Ba-lok sat with his back against a scrub oak, his knees pulled up against his chest and his blanket tightly tucked under his chin. He faced north with his back to the low ground. In a moonless sky the stars bathed the hilly steppe with cool, milky light.

Ba-lok snored like his grandmother, unaware of the mist rolling in from the northern horizon. It flowed over the distant hills, spilling over one hill, building in the low ground like milk in a bowl, and then spilled over the next. Sometimes, tendrils of mist twisted their way through the lowlands like pale serpents. The mist almost seemed to glow in the starlight as it quietly slipped south.

Ba-lok grunted, fell over, but didn't wake. He curled into a fetal ball below the tree and pulled the blanket over his head.

Above him, shooting stars began to streak across the sky. At first, only one or two per minute but soon, dozens, and then hundreds a minute blazed overhead.

The falling stars radiated outward from the Heart of the Dragon in sheets of dazzling light.

17. The Last Quest Of Fu Xi The Wanderer

I recounted the tale of my journey to Wu. Mother sat in silence, expressionless. Through my words I believe she relived the choices of her immortal life. Through my words I believe she finally understood the judgment of the Emperor of Heaven.

The Chronicle of Fu Xi

***

It was deep into the night before Fu Xi finished his account of the journey to Wu. He couldn't remain still as his tale poured forth like a confession. Fu Xi recalled each trial, each temptation encountered on his journey to the edge of the world and back. Sometimes he spoke in hushed, reverent tones recalling wonders beyond imagining. Often, he clenched his teeth in suppressed rage, reliving horrors he could not forget. Dawn was still an unfulfilled promise as he knelt before his mother, tears filling his eyes.

"I return from Wu with two magnificent horses, armor and a sword of red orichalcum metal. I also bring home shame and grief. Once again, because of my pride I have failed and all of Cin will pay." He bowed and placed his head in her lap.

Nuwa stroked his hair. "You have not failed. To the contrary, you have triumphed."

Fu Xi looked at his mother, his face wet with tears. "I don't understand. Paqua, the god-prince of Wu will come, and with him an army no force in Cin can stand against, even me. In the coming war of gods we will lose. I've placed all we love in peril. "

"He will not come nor will his kind ever threaten Cin. This god-prince, this Paqua...he and his kind are doomed."

Fu Xi looked up at his mother in shock.

"You *knew* of them, of the god-princes from the east?"

"Your journey was a test. I sent you east, knowing the temptations you'd face in Wu. Frankly, I had little hope you would return. You returned and, in doing, gained the favor of the Emperor of Heaven." Her stare intensified as she stood and held her face close to his. "You did what I could not; you resisted the temptation of pride."

Fu Xi searched his mother's face. Nuwa stood and held out her hand. "Come. Let us finish our journey together. We only have a little way to go."

He took her hand and they walked arm-in-arm into the night. When they came to the Place of Perfect Sorrows, Fu Xi saw his traveling clothes, cleaned and folded, along with a fresh pack of provisions, on the Altar Rock.

"Why?" he asked, pointing to his clothes.

"Paqua's father is my brother and, like me, has been known by many names. There more of us scattered across the world, charged by the Celestial Emperor to guide a fallen world back to redemption. In the end, it was we who fell."

Nuwa knelt down next to the northern canal and ran her hand in the water.

"We call this plane of existence 'The Water'. Time radiates...*flows* from the Throne of Creation." She motioned to the Eternal Tree. "It's intoxicating and seductive, much like you experienced in Wu. We forgot our purpose and turned away from our vows.

"But Mother, you've been steadfast in your service to the Celestial Emperor."

She shook her head. "What you see is but a moment; the last fallen grain upon the heap at the bottom of the hourglass.

"Long before your father was born, I fell in love with another. He was powerful and beautiful, and our passion was forbidden. I loved him, but I knew he would not, *could not*, return it. But I did not care. We were drunk on The Water and consumed with the sensual pleasures of our flesh."

Nuwa's eyes were distant. "I stole a mortal form which was not offered me so that my lover might ravish me. When my ecstasy ebbed I fled in shame. I bore a child, a son, whom I loved dearly. I was foolish to hide, for the Celestial Emperor found me. I begged him for forgiveness. He took my child that he should not be corrupted."

"I have a brother?" Astonished, Fu Xi held his head with both hands and paced about.

"Yes." Nuwa pointed to the clothes and provision on the Altar Rock. "And you must seek him out.

"For your entire life you've sowed seeds of wisdom across the land. Some of this seed has taken root, some has fallen among the thistles and barren rock. None of this matters now, for all your work will be like the soft clay under the spring downpour. It is destined to wash into the sea, forgotten under the slime of ages. Now you serve another destiny.

"Go west and harvest fruit sown by the Celestial Emperor himself. This fruit is precious to him. They are a lost people, a good people. Bring them to a promised place of safety and ensure their story is not forgotten. Do this not by my command, but for the Emperor of Heaven himself. These are your children now, my son."

Fu Xi paused. "How will I know them from other men?"

"There will be no other men," her voice was flat. "But you will know them by their leader, a man with hair like snow who carries the Two Dragons within his spirit."

Fu Xi stepped back. "What do you mean, 'no other men?'"

Nuwa stood and her voice once again took on the aura of a goddess. A blue light began to shine in her eyes.

"Before you rode into Nushen your head was full of questions of strange wonders and dark omens encountered along your return journey from Wu."

"Yes." Fu Xi feared what his mother might say.

"These signs proclaim the Emperor of Heaven has forsaken the earth. The world is hopelessly corrupt and he will destroy all who dwell upon it."

Fu Xi fell to his knees at her feet.

"No, Mother! Beseech him to turn his wrath, I beg you!" He thought of the hundreds of villages filled with good and decent people scattered throughout Cin. Images of children and their families flashed through his mind. "There is still so much goodness in the world. If I see this truth, certainly the Emperor of Heaven must see it, too?"

"This wrath is not only mankind's to bear. He will cleanse the world of my kind and our offspring. The world cannot be free as long as the Fallen and our children roam the earth."

Fu Xi rushed to the Altar Rock, yanked the Offering Blade from its hidden slot and held it to his chest. "So be it! Let us pay this price, but not the mortals. Let him wipe away us and the Black God, but spare mankind."

"In this matter the Emperor's will is set. He has hardened his heart. He stood here," she motioned to fountain, "and I begged for your life."

The Offering Blade clattered to the floor as he slumped against the Altar Rock. "How much time is left?"

"It has already begun."

"What must I do?"

She pointed to the pillars at the entrance to the Second Realm. "Mount the gray mare and ride west until the mountains scrape the sky. Climb the Roof of the World and do not stop. Do not sleep. Do not rest. Do not eat. Your mare will not survive. When she dies, leave her body and mount the black stallion. Ride him until you come to this place." She produced a stalk of wheat from the folds of her robe and handed it to Fu Xi. "This place is called the Navel of the World. Remain there until the curse is lifted.

"Be warned, the limits of your immortality will be tested. The Celestial Emperor only promised you a chance for life, not that your fate was assured. Now, get dressed. You haven't much time."

"How will I know the curse is lifted?"

"You will know," she whispered.

Fu Xi removed his robe and donned his travelling clothes. As he dressed, she continued her instructions.

"Fu Xi, you have one last gift to give the Tall Men, to these lost people you must seek out. This is a gift I do not possess. It lies with your half-brother."

"Where can I find him?"

Nuwa stepped over the eastern canal and motioned around the courtyard.

"Let the Place of Perfect Sorrows be your guide. If you survive to see the end of the scourge, depart the Navel of the World to the west. As you pass into unknown lands, keep the red sword close and always wear your armor."

"Why?" Fu Xi asked as he reached for the red sword on the table.

"In case your brother finds you first."

Fu Xi hesitated, and then slid the sword in his sash. "What is his name? How will I know him?"

"Totaresh, though I fear he has forgotten that name. Through him you will be tested." She laid her hand on his sword arm and whispered, "Your only hope is to recognize each other's kindred spirits before..." she trailed off. "That is all I can say."

Unsure what to say or feel, his mind swirled with more questions. This was all happening too fast, even for a god.

"Mother, I..."

"The time for questions is over. A new journey, a new quest awaits you. Flee! Your horses are fed and watered in the pasture below."

Fu Xi looked down at his hands as silent tears rolled down his cheeks.

"Will I ever see you again?"

"Do not weep, child. There will be many more days of sorrow before you see the sun again."

Fu Xi sobbed and reached to embrace his mother, but she pulled back. "I need you to understand everything I did, I did for love," she whispered.

"Will I see you again?" he repeated.

"When you depart, I will no longer be Nuwa, Celestial Goddess of the West. That grace has been stripped from me. The silver torches are cold and her light will depart forever. He has given me a new charge and a new name that I may be redeemed."

***

Nuwa stood at the stairs under the Threshold Dragon until she sensed her son enter the pitch black forest, riding hard away from the false dawn. Fu Xi dutifully obeyed her, but she sensed his tears drying in the cold air.

"Ride, son," she whispered. "Do not look back, for I have just begun to cry."

She lingered there a little longer and watched the dawn for the last time with human eyes. As she turned to go back inside the temple, the flame in the Threshold Dragon's eyes died.

***

As Nuwa straightened up the cottage, she noticed Heng's breathing growing more ragged.

"It's getting chilly in here, my love," she said and threw a few more faggots into the fire. She swept the floor and cleaned off the table. She carefully washed the ceramic cups in the cistern and placed them back on the wooden shelf built into the bamboo wall.

Nuwa looked around the cottage. Everything was neat and in its place. Newly born daylight glowed ruddy through oil-skin windows as she considered Fu Xi's bound bedroll.

Do not cry! I will not spend my last few moments in sorrow. The Emperor of Heaven made me a promise and I will trust him.

She lay down next to Heng on the couch. The plush couch and his silk robe represented her oath of service to mankind, an oath to place their needs above hers. The ancient oath held no power over her, her heart now burdened by another.

Nuwa snuggled up against Heng. He felt clammy. She reached down and pulled a thin wool blanket over both of them. His breathing became more labored. She wrapped her arms around him and held his hand. Nuwa heard his heart slowing and soon her heart beat in rhythm with his.

***

Nuwa could no longer bear the screams rising from Nushen.

"I chose Fu Xi!" she screamed at the Celestial Emperor's feet.

Nuwa could bear many of the temptations of the Water, even pride. The one she could not resist was love. For love, she betrayed her oath and her master.

"It is for love's sake I grant forgiveness," the Emperor of Heaven replied. "Out of love I spare Fu Xi. Understand, wayward servant, the price of forgiveness is blood. It is a price even I must pay.

"Keep your promise and I shall keep mine."

***

Heng drew his last ragged breath. She saw his spirit, young and handsome, slip away and float upward toward the door. Heng didn't look back; his face lifted up toward something else.

"Goodbye, my love," she whispered.

She would not need a mortal shell for her new duty.

"Let the spirit and the flesh be parted," she exhaled, and released the spirit from her shell. Lian's child-like spirit cloaked itself in the ghostly memory of her Offering Robes. She floated forward and took Heng's hand. He smiled down at her and together they faded away.

For the first time in countless millennia, Nuwa was truly alone.

A white mist materialized around Heng and Lian's dead bodies on the couch. Tendrils snaked away and flowed over the floor and began to swirl. After a few moments, the mist took a vague human shape. A light, like a blue flame, flickered over the swirling mist, then descended into the smoky form. The apparition's eyes showed forth with brilliant blue light as it turned and floated out of the hut.

The apparition's face briefly took on Lian's childhood form and then Mia's. With each step, it transformed into a new likeness. Each new face revealed the story of Nuwa's past, like the rings of an ancient tree. The blue flames in her eyes pulsed as her earthly forms flashed by.

As she passed from the Inner Realm to the Place of Perfect Sorrows, the faces flickered by faster than a hummingbird's wings, occasionally pausing on those who held special significance to the Goddess Nuwa.

One was the woman called Gaia, her shell when she gave birth to Fu Xi and founded the village of Nushen. That face faded and the lineage continued back into time, to Offerings that preceded the Nushen and the Acolytes of Nuwa. These faces belonged to girls from tribes so ancient they were forgotten even to the gods.

Two faces briefly flashed by, of an old woman and a young woman. These were not shells from her past, but souls she had very recently touched far to the west.

The misty form floated to the fountain at the base of the Eternal Tree and stopped. So, too, did the parade of faces.

The mist spun faster and faster until a howling gale blasted between the pillars. The form grew and stretched until it towered above the courtyard.

The mists congealed into a snakelike dragon writhing above the mountain like a tornado.

She looked down upon her temple, her home for so many thousands of years. She arched back her head and poured gouts of white flame into the crater. The cottage and the surrounding forests instantly incinerated. Flames shot through the courtyard and vaporized the Eternal Tree. The inferno flashed the water in the canals to steam and the resulting detonation blew apart the courtyard. Still, she continued to pour liquid fire onto the mountain until it flowed like lava between the columns and through the entrance below the Threshold Dragon. It flowed down the Silver Stairs like a waterfall of sunlight until it reached Nushen and the Tree of Immortality and wiped them from existence.

The golden spirit dragon lifted into the heavens, into the northern stars called The Dragon and vanished with the dawn. Nuwa, Celestial Goddess of the West, protector of mankind and bringer of enlightenment, took a new form for a new task.

She became Death.

18. The Gray Death

Rain was rare in that forgotten land. While thin clouds often covered their world, they were sterile. Ice and snow existed across the distant Adyghe Mountains, but not a drop of rain fell west of their slopes.

Shallow, cold streams irrigated the g'an. They originated in the unknown north and spilt into the Great Sea. What parts of the steppe the streams didn't quench, the ice mists did.

Sometimes the ice mists lasted only a few hours and sometimes they lingered for days. The Sammujad said the ice mists gave the grasslands life by stealing it from men's souls. Linger too long in the ice mist's embrace, the elders said, and the cursed fog would drag you to heli-dar.

The Chronicle of Fu Xi

***

Aizarg balanced precariously in his reed boat and tried to keep the mountains of water from swamping his tiny craft. His pole and paddle were gone.

He stood in the center of the boat, adjusting his weight by swaying right and left and trying to feel his way from crest to trough. In the darkness, he desperately searched for the next crest before snapping his bow around and surfing down the wave's face, survival from wave to wave his only thought.

Two titanic waves closed in on him, each building to impossible heights and squeezing him into a narrow channel. Aizarg reached out and touched the sheer cliffs of water on each side, but quickly pulled his hands away from the frigid water.

Lightning flashed across the churning sea. Aizarg ducked and cried. Another bolt struck the top of the waves. Then another, and another, until the sky flashed on and off in a never ending succession of strobes. With each flash came a clap of sound so loud Aizarg covered his ears.

The lightning parted the black curtain and revealed how high the surrounding waves truly were. From the bottom of the liquid canyon he could barely see the wave tops. Trapped between warring giants, the waves could collapse and crush him any second.

In a single flash he saw figures atop of the waves. In the next flash, they came into focus. Scythian Death Slaves floated above the turbulent foam. The skeleton warriors stared down on him with vacant eye sockets. The top of their skulls were shaved off, trophies for the Scythian warrior who slew them.

In another flash they were gone.

"Psatina, help me!" he gasped.

"The water is filled with the tears of the dead!" A voice faintly rose above the howling wind. Aizarg put a wet finger in his mouth and tasted salt. Something else covered his hands. In the lightning he saw they were covered with sticky, black pitch.

A new deafening rumble rose above the maelstrom.

Aizarg looked up to see the waves collapsing together, cutting off his escape. Then he saw an overpowering shadow atop the waves, riding high above the point where the waves tumbled together. Enormous and solid, the waves crashed harmlessly against it as it slid into the trough and hurtled straight for Aizarg.

A mountain within a mountain.

The waves suddenly overwhelmed Aizarg and he fell into the churning abyss. The frigid waters paralyzed him and he sank into the blackness. Black hands grabbed at his ankles and pulled him down.

***

"Aizarg! Wake up! Wake up!"

Aizarg opened his eyes, disoriented, and shivering uncontrollably. A thick fog enveloped everything.

"Sit up, Aizarg, ice mists are upon us!" Okta shook him again. The cold and Okta's fear cut cleanly through the haze in Aizarg's mind.

With great effort, Aizarg lifted himself into a sitting position. Water saturated his mat and dripped from his hair. Aizarg's clothes were soaking wet from a frigid humidity that burrowed deep into his bones.

I forgot about the ice mist! Aizarg shook off the terrible dream and tried to put the present reality into perspective. The War Council discussed and planned for many dangers on the quest. Unfortunately, the delegates failed to consider the ice mists.

I pray this doesn't prove a fatal oversight.

Aizarg only encountered the ice mists a few times in his life, but clearly understood their brutal truth. They killed by leaving nothing dry, nothing warm. For the Lo, being caught at sea enveloped in their ghastly embrace, unable to find the shore, was equally dangerous. That's what Aizarg felt like now, far out to sea with no sense of direction.

He stood and stretched his limbs. The soggy ground squished beneath his feet. As quickly as his numb fingers allowed, he folded his wet belongings and rolled them in his mat.

Once Aizarg packed his belongings, he stood and turned to Okta. "Do your people possess any lore which might aid us?"

"Very little, Uros. We call these mists the Gray Death. The War Council was hasty. We failed to consider this possibility," Okta said, teeth chattering.

Aizarg thought he smelled something. He sniffed the air, trying to get a better sense of direction.

"I smell the shore, the taste of where the sea and land come together. Do you?"

"I smell nothing," Okta said. "We are far from home, Uros."

"Perhaps I am imagining it." Aizarg shrugged it off and considered the corpse of last night's fire, now only a muddy, black pit. "We will restart the fire."

"Uros," Okta continued. "We both know there should be smoldering embers in the fire, but it is cold. The grass and dung are saturated and we have no wood. Flint and tinder will be of no use." Okta leaned in closer. "The Gray Death may last days. Our only hope for warmth is to keep moving."

Aizarg shouldered his pack and tried to peer into the mist. Pale figures moved slowly and stiffly as they packed their belongings. Okta's council sounded reasonable, but the thought of moving through the thick mist gave him pause.

I cannot even see their faces. It will be easy to lose someone.

"Let us gather everyone together while I consider your advice," he told Okta.

Aizarg bobbed his finger from silhouette to silhouette, counting his people. He recognized burly Ood-i and compact Levidi kneeling next to one another. Ghalen, tall and straight, assisted Setenay's thin, bent shade. Sarah stood apart, her back to the group.

Something about how she stood struck Aizarg as unnatural. Before he could ponder this further, Okta grasped his shoulder.

"Where is Ba-lok?" Okta said.

"BA-LOK!" Aizarg shouted. The men joined him, but the gray wall robbed their voices of vitality.

"He went up the hill on watch last night," Aizarg said. "Levidi, go up the hill and get him."

Levidi started off, but stopped and slowly turned around, "Yes, Uros, but...which way is the hill?"

Unable to regain his bearings, Aizarg knelt down and examined grass. The soggy ground eradicated any trace of Ba-lok's trail.

Setenay and the men gathered around Aizarg.

What do I do now?

"I think the hill is that way," Levidi said weakly and pointed. "I'm sure I can find him."

"No," Aizarg said. "I will go up the hill and look for Ba-lok."

"I caution against it," Okta said. "If you become lost..."

"I will not lose Ba-lok," Aizarg pushed past Okta. "I cannot ask any man to risk what I would not brave myself."

"No, Aizarg," Levidi begged. "Please, let me go!"

"No. That is my final word." Aizarg looked up to the sky, but the thick fog kept the sun's position a mystery. "Wait for my return until the cold becomes too unbearable, and then depart to the north. Stay to the low ground."

"Uros," Ghalen said softly. "We have no way to determine north. We could walk in circles between the surrounding high ground and easily become lost."

"I will not leave Ba-lok!" Aizarg said.

"If we do not start walking, we'll all freeze!" Okta gritted his teeth, barely able to keep his voice under control. He chewed his mud weed rapidly, nervously.

Ghalen spoke in a calm, measured voice. "Uros, we could *all* search for Ba-lok together. We may become lost, but we'll be as one. And we'll all be walking, keeping warm."

"Yes," Aizarg felt relieved. Ghalen's advice was a lifeline. Then a new thought occurred to Aizarg.

He remembered the Black River and his failure to string the rope across the river to pull everyone to safety. He reached into his pack and removed his rope.

"Everyone tie the rope to your waists and then each other. That way we can't lose one another. Prepare to march. We'll proceed slowly this way." He pointed to the grayness beyond the dead fire pit where he thought the ground went uphill. "Stay close enough to see each other. If you become separated, stop and we will backtrack to find you."

Without another word, the party shouldered their bundles and began tethering themselves to each other.

Setenay approached Aizarg in a slow, deliberate shuffle. She tightly grasped his arm. "We will not find Ba-lok," she said with a cracking voice. The mists seemed to attack her, leaving her skin colorless and lips tinged blue. She trembled as her eyes darted from place to place, focusing and then moving on. Aizarg peered into the mist, trying to see what she saw.

"What is it, old mother? Why won't we find Ba-lok?"

She swallowed hard. "Last night...I dreamt of the dead."

Last night's dream suddenly flashed in his mind's eye.

"Ba-lok remains in the world of mortal flesh," she continued. "It is we who are no longer upon the g'an. We are caught between the worlds of flesh and spirit. Wander all you wish, but you will not find him, and he will not find us."

"Setenay, these are common ice mists," Okta interjected, trying to sound confident.

"Your eyes behold one reality, mine another." She tightened her shawl over her shoulders, never taking her eyes off the gray curtain.

"What do you see?" Aizarg said.

"My eyes still slumber," she replied.

Clammy fingers of doubt crept across Aizarg's spirit.

"You heard the patesi-le," Okta whispered again, the fear still rising in his voice. "If she says we cannot find Ba-lok, then we should heed her council. We must leave."

Aizarg paused for a few moments, desperately hoping for a clear answer.

"Whether we are in the world of flesh or spirit, it does not matter. I must search for Ba-lok. Stay together and follow me and stay within an arm's length of the person in front of you. We'll proceed slowly and find the hill where he kept watch."

Setenay shook her head. "As you wish, Uros."

They fell into a loose line behind Aizarg and prepared to march into the fog. Sarah's back remained turned to the group.

Ood-i looked over his shoulder. "Sarah, come. Let me tie the rope around your waist."

She remained motionless. Aizarg couldn't detect a single shiver or even an indication she was breathing.

"Sarah," Ood-i repeated softly, with concern. "We must go." He approached within a few feet of her and stopped.

Head down, Sarah's wet, stringy hair hid her face.

"Sarah, are you all right?" Aizarg called out.

"Sarah?" Ood-i hesitantly reached out to touch her, his hand only inches from her shoulder.

Sarah suddenly spun around and raised her head. Ood-i gasped, stumbled back and fell. Sarah's eyes were white orbs, as blank and featureless as the surrounding mist. Her skin began to glow with a soft, electric blue aura.

"Do not touch her!" Setenay screamed.

"She is bewitched!" Okta cried out.

"No one touch her!" Setenay shouted again.

The blue aura surrounding her condensed into glowing tendrils that snaked around Sarah. They probed her, lifting and moving parts of her deerskin blouse and hair. Sarah gave no indication of awareness.

"We must save her!" Ood-i lunged forward, but Setenay snatched his tunic.

"No! She is possessed. The spirit is not harming her, but if you touch her it may not be so gentle with you."

"What is it? What must we do, Setenay?" Aizarg asked, rapidly feeling overwhelmed by events.

Setenay spoke with impatience as if Aizarg were only a child. "Sometimes there is nothing *to* do! This spirit has chosen her and we are powerless."

"Chosen her for *what?*" Levidi asked.

"I thought you said the spirits were gone from the world?" Okta spat his words at the patesi-le.

Setenay turned a merciless gaze on Okta, "The spirits are gone from *our world*. As I told you before, we are now in their realm!"

"Are we dead?" Ghalen said stone like.

"Not yet. Whether we stay alive depends heavily on what we do next."

Levidi grabbed Aizarg's tunic. "Sarah's feet do not touch the earth!"

The men shrank back except for Ood-i, who stood shoulder to shoulder with Aizarg. Setenay also held her ground.

Sarah hovered inches over the ground, as if lifted by strings stretched between worlds. Her arms were slightly outstretched with palms up. Her head tilted back as glowing tendrils swirled around her with greater intensity. Her blank eyes frightened Aizarg the most, as if her soul had fled.

"We must run!" Okta shouted. "We must run before this demon kills us all!"

Like an anchor that suddenly finds purchase in a swift current, Aizarg found his courage.

"Hold your ground!" Aizarg called to his men. "If your patesi-le does not flee, neither will you!"

As Sarah glided past them, the air seemed to warm.

"She is leaving!" Ood-i untied the rope from his waist and followed her before Aizarg could stop him.

"Ood-i! Come back!" Aizarg shouted after him.

Setenay looked up at Aizarg. "Ood-i follows his heart. Love is his faith and guide, a torch thrust ahead of him into the unknown." She paused. "What do you have faith in, Uros of the Lo?"

The farther Sarah floated away, the brighter she glowed. The spirit possessing Sarah illuminated the fog around her, silhouetting Ood-i's broad frame as he melted into the blue glow.

Aizarg made up his mind. "Love...yes, and hope. Hope is my faith, hope that this mysterious spirit beckons us for good." He raised his voice and his boar spear and motioned forward. "We follow Sarah. Come!"

Setenay followed her Uros into the gray wall and the men filed in behind them.

***

Aizarg trailed several paces behind Sarah while Setenay and Ghalen brought up the column's rear. Ghalen carried Setenay's bundle and walked close by her side, his extra tunic wrapped around her shoulders. The ice mist seemed to renew its attack on her. Sometimes she murmured strange chants under her breath. Occasionally, Ghalen wrapped his arms around her frail body, trying to warm her and whispered tender words of encouragement. When Ghalen and Setenay fell behind the rope grew taut and Aizarg ordered the group to slow. The spirit possessing Sarah seemed to sense this and also slowed down.

The damp, heavy cold robbed them of the will to speak. Aizarg couldn't feel his toes; his soft deerskin shoes were soaked. His clothes were completely drenched and the bottoms of his breeches were splattered with mud. Every breath seemed to freeze his lungs and chill him from the inside out.

The men trudged forward like deathly shades. Hair pasted to their faces, they appeared as if freshly emerged from the water. Okta, the most affected, looked ashen and struggled to keep up.

Perhaps the mist is stealing our souls, Aizarg thought as he watched Okta's vaporous breath melt into the fog. *Maybe it has already taken Sarah's.*

Aizarg's thoughts turned to Ba-lok. He felt guilty for leaving him, but at this point, every step, every decision he made on faith.

Faith in what? A glowing spirit that has seized my daughter?

The line suddenly snapped tight around Aizarg's waist.

"Levidi! Help me!" Ghalen called out.

Aizarg looked back to see Setenay stretched limply over Ghalen's forearm. Levidi hurried over to take Ghalen's sagar, but Ood-i stopped him.

Ood-i took Ghalen's sagar. "Levidi, you have enough to carry already."

Ghalen swept Setenay into his arms and held her close to his chest. "She's freezing. She won't last much longer," Ghalen pleaded to Aizarg.

I cannot do this without Setenay.

"We must keep walking, it's our only hope." Aizarg turned to go.

Sarah was gone.

Now the spirit has abandoned us.

Suddenly, Okta slumped to the ground.

"Okta! You must get up! We must keep walking," Aizarg tried to lift Okta, but he sagged to his knees.

"It's all right, Uros." Okta's speech slowed and slurred. Black mud weed juice dribbled down his beard. "I only need a few minutes to rest. I'm getting warmer. Perhaps the ice mist is lifting."

It wasn't getting warmer and the mist was as thick as ever. He tried again to pull Okta up by his tunic, but Okta fell over and squished onto the saturated ground.

"Please, Uros," Okta murmured, losing consciousness. "Give me a few moments to rest."

"Levidi, help me!" Aizarg shouted. Together, they put Okta's arms over their shoulders and lifted him.

"Walk!" Aizarg ordered the party. "Ood-i, you will lead."

"Sarah is gone. Which way, Uros?" Ood-i asked.

Despite Aizarg's best efforts, panic seeped through his voice. "I don't care..." he waved his hand. "Straight ahead."

Ood-i grasped Aizarg's bicep. "Strength, Uros."

Aizarg suddenly noticed Ood-i wasn't stuttering. *Who is this clear-eyed, lion of a man?*

Without another word the group shambled on.

Gruesome images filled Aizarg's imagination; the party falling, one by one, and freezing to death as he helplessly watched.

Then, a new image flashed in his mind, of Atamoda and the boys waiting for him to return. He tried to grasp Atamoda's li-ge around his neck, but his numb hand couldn't feel it.

"Uros!" Ghalen shouted from behind him.

Aizarg turned and saw Ghalen looking away into the nothingness.

"Hold him and don't let him fall," Aizarg ordered Levidi and slid out from under Okta's arm.

Aizarg came alongside Ghalen. "What's wrong? What do you see?"

"There, Uros!" Ghalen nodded into the nothingness. "Someone is coming."

Ba-lok! He hoped against hope.

"Who?" I see noth—" Aizarg rubbed his eyes and looked again.

The fog plays tricks on my mind, Aizarg thought as the blank wall of gray seemed to congeal at certain points, like pulling a string on a garment and watching the material bunch up. The apparitions didn't approach from within the fog as much as they gelled into existence. At first he saw one, and then two, and then many. The shades were barely discernible, melting into one other and then reforming.

Without a word, Ghalen gently put Setenay down. Levidi did the same with Okta. They grabbed their sagar spears from Ood-i and shuffled abreast of one another into a battle line.

"Who are they?" Levidi whispered.

"*What* are they?" Ood-i said.

One after another, the strange figures sharpened into focus and drifted forward. They were once Sammujad warriors. Their colorless clothes and leather armor hung in shambles and their sagar spears were broken and splintered.

"Aizarg! Their heads! Look at their heads!" Levidi's voice quaked.

Above the black pits of their eye sockets their skulls were cleanly cut off.

"These are the Scythian Death Slaves, the ones who lined the ridges," Aizarg whispered as his nightmare become reality. "Setenay is right, we are between worlds."

"How do we get back to our world?" Ghalen asked.

"I don't know," Aizarg stole a glance behind him. Setenay still lay on the ground. He desperately wished she stood by his side, telling him what to do.

"They've come to steal us away, to exact vengeance on us for desecrating their bones!" Levidi jabbed his spear at the army of the dead and shrieked. "Get back! Back, I say! You will not drag me to heli-dar!"

Aizarg knew they all held their ground by a frayed thread of courage. Levidi's bravery in the mortal realm did not guarantee courage against the terrible powers of the spirit world.

"Hold!" Aizarg said firmly, placing a hand on Levidi's shoulder.

The battle lines were about thirty feet apart, but the dead vastly outnumbered the living. Aizarg glanced left and right. Ghalen leaned out slightly ahead of the line, as if he'd been ready for this moment his whole life. Ood-i was unexpectedly calm.

Men of the Lo hold their ground against the forces of hell, he thought with unexpected pride and hope.

Behind them, Setenay suddenly moaned.

They all turned.

Ghalen cried, *"Setenay! She is possessed, too!"*

Sarah had mysteriously reemerged from the mist. She stood hand in hand with Setenay, whose eyes were as white Sarah's. They faced the men as the blue aura engulfed them both.

"Quickly, form a circle around Okta!" Aizarg commanded.

The men formed a circle, spears outward, trapped between the ghosts and the possessed women.

"We are doomed!" Levidi cried out.

"Calm yourself!" Aizarg scolded him. "I'm frightened, too, but we must think clearly."

"Aizarg, the ghosts do not attack," Ood-i said.

The shades hovered at the edge of the mist but didn't move toward them.

"Yes," Ghalen whispered. "Why don't they attack?"

Then, in the center of the spectral line, a tall figure stretched out his sagar toward the men.

Aizarg looked at the apparition, trying to discern its purpose. Unconsciously, he reached up and clutched Atamoda's li-ge.

"He's pointing," Aizarg whispered, suddenly understanding what the ghost wanted. "He's pointing behind us."

Aizarg looked back. Setenay and Sarah were slowly drifting away, hand in hand. The blue aura bridging them brightened.

"They want us to follow the women. Levidi and Ghalen, get Okta. We must hurry," Aizarg commanded.

The women floated above the grasslands as the men stumbled after them like moths chasing a flame. The dead marched forward as their ranks split and flanked the men on either side.

***

Time lost all meaning as they walked in silence. While still cold, the air didn't carry the same bone-numbing chill.

Every so often Aizarg spied dark, silent shadows paralleling them beyond the ghostly army. They were hulking, monstrous forms. The hair on Aizarg's neck stood up when they appeared. The black forms retreated only when the dead lifted their sagars toward them, only to reappear at different points.

Aizarg didn't know the intentions of the army of the dead or the spirits possessing Sarah and Setenay. However, he had no doubts the black shadows were malevolent and the only thing standing between them and his men were the dead.

The others didn't seem to perceive the lurking shadows and Aizarg thought it wise not to mention them.

"This is the march of the damned," Levidi muttered to himself. The fear remained, but without the panic.

"No, it isn't," Aizarg said as a strange calm settled over him. "The dead could easily overwhelm us. I feel no malice..." ...*at least not from the dead.*

"I don't feel as cold," Ood-i said from behind.

"Neither do I," Ghalen huffed and readjusted Okta's arm over his neck.

"I think the dead are protecting us," Aizarg said.

"From what?" Levidi asked.

"I don't know," Aizarg lied as another black shadow darted beyond the ghostly escort.

Without warning, bloodcurdling shrieks, an unholy blend of animal rage and frustration, rang out from the mist. They were so loud Aizarg flinched.

The women released their hands and the blue aura connecting them thinned and parted. Setenay settled to the ground and stopped. Sarah drifted a few more paces before also settling to earth. The ghosts halted, surrounding the men on three sides.

"What now?" Levidi whispered as he looked around.

The shadows beyond the dead grew in size and number. They merged into a black mass like an imposing wave threatening to break over them. Then, with another hideous scream, the dark entities scattered and vanished into the mist like bats fleeing the dawn.

Aizarg winced again, their malignant screams almost too much to bear.

"I thought I heard something," Ood-i said. "Did any of you hear that?"

Ghalen and Levidi shook their heads.

Something has driven away the evil spirits, Aizarg thought with relief. *Why didn't the other men see or hear them?*

Sarah and Setenay slowly rotated to face the men. The blue aura intensified as misty tendrils twisted and wrapped into tight, brilliant balls of light over each woman's head. The light intensified and elongated into tongues of blue flame, which slowly drifted away from the women, one floating to the left and one to the right.

The women collapsed as if invisible strings had been cut. Ghalen and Ood-i began to walk to them, but Aizarg barred their way with his spear.

"Wait. Keep your spears up and be patient. The women will be all right." Aizarg didn't know that, but he didn't want the men to let their guard down.

The blue lights floated soundlessly over the ranks of the dead. As they passed over the ghosts, the blue aura briefly transformed each apparition, providing a glimpse of what they were in life. Their spears suddenly became whole. Sawed off heads were instantly covered with full heads of hair. Empty sockets were filled with mournful eyes. Their sorrowful expressions disturbed Aizarg more than the empty, ghastly skulls. As the blue flame moved on, each spirit reverted to a deathly apparition.

"What does this all mean, Uros?" Ghalen gasped.

Aizarg shook his head.

Finally, both flames came full circle in front of the men and fused together as one over a single ghost. This ghost became life-like and stepped forward. The light followed him, bathing him in shimmering blue light. Aizarg recognized the man and caught his breath.

His name was Tuma.

This was not the mangled corpse they buried yesterday, but what appeared to be a living, breathing young man. The Scythian prince's feet hovered above the ground. His head was shaved except for a top-knot of long brown hair falling over his broad left shoulder. His clothes, no longer shredded and in perfect condition, covered a tall and handsome body. Bronze buckles firmly clasped black leather armor over a pale red cherkesska. No longer covered in hideous tattoos, the scars of his earthly life were washed clean.

There is something familiar in his eyes.

The men stared slack-jawed as the ghost slowly drifted past, paying them no mind. The ghost briefly considered Setenay and then floated to Sarah, where he stopped and looked down upon her.

Ood-i pressed forward, but Aizarg held him back. "We are now only spectators to our fate," Aizarg whispered.

The ghost didn't have the haughty look of a man who once wielded great power. Instead, he gazed upon Sarah's form with tender adoration. The Scythian lingered over Sarah only for a moment, and then stepped back to Setenay and knelt down. He touched her and a bolt of blue flame arced throughout Setenay's body. She arched and let loose a primal scream that made Aizarg want to rush to her side.

"What is he doing to her?" Ghalen cried.

Setenay moaned as her body settled.

"She's still alive," Aizarg tried to calm Ghalen.

The ghost stood and skimmed across the ground until he came within arm's reach of Aizarg.

"Aizarg of the Lo, I come to deliver a message," the Scythian's voice shifted and floated like the blue flame dancing over his head.

"A message? Who sends this message?"

The blue flame above the ghost's head suddenly brightened. "Aizarg of the Lo, only you and Sarah may enter Hur-ar and the fortress of the Narim. The others may not cross beyond the Dead Forest."

"Does this message come from the Narim?" Aizarg said with sudden hope. "What can you tell us of them?"

The ghost ignored him and continued to speak.

"Once you return to the other side of the Black River, you shall no longer accept strangers into your midst, lest you share in their judgment. In exchange, a new land shall be granted to your people. Do you accept this covenant, Aizarg?"

"A covenant? With whom do I make this covenant...with you?" Aizarg stepped closer to the ghost, desperate for answers. The flame suddenly brightened and Aizarg turned away.

"You make this covenant with the spirit who sends me. I ask again. Do you accept this covenant, Aizarg of the Lo?"

A new land?

"What if I do not accept this covenant?"

"Then you and your people perish."

One by one, Aizarg looked at his men.

The decision is mine alone.

He looked out over the horde and felt the same sensation as last night's dream. *Everything has changed.*

A new reality dawned on Aizarg. He suddenly realized this was no longer about his people avoiding, or even surviving, a coming doom. He and the Lo were caught between worlds, the playthings of gods.

We are caught between two waves, our only chance of survival is to descend deeper into their embrace.

Aizarg exhaled and plunged forward.

"Aizarg, Uros of the Lo, accepts this covenant, but only if it will save my people."

"It is done," the ghost said with finality and drifted away, but the blue flame did not follow him. As the ghost slipped out from under the light's aura the pastel colors of life faded to animated gray. The ghost's armor and clothes were once again shredded as it rejoined the dead.

The blue flame flickered and split into two parts. Each began to slowly rotate and sparkle. They spun faster and faster and intensified. The men backed up and shielded their eyes.

The mist lightened and started to pull toward the flames like a curtain being tugged from one end. The ghosts washed out and faded away as their forms stretched and distorted with the mist. The mist swirled around the dazzling orbs like a whirlpool, a vortex which sucked the air until it roared like a thousand rushing waters. Aizarg and the men fell to their knees, tunics flapping and blowing in the wind.

The vortex finally engulfed the ghostly horde and ripped away the icy curtain, revealing a pale blue sky and approaching sunset. The sun backlighted the swirling vortex, gilding the white whirlwind with crimson fire.

Levidi buried his head under his arms and shrieked. The rest of the men bowed their heads to the ground, too terrified to look upon the supernatural power. Only Aizarg did not avert his eyes as tears streamed down his face.

Then the blue orbs blinked. And blinked again. An immense human-like form materialized from the vortex with the orbs as its eyes. Outstretched arms formed, collapsed, and reformed in the whirlwind.

For a moment, Aizarg thought the form resembled a robed woman. Then great bird-like wings emerged behind the entity and partially obscured the setting sun. Lightning flashed within the entity and erupted from its fingertips. The blue orbs intensified and captured Aizarg in their power.

"Have mercy on us!" Aizarg pleaded.

The entity's white, misty body suddenly darkened to a smoky gray. It grew and transformed as arms morphed into fore and aft claws. The soft wings sharpened to bat-like forms that engulfed the sky. The entity's snake-like neck arched back as if about to strike. Massive jaws opened to reveal eternal blackness.

Inside the blackness, Aizarg saw endless stars, from which emerged a brilliant light that consumed him in a sea of white fire.

19. To Dance With Madness

The old Uros spent his last years warming his bones under the sun or in front of a roaring fire. It did not matter if a snowstorm blew down from the mountains or a dust storm rolled in from the desert, Aizarg would rather sit in front of his tent than in it. He only sought the shelter of his yurt when it rained. He hated the rain.

I rarely left his side during that time. My scrolls and paintbrush were always nearby, ready for me to capture his words, whatever they may be. It was my purpose and I had time.

More often than not, we sat in silence and enjoyed a good cup of fermented barley. Sometimes, we spoke of children or fishing or the proper planting of crops. He avoided talking about women. On that subject he said gods had no special knowledge over men.

One autumn night he sat on his blanket and drank his barley ale and chewed on bitter root, as it often made his gums feel better. The wind blew down from the northern mountains and Aizarg had a distant air of remembrance. Perhaps the cool mountain air took him back to that previous age when he didn't carry the weight of a life lived for others.

He put down his ale and spit out the root. I picked up my brush and scroll and waited for him to speak.

"It was on the morning of the seventh day after Levidi and I found the Valley of the Beasts that I looked upon Hur-ar," he began. "Sarah told me much about Hur-ar on the journey.

"A great deal of what she said I didn't understand, but some I did. I assumed I would come to understand once I saw these things with my own eyes." Aizarg leaned over like a confidant. "But when I crested that hill, I realized I knew nothing. That...!" he shook his bony finger, "...that is when I was the most frightened. The unknown became real, it had a face. It was the face of mountains. It was Setenay's face." The Uros looked down at his arthritic hands. "The unknown is a pit. If we see the bottom, we fill it with our hopes. If we see blackness, we feed it our fears.

"I stood between the endless g'an and the mighty mountains, between the worlds of flesh and spirit, and saw the pit."

The Chronicle of Fu Xi

***

"Wake up, Father!" A hand nudged Aizarg's arm.

He swatted the voice away and mumbled, "Bat-or, tell your mother I'll get up in a moment."

A sweet, light voice giggled, but it was not Bat-or. The hand shook him harder. "Get up!"

Another voice, low and heavy, came from beyond the first. "He's fine."

"His hair, it is like yours, Sarah," said another familiar voice.

Sarah...quest...dead...

Aizarg's eyes flew open and he bolted into a sitting position. *"The light!"* he screamed as several pairs of hands restrained him.

"It's over," Sarah pushed him back down. "Lie down and recover your strength."

Aizarg squinted against a clear, cool sky, but he remained in shadow. Sarah, Okta, and Ood-i came into focus, huddled over him. He was disoriented, but took comfort in their familiar faces.

"How long have I been asleep?" Aizarg ran his hands through his hair and rubbed his eyes. His stomach growled.

"It is morning. You are the last to wake," Okta responded. "Judging by the sound of your stomach, both you and your appetite are none the worse for the experience."

"I'll get you something to eat," Ood-i trotted off to retrieve his pack as Aizarg looked around.

They were surrounded on three sides by steep hills far larger than anything they'd encountered thus far. The hills blocked the morning sun. They couldn't proceed east without a steep climb.

Are these mountains?

Ood-i returned and gave Aizarg a chunk of dried fish and a water skin.

"Thank you." Aizarg took several hungry bites between healthy gulps of water. "Is everyone all right?" he mumbled between bites.

Except for Okta, they all looked down at the ground. Aizarg stopped in mid-chew.

"Ba-lok is still missing," Okta spoke up. "Otherwise, we are all here." Okta lowered his voice, "Levidi is...disturbed."

Aizarg peered around Okta and saw Levidi squatting several yards away with his back to them. Levidi rocked back and forth with his arms wrapped around his shoulders.

"I am disturbed, too," Aizarg said dryly. "I can safely assume we are all disturbed."

Aizarg finally noticed Sarah's pure white hair. "Sarah!"

Sarah smiled weakly. "The mist is still in our hair."

"Yours is the same, Uros, even your beard," Ood-i said. "Only you and Sarah were affected."

Aizarg frowned and pulled at his hair, trying to spy a white lock through the corner of his eye.

"Where are Ghalen and Setenay?" Aizarg asked.

Okta nodded to his right and Aizarg followed his gaze. Ghalen knelt over Setenay, who lay under a blanket at the base of the eastern hill.

Aizarg hurried to her side.

Ghalen held Setenay's hand and looked up at Aizarg with a forlorn expression. "The mist...the spirit, they took a heavy toll. She cannot travel until she is well."

Setenay's eyes were still sharp, but were sunken in dark pits above hollow cheeks.

She looks depleted, as if the spirit stole something from her...or gave her a heavy burden.

"What do you remember, Uros?" Setenay's voice carried only a shadow of its former power.

"We walked with the dead." Aizarg glanced about as if the mists would suddenly reappear. His voice quivered. "There was mist, wind, and a voice of fire. If I try to speak of what happened, I fear I will slip into madness."

"It's often the duty of the patesi-le to dance with madness," her voiced cracked. "Such is the way of the spirit world."

Aizarg swallowed hard. "You were not yourself. Neither was Sarah."

"The spirit took us. Sarah remembers nothing." Setenay's eyes darted left and right as if reliving the moment.

Aizarg frowned at Sarah, kneeling across from him. "Nothing?"

Sarah shrugged. "My last thoughts were going to sleep the night before. That is all."

"Count yourself fortunate." Ghalen shuddered.

"What do you remember, old mother?" Aizarg whispered.

"Everything and nothing. The spirit revealed different truths to my eyes. I beheld visions without understanding, images for which I have no words. The spirit bestowed the cruelest gift of all, prophesy without wisdom," her voice trailed off.

"Ood-i, Levidi, and I remember the dead Scythian prince and the covenant you made with the dead, but hid our eyes when the terrible spirit appeared," Ghalen said.

"My covenant was not with the dead," Aizarg said as yesterday's events played out again in his mind. "The ghost was only a messenger from an unknown power; one I believe holds the key to our salvation."

"I remember only bitter cold," Okta said.

Ood-i nodded. "You should be thankful. I would rather be pulled apart by Scythian horses than live through that again."

"Why can't I remember anything, Setenay?" Sarah softly stroked the old woman's brow.

Setenay grasped her arm with both hands. "Oh, dear Sarah!" Her lower lip trembled. Tears formed at the corner of her eyes and rolled into her hair. Setenay squeezed her eyes shut and, after a few moments, regained her composure.

"Uros, come closer," Setenay whispered.

Aizarg leaned in closer.

Setenay peered into the sky and reached straight up as if trying to touch something. "I do not know if these visions are of this world or the next. I am too small a cup for what the spirit has poured into me!" Setenay trailed off.

Aizarg leaned within inches of Setenay's face. "What did the spirit show you? Tell me, Setenay!" Despite his best effort, his desperation broke through.

Setenay slowly turned her head left and focused beyond the hill. Her hand fell until she pointed to the east. "The spirit and the flesh shall be parted," she groaned. "And the sea will overflow with the tears of the dead."

The dream from two nights ago rushed back into his mind.

"The water is filled with the tears of the dead!" the voice in his dream had said.

"Father, are you all right? You are ashen," Sarah said.

"No, Sarah. I don't know if I will ever be all right again." He regretted the words the moment they left his lips.

Several paces away, Levidi still squatted and rocked.

Setenay took Aizarg's hand and she tried to pull herself up. Ghalen and Sarah reached behind her back and helped her sit. "I want to tell you, Uros, but I don't know how. I am mute before the horrors in my mind's eye. What is certain is time is short. You and Sarah must go to the Narim, now! They are our only hope."

"Setenay, I am afraid," Sarah whispered.

"You should be," the old woman rattled. "We all should be. I see a terrible shadow approaching, but not its form. Go now, both of you."

Aizarg stood and found his pack. "All of you, come here!" he said.

The group surrounded Aizarg, but Levidi didn't move.

"Sarah, do you know where we are?" Aizarg motioned to the hills.

"Yes. This is the canyon I spoke of. When we climb that hill," she pointed east, "we will look upon the Hur Valley."

"There are deep foot tracks over there." Ghalen pointed to a faint trail of flattened grass and exposed dirt several yards away. "Many have repeatedly passed this way."

"Those must be from Virag's caravans," Ood-i said.

Aizarg peered up the hillside. "The spirit led us here. Strange powers guide our ways. To what purpose, I can only guess."

Aizarg glanced at Levidi and took a deep breath. "I have a plan. All of you wait here." Aizarg walked over to Levidi and knelt down.

Levidi's eyes, red rimmed and wide, looked through Aizarg.

"Levidi." Aizarg touched Levidi's shoulder and spoke softly. "Levidi, I need you to look at me."

Levidi continued to rock back and forth.

"Levidi! Look at me!" Aizarg commanded.

With a faint shift Levidi's gaze focused on Aizarg.

"Aizarg." Levidi briefly smiled with recognition before his smile crumbled along with Aizarg's short-lived relief.

"I want to go home, Aizarg. I want to go home!" Aizarg embraced Levidi and held him tightly. Levidi sobbed into Aizarg's shoulder like a child. Aizarg would rather face all the tribulations of their journey again than see his friend like this.

"The dead, Aizarg! The monster...the winds..!"

Aizarg patted his back. "Peace, peace! It's over. I want to go home, too. But home is forward, not backward. The spirits showed me the way, but if we go back now, all is lost. I need you to be strong."

Levidi quieted. As he slowly regained his composure, he could not meet Aizarg's gaze.

Aizarg thought about Setenay. "Do not be ashamed. You were brave. Even a patesi-le should never see the things we beheld."

Aizarg stood and lifted Levidi by the arm. Ghalen stepped next to them and held out Levidi's spear. "Here, take your spear. I'm not turning back, and that means you can't turn back. You have to carry my things, remember? I'm not going to let you off that easy."

Levidi grimaced at Ghalen and snatched his spear. He looked around at the group as if seeing them all for the first time. Levidi frowned at Aizarg. "Your hair?"

Aizarg shrugged and shook his head. "I don't know. Sarah is the same."

Levidi glanced over at Sarah and then back to Aizarg. "It looks better on her. It makes you look like an old woman."

Aizarg smiled. *He'll be fine.*

Aizarg absently clenched his right fist.

"My spear. Has anyone seen my spear?"

"You tell him," Ood-i said to Okta, his meaty face twisting in discomfort. "You found it."

"It's over there." Okta pointed downhill toward the west, where the canyon opened up toward the open g'an. "Something destroyed your spear."

Aizarg saw a black streak in the grass only a few yards away.

It was still intact, but the heavy iron point and cross piece were melted into a graceful tear drop-shaped glob. The glob's narrow end thinned and twisted around the shaft like a serpent until it terminated a third of the way down.

Aizarg wouldn't have recognized it if it weren't for the familiar scratches on the shaft.

"What new wonder is this?" Aizarg marveled. "The metal is blood red!" Aizarg knelt down and reached for it, wondering how the black iron transformed to a metallic crimson.

"It is hot!" Ood-i cautioned. "I tried to pick it up shortly before you woke, but it burned me." Ood-i showed Aizarg the blisters on his thick fingers.

Aizarg lightly touched the red teardrop. "It's not even warm." He ran his finger cautiously across the entire surface, both wood and metal, before he grasped it and stood.

"It's lighter and better balanced," Aizarg marveled.

"This cannot be!" Ood-i frowned. "It was like fire only moments ago." He reached out to touch the spear, but jerked back and winced. "It still burns!"

"Bah! Let me try!" Okta stepped forward. He touched the red metal orb, but snapped his hand back as if bitten. He shook his hand and watched the blisters rise. He gasped. "What manner of witchcraft is this? Ghalen, Levidi...touch it and see what I mean."

"I already see what you mean!" Ghalen exclaimed. "I'm not getting near it."

Sarah held her hand close to the red metal. "I can feel the heat radiating from it like a hot coal. It is plain to see the spear of the Uros is for his hand alone."

Aizarg looked at his people. With the exception of Sarah and Levidi, the rest wouldn't look at him.

They are afraid of what is happening to me. He looked at Sarah's hair. *I am, too.*

Aizarg suddenly felt overwhelmed and isolated.

Levidi smiled weakly and stepped up next to Aizarg.

"Well, I better find out what all this fuss is about. Maybe we can use Aizarg's fancy new staff to start our dung fires, eh?"

"Levidi, please," Aizarg said, remembering Levidi's terror only moments ago. "You don't have to prove anything..."

Levidi ignored him and held a shaking hand close to the staff. And then he held it closer.

"I don't feel anything." He grinned and grasped the staff with both hands over Aizarg's fist. "Your staff likes me, Aizarg!"

A knot released in Aizarg's stomach and he gave Levidi a tight hug.

"Uros." Okta grimly stepped forward. "What is your command?"

The words of the Scythian ghost rang in Aizarg's mind.

Aizarg of the Lo, only you and Sarah may enter Hur-ar and the Fortress of the Narim.

"I do not know what we experienced yesterday, but for better or worse, our circumstances have changed." Aizarg hefted his strange new staff. "I have entered into a covenant with a power from the spirit world, one I must fulfill.

"We make a base camp here. Ghalen, you remain with Setenay. Okta, you take the rest of the men and search for Ba-lok."

Sarah touched his arm. "Virag never made camp at the bottom of the canyon. He said it wasn't safe."

"She has a point," Ghalen said. "We are protected from the wind down here, but also trapped."

"Virag often camped at the top of the hill." Sarah pointed uphill to the east. "The wind is harsh, but you can see approaching danger."

"So be it. Gather your things, we climb the eastern slope and make camp there. Sarah and I will depart for Hur-ar once camp is established."

"I don't think Setenay can make it up the hill," Ghalen said.

"Your pack has already worn a blister in my shoulder, so why should anything change now?" Levidi huffed with a half-hidden smile. "Carry her and I will haul your junk."

Sarah gathered her things and approached Aizarg. "Father," she whispered and looked about to make sure no one was listening. "Let us climb the hill alone first. They can wait a few moments before they follow us."

Aizarg nodded.

***

We are finally here.

Aizarg wanted to climb faster, but his thighs burned. Occasionally, he reached down and steadied himself against the gusting wind, which intensified and shifted out of the north as they climbed above the sheltered canyon.

About halfway up the slope the morning sun crested over the hill. Sunlight shimmered up and down his staff's red metal coils. He didn't know why the spirit transformed his spear, but it made an excellent walking stick. His hand fell comfortably on his normal grip point, just below the metal.

The hill rose higher than he suspected. The group below looked like insects in the canyon's shadow. Near the top, coarse grasses gave way to worn rock and the wind lightened.

Sarah pulled him forward like a little girl. "Come, I want to show you!"

Out of breath, Aizarg smiled and they locked arms as they crested the hill.

Aizarg couldn't take it all in at first. The magnitude overwhelmed his senses and made him dizzy. He braced himself against the staff.

"I wanted to share this with you first!" She spread her arms wide and twirled around. "These, Father, are *mountains!*"

They stood along the crest of a long line of hills stretching north and south, horizon to horizon. The eastern slopes dropped steeply in front of them and flattened out into a brown, grassy valley far lower than the canyon behind them. A wide, black river meandered through the center of the basin. Aizarg only noticed the sprawling valley as a fleeting afterthought, a footnote to the immense glory lording over him.

On the opposite side of the river the grasslands sloped up to a narrow blanket of dark green trees. Beyond the trees sheer gray cliffs vaulted skyward until they scraped the roof of heaven.

Boldness. That was the only word Aizarg could summon. He found it difficult to crane his head back to see their tops. Tears trickled down his face and were quickly stolen by the wind.

How does the sun climb over them?

The image of the swirling spirit suddenly jumped into his mind. The mountains were like the spirit frozen in timeless stone.

Above the stony mountain cliffs, blankets of white-capped peaks reminded Aizarg of teeth. Clouds danced and shot off the summits, their billowing edges catching the sunlight like silver streamers.

"The clouds," he gasped. "It tears them apart. Look how their tattered remains rest on the tops."

"That is called *snow.*" She leaned over and placed her head against his chest.

"Snow? Is that what clouds are made of?"

"Maybe. I never thought of it before."

"I cannot find words for what I see," he stuttered. "Now I understand what you were trying to tell me. The Narim must truly be gods to dwell in such a place."

Sarah reached up and hugged him tightly around the neck. Aizarg tore his eyes away from the majesty to the small woman-child. She smiled up at him with glowing contentment.

"What was that for?" he asked.

She smiled through fresh tears. "Growing up in Hur-ar, I was always afraid. The only time I was ever happy was when I wandered the mountains surrounding my home. These mountains were my refuge." She hesitated, trying to control her emotions. "When Virag made camp, I would often stand and gaze at them. Surrounded by Virag's evil, they gave me hope. Now, I wanted to see them again through your eyes."

Aizarg smiled and placed his finger to her lips. "You've never been able to share that love with anyone until now?"

She nodded, tears starting afresh.

"The mountains are your place of beautiful solitude." Aizarg wrapped his arm around his daughter and focused his attention on the valley. On this side of the river, fields of broken, gray landscape lined the long stretches of the shore.

"What is that?" He pointed to the strange landscape.

"That is the Dead Forest. It will take us the remainder of the morning to reach it." Sarah held her hand to her mouth in surprise. "The Hur River is flooded! Oh, please, no..." She peered north of the Dead Forest, as if trying to find something until her eyes suddenly lit up. "The Kupar Bridge is still intact!"

"Where is it?" Aizarg leaned in and squinted, trying to see what she saw.

Sarah held her finger out ahead of Aizarg's face. "Look to the far left of the Dead Forest on this side of the river. There you'll see an oxbow in the river that bends toward us. Do you see it?"

"I do, but I don't see the bridge...Ahh! I see it!" He shouted. Two tall structures stood on either shore with a thick gray line crossing the river between them. Aizarg felt a little disappointment.

"From your descriptions, I thought it was bigger."

"It's every bit as big as I described, Father. It is just that we are very far away."

She said twenty men could walk across that bridge shoulder to shoulder! How far away are we? He looked from the bridge to the mountains and then across the valley. He shook his head with new understanding.

"Look beyond the bridge," Sarah said. "Do you see that faint, brown line twisting away from the bridge on the opposite shore?"

"Yes."

"That is the road to Hur-ar."

The road cut to the right and snaked south along the river until it came to a point immediately across the valley from where they stood. Then the road turned sharply east until it came to a point just short of the mountains. Dozens of light and dark green squares and rectangles of strange grasses surrounded the road as it approached Hur-ar. The road ended at a deep, box-like canyon where the impregnable wall of mountains parted. A dark brown line stretched from cliff to cliff at its mouth. Beyond the line, in the heart of the canyon, were hundreds of dots and squares arranged in geometric patterns.

Sarah pointed at the canyon. "That is Hur-ar, my former home." Her soft expression evaporated with a voice as sharp and cold as the wind. "The road ends at the city wall, which seals the city against the mountains. It is the only way in."

Now Aizarg saw the countless dots were structures, perhaps huts or tents.

"Amazing." Aizarg could not have imagined such a place existed.

The sheer cliffs surrounding the city rose halfway to the snowy peaks. Golden morning sunlight bathed the valley, except for Hur-ar recessed deep in the blue shadows of a canyon.

"They mustn't get sunlight until noon!" Aizarg gasped.

Sarah nodded. "It's even worse in the winter. Hur-ar is often a dark, cold place, but the canyon provides excellent protection. Hur-ar has never been invaded. They have a saying...'Who needs the sun when our homes are lit by gold's luster?'"

The towering cliff behind Hur-ar, the tallest of the canyon's sides, drew Aizarg's eye. He saw a faint line zigzagging up the cliff and traced it up until the cliff terminated high above the city, just below the snowline. A thick, dark line outlined the top of the cliff. At first, he took the line for trees along the top of the cliff, but realized it was another wall. It paralleled the thinner, less imposing, city wall below. A giant shape, dark and ominous, jutted from behind the black wall. Aizarg thought it might be a rock outcropping below the main peak. He squinted and shielded his eyes against the sun to get a better look.

The promontory stood in stark contrast against the snowcapped peak beyond. Like the wall, its blackness soaked up the sunlight and rivaled the mountain itself.

The lines are too straight. The top is too flat. A chill ran down Aizarg's spine.

It wasn't a rocky promontory, but a structure, an incomprehensibly immense black rectangle.

Sarah pointed. "That is what you seek. Behold, the fortress of the Narim."

Aizarg slowly sank to one knee and ran a hand through his hair. "A mountain within a mountain!" He muttered. Now Aizarg realized the black wall didn't protect Hur-ar's eastern flank, it enclosed the realm of the Narim.

Aizarg closed his eyes and rubbed his temples. He suddenly felt like Levidi. He wanted to turn and run.

Sarah knelt next to him and placed her arms around his shoulders. "What are you thinking?"

"I cannot smell the sea."

"I don't understand," she said.

The words rushed out all at once, "This is all...too big. I want to pray for courage, but to what god? I want to shout, but who will listen?" Aizarg looked over his shoulder and motioned to the group below. "They are all looking to me to lead, but I am only a man. I don't know if I can do this."

Sarah leaned her head on his shoulder and they stared at the mountains in silence for several long moments.

Sarah finally spoke. "I am small, too. I know what awaits us in Hur-ar, and I know I should be afraid. Setenay says I should be afraid. But I won't be, because the last few days have been the happiest of my life. I found my family.

"I have you. I have the others. I have a new mother and brothers I have yet to meet. I've only been given this breath and this moment to love. I will not corrupt it with fear.

"So, please, Father, let us not say a prayer for tomorrow, it will only carry our fears to heaven. Those prayers are always answered with worry. Let us say a prayer for today, for those are lifted on wings of gratitude and will always be met with hope."

"You sound so much like my Atamoda!" Sarah's hair reminded him of the snow on the mountains.

"What would Atamoda say to you right now, if she were here?" Sarah put her hands on her thighs and leaned back. Her eyes twinkled.

Aizarg looked back over his shoulder. The g'an stretched back to the west in an endless succession of rolling hills. He saw Okta, Levidi and Ood-i climbing up the hill behind them. Ghalen followed, carrying Setenay.

The panic ebbed away. Aizarg smiled at his beloved daughter and reached out his hand.

"She would say, 'Take my hand and we will walk together, come what may.'"

***

Ood-i dropped his packs and fell to his knees next to Sarah, panting for breath. "I...I...it is more beautiful than you described, Sarah."

Sarah patted his back.

Levidi bent over against his spear. "Is this the end of the world?" he gasped.

"No, it's the beginning of mine." Sarah stretched her arm out across the valley. "This is the Hur Valley and the Adyghe

Mountains beyond. Aizarg and I should reach the city gates before nightfall."

Aizarg stood up and looked over his shoulder, where Okta gazed stoically across the valley. Behind Okta, Ghalen and Setenay were almost up the hill. If Ghalen struggled, he didn't show it.

Aizarg took a closer look at the well trampled grass and dirt on the hill top around them. Several stone circles filled with gray ashes lay about with piles of sticks, dried dung, and animal bones strewn near the fire circles.

We can quickly start a fire. This is a much needed blessing.

While the men gawked at the view, Sarah pulled Aizarg aside.

Sarah only spoke loud enough to be heard over the wind. "We must cover our heads before we descend into the valley."

"Why?"

"My people believe pure white hair among the young is a sign one has been touched by the gods. It can be taken as an omen for good or ill and will attract unwanted attention."

Aizarg chuckled. "I think we *have* been touched by the gods. But, yes, we will cover our heads. What of my beard?"

She frowned. "A white beard is not as uncommon as white hair. Perhaps it will pass without too much scrutiny." Sarah paused, as if thinking deeply. "We will need something to trade. The guards extract a toll for crossing the Kupar Bridge, and we have no gold..."

An ear-splitting scream made them jump. Aizarg spun around to see Setenay thrashing in Ghalen's arms. She screamed again, a soul-splitting sound. Setenay kicked and pushed against Ghalen like a child trying to get out of her father's arms.

"Setenay, what is wrong?" a shaken Ghalen asked as he gently put her down.

"Let go of me!" She pushed away with a bizarre mix of impatience and panic.

Setenay ran to the edge of the eastern slope, jaw agape and hands clutching her wild, gray hair. She paced back and forth, transfixed on the mountains in disbelief.

"No, no, no, no..." she chanted as tears welled and flooded the deep canyons in her cheeks.

Sarah rushed to her side. "Setenay, what is it?" She placed a calming hand on the old woman's shoulder, but Setenay flung it away and ran to Aizarg. She clutched his tunic and pulled his face down to hers.

Even when he consoled fathers who had lost sons and mothers who had lost babies, Aizarg never witnessed such utter dejection, such abject horror. Setenay teetered on the edge of madness, if not already past the tipping point. She shot an arm toward the mountains as if accusing them of murder.

"Do you see them? *Do you see them?* No, it cannot be!" she hissed into his face. "It cannot be!" Primal terror gushed from Setenay like blood from an gaping wound.

Her terror infected the men. They looked at one another with grave uncertainty.

Aizarg would have been less afraid if the mountains suddenly crumbled. "Calm down, old mother. It's all right, but you have to tell us what's wrong," he said softly.

"No!" she shrieked and ran back to the edge of the hill. She jabbed her finger at the mountains. "No! It isn't all right!"

Setenay doubled over, fell to her knees and wrapped her arms around her waist. She shrieked at the top of her lungs as if trying to vomit the fear from her soul. She pounded the earth with her frail, gnarled fists until they bled. Sarah fell down next to her and tried to console her, but Setenay would have none of it.

"Help her, Uros!" Ghalen begged.

"I...I do not know how," Aizarg said helplessly.

Setenay leaned back and raised her arms to the sky. "Blind me! Strike me deaf and dumb so that I may not see, so that I may not hear, so that I may not speak!" She released a long, terrible moan as if all those who ever died, who ever suffered, who ever knew pain and suffering, rose together in a chorus of hopelessness and despair from the pit of hell.

Levidi covered his ears and closed his eyes.

Then there was only the wind. Setenay hunched over, face down to the ground. Sarah sobbed next to her, slowly rubbing Setenay's back. Aizarg knelt down next to her. The rest of the group bent on one knee behind them. They faced the mountains as if worshipping them. The dry wind whistled around them. No one spoke. Aizarg didn't know what to say.

"The mountains..." Setenay whispered into the earth.

"What about the mountains?" Aizarg said.

"You see them as they are. I see them as they will be. The tears of the dead are almost upon us."

Aizarg picked up his pack with one hand and lifted Sarah with the other.

"You know my orders," he shouted to the men. "Find Ba-lok! We will return as soon as we can."

Hand in hand, Aizarg and Sarah ran down the steep trail into the Hur Valley.

***

"Wake up, Mother!" A small hand nudged her arm.

Atamoda swatted the voice away and mumbled, "Bat-or, the sun isn't up. Tell your father I'll make breakfast in a moment."

"It's Kol-ok, Mother," the voice came again. "The sun is up and Bat-or is on the dock."

Atmoda stirred. Kol-ok stood over her, grasping the crudely sharpened stick he called a spear.

Within hours of Aizarg's departure, the spear appeared in Kol-ok's hands and never left. He even slept with it.

He's trying so hard to fill his father's sandals, to be the son of the Uros.

Unfortunately, that included being extra bossy to his little brother, resulting in the expected pushing, shoving and yelling. It never happened during Aizarg's extended fishing trips, then Kol-ok never tried to be a man. Things were different now.

Aizarg had been gone for much longer stretches of time, but always to places she knew about, like the western shoals or the deep marshes. Atamoda could visualize where he was, what he was doing and could go about her daily routines with a reasonable expectation he would return. Now, he was 'someplace else.' Uncertainty and fear plagued her every waking thought.

She wanted to sleep more, to hide under her furs and pray time would pass quickly. Only her children and her duties as patesi-le gave her reasons to get up every morning. Atta had been there, too.

Aizarg placed Atta in charge in his absence. The venerable old fisherman took to the role with gusto and seemed to grow younger with his new responsibilities. Every day he consulted with Atamoda, keeping her focused on her role as the village's spiritual guide. He pestered her to make daily visits to each hut, especially those of Alaya and Ula, the wives of Levidi and Ood-i. Atta felt it important Atamoda keep a close eye on the village women and squash any corrosive, idle talk.

"Keep them busy!" he said. Atamoda appreciated his wisdom. Atta also kept the men busy searching for the vanished fish in defiance of Setenay's prophesy.

"Fish or no fish, the men are better off on the water than in their huts," Atta insisted. "We only have a few weeks of food left. Maybe we'll get lucky."

Atta's wisdom and calm demeanor not only strengthened the villagers' courage, but was a blessing to her family.

Atta took Kol-ok with him as he scouted for fish with the other men.

"He's at that difficult age between boyhood and manhood, Atamoda," Atta had told her in slow, confident tones. "He needs to be with the men, not fretting with the women. You tend to little Bat-or and the women. I will keep Kol-ok's mind off his father."

Atamoda stretched again and sat up. She rubbed her eyes and focused on pale Kol-ok. His eyes darted nervously toward the hut's curtained door. She heard Bat-or giggling outside. Every few seconds something slapped the water and his laughter resumed.

The brazier still smoldered, but a chill seeping up from the floor overpowered it.

"What is the matter?" she asked.

He pointed outside. "The water is wrong."

Wrong?

She looked back at the door where blue sky peeked around the curtain. She slept late again. Atamoda stood, threw the curtain aside and stepped onto the outer platform. She could barely contain her scream.

The black water came up almost level with the dock, a full four feet higher than normal.

Kol-ok held her hand. "The water was like this when we woke. Atta was supposed to come get me. We were going to look for shellfish, but he didn't show up." Kol-ok looked up at her. "The water is so cold! I was going to swim to Atta's hut to look for him, but I can't stand to get in."

Bat-or ran up and down the dock, giggling and slapping the water with a short stick. "Mommy, look! Funny fish!"

Atamoda released Kol-ok's hand and climbed down to the dock.

"Has the water ever done this before, Mother?" Kol-ok followed her down.

The water looked still at first, but as she looked closer, Atamoda saw the surface tug and crease around the dock's pilings.

She snatched Bat-or away from the edge. "Stay back! The water is swift."

Atamoda transfixed on the water. She knew of no lore of the Great Sea rising like this, even under a strong south wind when the waves were high. The flat and mirrored water moved with deep power. Atamoda lifted her head and looked out across the arun-ki.

Everything looked disjointed and out of place, as if the world had shifted downward. Some docks were even partially underwater. People stood on their platforms. A few paddled to and fro in their boats, faces slack with disbelief. Across the water, she heard muted cries and sobs.

Kol-ok sought out her hand once again.

A branch with green leaves floated by with great speed and instantly gave her a sense of the current.

The current comes from the shore. Atamoda's stomach tightened and she slowly turned north. Her knees suddenly gave way and she slumped to the dock.

The shore was gone. Trees and the highest marsh grasses poked above the surface, bent in the current.

"The black tide comes from the land!" Atamoda could not believe her eyes.

Shore camp! How many people were in shore camp last night?

A loud bang startled her. A large chunk of dirty ice slid across the dock in front of her. Atamoda turned around as Xva's boat slid alongside the dock with Atta standing up front.

"Yes, it comes from the shore," Atta grimly said as he stepped out of the boat dressed in his winter clothes, not his usual loincloth. "And it's cold as winter's breath."

"Atta!" Kol-ok shouted and rushed to hug the old man. "Where were you?"

Bat-or pulled away from Atamoda and returned to the edge, happily pacing back and forth, slapping the water and giggling.

"I'm sorry. Xva saw the water rising late last night and fetched me. We went to investigate." He motioned to Xva, who sat in the boat and strained to hold onto the dock against the current.

Atta continued. "The streams that spill into the marshes are swallowing the shore and invading the sea. Xva and I barely warned those in shore camp before it was overwhelmed. They are all safe in their huts now."

Atmoda exhaled with relief.

"I would have woken you earlier, patesi-le, but we were very busy. Do you have any idea why this is happening? Is it Setenay's prophesy?"

Atamoda shook her head. "Perhaps."

Atta ran his tongue around his missing teeth and pointed to the chunk of ice. "These are floating everywhere. Farther east and west they are much bigger, like islands."

"If one of those should drift through the arun-ki, it would crush any hut in its path," Xva said.

Kol-ok looked up at Atta and then pointed to the shore. "Atta, Father is out there. Is he okay?"

Atamoda's stomach tightened.

Atta looked sternly down his nose at Kol-ok and stroked his beard, as though the boy should have known better for asking such a foolish question.

"Young man, we are Lo. We are born of water and will die upon the water." He flicked the back of his hand over the flooded shore and pursed his face dismissively. "If this is the nature of the doom Setenay spoke of, then it is not our doom. And for that I am much relieved." Suddenly, Atta released a jolly laugh. "If there is water where Aizarg is, he has probably built a boat and is sailing to the Narim and wondering what all the fuss is about. Perhaps it's our job to save the Narim!" Atta laughed again. "Maybe the Great Mother is finally washing away those damn Scythians. This all might be a blessing."

Atta watched Bat-or happily slap the water. "Now, there are the makings of a great Lo man!" He bellowed.

"Bat-or, I told you to get away from the water!" Atamoda shouted.

Atta laughed. "He is fine, Atamoda. Little Bat-or knows he has nothing to fear from the water. We should be more like him."

We are Lo. We are of the water. Please, Great Mother, let Atta be right!

"Patesi-le," Atta continued. "It is still wise to be prepared. Everyone must be ready to take to their boats and rafts should the waters continue to rise."

"Yes." Atamoda stood, feeling better about doing something. "Kol-ok and I will load our raft. Atta, will you warn the rest of the village?"

"Of course. I'm sure the water will recede as quickly as it rose. Kol-ok, take care of your mother and brother and use your paddles, not your poles." He looked down into the water. "It might get too deep for poles." Atta looked back at Atamoda. "If it gets too deep, tie your raft to the dock. This way you will not get swept to sea."

"Atta," Bat-or grabbed his big, calloused hand. "Come see the funny fish!"

"Why, certainly!" Atta opened his mouth in mock wonder and surprise. "I think I would be happy to see any fish right now, funny or sad." Bat-or led him to the edge of the dock.

"My, those are amazing fish!" Atta remarked as he considered the water with convincing seriousness. "I wish I could catch some of those."

Irritation flashed across Ba-tor's little face. He frowned up at Atta. "No, over there!" He pointed to a different spot on the water from where Atta looked.

Kol-ok rolled his eyes and whispered up to Atamoda. "He's been doing that since dawn. He got mad at me when I wouldn't play along."

Atamoda didn't need to deal with another bout of petty arguments between her boys. "If you want to carry the spear of a man, act like a man. Bat-or is the child. Do you see Atta getting angry at Ba-tor?"

"No, Mother." Kol-ok sighed mechanically.

"Oh, I see!" Atta stifled a laugh. "Yes, fine fish. Why don't you try to catch one for supper?"

"No, no!" Bat-or said with all seriousness and shook his head. "They aren't for eating. They want to play. They asked me to go swimming." He turned back and shouted to Atamoda.

"Mommy, can I go swimming with the funny fishies? PLEASE?"

"No! The water is too swift right now."

"Oww! No fair!" Bat-or stomped his foot and hurled his stick into the water.

Atamoda absently watched the stick while she thought about what they needed to load onto the raft. It landed lightly with a small ripple, and then snapped underwater like a crumb snatched by a carp.

"Atamoda, I will be back later this morning," Atta called as he stepped back into the boat.

"Thank you, Atta." Her heart brimmed with gratitude. Some of the villagers, especially the men in their prime, chaffed at having to follow one so old. None of them could remain as calm and inspire so much courage as dear Atta. With Atta, they would be safe.

Xva and Atta paddled out towards the center of the arun-ki near the köy-lo-hely. Even with both paddling, the boat cocked off in the powerful current.

"Atamoda!" Someone called from across the water. She looked up and saw Ula standing outside her hut. Even from where she stood, Atamoda saw the shock on Ula's face.

She must have just awoken, too. Atamoda knew Ula was alone. Su-gár had spent the night with Alaya. Su-gár and Alaya were close in age and good friends. Su-gár often took refuge there when Ula and Ood-i fought.

Atamoda shook her head and gave an exaggerated shrug.

A sound like the faint hissing of grease just beginning to drip into the fire tickled Atamoda's ears.

"Mommy, can I play out here with the fishies a little longer?"

"Yes, dear," she said absently as she looked around for the source of the noise.

"Can you get me a new stick, mommy?"

"Not right now, dear." The sound grew louder. "Kol-ok, do you hear that?"

"What?"

"It's..." She strained to listen closer. "...It's coming from the water." Atamoda stepped to the edge of the dock next to Bat-or and looked down into the lagoon.

At first, she thought they were discolorations, a trick of light and shadow. *Have the fish returned?* Atamoda bent over and squinted. The hissing suddenly grew louder, like the dark whispers of a thousand conspiracies.

Just below the surface two flat, yellow eyes opened and peered back at her. Atamoda shrieked and jumped back. She grabbed Ba-tor's hand and yanked him away from the edge.

"Mommy sees the funny fish!" Bat-or giggled.

Hundreds of slithering shapes suddenly came into focus. A thousand lifeless eyes darted back and forth, hungrily boring into her. A feeling of malignancy suddenly overpowered Atamoda and she screamed.

"Mother!" Kol-ok rushed to her side. Atta and Xva brought the boat about.

"Atamoda! Are you all right?" Atta called out.

The collective hissing took on a broken quality; a stuttering, ragged cackle. One of the shapes swam to the edge of the dock and looked up at her. A hungry gash full of icy needles opened below the narrow, yellow eyes.

Atamoda screamed hysterically, over and over. She squeezed Ba-tor's hand until his screams joined hers.

Kol-ok tried to pull her away and began to cry, too. "Mother, please! You're scaring me...what's wrong? Please tell me, please?" Confused, he looked into the water and then back to her.

"Kol-ok, what's the matter?" Atta shouted.

"I don't know! Help us, please!" Kol-ok sobbed.

"Atamoda!" Ula shouted across the lagoon and stripped off her tunic. "I'm coming!"

Somehow, Ula's voice penetrated Atamoda's terror. She looked up just in time to see Ula dive into the water. The instant Ula splashed into the water, the creatures turned and darted toward her like a pack of famished wolves. They moved with such speed they stretched and distorted into long oily streaks under the water. They were black spears aimed right for Ula.

Ula didn't come up for air.

"No!" Atamoda screamed and pointed at Atta and Xva. "Atta, get Ula out of the water! Now! Hurry!"

Instantly, they turned the boat and headed toward where Ula dove in.

"I will get her!" Kol-ok moved to the edge.

Atamoda snatched him back so hard he winced in pain. She put her face inches in front of his, eyes wide and shaking. "No!" You will take your brother and go inside the hut! Do not come out."

"But..."

"Now!"

Kol-ok pushed Bat-or up the ladder and into the hut without another word.

Ula broke the surface, but far downstream from her hut. She reached up with a pale blue hand as her eyes rolled back into her head. She slipped back down and vanished.

Atamoda ran to the end of the dock as Atta and Xva paddled hard to Ula. Demons seethed around their boat, but Atta and Xva were oblivious to the monsters inches away.

They can't see them!

Before she could react, Atta dove in.

Black forms instantly swarmed under the ripples of his splash like a knotted ball of marsh vipers. They rolled over him in a silent frenzy.

"Xva! Get him out of the water!" she shouted. Xva didn't acknowledge her and calmly paddled the boat back and forth, clearly expecting Atta to break the surface with Ula in his arms any second.

Atamoda watched helplessly as the disaster slowly unfolded before her. Villagers gathered in front of their huts and on their docks. Atamoda saw a few prepare to jump in.

"Do not enter the water!" she shouted to all who could hear. What could she tell them? How could she explain this? "The water is cursed! Stay out of the water!"

A few of the dark shapes drifted away from around Xva's boat. Atamoda instinctively knew the demons had made their kills. Atta and Ula were dead.

She fell to the dock and released a long, desperate moan, powerless as death unfurled before her.

Xva put the paddle in the boat and flipped over the side into the water. Atamoda squeezed the sides of her head and prayed for this nightmare to end.

"Stay out of the water!" she screamed over and over.

Xva's empty boat drifted by on the current, turning around and around like a dead leaf on a winter pond. Atamoda placed her head against the dock and sobbed. Concerned villagers called her name from across the lagoon. A few shouted for Atta, Xva and Ula. Then their shouts became cries and screams.

Suddenly, a pale hand shot out of the water and grabbed the dock. Atmoda lunged and grabbed Xva. She pulled with all her strength, but black ice formed and cracked around where his shoulders emerged from the water.

Desperate, she plunged her upper body into the water and grabbed under his armpits. The cold seized her, almost making her inhale a mouthful of water. She opened her eyes and faced dozens of yellow eyes, but her courage held. Atamoda locked her arms around Xva's back and pulled with everything she had. The demons shrank back for a moment, perhaps surprised at her audacity. In that moment she managed to pull Xva out of the water. They both flopped backwards onto the dock.

She pushed Xva onto his back and knelt over him. His eyes were closed and his breaths where short and shallow.

The young man shivered violently. Dozens of bloody slash marks and needle-like bites peppered his body.

"Kol-ok!" She shouted up to the hut. "Bring blankets, now!"

She looked back at the lagoon for any sign of Atta or Ula, but only saw Xva's empty boat, a dot drifting on the far southern horizon.

The hissing returned. Something bumped the dock. Atamoda placed her hands against the wood and felt a rough, ragged vibration. Another sound rose above the hissing, of wood being chipped away, of a thousand needle-like teeth gnawing away the pilings.

20. In The Land of Giants

The legend does not say when the Narim appeared in the Hur Valley; only that it was long ago. The tribe of immortals came from a perfect land far beyond the mountains.

A tree with golden apples grew in that paradise. Women who ate from that tree gave birth to immortal sons and daughters with silken white hair. They were deceived by a trickster into betraying their god and, as punishment, were cast out. In his mercy, their god sent them a swallow.

"Of all the blessings of this land, ye may take only one," the swallow said.

"We do not want to be like cattle. We do not want to reproduce in great numbers. We want to live with dignity. Let us not depart from truth! Let fairness be our path! Let us not know grief! Let us live in freedom! Give us wisdom," the Narim answered as one.

Their god saw this was good. "Only with wisdom may ye find the path back to paradise through a fallen world."

The Chronicle of Fu Xi

***

They followed the road north until mid-day, when it came to an intersection of another road running east and west. To the east, a wide, well-rutted road led to the river. The west and north roads were only overgrown footpaths. Here they rested on a stump and prepared to cross the bridge.

Aizarg's toes barely touched the ground. He felt like a child as he sat on a gray stump bigger around than his hut. When Setenay said the Narim laid waste to entire forests, he had humble willows and marsh oaks in mind. These kupar stumps must have once been enormous trees.

Aizarg tried to peer around Sarah at the Kupar Bridge, looming behind her.

"Hold your head still! I'll be done in a moment." Sarah grabbed his chin and made him face her. She paid scant attention to the surrounding wonders as she arranged a blanket over his head.

"My people often cover their heads like this," Sarah said as she worked. "It is something passed down from the Narim. We call it a *kaffiya*. It keeps the sun off our heads and necks when we work in the fields. Brown Lo blankets are different from the white Hur weave, but it will cover your hair and make you stand out a little less."

She secured it around his head with a twisted piece of cloth and then stepped back to examine her handiwork. Sarah rested her chin in her palm, narrowed her eyes and tapped her foot.

"I think it will do," she said after a few moments.

Aizarg looked to his right from whence they came. On either side of the road, an endless expanse of giant gray stumps dotted the southern landscape. They reminded him of the Sammujad ghosts. Aizarg ran his hand over the stump's flat surface. It didn't show a single axe stroke. *The Narim sliced off these trees as cleanly as Scythians slice off the tops of their victim's skulls.*

The wood was solid under his hand. *If they took their forest so long ago, why aren't the stumps rotted out?*

Sarah held out her hand. "I need your pack, please."

Aizarg thought about asking why, but handed it over without a word. Sarah considered the pack and then looked nervously over her shoulder at the bridge.

"Aren't you going to cover your head?" Aizarg asked. Sarah didn't respond and started to rummage through his pack. She pulled out some dried fish jerky and his water skin.

"Eat and drink. It may be your last chance for quite some time." He took them, but she wouldn't meet his eyes and resumed digging through his pack.

She'd been distracted since they descended into the Hur Valley. At first, Aizarg thought Sarah was still disturbed by Setenay's terrified outburst. Now, he suspected Sarah preoccupied with trying to find a way into the city.

They encountered this road not long after they entered the valley and followed it into the Dead Forest. Aizarg was curious about the mysterious trenches cut into the earthen road. Sarah tried to explain these ruts were formed by something called 'wheels', but Aizarg couldn't grasp the concept. Occasionally, he hopped into the deepest ruts, which often came up to his mid-thigh. The packed soil felt like stone. Sarah said they were made by the Narim in ancient times. His imagination ran wild as he tried to picture what a wheel might look like.

Aizarg slowly chewed his food and gazed down the eastern road. He tried to stay focused on the journey ahead, but he could only stare in awe at the twin towers of the Kupar Bridge.

It looks so strong, yet graceful. Only gods could build such a wonder.

"Why would they need something so big?" Aizarg whispered, not really talking to anyone but himself.

Sarah looked up from the pack. "My people have asked themselves that for generations. The Narim never told my ancestors why they built it. For most of the year, the Hur

River is so shallow a child could wade across. Some say they did it to honor their god."

Sarah continued to talk as she placed Aizarg's pack on the stump next to him. "Once, in the time of my grandmother, King Yontel ordered the entire population of Hur-ar onto the bridge. The census was the official reason, but the real reason was a wager with one of his nobles, who was sure the bridge would collapse under the weight."

Aizarg turned to her, horrified. "Why would a leader take such a risk with the lives of his people?"

"For gold and pride, of course."

"Obviously, it held," Aizarg said.

"Thousands of people packed the bridge from end to end. Grandmother said the bridge didn't even creak."

Sarah straightened up and considered Aizarg's pack. "It will do."

"What will do?"

Sarah pointed to the bridge. "The road climbs a gentle bluff overlooking the river. Do you see it?"

"Yes."

"That is the western access to the bridge and the first guard shack. There will be two warriors there. They collect the king's toll...and a hefty bribe."

Aizarg tore his eyes away from the bridge and fully focused on Sarah. She stared at him so intensely it made Aizarg uncomfortable, as if she were taking his measure.

"Are you going to cover your hair, daughter?"

She ignored his question. "Do you trust me, Uros?"

She has not called me Father since we entered the valley.

Aizarg cocked his head. "What?"

"Do you trust me?" Sarah reiterated.

"Absolutely."

"Then do what I say without question."

Sarah pulled the leather drawstring, about a finger in thickness and a yard long, from Aizarg's pack. She wrapped the leather strap twice around her neck and then tied it with just enough slack so it wouldn't bind her skin. With a few quick, well-practiced movements, she tied a series of square knots with the two loose ends until they formed an ornate cord about four inches long. With the remaining slack she created a wide loop and then tied it off.

She rummaged around Aizarg's pack until she found his rope and flint knife.

"Uros, I need to cut some of this rope. May I?"

"Yes." Aizarg burned with curiosity.

He watched as she cut a piece four arms in length. She cut another smaller length and placed it on the stump next to the pack.

Sarah pointed to the short length of rope. "Use that to secure your pack."

Next, Sarah took the flint knife and sliced her sheath dress just below her left hip.

"Sarah?" Aizarg gasped.

Sarah continued to hack at her skirt. "I hope Setenay will forgive me for ruining her dress."

After a few minutes of work she cut her skirt diagonally from her left hip to just above her right knee. She then cut a vertical slit revealing a long stretch of her right thigh.

She tossed the excess deerskin to the ground.

Aizarg considered the spare material, thinking it a shame to waste it. He stood, picked it up, and started to wrap the deerskin around his staff. "This will attract more attention than our hair."

"No, leave it unwrapped," she said. "Your staff could be seen as a sign of wealth. It will attract the right kind of attention."

Aizarg warily put the strips in his pack. He had a bad feeling about this.

Sarah took the long length of rope and tied one end around the loop on her new necklace.

"Your hair will be taken as one touched by the gods. My hair could also be taken as a desirable oddity by men willing to pay gold." Sarah placed the other end of the rope in

Aizarg's hand. "You are now a flesh trader from the steppe and I am your slave."

"Sarah, no!" Horrified, Aizarg pushed the rope away.

"Listen! You said you trusted me, so trust me. My people say only a fool or a slave enters Hur-ar without gold or trade. We have no gold. We have no trade. If we cross the bridge without either, the guards will kill you and take me *and they will be fully within their rights to do so!* The Hur-po are cruel, but they live and die by the law. A poor man and his daughter have no protection under Hur law, but a slaver and his pleasure wares do."

"Absolutely not! We will swim the river. We will climb the wall—I don't care, but I will not see you defiled. You are my blood..."

"No!" she screamed and pushed him back with such ferocity Aizarg stumbled and slumped down onto the stump. "I am not your blood! I am a daughter of Hur-ar and a pleasure slave to Virag the Terrible." Wide-eyed with clenched jaw, a knife-edge intensity replaced her sweet tenderness.

"Every day I was a slave I was tortured, humiliated and did things for which I can never forgive myself. But each day I wore Virag's collar I thanked the spirits I was not a slave in Hur-ar." Sarah pointed to the bridge. "There is no love and no hope beyond those towers for slaves or those without trade."

She poked angrily at his chest. "I know what we are about to face, you don't! My body will be our trade. I will pave our way to the Black Fortress. Accept it, for there is no other choice."

Aizarg sat in stunned disbelief. Sarah, his daughter, vanished, replaced by Sarah the survivor. He assumed he knew the torments Sarah must have suffered, but until now he never saw the scars.

He clasped her hands, kissed them and held them to his cheek. "I am sorry, dear Sarah. I am so sorry, so sorry..." Aizarg wanted to take away her pain and make everything good again. Seeing her like this broke his heart. Atamoda and his children flashed into his mind. He thought of Setenay's madness and of lost Ba-lok. He held his face in his hands and tried to squeeze his eyes shut and hold back the tears, but they broke through anyway.

She knelt over Aizarg, kissed his forehead and held him to her bosom. Sarah spoke with an air of resignation. "Until we make it to the Black Fortress, you will see me do things and say things which might make you despise me, even hate me. Please, do not judge me too harshly. When this is all over, I will understand if you want to disown me."

"I will never disown you!" he cried and lowered his head into her arms.

Sarah's voice darkened. She sounded like a stranger. "Be warned, Aizarg of the Lo, the man you are now will not be the same man who returns from Hur-ar. Cry now, but leave your tears in the Dead Forest."

She lifted Aizarg's chin. A wave of relief washed over him when he saw her radiant smile return.

Follow her light.

Sarah wiped Aizarg's face and helped him stand. She placed the end of the leash in his hand. "I will do what I must, but I promise I will do so out of your sight. The only way back is forward. Isn't that what you told Levidi? I love you, but do not try to save me. I must save you, all of you. For me, it is the only way home."

***

They walked onto the bridge with Sarah in the lead and Aizarg holding the leash. He wanted to take in the full magnitude of the bridge, but his eyes kept falling on Sarah. Back straight and head held high, she betrayed no fear. Her bravery amazed him.

I am frightened enough for the both of us.

Aizarg made up his mind. He could not permit Sarah to sell her body. He prepared himself to kill the guards if necessary. He didn't know how he'd do it, but perhaps the staff held the key. The thought of killing another human made his knees weak, but the thought of Sarah sliding back into degradation, especially for his sake, filled him with shame. He took a deep breath and steeled himself for what was to come.

The first set of gray towers soared high above his head. The support towers on each side of the bridge were composed of four massive tree trunks lashed together with rusted iron bands thicker than a man's chest. The support towers were joined over the bridge by five crossbeams of heavy timber and lashed into place with more iron bands. Coiled ropes of a material Aizarg didn't recognize were tied to the tops of each support and then strung the length of the bridge on both sides. These cables were as thick as a man's leg and drooped gracefully, almost touching the bridge at mid-span. Additional heavy coiled ropes were tied to the long cable at regular intervals, and then tied off to iron loops on the bridge's sides. Thick, flat boards ran crossways over heavy logs to create a continuous, flat surface.

Aizarg pulled his eyes off the majestic bridge to see Sarah staring at a small, rickety hovel about twenty yards ahead on the left. It obviously wasn't a part of the original bridge construction. It was a little thing, obviously built by men. A similar shed stood on the opposite side of the bridge, between them a long empty expanse.

Sarah whispered to Aizarg, "Something is wrong. The sentries should have challenged us by now."

Leading him by the rope, Sarah walked around the side of the shack and peered inside. Other than a rough bench and an empty brass pot, the structure was empty.

Sarah looked around, astonished. "I have never heard of either post being deserted, ever."

Aizarg let go of the leash and stepped around the shack to the edge of the bridge. He leaned against the rope cable and peered down. The Hur River ran dark and deep, like the Black River they crossed two days ago. The eroding bluffs spoke of a river in violent flood, but the bridge rose so high it felt impervious to its power. Shattered logs and twisted branches piled high against the base of the towers. Aizarg thought he saw chunks of black ice bobbing in the current.

Sarah leaned over next to him and looked down. "The towers never stand in the water, the river always trickles between them. I've never seen or heard of it running so high."

A rumbling to their right, like firewood rolling over a dock, caught their attention.

Sarah looked across the bridge. "Someone approaches!" She placed the leash back in his hand.

The sight of what looked like a large beast alarmed Aizarg at first, but Sarah made no move to run. What he saw was a man grasping two poles, dragging a large object with another man perched on top.

"It is a cart, Uros. You are about to see wheels. Quickly, you must appear haughty and arrogant."

Aizarg puffed up his chest, crossed his arms and frowned.

Sarah didn't look impressed. "I guess it will have to do." The corner of her mouth lifted in a suppressed smile. "Balok would actually be useful right now."

Aizarg didn't know if he should take that as a compliment or an insult.

The cart rumbled across the bridge, pulled by a naked young man. Aizarg did everything in his power to not react to the sight of the miserable soul pulling the cart. Gaunt and wiry, with lifeless eyes, the lash marks scarring his back reminded Aizarg of a turtle shell. He wore a thick leather collar with two long reins attached and held by the man sitting on the cart.

So those are wheels. Now the ruts made perfect sense. Wooden spokes radiated outward from a central hub. The outside of the wooden wheels were sheathed in bronze and reminded Aizarg of the sun.

What did Setenay say? 'The Narim lay waste to entire forests, and then commanded the full moon and sun to descend from heaven to gather the wood.'

Aizarg wanted to further examine the wheels and cart, but he had to keep up the charade.

Sarah whispered to Aizarg, "He is a stump farmer, the lowest caste of freemen in Hur-ar. They farm the lands west of the river. I will do the talking. Follow my lead and do what I say. If I tug the leash once, nod 'yes'. Twice, shake your head 'no.' An occasional grunt might be appropriate, too. Please, Uros, try to look imposing!"

An old man, hard but capable looking, drove the cart. He wore a soiled, rough-hewn white shirt and trousers of the same. A plain white kaffiya encircled his head, secured with a black band. He pulled back on the reins and stopped the cart next to Sarah and Aizarg.

His beady black eyes slowly walked up and down Sarah's body and then threw Aizarg a distrustful glance. Aizarg cringed as the old man snapped back on the reins, jerking the slave down onto all fours. Without a word, the old man climbed down using the slave's scarred back as a step-stool. He slowly walked to the back of the cart, all the time eyeing Aizarg and Sarah. His slave remained on his hands and knees, heaving for air.

Sarah cleared her throat and bowed to the stranger. "My master and I are on our way to the city to trade. We have spent many days trading on the steppe. Can you tell my master what has become of the bridge guard?"

The old man rummaged through the back of the cart, filled with strange implements and stacked reed baskets.

Those are Lo baskets. Aizarg remembered that Hur traders frequented Ba-lok's shore camp.

The old man pulled out a wooden mallet and continued to eye them, occasionally glancing at Aizarg's staff.

"Why can't your master speak for himself?" the old man said and struck the wheel hub with the mallet. The stump farmer spoke with a strange accent, as if some of his sounds were grinding in the back of this throat. Aizarg had heard this accent very faintly in Sarah's voice during their journey.

Sarah put her hands on her hips and lifted her chin. "My master is a powerful outlander and trader. He reserves his words for those who can afford his wares. I speak to those who can't."

The old man harrumphed and threw the mallet back into the cart. "If you say so. My business is among the stumps, where I hope the world is still sane. If your business is in the city, well, good luck. That's where you'll find the guards."

"I don't understand," said Sarah.

The old man took a gourd from the cart and walked forward to the slave, still on all fours like a beast. He lifted the slave's chin and poured water down his throat. The slave greedily gulped it down.

"Don't drink it all!" the old man chastised and harshly slapped his slave's cheek. The old man shook the gourd and shot the wretch a nasty look. "Or do you want to have to refill it from that infernal river?" He put the gourd back in the cart and returned his attention to Aizarg and Sarah.

The old man motioned to the east, toward the mountains and the city. "All the warriors are needed in the city to maintain order and keep the market open. Terrible omens have visited the Hur-ar. The people are panicked. It started when the beasts fled the city and fields many days ago, including my ass!

"Now I have to use my field slave to get my grain to market. I should be thankful there is still a market." The old man scrunched up his face, wrinkled his nose, and spoke in a high, mocking tone. "'All is well,' the king says. 'Continue to buy and sell!' he said as the animals stampeded out the gates. The king ordered the city gates closed to keep the rest of the animals from escaping." The stump farmer spat on the ground.

"Bah! Lot of good that did! The trapped beasts were taken with madness and had to be slain. Not a chicken or a rat remains in Hur-ar. The king's scouts have scoured the surrounding mountains and steppe for game, but the wild beasts are gone, too. The city still has meat, but not for much longer. Thieves are already raiding the nobles' fields along the east bank. What the thieves haven't taken, the river has flooded. Some nobles are harvesting their fields early and burning the rest to keep the prices high, looking for a quick profit. Madness! I'm going to my fields before it gets worse."

The old man let out a loud, wicked laugh. "Ha! It finally pays to be a lowly stump farmer! My scrabbly fields are still untouched by thief or flood...for now."

The farmer stepped on the slave's back and climbed onto his cart. He gave the reins another sharp tug and the slave stood up and grasped the poles.

The stump farmer leaned down toward Aizarg. "Master slaver, did you happen to see any strange sights upon the steppe?"

Aizarg shook his head.

"Hmm, well, is that so? My tale gets worse. For days now the earth has trembled, and two nights ago, thousands of stars fell from the sky." The old man shook his head and whispered. Aizarg saw fear behind his gruff mask. "The worst omen came when the Narim didn't open the Black Gate. Never have the Narim refused trade."

Sarah gasped, and then quickly composed herself.

The stump farmer gazed west. "I do not know what is more expensive these days, gold or food. You can't eat gold, so I'm off to my fields until the danger passes." He looked at Aizarg. "Only two things are free in Hur-ar, advice and death. Take my advice. If you know what's best, you'll turn around."

Sarah gave the leash one gentle tug. Aizarg nodded once and grunted.

"You are strange, even for an outlander." The old man pointed to Sarah. "But even in these dark days she will bring a good price, especially with that hair." He sighed and sat up.

"If I were younger, I'd pay an honest ounce or two for a night with her. Now I will pay twice as much for another good field hand...or an ass." He popped the reins and the slave strained against the cart. "Good luck, outlander. May you find profit in these evil times."

Aizarg watched the cart rumble off the bridge and onto the road. The slave drifted to the side and avoided the deepest ruts.

The wheels amazed Aizarg, but he didn't think them much good to the Lo. *The marsh is too soft for such contraptions. And where would we go in a cart that we can't go more quickly in a boat?*

He turned to Sarah. She looked toward Hur-ar with a worried expression.

"What's wrong?"

"He said the Narim aren't trading. That's how I planned to get us into their fortress." She looked at Aizarg. "I don't know what to do now."

"I thought you said the Narim sealed themselves in and never came out?"

"They don't come out and no one sees them. The Black Gate has an inner and outer gate. Once a week, the king's traders load large carts full of wares they buy from the vendors in the market. Oxen pull these carts up the Cliff Road to the Black Gate. The traders ring an iron bell and then the outer gate opens. The traders roll the carts into a holding area between the inner and outer gates and then ring a smaller, brass bell which tells the Narim they have vacated the holding area. The outer gate closes. Soon, the iron bell rings again and the outer gate swings back open. The wares are gone and the carts are filled with gold ore."

"Ore?"

"Its gold mixed with rock. Gold is sunlight stolen by giants and buried deep in the ground to hide it from the God of the Narim, who wants it back. There are giants in the earth and that is why it sometimes trembles. In the ground, the sunlight mixes with the rock and forms gold ore. It is said the Narim enter the bowels of the earth and do battle with giants to win the gold. The Narim hope to curry their god's favor by freeing the gold from the mountains. The old temples to the god of the Narim were once covered in gold."

Aizarg thought about this. "So how do the king's traders know what the Narim want?"

"The Narim leave clay tablets with the gold. The tablets have magical markings which speak only to traders and tell them what to bring next time."

Something didn't make sense to Aizarg. "If the Narim are wise immortals, why would they give the Hur-po the very substance that corrupts them?"

"I don't know, Uros. Now my thoughts dwell on how we are going to enter the Black Fortress."

"No one has entered their dwelling before?"

"The penalty for entering the Black Fortress is death. Those who've tried are never seen again."

"Providence has brought us this far. Perhaps the spirit of the mist knows providence will carry us the rest of the way. Come, let us cross the bridge."

***

The mountains thrust high ahead of them, bright and hazy in the dusty autumn sunlight. The day waned and the shadows lengthened. Sarah and Aizarg walked on the road between two golden fields of grain. Aizarg held his arms out and barely touched the top of the stalks. He remembered another of Setenay's stories about the Narim.

Food springs from the ground at their very command.

Aizarg wasn't convinced about the usefulness of the wheel, but vowed to bring the ability to grow food to his people.

"Uros!" Sarah hissed. "Please, get away from the field. They belong to the nobles. They may think we're stealing grain."

"Just a few more moments." Aizarg studied the lay of the land, trying to memorize how the fields looked. Deep canals were cut from the river to the fields, which in turn, divided into smaller channels running between the rows. At regular intervals, small wooden slats controlled the flow of water to individual fields.

Aizarg smiled enthusiastically. "When we get home, I'm going to do this!" He plucked a handful of stalks and stuffed them into his pack.

"We harvest wild grain, but I never thought it could be summoned from the ground." Aizarg stepped away from the field. "With this 'farming,' we will not have to worry so much about fishing or hunting. If they can grow this here, I know we can grow it in the marsh."

The fields of grain gave Aizarg hope. Maybe that's why he was led here, to learn this craft.

Sarah smiled weakly. "Yes, of course." She handed him the leash and pulled him toward the city.

Aizarg looked over his shoulder one more time at the fields stretching along the eastern bank of the river. The lower fields were flooded and the fields to his left were flat and blackened.

The stump farmer's words aggravated his already growing sense of unease.

If the Narim have turned their back on the Hur-po, why would they help me?

The light brown wall enclosing Hur-ar, taller than five men and as smooth as polished stone, brightly reflected the western sun. Dozens of metal clad warriors stood atop the wall, their long spears glinting in the sun.

I cannot protect her in there. If we enter those gates, I condemn her. If I don't, I may condemn my people.

The gates were open and Aizarg heard the din of thousands of voices that reminded him of the black river's rushing waters.

"Sarah?" Aizarg whispered.

"Yes, Uros?"

"Did men or Narim make this wall?"

"Men."

Aizarg craned his head back and looked up the cliff behind the city. He clearly saw the zigzagging road leading up the cliff, with its dozens of switchbacks. Easily twice as high as the city enclosure, the wall of the Narim appeared black and featureless in the direct face of the late afternoon sun.

Even the Scythians fear this place. I am an ant in the land of giants. Oh, Great Mother, what are we doing here?

Sarah stepped out ahead of him, whispering as she passed, "I will lead you. Remember what I told you and be strong."

Aizarg swallowed hard. *The only way back is forward...The only way back is forward...The only way back is forward.*

He wrapped the leash around his fist and held on.

21. Hur-Ar

The Narim wandered for many years, doing good works until one day they crossed over the mountains and descended into a fertile valley filled with savage men. The Narim took pity on them and taught the valley dwellers many crafts to lift them out of ignorance.

Under the Narims' tutelage the mortals became a righteous and prosperous people. Pleased with the fruits of their works, the Narim moved on to other lands. However, having come to love the valley, a handful remained.

There came a day when the Narim showed the people a beautiful yellow metal they called hur, or gold.

"Give us more of this yellow metal," the people told the Narim. "And we shall give you all you need."

The valley dwellers grew in power and wealth and became known as the Hur-po, the People of Gold. Soon, they coveted gold above all else and took the blessings of the Narim for granted.

One day the Narim said to the Hur-po, "Repent and turn from your evil ways." Possessed by lust and wickedness, the Hur-po ignored them.

"If gold is what you love, then have your fill," they told the Hur-po. "You shall drown under its weight."

The Narim built the mighty bridge and the Black Fortress. They sealed themselves inside and were never seen again.

The Chronicle of Fu Xi

***

Aizarg was drowning in a sea of filthy faces and hands, assaulted by a cacophony of screams and shouts. Dust choked his throat and his chest tightened with anxiety. *I am suffocating.* Worse than drowning, he couldn't swim out of the crush of bodies.

"Sarah!" he screamed, with no regard to the charade of being a slave trader. Now his lifeline, he wrapped the leash tighter around his wrist, terrified Sarah would lose him.

Occasionally, he felt a tug against his staff, which was always followed by a scream. He knew some of these people were attempting to wrest the staff from his hands and then melt into the crowd. Each time they were rewarded with pain for their efforts.

The imposing walls rose high above the crowd. The gates to the city were open as conflicting masses of humanity tried to simultaneously enter and exit the city. A line of warriors lashed the mob with long whips, trying to keep some semblance of order.

The leash pulled him through the throng until they came to the city gates. The gates were made from crudely hewn planks of a lighter-colored wood than the Kupar Bridge. The gates were banded with bronze and topped with iron spikes. They were pushed outward, perpendicular to the walls, and channeled the throng into a dense chokepoint. The warriors formed a picket of bronze and spears across the open gates. The crowd ebbed and pushed against them like the tide.

Sarah's white hair became a beacon as she pushed through the crowd.

She moved as effortlessly as a mouse through marsh grass.

The crowd thickened and he lost sight of her. He felt violent tugs against the rope, like a big fish struggling against a line and the leash began to slip from around his sweaty wrist. Aizarg knew if they became separated he may never find her again. On impulse, he began striking out with his staff. Someone yelped wherever the red orb made contact with their flesh. The tension on the leash abated as the crowd cleared a small space around Sarah and Aizarg. Aizarg took a deep breath, thankful to be out of the worst of it. But his gratitude faded as they were confronted by a wall of flesh and bronze.

A line of burly guards stood with folded arms. They considered Aizarg and Sarah with hostile indifference.

"Back, dogs!" A warrior stepped from behind the middle of the line and cracked a whip. "Show your wares or gold. No one enters Hur-ar without trade and NO ONE enters without paying the king's tax!"

The warriors wore pleated chest plates over ornate ocher and yellow robes. The robes were tightly wrapped over their muscled torsos and extended just above brass-shod greaves. They had long black hair and wavy beards similar to the Sammujad, but with dazzling yellow jewelry interwoven into their beards.

So that is gold.

"You!" The center guard pointed his whip at Aizarg. "What is your business? Speak quickly or feel my whip!"

Aizarg opened his mouth, but Sarah stepped in front of him and lightly walked toward the warrior. With each footfall, her curves rose and fell in a slow, sultry rhythm. Her fingertips gently brushed up her hips, catching her dress with just enough tension to lift the ragged hem a few tantalizing inches before it slipped back down over her hip. Her fingers continued up through her long, white hair before letting it spill over her shoulders again.

The crowd grew silent as Sarah stalked the warrior like a lioness. She pushed as achingly close as two humans could without touching. Aizarg felt the heat building between them. Sarah demurely tilted her head and flashed musky eyes. He glared down at her as if about to snap her neck. But Aizarg saw the man's breath deepen and slow and knew the warrior had already ravished her a thousand times in his mind.

Aizarg suddenly appreciated Ood-i's strong attachment to Sarah. *Yes, we are going to marry her off to a distant arun-ki. Very, very far away. I'm confident I'll have no problem finding suitors.*

The crowd leered hungrily, anticipating what might happen next.

Sarah didn't raise her voice, but was clearly heard. "My master comes from far away to trade in Hur-ar. He brings no gold..." She shook her head and let her thick, white locks fall seductively across half her face. "...but he brings the finest silver."

For a long moment the warrior's expression didn't change, and then a grin spread under his greasy beard. The tension broke and the crowd let out a burst of approving cheers.

"Your master is most welcome in Hur-ar." The warrior never took his eyes off Sarah. "Bring your wench, slaver, and follow me to the perimeter barracks. There you can pay me the entry tax."

"Go easy, Gilga, and save some 'tax' for us!" One of the guards bellowed and slapped his thigh.

Sarah looked back over her shoulder at Aizarg and mouthed "come."

Before Aizarg could take a step, a spear sank deep into the dirt inches in front of the warrior called Gilga.

Gilga jerked his head up to see who threw the spear. Another warrior stood high above them on the wall. This one wore a conical helmet and more gold in his beard and around his neck. His features were obscured by his helmet, but he stood with an air of relaxed confidence with one hand resting on the hilt of his short sword.

"Gilga," the warrior called down in a commanding voice. "Take the slaver and his bitch to the commander with my compliments. She gets there clean, do you understand? You can purchase her favors only after the commander has his fill."

Sarah caught sight of the man on the wall and quickly lowered her head and brushed some hair over her face. Aizarg glimpsed a flash of fear and recognition in her eyes.

She knows him.

The man on the wall tossed down two small, circular objects in the dust in front of Aizarg.

"Slaver, this should cover your cost minus the king's tax." The man turned and walked away.

Sarah fell to the dust and snatched the objects. She held them close and looked around warily, as if someone might take them away from her. She dusted it off and bit down on one. Sarah smiled greedily and held up the gold disks so Aizarg could see. "They are real! Two shequels!"

For a fleeting moment, Aizarg didn't recognize her. Seeing Sarah grovel in the dirt after the shiny metal disturbed him more than her seduction of the warrior.

They are just little things, these pieces of gold.

Sarah must have seen something in his face, because she lowered her head. She stood, walked behind him and put the gold disks in his pack.

"We may need them later," she whispered.

Gilga snarled and kicked over the spear. He growled at Aizarg and Sarah. "Come!"

As they passed through the line of warriors, Aizarg heard one of the guards comment to another, "The Captain of the Gate is at it again. His efforts to buy the commander's favor may earn Gilga's knife in his back, instead."

With the entertainment over, the people in the throng pressed against the line of warriors again.

Sarah and Aizarg crossed out of the late afternoon sun into the chilly shadows of Hur-ar.

Inside the city the smell suffocated Aizarg. He covered his mouth and tried not to vomit.

The wind doesn't reach the bottom of these strange canyons.

Piles of garbage and human waste lined the streets. Aizarg saw someone sleeping in the gutter. *Why would anyone lie down in such filth?* He stumbled and almost fell with the realization it was a dead body. Soon, he saw more corpses.

Why would anyone want to enter this city? There isn't enough water in the Hur River to cleanse the filth from this cursed place.

Aizarg noticed the bodies were devoid of flies. He remembered the stump farmer's tale about the animals fleeing the city.

The strange curse infects this place, too.

Countless faces passed by, but they reserved their glances for Sarah. None of them seemed the least bit concerned with the stench or the bodies. Most of the men only wore loin cloths and an occasional rag wrapped over his head. They looked sickly, with thin legs and knobby knees. Some rushed towards Aizarg with pleading faces and cupped hands shouting, "Alms, merciful master, alms!" Gilga occasionally cracked his whip across the beggars' flesh to drive them back. Aizarg wanted to help, but he didn't know how. Sarah's leash pulled him mercilessly forward.

Sometimes they passed men who wore ornate robes in a variety of colors. These men decorated their bodies with golden jewelry. They walked quickly and with purpose, indifferent to the suffering around them.

Why do they wear scowls on their faces when it's so obvious they have enough food? Do they not see the need of those around them?

Hur-ar was an enigma, but its children provided the greatest mystery of all.

A horde of ragged, filthy children followed behind them. They were all boys and mostly naked. A lucky few (the oldest) had rags wrapped around their waists. They begged just like the men, but were far more malnourished. Their bellies were distended and their eyes bulged.

These are the children of their arun-ki! Their flesh, their future! Why do they not help?

Aizarg wanted to rip off his pack and give them all his food. He wanted to scoop them into his arms and carry them far away. He lifted his sleeve and wiped away the mist forming at the corners of his eyes. He knew to cry here would be an invitation to death.

Sarah tugged the leash and spoke over her shoulder. "This is the Avenue of Kings. It leads to the market district."

Kings? If I were a king here I would be ashamed.

As they moved away from the city wall's shadow, sunlight warmed his back and lit the long, crowded avenue. Tall, wall-like dwellings lined each side of the street. Aizarg craned up to see their tops and almost tripped on the strange, rectangular rocks that formed the street's surface. The tall stone huts were smooth and brown, like the perimeter wall. Each hut seamlessly joined the next. Some had windows above other windows. Aizarg didn't see ladders on the outside; he wondered how the people got up that high. Ropes with clothes pinned to them were strung high over the street.

Women leaned out of the upper windows or sat on the front steps, watching the comings and goings. Most women wore faded wraps with the occasional piece of gold imbedded in holes in their ears or through their nose. Some carried babies and sometimes children clung to their legs. Like everyone else, neither the women nor the children smiled.

They passed several intersections that led to narrow, murky alleys. Aizarg felt the air chill as he passed them. He shivered and wanted no part of those places. Now he knew why the Scythians called Hur-ar the Place of Mazes.

The nature of the avenue quickly changed, as if they passed through an invisible barrier. The clothes hanging over the streets were gone, along with the garbage and corpses.

The street grew wider as the dingy, packed hovels gave way to grand structures. These buildings were clean, white and much larger. Sometimes they were surrounded by walls, above which rose exotic trees and shrubberies.

It looks better, but doesn't smell any better.

The beggars and feral children were gone, replaced by warriors at every crossroad. They brandished spears and clubs, but appeared bored and lethargic.

A flash to his right caught Aizarg's attention. He looked over his shoulder and caught a glimpse of a filth-covered boy a few years older than Kol-ok darting into an alley. The boy kept to the shadows, careful not to be seen by the guards, but Aizarg knew the boy trailed them.

Aizarg turned around. A din rose ahead that sounded like the wind, or maybe rushing waters.

"What is that sound?" he asked Sarah.

She turned her head and spoke out of the corner of her mouth. "We are approaching the Grand Market. The barracks lie on the far side of the market, beyond the Temple of Ba'al. Do not let go of the rope or we may never find you!"

The din became a deafening roar as the avenue ended on a platform overlooking an enormous public square. Gilga stopped and surveyed the scene below as Sarah and Aizarg came alongside him.

"The crowds are thinned since the omens began," Gilga commented. He pointed his whip to the right. "We'll stay along the south wall and circumvent most of the market."

Thinned?

More people packed the market than Aizarg thought existed in the world, than *could* exist in the world. Aizarg's head swam at the staggering scene. Sunken below street level, the market stretched for almost a mile. A broad, fan-shaped stairway spilled down to the market level. Row after row of stands and stalls packed the square, many covered with colorful tarps or pennants flapping in the breeze.

People flowed in the narrow alleys between the vendor stalls like water through the irrigation channels in the fields.

A Great Sea of humanity.

Four stone walls enclosed the market with four wide avenues radiating from the market's corners. Stairways descended from the avenues to the market. Above the market wall, splendid mansions hemmed the square in on all sides, blocking Aizarg's view of the rest of the city. Beyond their flat rooftops, Aizarg beheld the sheer cliffs that boxed in the city.

A square within a square within a square.

To his right, Aizarg clearly saw the road, much steeper than he originally thought, zigzagging up the cliff to the Black Fortress. High atop the Cliff Road, the Black Fortress loomed over the city. The fortress felt apart from Hur-ar, as if the city and fortress seemed oddly divorced.

The Black Fortress looks as if it is protecting itself from the city.

An enormous, black object rose above the far side of the market. Aizarg gasped and almost cried out before realizing it was only a statue. A terrifying serpent-like creature, standing twice as high as the surrounding palaces, stood on its hind legs and stretched its bat-like wings over the market. The monster's fore claws were outstretched, as if to attack. Real fire licked out of its mouth, creating a trail of greasy smoke that settled over the market.

Aizarg pointed to the statue and whispered to Sarah, "What is that?"

"That is the Temple of Ba'al, the Black Dragon. He is the god of the Hur-po."

"I almost expected the Hur-po to worship the Narim."

Gilga heard them over the din and threw his head back in booming laughter. "You are an outlander, aren't you? Narim only give us gold, but Ba'al shows us how to use it!" Gilga held out his arms over the market. "Through Ba'al we are granted all desires of our heart." With that, Gilga descended into the sea of flesh.

***

Gilga didn't beat his way through the crowd as he had done before. He used his bulk to bully his way through the masses. Aizarg felt disoriented by the blur of chaos as vendors hawked their wares with animated gestures. Aizarg tried not to flinch, assaulted and surprised by their loud voices.

Most of the people in the market were Hur. Like Gilga, the men sported dark, curly beards. They were bare-chested and wore tight-fitting quilted skirts and kaffiyas decorated in reds, oranges and sometimes blue weaves. The women wore equally tight linen robes, but of only pure white or black. While some women wore kaffiyas, most used golden headbands to keep their rich, black locks away from their face. Both men and women outlined their eyes with black pigment. All of them wore the yellow metal.

Gold glittered everywhere. Men wore it on their wrists, around their necks, and woven into their beards. It dangled from women's ears and through their noses. It changed hands, clinked in copper bowls and sat on brass scales. Aizarg could not turn his head without seeing the shiny metal.

He looked over his shoulder to see if the beggar boy still followed, but the boy, or any of the poor, had vanished. Aizarg suspected the poor were forbidden from the market, as armed warriors were in abundance among the vendor rows. The people of the market were well fed, richly clothed, and indifferent to the suffering of their own.

In Hur-ar, one is not a human without gold. Hatred for the city fermented in Aizarg's heart with each step.

But not all those in the market were Hur. He caught flashes of wild Sammujad nomads hawking weapons and animal skins, or the sunbaked Aryans selling copper and iron. Some faces were completely alien. A group of small, compact men wore heavy fur garments and pointed fur hats. They had bizarrely slanted eyes and skin the color of dusty spring pollen. These men held a beautiful, glimmering fabric over their outstretched arms and attracted a large crowd.

The market simultaneously repulsed and fascinated Aizarg. Instinct told him to flee the oppressive crowd, yet he wanted to explore the market. His eyes were not only wide in amazement at the sights, but his stomach growled at the smells of roasted meats and exotic spices.

The treasures of Hur-ar went by in a blur as Gilga plowed a path for them. The leash stayed tight as Sarah relentlessly kept Aizarg moving onward. Thankfully, Gilga kept the low, southern wall on their right. Deep in the market pit Aizarg couldn't see the cliffs and therefore couldn't keep his bearings. If they ventured left, into the heart of the market, he would surely lose his way.

They emerged into an open area where the southern and eastern walls converged and another stairway ascended from the market. To their left, the crowd thickened around a long platform erected against the eastern wall between the obsidian feet of Ba'al.

The statue, even more sinister close-up, looked as if it were about to descend upon the market and devour everyone.

Why would anyone worship something so foul? Are they blind to its evil?

Gilga paused at the base of the stairs and considered the spectacle. Aizarg caught the warrior briefly watching him out of the corner of his eye, the way a hunter assesses his prey. Gilga quickly looked away and then jovially slapped Aizarg on the back and pointed at the platform.

"Even in these times, business is good on the slavers' block! If the commander is pleased with your white-haired wench, his endorsement could double, even triple, her price on the block."

Aizarg fought not to recoil at Gilga's touch.

A tall, fat man carrying a whip stood on the slaver's block. His belly bulged over his waist wrap and his chins fell under a scrabbly beard. Aizarg had never seen a fat man before, and thought he looked like a monster spawned from between Ba'al's legs. A line of naked girls and boys, some as young as little Bat-or, sulked in front of the slaver.

Richly dressed men and women in the crowd occasionally raised their hands. An old woman standing on the platform pointed to them and made marks on a clay tablet. Several men and women lounged on gold-gilded litters carried on the shoulders of naked male slaves. They occasionally lifted a lazy finger and the woman on the platform smiled and nodded eagerly.

The children's faces were downcast as the fat monster occasionally grabbed one and spun them around to show the buyers. Many faces of the crowd wore the same lustful expression Gilga wore when he considered Sarah.

Revulsion overwhelmed Aizarg and, in an instant, he knew the reason the gods abandoned the world. Hatred burned hot in Aizarg's heart.

Now I understand, Great Mother.

Hur-ar deserved the worst of heavenly judgments, but Aizarg feared Hur-ar's sins were so great they would drag down the rest of the world.

Aizarg looked at the poor children being sold into suffering and then he looked at Sarah. She looked away from the auction block, her arms were folded tight, pain swimming just below the surface.

She's been there.

At that moment, Aizarg made up his mind. He would not turn Sarah over to the commander. Setenay said the Narim were the key to their salvation, but if he surrendered Sarah to Hur-ar's clutches, then he and the Lo shared in Hur-ar's judgment. Perhaps Aizarg could not turn the wrath of the gods, but he would meet the next world with a clear conscious.

Aizarg gripped his staff tighter. At the first opportunity he would strike Gilga over the head and they would make a run for the Cliff Road.

"As much as I'd like to stay and enjoy the auction, the commander awaits." Gilga sighed and pointed his whip up the stairs. "The commander's barracks are at the top of the stairs on the Avenue of Ba'al." He turned and started up the stairs.

Sarah took Aizarg's arm when Gilga drifted far enough ahead to be out of earshot

"The worst is behind us," she whispered. "We can be at the Black Fortress before sunset, but you must control your anger! I can see you seething. It will draw suspicion."

How can one man's anger draw any attention in this foul place? Aizarg looked up at the Black Fortress looming high above them.

"No, Sarah, the worst is not behind us," he whispered. As Gilga led them up the stairs and out of the market, Aizarg began to doubt the Narim could save them.

Gilga pointed them to a dark side street and waited for them to pass. "This way."

Sarah glanced at Aizarg with a confused look before she turned to Gilga. "Great warrior, I have been this way many times. Isn't the entrance to the Central Barracks around the corner?"

Rage crossed Gilga's face, but he quickly suppressed it. "Of course it is, but I'm not leading a choice morsel like you through a den of wolves. I don't feel like fighting half the garrison and I don't want to be responsible for delivering a bloody and bruised harlot to the commander." Gilga smiled like a serpent. "He likes to deliver the blood and bruises himself.

"The entrance to the commander's quarters is this way. I will discreetly deposit you there and then retrieve the commander." He turned to Aizarg. "You can wait outside the commander's door until he is done. After that, your affairs are your own."

Gilga once again motioned Sarah and Aizarg ahead down the alley. Sarah went ahead, but gave Aizarg a worried expression.

"Go, I will follow you," Aizarg said. He wasn't about to let this dangerous man get behind him.

Gilga laughed and went ahead of him. "As you wish, outlander. I admire your caution, I'm sure you learned that on the steppe."

With Gilga between Sarah and Aizarg, they entered the narrow recesses of the alley. The brick pavers gave way to dirt.

Aizarg readied his grip on his staff.

Gilga pointed to the right. "It is the third entrance on your right. Enter, and then take the first door on your left."

Aizarg looked back over his shoulder. In a few more paces they would be deep enough in the alley where he could deliver a blow to Gilga's head without being seen from the street.

Aizarg turned back just in time to see Gilga's fist slam into his face.

22. The Fisherman's Farewell

The Fisherman's Farewell was performed by the Lo wives the night before their husbands departed on the arduous winter fishing expedition. When autumn's color gave way to the gray winds, the giant trout migrated from the shallows to the deep waters beyond the Silt Flats. The expedition could last weeks and often netted a bountiful catch, but the winter sea was dangerous and fisherman often never returned. It was so perilous that, if the summer fishing season was plentiful, a wise sco-lo-ti wouldn't chance a winter expedition.

Two days before the expedition, the wife would fast to acknowledge her husband's sacrifice and the consequences if he should fail. She prepared a feast the night before her man's departure, but she would not eat during the ceremony. Instead, she fed her husband by hand until he could eat no more.

The spirit of the Fisherman's Farewell was captured in the Lo chant, "Remember", recited by the wife at the conclusion of the ceremony. The chant was meant to nourish her man's spirit and give him strength for the long journey ahead. More importantly, it was a way to say goodbye.

The Chronicle of Fu Xi

***

Setenay woke with a gasp. "Aizarg!"

"Do not be afraid. I am here, old mother." Ghalen reached under the blanket and held her hand. He'd been sitting next to her since the rest of the party departed.

She looked about as if she didn't know where she was. Finally, her eyes focused on Ghalen. The way she looked frightened him. Her cheeks were sunken and dark circles surrounded her eyes. Her breath carried a slight wheeze.

"Are you all right?" he asked.

"Yes. It was just a dream...it has passed." She reached up and caressed his cheek. "Ghalen, I need you to do something for me."

"Anything."

"Build me a fire; a great, roaring fire."

Ghalen cautiously looked over his shoulder. They were on the highest ground on this side of the river. A fire could be seen for miles.

As if she understood his thoughts, Setenay touched his arm. "Trust me."

"Yes, I will see to it." Ghalen pulled away to start the fire, but she held his arm.

"And Ghalen...if there is enough wood, can you fashion a spit?"

"Yes, old mother." He pulled away, but she pulled him back again.

"If you can, try to find a good, flat cooking stone."

He patted her hand. "Yes, old mother. I will see what I can do." Ghalen leaned in. "What am I cooking?"

Setenay winced as she pulled herself up on her elbows, took a deep breath and exhaled. The wheezing didn't go away. "You are not cooking anything. I am."

"Are you up to it, old mother?" he asked, doubtful of her ability to even stand.

"I am. I have one more request, Ghalen. Do not call me 'old mother' anymore. I know it is proper and you do it out of respect, but my name was Setenay long before my hair turned white and my skin turned to leather. It will please me to hear my name from your lips."

"So be it...Setenay."

In a few minutes, Ghalen gathered all the available wood from beside the old fire pits and placed them in a large pile.

Setenay managed to stand, though she swayed unsteadily. He rushed over to help her, but she shooed him away.

"I am fine. Make the fire."

Ghalen watched her out of the corner of his eye as he worked. She stood on the edge of the hill, her arms wrapped tightly around her shoulders, gazing at Hur-ar with a haunted expression. He worried she would lose control again. Without Aizarg and Sarah here to help he wasn't sure how to handle it.

"When did they leave?" Setenay asked, not taking her eyes off the city.

"Not long after your..." Ghalen paused to carefully consider his words. "...after you passed out. Aizarg and Sarah went into the valley and the rest went east searching for Ba-lok."

Ghalen motioned to the wood pile. "We are fortunate. If we are careful there is enough wood for three days."

Setenay considered the wood pile. "Burn it all," she calmly said, returning her gaze to the city. "We will not be here for three days and I do not wish to be cold."

Ghalen opened his mouth to protest, but thought better of it and threw another pile of sticks onto the fire. Soon, he fashioned a spit and even managed to find a fairly flat, broad rock to serve as a cooking stone.

He looked up to see Setenay inspecting the fire. She jiggled the spit to test its sturdiness and poked the cooking stone, judging its quality. Her demeanor dramatically changed from only a few minutes ago. The old Setenay returned, complete with the twinkle in her eye.

"Yes, that is a fine fire. Now, get up."

"What?"

"Yes, you heard me, get up!" She clapped her hands rapidly to accentuate her point. Setenay took his hand and led him with authority to the upwind side of the fire. "Stand here, don't move." He obeyed, not knowing what else to do. She unfurled her blanket at his feet and then folded his blanket into a thick square and placed it against his pack as a crude backrest.

"Sit," she commanded

Ghalen felt ashamed. It was Setenay who should be sitting in front of the fire, not him. "Please, Setenay, let me..."

"Sit," she repeated stubbornly. He searched Setenay's eyes, trying to see behind her weathered mask.

"All right, I will sit down." Ghalen relented, and that seemed to make her feel better.

At first, he felt guilty for enjoying the way the roaring fire felt against his skin. As the shadows lengthened, Ghalen finally relaxed and let the flickering light hypnotize him. He plucked a piece of long, dry grass and put it between his teeth and idly twisted another between his fingers. For a moment, he was home, perhaps in shore camp after a hunt. He almost smelled the sea and heard the water lapping against the shore. Setenay hummed a happy tune as she set her pack down and removed bundles of food wrapped in leaves, bound with leather strips.

A man content with the simple pleasures of fishing and hunting, Ghalen often heard the whispers about what a good sco-lo-ti he would be, but he had no ambition to fill his older brother's role in the Turtle Clan. While he didn't want to be a sco-lo-ti, he desired a wife worthy of a sco-lo-ti.

Perhaps that is why he declined all attempts to marry him off. The girls of his arun-ki were pretty maids all, but they were just girls. Even across the Lo nation he couldn't find the woman of his dreams.

Sarah...now that is a woman! Even though he respected her, Ghalen found no desire in his heart for Sarah. She loved Ood-i and Ghalen sensed she had another destiny to fulfill.

His future wife must have a fire in her soul, the strength of the sea in her flesh, and the wisdom of a goddess in her heart. These were all the traits which made a strong patesi-le.

Patesi-le are only married to sco-lo-ti.

Ghalen sighed and threw the mangled piece of grass into the fire.

He looked up and caught Setenay staring at him with a sad, sweet smile.

"It won't take me long to prepare the meal," she said and went back to work.

My wife will have to be like her. He knew he harbored a fool's hope. A woman like Setenay came along once in a generation. The closest the Lo had come to producing a patesi-le like her was Aizarg's wife, Atamoda.

Over the next few minutes she had all of her food, a week's worth of dried fish and crushed wild grain, laid out in an orderly row. She untied the bundled leaves to reveal dried brine salt, crushed plant roots, and dried yellow marsh peppers. One of the leaves contained several strips of dried pig fat, which she tossed onto the cooking stone. It sizzled and began to melt over the rock.

In rapid succession, she sprinkled the grain and crushed the spices into the sizzling fat and then carefully laid a third of her fish ration over the concoction. The dried fish began to swell with the fat and turn delightfully brown. The fat and crushed grain stewed into a thick, brown sauce, which she smeared over the top of the fish.

"It smells so good." Ghalen's mouth watered and his stomach grumbled.

She smiled warmly and softly touched his knee. "I hope you enjoy it. I'm the best cook in the Minnow Clan."

Ghalen believed it. Having a wife that could cook was important, too. He noticed how much food she cooked and would make sure he replaced her rations from his supply.

With two sticks, Setenay lifted the fish off the cooking stone and, one by one, laid them over the spit where they would slowly finish cooking. She reached down and picked up the rest of her food, and instead of putting it into her bag, she quickly placed it all on the cooking stone.

Ghalen bolted upright. "Setenay! What are you doing? That is all your food!"

"Yes," she said as she stirred the sauce over the fresh strips.

"Once you cook them they have to be eaten or they will spoil by morning. Take them off!" He tried to pick them off the rock.

She slapped his hand. "Let them be."

Ghalen leaned forward. "You won't have enough food for the journey home."

She continued cooking, but her unspoken words were clear to Ghalen.

"Don't think that way!" Ghalen scolded her. "You will make it home, all of us will."

Setenay gently pushed him backward into his lounging position. She crawled next to him and knelt with her hands on her thighs. Large tears formed under her baggy eyes and rolled down her cheeks, but Setenay spoke softly and patiently.

"Tomorrow we will talk of the needs of the flesh and of what we can or cannot do with the time we have. Tonight, it is the spirit that needs nourishment. It is my spirit that needs tending, Ghalen."

Crushing sadness washed over Ghalen at the realization of what Setenay was about to do.

She's performing the Fisherman's Farewell.

Ghalen tenderly wiped the tears from her face, leaned back, and surrendered to her will.

***

As the sun died in the west, Setenay tended to her fisherman as Lo women had for generations. She knelt next to him and fed him by hand until the food and sunlight were gone.

Setenay pulled a blanket over the both of them. Without hesitation Ghalen pulled her close and put his arm around her. Soon, laughter rolled down the hillside and into the night. They spoke of the small things in life, of the everyday, as if tomorrow was just another day. She spoke of her late husband, about her children, and of a hundred things about her clan and the Lo she hoped would never be forgotten.

As the night wore on her tone became more subdued and she told him secret things, knowledge only reserved for a sco-lo-ti...for an Uros. Ghalen listened quietly. She needed him to listen. She needed him to remember. Mostly, she needed this moment to last forever.

One subject Setenay didn't speak of was her vision. Tomorrow fast approached and that thought threatened to drag her into madness. Setenay the woman wanted to bury her head into Ghalen's chest and cry like a child, hoping against hope tomorrow would never come. Setenay the venerable patesi-le was simply thankful for the fire, the blanket and the man next to her.

She snuggled closer to him under the blanket, put her head on his chest and listened to his heartbeat. Ghalen reminded her so much of her late husband. He even smelled like him. She found his hand and she squeezed as tightly as her arthritic joints permitted.

The fire slowly faded and the noose of darkness tightened around them.

I have tonight.

Ghalen's breathing became more regular. She looked up and saw his eyes were closed.

"The ceremony isn't over," she whispered, but he was already fast asleep.

Setenay looked upon Ghalen's tranquil face like a maiden adores her husband on their wedding night. She lightly kissed him on the lips.

As Ghalen slept, sadness swept over Setenay. As an unmarried man, he never heard the chant spoken in love.

And she knew he probably never would.

"Remember, my love..." Setenay began the chant that completed the ceremony.

"When the waves strike hard against the bow, let the memory of my soft embrace protect you,

"When the wind blows cold against your skin, let the memory of our hearth warm you.

"In the endless silence of night, let the echo of our children's laughter fill you with joy,

"In the starless darkness, remember the light in my eyes and let it guide you.

"When your weary arms sag and your shoulders ache, let the memory of my strength inspire you,

"If your beautiful solitude turns to loneliness, remember my love and let it fill you with hope.

"When you are adrift in the vast emptiness do not despair, remember your home lies beyond the waves.

"Remember me, my love."

23. The Black Fortress

"I put my faith in a stranger's voice. He told me to move, and I moved. He told me to stop and I stopped. I didn't look ahead and I didn't look behind. The world ended with his voice and my fingertips. That is the true meaning of faith, of trust. I had to believe and hold on for only a few minutes.

"The Narim had been holding on for centuries." - Conversations with the Uros.

The Chronicle of Fu Xi

***

The screaming burned into Aizarg's throbbing head.

He commanded his eyes open, but only one obeyed. The blurry scene beyond came into focus. His left cheek lay in the dirt as blood pooled in the dust before him.

Sarah!

Gilga's armor and sword belt were strewn across the dim alley and his quilted skirt hung loosely over his broad back.

He had Sarah pinned high against the wall, one hand squeezed her neck while the other tried to pry her legs apart.

Sarah fought like a cornered wildcat. She kicked, scratched, and slapped with all her fury, but her struggles only excited him further.

"I could turn you around and take you, bitch, but then I wouldn't be able to enjoy that white hair spilling over your pretty face!" Gilga unleashed a hard backslap across Sarah's face. She slumped and ceased struggling.

Aizarg struggled to pull himself on one elbow, but his vision swam and nausea overwhelmed him. He vomited into the dust and collapsed again.

Gilga looked over his shoulder. "Ah, the slaver awakens, if that's what you really are." He spat on Aizarg. "I've seen every manner of snake slither through my gates. You do not mask your intentions very well, outlander. I saw the treachery on your face."

Gilga's smiled like the snarl of a swamp fox.

"Your arrival was most fortunate. I will deliver you to the commander as a Scythian spy, permitted to enter the gates by none other than my watch captain himself, and in front of a dozen fellow warriors, no less! I've even placed a Scythian knife in your pack next to the captain's gold to seal your doom."

Gilga leaned his head back and smiled as if savoring his victory to come. He lifted Sarah's body higher, hiked her dress and began to work his way between her legs.

"First, I'll enjoy my new slave. She will fetch a glorious price on the block."

Aizarg saw his staff and pack lying within arm's reach. He reached out, grasped the staff, and struggled to stand. Another wave of dizziness incapacitated him and he collapsed.

Sarah cried out with a quick gasp of pain as Gilga found his mark. Aizarg clenched his eyes shut.

I failed.

A small, dirty foot materialized next to Aizarg's face. A little hand snatched his pack. In quick succession, waves of feet silently tread between the Gilga and Aizarg. Several stooped to snatch Gilga's armor and weapons before scurrying into the shadows.

Gilga, too engrossed in violating Sarah's limp body, didn't notice the newcomers. Sarah stared into nothingness, hiding in her thoughts until Gilga finished his vile deed.

Another pair of feet landed next to Aizarg's head. A child's hand reached down for his staff, but suddenly pulled away with a yelp.

Gilga snapped around at the sound. "Be gone or I'll gut the lot of you!" He dropped Sarah and reached for his sword, but it was gone. Shock and rage flashed across the warrior's face as he simultaneously tried to close his robe and chase the children.

A shadow darted from Gilga's left and leapt onto the warrior's back. Gilga stumbled backward and reached over his shoulder, trying to pull the assailant off. He spun and danced around, unable to shake his attacker. In a flash, a hand blurred under Gilga's beard and briefly exposed his thickly corded neck. Like a cat, the attacker slid off and lightly landed behind the warrior.

Gilga calmly looked down at Aizarg for a long moment. His naked front, including his still excited member, fully exposed as blood poured from under his beard like a waterfall. It painted his body bright red and loudly splattered into the dust. Gilga's eyes rolled into the back of his head and he dropped like a felled tree.

Now Aizarg saw the attacker in full. It was the boy who followed them through the city. He wore a loin cloth and had long, sandy brown hair. His gray eyes were piercing and cold.

No one that young should be capable of such coldness.

The killer dispassionately turned to Sarah, the bloody bronze knife still in his hands.

Aizarg struggled to stand yet again, but an unseen hand snatched back his head. A knee dug into his back and a cold blade kissed his throat. The boy turned to Aizarg's unseen attacker and held up his hand. The blade relaxed against Aizarg's skin.

Some of the feral children came into view and tried to steal Aizarg's staff, but cried out at the slightest touch. One child, naked, grime covered and with long, tangled hair, could not have been more than six. It shocked Aizarg how efficiently the child stripped the skirt and sandals from Gilga's bloody corpse.

Sarah recovered her senses and focused on the boy lording over her. Her forehead wrinkled for a moment and then her eyes flew wide open with astonishment.

"Ezra!" she cried and leapt to her feet. She embraced him so tightly Aizarg thought she would snap his back. He stood rigid, as if unsure what to do, then the knife slid from his grip. He slowly wrapped his arms around her waist and laid his head against her bosom. She cried and kissed the top of his head over and over like a mother might do to her child. His steely eyes softened, closed and the killer vanished.

The little boy's jaw was agape in wonder as he looked up at the embracing figures. He held Gilga's bloody skirt and sandals all bunched up in his arms like meat gleaned from a kill. Blood streaked the child's body like mud, as if he'd only been playing along the shore all day in the autumn sun.

"Ezra," the little boy said with shy tenderness. "Your sister is pretty!"

***

Sarah convinced her brother not to slit Aizarg's throat, but that was as far as their conversation progressed before Ezra cut her off.

"Sarah, there is no time to talk. It's too late to hide the body, we must flee."

Aizarg's pack vanished into the hands of the feral children, payment for saving their lives. Ezra could only retrieve Aizarg's water skin before his gang scattered into the shadows like rats. If the food in his pack would feed a few of the children for another day, Aizarg was glad of it and thankful he still had his and Atamoda's li-ge around his neck.

Sarah wiped as much of the dried blood from Aizarg's face as she could. He gulped some water, which seemed to abate some of the dizziness.

With his staff in one hand and Sarah supporting the other arm, Aizarg followed Ezra deeper into the alley and the depths of Hur-ar.

***

They stumbled through Hur-ar's dark heart as fast as Aizarg's wobbly legs permitted. He tried to retain some sense of direction, but as they twisted and turned through the maze of narrow alleys, Aizarg became hopelessly disoriented. Daylight still peaked between the rooftops, but he sensed nightfall approaching.

Sarah supported much of his weight without complaint, but Aizarg wondered if she was all right. The vision of her rape burned in his mind.

She's already hidden that suffering away in the secret place she hides all her pain.

Ezra halted and held up his hand. He looked about to make sure they were alone. The empty alley reeked of sewage. Ahead, the alley opened to daylight. Aizarg saw what looked like a cliff just beyond and deduced they were near the edge of the city.

"Rest, but only for a few moments," Ezra whispered.

Sarah slowly helped Aizarg to the ground and gave him the water skin.

"Ezra, where are we?" Sarah asked.

Ezra knelt next to them and pointed to the daylight. "We will come out at the base of the Cliff Road. The way to the

Black Fortress is unguarded and perhaps the last place they'll look for us." He looked around in the alley. "But it won't be long before the guards start searching the backstreets and asking questions.

"You and your..." Ezra gave Aizarg a quizzical glance, "...*companion* were seen with the warrior. When his body is discovered, they will be looking for you. The city guard is relentless enough without vengeance spurring them on. With an outlander involved, they will seal the front of the city first."

Aizarg always thought Sarah well-spoken, especially for a slave. This man-child was also well spoken, perhaps more so than his older sister. Definitely more than Aizarg would have expected of a street beggar.

Ezra looked to the cliff and his voice became hard. "Hiding in the shadows of the Black Fortress might buy us a day, after that I might be able to make other arrangements; but ultimately, there is no safe place for you. No one will take you in and there will be a bounty for your heads. It's likely my own gang will betray me for such a bounty. You are already dead, as am I."

Aizarg knew the cruel fires of Hur-ar had refined Ezra into a cunning leader.

"Then why did you help us?" Aizarg asked.

"Sarah is my only family. I thought I had lost her once, I will not lose her again." He smiled and touched her hair. "I couldn't believe it was really you. I recognized you, even with this."

Sarah stroked his cheek. "You are a prayer answered."

Ezra looked Aizarg up and down suspiciously. "Who is this 'master,' that you would spare his life?"

Sarah smiled mischievously. "He's not my master. He's my father."

Ezra frowned.

Sarah smiled adoringly at Aizarg and held his hand. "It's a long story, Ezra. I will tell you everything as we climb the Cliff Road." She studied Aizarg's face and frowned.

"The warrior certainly landed a solid blow, but I don't think your nose is broken. Most of your wounds came from your fall." She took his water skin, poured a few drops onto the corner of his kaffiya, and then lightly dabbed the cuts on his face. "I'll tend your wounds properly when we get to the top."

The coldness returned to Ezra's face. He stood and turned away. "Mother is dead."

Sarah winced, but kept dabbing Aizarg's face. "How?" Sarah said.

"Not long after Father sold you off, he made Ashtoreth his First Wife. Mother was dead within a week." Ezra swallowed hard, the steely façade cracked ever so slightly. "Our 'dear' half-brother, Bal-eeb, tried to slit my throat, but I escaped. The gutters of Hur-ar are my home now. Now Father is dead and Ashtoreth is a wealthy widow. They call her the Snake of Hur-ar. She'd plotted it all along. With Father's gold, Ashtoreth bought Bal-eeb a command in the city guard."

"Sarah, I'm sorry," Aizarg whispered.

"I saw Bal-eeb at the gate, though thankfully he did not recognize me." Sarah fought for composure. "Ezra only confirmed what I already knew in my heart. I shall mourn for my mother and father later. We must go."

Ezra turned to them and bit his lower lip for control, just like Sarah. Aizarg saw the wound still fresh in Ezra's heart.

They look so much alike.

"The Cliff Road will be deserted," Ezra said. "But the king's traders will attempt another exchange with the Narim tomorrow. They'll bring a host of guards to protect the wagons. We'll have to depart the cliff before dawn and slip into the sewers. In the sewers we risk discovery by other thieves, who could either kill or betray us."

"Why isn't the Cliff Road guarded?" Aizarg asked.

Ezra shrugged, as if the answer were simple. "The road is a dead end. No one fears the Narim, and they need no protection. The poor don't go up there because there is no water or shelter."

"The Cliff Road is perfect," Sarah said as she stood up. "Because that is where we want to go. We are here to see the Narim, brother."

Ezra shook his head. "The Narim? I don't understand."

"We will tell you as we climb." Sarah helped Aizarg to his feet. "We must devise a plan to sneak into the traders' wagons and hope the Narim will open the outer gate tomorrow. Father, can you walk without help?"

Aizarg nodded. They turned to Ezra, who hadn't budged. He eyed them as if trying to make a decision.

"What is it, Ezra?" Sarah asked.

"I know a way into the Black Fortress."

***

Aizarg hugged the side of the road away from the drop-off and tried not to look down. Each time he glanced over the precipice, he became light-headed. They were only halfway up the cliff and he saw the entire city spread out before him. Aizarg peered into the heart of the grand market where the people milling about appeared as insignificant as ants.

Is this how the gods see all of us?

Aizarg saw clearly across the Hur Valley where the Kupar Bridge and the hills beyond stood as vanguards against the immense grasslands stretching west under the sunset.

Could I climb but a little higher, perhaps I could see the Great Sea.

Switchback after agonizing switchback they climbed. Aizarg's thighs burned and his lungs screamed. Sarah seemed to breathe heavier than normal, but Ezra wasn't even sweating.

"The air!" Aizarg took heaving gulps, but couldn't seem to fill his lungs. "It is difficult to breathe."

Ezra smiled at Aizarg for the first time. "It takes a while for an outlander to get used to it."

The late afternoon grew cooler even in the face of a strong setting sun. They approached the level of the tree line, and above that, the white blanket Sarah called snow. He so badly wanted to touch it. Was it soft? Was it cold? His imagination ran wild.

Too bad I don't have my pack. He wanted to stuff some snow inside his pack to show his family.

It wasn't just the thin, nippy air or the arduous climb that occupied his mind. Aizarg felt the weight of the Black Fortress pressing down on him.

As they climbed, Sarah told Ezra about how she came to know Aizarg. With each new turn of her tale, Ezra looked back at Aizarg in astonishment.

"Now you know our tale, brother. Tell us how we can get into the Black Fortress."

"It will be easier to show you," Ezra said.

***

The sun almost touched the western horizon when they reached the top. Aizarg bent over with his hands on his knees and tried to catch his breath, partly from exhaustion, and partly from the immensity of the Black Fortress.

"I have never seen it so close," Sarah whispered.

The Cliff Road emerged in the center of a ledge running the length of the wall. The wall was made of whole Kupar logs driven into the stone ledge, so tightly spaced there wasn't room for even a knife between them. The titanic logs were bound together with heavy iron bands, much as they were on the Kupar Bridge. This wall, black as night, stood three times higher than the city wall.

The gate stood in the center of the wall, indistinguishable except for a large bronze bell affixed to its surface with two heavy wooden crosspieces.

What are the Narim trying to keep out?

The ledge ran the length of the wall in both directions for at least two hundred feet. A dozen men could stand shoulder-to-shoulder on the ledge from the wall to the cliff. Crushed gray stone covered the ledge, making the wall appear even blacker. At the ends it tapered and vanished where the wall and cliff joined. There, it plummeted to the city thousands of feet below.

Legs aching, Aizarg hobbled to the gate and touched it. He pulled his hand back and examined the sticky, black substance covering his fingers.

Aizarg turned to Sarah and Ezra. "I've seen this before. I can't remember where, but I'm sure of it."

Sarah touched the wall with one finger and rubbed the substance between her fingers.

"The strange, black substance sometimes seeps over the wall," Ezra said. "Though no one knows what it is, but it gives the Black Fortress its name."

Sarah sniffed it. "It has a strong smell, like pine trees."

"It reminds me of the tree resin we use to seal our reed boats, but this is much darker and thicker."

"Why would the Narim put it on their wall?" Sarah asked.

"Maybe to preserve the wood, to keep it from rotting or keep termites out," Aizarg shrugged.

He turned to Ezra. "Show us how to get in."

***

They stood where the southern ledge terminated at an abyssal drop off. One more step and they would drop to the city below.

Aizarg peeked over the ledge, but snatched himself back. "You climbed out *there*?" Aizarg couldn't fathom anyone being able to hold on to the sheer cliff face.

"It was either that or get shot. I didn't think the guards would pursue me all the way up here. Usually, they get winded and abandon their pursuit halfway up." Ezra beamed with pride and continued. "They are starting to know my name. I'm a damn good thief and I suspect there's a bounty on my head."

Sarah considered the rock face. "I think I see where you gripped the rock and placed your toes." She pointed. "There...there...and there."

Aizarg squinted, but only saw smooth, vertical rock.

"That's right," Ezra nodded. "Can you still climb?"

Sarah grinned mischievously. It was easy for Aizarg to forget she was raped only a couple of hours ago.

"I haven't climbed since Father sold me, but that only means I might be *slightly* better than you now."

"You are as deluded as ever," Ezra teased and poked at her.

Aizarg kept safely away from the edge, but felt like he would plummet to his death if he got so much as one inch closer. His knees shook. He flattened his back against the cliff and fought the vertigo.

Mountains are no place for a fisherman.

He swallowed hard, trying to hide his fear. "You crawled out there and they pursued you?"

"No, they stood where we are now and fired arrows at me. You can still see where the arrows scraped the rock. I was barely able to slip around the corner in time. That's when I found the small ledge. You can't see it from here, but it's actually easy to reach and big enough for the three of us. I was going to wait until they grew tired, but then I had a plan." Ezra cupped his hands and shouted, "Ahhhhhhhh...!" as if he were falling. "They fell for it and I heard them laugh and leave. I thought it might be a trick, so I sat down to wait. That's when I saw the crack.

"I thought it was just a shallow indentation, but then I saw daylight shining through. I crawled in and realized it led inside the Black Fortress. That's when I heard voices and turned around as fast as I could."

"Did you see anything?" Aizarg asked.

He shook his head. "The Black Fortress is death."

He's not afraid to crawl across the cliff like an insect on a wall, but he wouldn't go inside the Black Fortress?

Sarah looked to the setting sun. "We must go now, or wait until morning. Uros?"

Aizarg stared at the cliff, one hand gripping the rock face, one clenching his staff.

"Father, are you all right?"

"I can't do this, Sarah," he blurted, the fear gushing out all at once. "I can't. Climbing out there is impossible. I will fall."

"You must do it!"

"I cannot!" Aizarg closed his eyes, unable to look at the chasm. Fear paralyzed him in a way he'd never experienced.

I must be under an evil spell. Oh, if only Setenay were here to ward it off.

Sarah ran her hands through his hair.

"Open your eyes," Sarah said softly but firmly.

"I cannot smell the sea!"

"Father!"

Aizarg's eyes snapped open. Only inches from his face, Sarah's eyes bore into his.

"I cannot swim, but I went into that icy river anyway, didn't I? You and Ghalen and Okta, I knew you would not let me drown. I trusted you. Now, trust me." She motioned to Ezra. "To us, these mountains are like water and climbing comes as naturally as swimming."

She lowered her voice, and for a moment, Sarah had some of Ezra's iron in her voice. "If you don't do this, Atamoda and your children will die. Our people will die. Hope is in there, death is out here. If you are ready to accept that, then forget they once called you Uros and throw yourself off the cliff now."

Aizarg took a deep breath. Fear gave way to shame, and courage found a toe hold in Aizarg's spirit.

"I will try."

"Good." Sarah patted his chest. "Ezra will go first. I will go last. He will tell you exactly where to place your feet and hands, just do what he does. Whatever you do, do not look down."

Don't look down...I think I can do that.

Ezra grabbed Aizarg's staff. Aizarg started to pull it back, fearing it would burn Ezra, but the boy continued to grasp the shaft. "Give me your staff. I will carry it on my back. I promise, I will not drop it."

Aizarg opened his mouth, but thought better of it. He began to think the staff had a mind of its own.

The boy reached into his ragged loincloth, and from some hidden pouch, pulled out a length of leather string. Ezra secured one end around the base of the orb. He then created a wide loop and placed it over his neck so the staff would dangle over his back.

"Are we ready?" Ezra asked.

"Father?"

Aizarg nodded and swallowed hard, but didn't have any spit.

Ezra gracefully pivoted and stepped off the ledge. His hands found niches and bumps Aizarg didn't notice before. Without hesitation, the boy hugged the cliff and slid to the right.

He makes it look so easy.

"You are much taller than me. You will have no problem reaching the handholds." Ezra nodded enthusiastically. "It will be easier for you."

Sarah gently nudged him to the edge. "Remember, don't look down," she whispered.

"Put your hand right here, where mine is," Ezra said encouragingly. "Same with my foot."

Aizarg felt weak and his legs shook uncontrollably.

"Look at me, Aizarg. Look at my eyes." Ezra's tone reminded Aizarg of a father teaching his children to swim. A sudden calmness swept over him.

"Good. Look at my hand, reach out and touch it."

Aizarg reached out, placed his hand next to Ezra's and felt for the grip.

"Now, your right foot, place it where my left foot is now. Don't look beyond my foot and don't worry. I'll move it in time."

Aizarg obeyed, pressing himself as close to the rock face as he could.

"Relax," Ezra said. "If you squeeze against the cliff any tighter you're going to crush your shadow."

The setting sun warmed the stone and it felt good. The trembling in Aizarg's legs lessened.

"Good. Now put your left foot in the same footing. Don't worry, its large enough even for your big feet." Aizarg gave Ezra a sharp look and the man-child grinned back.

Aizarg shifted his left foot away from the ledge and placed it in the narrow crack. With a death grip on an inch of rock and a mile of faith, Aizarg clung to the mountainside. His panic fell away as Ezra's soothing, calm voice guided him from cranny to nook, crack to bump.

"Look at me," Ezra commanded. He had Sarah's mischievous grin and Aizarg couldn't help smiling back. "What?"

"What am I supposed to call you? Aizarg or Uros or sco-yo...*sco-po-tee*?"

Aizarg smiled with his forehead against the rock. "Ezra, you can call me whatever you want if it will get me safely off this cliff."

"That's reasonable." Ezra giggled. "Let go."

Aizarg's fear suddenly returned.

"Trust me." Ezra winked at the Uros of the Lo Nation.

Is this kind, sympathetic soul the same person who slit Gilga's throat ear to ear?

Aizarg closed his eyes, held his breath and let go.

Nothing happened.

Sarah's voice came from his left, "Open your eyes and look at your feet."

Aizarg stood on a narrow ledge, just big enough for his feet to fully fit lengthwise. He looked back at Sarah beaming at him. Behind her, he no longer saw the Black Fortress. They had slid completely around the corner.

"You did it!" Sarah beamed.

"Yes...yes I did!" Aizarg clasped Ezra's hand. "Thank you, friend."

Ezra grasped his hand tightly, as a man would. "This place you come from, the sea. Will you take me?"

Aizarg nodded, overcome with a wave of joy. "You will be welcome among my people."

"The sun is almost down," Sarah said. "We must hurry." She carefully knelt down, holding onto the rock face. "Is this it?" She pointed to a vertical crack in the cliff, perhaps three feet high and two feet wide.

"Yes," Ezra said. "It's well hidden from the city below and the Black Gate. We might be the only ones who know of its existence."

Aizarg watched the last of the sun slip behind the western side of the valley. On top of the far western hills he thought he saw a flicker, like a bonfire on the shore seen from far out to sea. His courage returned, greater than before.

Aizarg carefully knelt down and reached into the crack.

"Will I fit, Ezra?"

"Easily. It's not very far."

"Good. Thank you, Ezra, but I ask you to go no farther. Should I meet my doom in there, I do not want you to share it."

Ezra nodded and gave Aizarg his staff. "I will wait here."

"Ezra." Sarah touched his hand. "Wait as long as you can. If we do not emerge, leave the city and travel beyond the bridge. Our party is camped there. Find a man named Okta and tell him what happened."

Aizarg put his hand on Sarah's shoulder. "You don't have to come with me. I think this part of the journey is mine to make alone."

"It is my journey, too. The only way home is forward."

Aizarg kissed her on the forehead and then slid into the crack and passed into the Kingdom of the Narim.

24. The Great Hall Of The Narim

Truth brings liberation, but seldom happiness. For both the Lo and the Narim, the truth was terrifying.

The Chronicle of Fu Xi

***

The passage narrowed, but Aizarg had no trouble wriggling through. He spotted a dim light ahead.

Ezra was right, it isn't very far.

"I am right behind you," Sarah whispered.

They emerged into cool twilight at the base of a narrow and steep defile, which widened a few yards ahead.

"Are you ready, daughter?"

"Hold my hand and I will not be afraid."

Hand-in-hand, they climbed the defile, careful not to slip on the loose shale. They came to the base of a huge pile of scrap wood that completely blocked the mouth of the defile.

Aizarg picked up one of the chunks of wood. It had been hacked with an axe and looked very old.

"It's kupar," Sarah said.

Aizarg dropped it and examined the pile. "We'll go left, against the cliff, where the pile is the lowest. We must be careful not to twist an ankle or break a leg."

Using his staff to steady himself, Aizarg started up first. He almost reached the top when something caught his eye, the last thing he expected to find here. He picked it up and examined it.

"What is it?" Sarah asked.

He held up the half-rotted reed bag for her to see. "It's a Lo sack. Ba-lok's clan trade with the Hur-po."

Sarah shrugged. "The king's traders likely use them to pack the goods they send through the Black Gate."

Aizarg dropped the sack and resumed climbing, but stopped again at the sound of approaching footsteps from the other side of the wood pile.

"Do you hear that?" he whispered. "Something is coming!" A moment later a head materialized over the crest, silhouetted in the dusky twilight.

Aizarg almost laughed as the goat bleated and proceeded to munch on the discarded sack.

Aizarg's smile faded. "This is the first animal I've seen since the Valley of the Beasts."

As they rounded the top of the wood pile, any doubts Aizarg had about the divinity of the Narim melted away as they gazed into the heart of the Black Fortress. Tears of awe streamed down his face.

A mountain within a mountain.

"The Great Hall of the Narim!" Sarah whispered.

The enormous structure overwhelmed his senses. Blacker than the pit of the sea, the titanic Great Hall rivaled the mountains. The rectangular hall almost reached the other side of the box-like compound, over 500 feet away and easily exceeded 150 feet wide. Taller than ten men it vaulted as high as the surrounding cliffs. It defied the dominion of heaven, as if daring the gods to strike it down.

It's larger than my Arun-ki! It would hold the entire Lo nation.

Aizarg and Sarah climbed down the wood pile to the southern corner of the compound, next to the black wall. The goat followed.

Sarah pointed to the center of the Great Hall, opposite the Black Gate, and whispered, "The way into the Great Hall." A wide walkway led from the ground to a giant doorway halfway up the wall. The entrance stood easily twenty feet across and thirty feet high. Blackness waited beyond. "It must be as the legends say, they are giants."

Sarah shivered and drew close to Aizarg. Her voice cracked. "I don't see anyone. Should we call out to them?"

"Not yet. I want to look around for a moment."

The inside of the black wall was strikingly different from the outside. Thousands of stuffed reed bags formed a giant ramp. A man could easily scale it and look down on the cliff and Hur-ar. The ramp filled most of the gap between the wall and the Great Hall. The solitary break in the ramp opened near the wall's center, about two hundred feet away. The ramp parted, forming an enclave to the outer gate. An inner gate, half the size of the outer wall, enclosed the enclave. Cabled ropes, like those on the Kupar Bridge, were strung through a series of blocks and pulleys. The rigging ran to wooden towers on either side of the enclave.

Aizarg knew the enclave must be where the kings' traders rolled in their wagons. Using the ropes and pulleys, the Narim manipulated the inner and outer gates.

It's not unlike the rigging on a sail, only on a god's scale.

Sarah knelt down next to the ramp and examined one of the sacks. She fingered a tear in the material. "These are your people's sacks. They are full of dirt." She shook her head. "Why would they build this?"

Aizarg put his hands on his hips, took a deep breath and slowly released it. "One can quickly run up this ramp and defend any portion of the wall. From up there, a defender could pour arrows, spears or rocks down on any enemy."

"The Narim have no enemies," Sarah said.

"They must think they do." Aizarg craned his head back and examined the wall and followed it until it met the cliff. There, high above their heads, a large cave opened into the cliff. A narrow walkway spanned the distance from the cave to the top of the hall.

Is that where they enter the earth to battle the giants?

"I want to examine the hall closer." Aizarg took her hand and led her away from the wall. "After that, we will approach the entrance and summon the Narim and hope they will be merciful."

The goat followed.

A thin veil of fog hung near the top of the giant hall. The silence unnerved Aizarg. Sarah felt it, too. "I don't know why, but it feels like this place is *waiting* for something."

Aizarg sniffed the air and realized the fog was actually wood smoke. His stomach suddenly growled at the smell of roasting meat. He looked around for the source and spotted something he'd missed before.

"Look!" He pointed to the far end of the hall, where a small stone cottage nestled against the opposite cliff. A warm, dim light glowed through a window and a tendril of smoke rose from chimney.

"Someone lives there!" Sarah exclaimed. "Maybe they serve the Narim. Should we approach them and ask for help?"

"Yes, but first I want to see the hall up close, before it's too dark."

With a trembling hand, Aizarg reached out and touched the hall. The individual boards, running left to right, were expertly joined with what looked like small circles of metal. The same black resin that coated the outer wall also covered the hall. This close the piney odor overpowered the smell of food.

He held his palm out to Sarah. "I dreamt this! The night before the ice mist, I dreamt this!" Aizarg rubbed the thick, black substance in his hand and looked at the ramp leading into the hall.

Sarah searched his face. "What is it, Father?"

"Something eludes me. It stands naked before me, but I cannot see it." The goat brushed by Aizarg and disappeared under the hall. Aizarg knelt down, put his staff on the ground, and followed the goat.

"Father?"

The narrow crawl space underneath the hall forced Aizarg to stoop. Massive wooden support beams, cut square and spaced about every twenty feet, ran the width of the floor. The ground sloped uphill from the black wall, so the supports were shimmed on his side to level the structure. Globs of sticky resin caked the ground. The goat made its way farther into the dark shadows beneath the floor, heading for the gray light on the other side. Halfway across, the goat crawled under an enormous cross beam, perpendicular to the square supports, and running the entire length of the hall.

It cannot be.

Aizarg blinked and rubbed his eyes. When he opened them he saw everything differently. A line here, a curve there, a board, a smell, a shape...all of it instantly gelled into place. Aizarg, Fisherman of the Lo, saw the truth.

He scurried from underneath the hall as if he were afraid it would suddenly crush him. He gasped for breath, trying to grapple with the reality suddenly forced upon him. Aizarg flattened his back against the hall, like he had against the cliff with Ezra. But it was too late.

Aizarg knew he'd already fallen.

Sarah grabbed his arms, trying to get him to look at her. "What did you see under there? What is wrong? Tell me!"

"I see what Setenay saw," he whispered.

Aizarg barely registered a dull *twang* the instant before something slammed him against the wall.

Sarah screamed as excruciating pain ripped through his right shoulder. He slumped, but could not fall. Aizarg turned his head and saw an arrow protruding from his shoulder, pinning him against the Hall of the Narim.

A voice drifted out of the dusk, "I think I hit one of them!"

***

Panic overwhelmed Sarah. She turned and placed her body between the voice and her father, trying to shield him.

"Please!" She shouted in the direction of the voice. "Do not hurt us! We come for help! Please!"

"Stay where you are!" the deep male voice commanded. "Take a step and I will loose another volley."

"One of them is a woman." A young female voice drifted out of the darkness.

Two forms materialized from the twilight, a tall and powerfully built man and a woman. He had a sturdy bow trained on Sarah, an arrow notched and ready to fly. The woman lingered behind him, timidly poking her head around to look.

"Who are you? How did you get in?" the man, perhaps in his late twenties, demanded. With a short beard and thick black hair, he wore a simple, motley wool robe that fell to his sandaled feet and covered wide shoulders. His powerful arms effortlessly kept the bow pulled back.

The slightly younger woman wore a similar robe, except with a long shawl partially covering her hair. Her large, doe eyes fit her timid movements.

Sarah shielded Aizarg, ready to take the next arrow. He groaned behind her.

"We seek the Narim!" Sarah begged. "Help us, please!"

He ignored her plea. "How did you get in?"

Sarah pointed to the woodpile. "There is a passageway through the cliff."

The man gritted his teeth and shook his head.

Aizarg slipped and groaned. "Aghh!" he shouted and straightened up again.

"I beg you!" Sarah didn't know what to say; only that she had to protect Aizarg.

"Look at her hair!" The woman pointed at Sarah.

The man peered at Sarah and then his eyes widened. "Get the rest," the man told the doe-eyed woman.

"But Father and your brothers are in the mine," she said.

"Then go into the mine, Zedkat!" Frustration cut through his voice. "And bring back torches."

"You know the rule on torches! Father will not allow it."

"I know Father's rules, but we need to see. I will be careful. Now hurry!"

She frowned and slipped back into the darkness.

He returned his attention to Sarah. "Are there any more of you?"

"No." She briefly thought of Ezra waiting on the ledge. "We mean no harm." Sarah examined Aizarg's wound. His eyes fluttered as he slipped in and out of consciousness. Blood soaked his clothes and dripped down his leg. "He needs help!"

The man tightened the bowstring. "He will stay exactly where he is until I say otherwise!"

Sarah's frustration grew. *Aizarg is going to die.*

Torchlights materialized from the cottage and bobbed toward them.

"Son?" a new voice called from the torches.

"Over here."

Two different women approached, one older with strong features and wispy gray hair poking from underneath her shawl, the other a young woman, tall and slender with almond eyes.

The older woman took one look at Aizarg and inhaled sharply. The crow's feet and lines around her mouth spoke of a woman just entering old age. She shot the man with the bow a stern look. "Shem, what have you done? Put that bow down this instant!" the old woman scolded. The man sighed, slowly released the tension, and pointed the bow at the ground.

"Mother!" Shem looked to the other woman, as if wanting her support. "I was protecting our home. I was enforcing the law!"

The old woman handed her torch to the younger woman and rushed to Aizarg.

Sarah thought she saw pity in her eyes. "Please," Sarah beseeched her. "He's hurt."

The old woman squinted at Aizarg's wound. "My eyes are not what they use to be, but I think he will live if we can get him down and staunch the bleeding."

"Thank you, thank you!" New hope sprung in her heart. Maybe she could get this kind woman to listen.

These are just people. Are they servants of the Narim?

"Don't thank me," the old woman said dryly. "Any mercy shown now may be taken by the law later." She took Sarah's hand and placed it against Aizarg's chest. "Hold him here and don't let him slide or shift. I will break the end of the arrow and then we will slide him straight off." She looked up at Sarah. "Do you understand?"

Sarah nodded vigorously. "Yes!"

The old woman froze, transfixed on Sarah. "Shem, bring the torch closer."

"Mother, it's too risky!"

"Bring the torch closer." The old woman spoke with a low, flat voice. Her expressionless stare locked uncomfortably on Sarah.

Shem leaned in with the torch, his eyes nervously scanning the hall. "I dare not bring it closer, mother."

The old woman reached out and touched Sarah's hair. Then she snatched off Aizarg's kaffiya. His white hair tumbled down over his bloody shoulder.

The old woman threw the kaffiya to the ground and backed away, almost tripping over Aizarg's staff. The old woman knelt down and picked it up. She cried out in pain and forcefully cast it down. The staff bounced and rolled into the shadows under the hall.

The old woman shook and blew on her hand. She stared at Sarah with ice where only moments ago dwelt pity.

"Kill them," the old woman said.

"Mother?" The man named Shem seemed genuinely shocked.

"It is the law," she said coldly.

Sarah fell to the old woman's feet. "I beg you, we came for help! We have traveled so far, do not forsake us!"

Shem hesitantly began to pull back his bow.

The woman with almond eyes whispered to the old woman, "Emzara, perhaps we should wait for Father. He might..."

"It is not Father's law, Arathka!" The old woman called Emzara snapped. "It is God's law!" She pointed at Sarah. "They are intruders and have brought death upon themselves."

Sarah didn't see hate in the Emzara's eyes. She saw fear, the same fear she saw in Aizarg moments ago.

Shem notched his arrow and pointed it at Sarah's heart. This time his arms were trembling.

"Who knows the law so well they can dispense justice so quickly?" A deep voice boomed around them and echoed off the canyon walls. Sarah looked all around, trying to find its source.

A form materialized around the voice and stepped out of the darkness. "God wrote the law in all our hearts, but it is I who dispense justice."

A Narim!

Taller than even Aizarg, he towered over them all, including the two men and two women who followed him. His hair wasn't white the way an old man's hair might be, but snow white like Sarah and Aizarg's. It flew about like a mane, his bushy beard and eyebrows equally wild.

He wore a leather apron, covered in grime and wood chips, over a bare chest and a plain, Hur-style wrap. His thick arms were like tree trunks, his mighty chest like the iron bands binding the Kupar Bridge. In his right hand he carried a massive axe made of strange, gleaming white metal. His face flushed pink as if he'd been working. His hazel eyes burned through Sarah's flesh and laid her soul bare.

Sarah bowed at his feet, her forehead to the ground. "Please, great Narim, spare us. Please, save my father. We've come seeking your help."

The white-haired man reached over and gently lowered Shem's bow, to Shem's obvious relief, and handed him his axe.

"What do we have here?" he said casually. He knelt down and lifted Sarah's chin. "What is your name, child?"

"Husband, I beg you! Do not speak to them!" Emzara hissed.

"Hush, woman! I see their hair," he chastised her. "Its color is obvious, but its meaning is not, so calm yourself." He turned his attention to the men and women gathered around them.

The torchlight cast giant black shadows against the Great Hall that seemed to surround and bear down upon Sarah and Aizarg.

"Move those torches away, or we'll have so much light the Hur-po will think the sun is rising!"

The group took a few steps back and the Narim returned his attention to Sarah.

"Look at me. What is your name, child?" he repeated.

"Sarah," she said through her tears. "I've come here with my father, Aizarg, Uros of the Lo. We seek the aid of the Narim."

"The Lo?" The Narim man said in genuine shock. "I've heard of them, but never seen one before." He stroked his beard and studied Aizarg, whose eyes were closed and head rolled over to the side.

Sarah feared this Narim, but she didn't see any malice in his eyes.

"Do the Lo know this place is forbidden?" he continued. "Did your father ask the Hur-po what happens to those who violate the Black Fortress?"

"Yes," Sarah sobbed. "Yes, we knew, but you are our only hope!"

"Hope for what? Why did you come here, knowing it would lead to your death?"

"Please, husband!" Emzara interjected. "Haven't we heard enough? The law is the law!"

The Narim turned to the old woman. "What is it you fear?"

"Them!" Her eyes flashed. "Though why, I know not." She wrung her hands. The young women surrounded her and tried to give comfort, but Emzara kept her arms tightly wrapped around her shoulders. The young men looked to one another with deep concern.

Sarah sensed their discomfort at her and Aizarg's presence. *They are afraid of us.*

The Narim held up his finger, signaling his wife to be quiet. "Sarah of the Lo, tell me why you and your father came here."

It all rushed out at once. Over the next few minutes, Sarah told them the tale of their journey. The Narim knelt before Sarah, listening intently without expression or reaction.

As she spoke, Emzara broke down and fell to her knees, sobbing. The other women supported her, but their faces were pale. Zedkat began to cry, too.

Sarah was thankful they were at least listening. Perhaps now they would help Aizarg. Every few minutes she glanced over at his motionless form and her desperation grew.

"These are signs and omens," Sarah said as she came to the end of her tale. "The animals have fled, the fish are gone! Our holy woman says the gods have abandoned the world and you hold the key to our salvation. My father has seen these omens. He can tell you more. Won't you help him?"

The Narim stood.

"Your gods did not abandon you, Sarah. They betrayed you. They have been judged by a greater power and have been found wanting. These *gods*..." he spat the word out,

"...will suffer a terrible wrath for their sins. All the world shall suffer with them. Your tale heralds this coming judgment."

Hope and dread raced through Sarah. Here were answers to their questions, and perhaps the key to their survival.

Sarah put her hands together pleadingly. "Then you can help us?"

The Narim's face turned to stone as he signaled to the men who accompanied him. "Get me a large stump off the pile and bring it here."

One of the young men leaned in and whispered, "Father, if what she said is true, can't we just let them go? Won't the law take care of itself?"

"Judgment passed here will be quick and merciful. There will be no such mercy beyond these walls."

"No!" Sarah's stomach suddenly dropped. She knew they were being condemned. She sprang to Aizarg and threw herself over him. "We've broken no law! We only wanted your help!"

The two other men dragged a flat, heavy stump into the ring of torches. The Narim took his axe from Shem and placed it next to the stump. The young women wailed and covered their faces.

Don't let it end like this!

"Please..." Aizarg called weakly.

Shem and the young woman named Arathka gently pulled her toward the stump. Sarah fought with all her strength, but they easily overpowered her. Even through her tears and terror, she saw their dejected expressions. They did not relish this task.

"Your father is suffering, and for that I am truly sorry," the Narim said as he approached Aizarg. "I also regret that we cannot help you. The law is the law. There are no answers here, only those who do God's work..." he shook his head with genuine sadness. "...and obey God's law."

"Please..." Aizarg croaked again. The Narim held one hand against his chest and snapped off the arrow with the other. Then, as carefully as possible, he slid Aizarg off the arrow. Aizarg clenched his teeth and groaned. The Narim then gently lowered Aizarg to the ground.

The Narim strode over to the stump and hefted the axe. "Bring him here," he said to the other men and motioned to Aizarg. "Take Sarah around the side so she won't have to witness this."

"No!" Sarah screamed defiantly as anger replaced fear. "If you plan to execute us, we die together. If this is what your god calls mercy, then the hell with him...and you!"

She saw the impact of her words on the Narim's face. Sarah did not know why, but suddenly she felt pity for this powerful being about to end her life. She recognized the look in his eyes.

Fate.

The old woman jumped up and snatched Sarah by the arm. "You will not talk to him that way!" She reared back to slap Sarah. The Narim gently removed his wife's grasp from Sarah's forearm. "There will be no wrath here! Let her be angry at God. She is entitled to that."

Aizarg reached up for the white-haired man. "Please..." he beseeched again. "I must know..." His voice and his strength were rapidly fading.

The Narim stepped back to Aizarg and knelt down on one knee. "Speak your last words and be at peace, man of the Lo." The Narim placed his ear near Aizarg's mouth.

Sarah couldn't hear what Aizarg said. She closed her eyes and sagged between the arms of her captors as the last of her hope drained away. Resigned to her fate, but not at peace with it, Sarah regretted not meeting her new mother or brothers. Mostly, she wanted to be in Ood-i's arms one more time.

She was also thankful Ezra did not enter the Black Fortress. *Maybe he will find happiness among the Lo.*

Sarah heard the crunch of the Narim's sandals on the gravel and knew he had stood up. *It won't be long now.* She thought of the pile of cleaved kupar wood and the Narim's mighty arms and powerful axe.

I will not suffer.

"Father?" one of the men said.

She opened her eyes. The Narim stared at the Great Hall in shock. He stumbled backwards from Aizarg and snatched a torch away from one of the men.

"Father?" the man repeated. "Are you all right?"

The Narim ignored him and strode parallel to the Great Hall. He held the torch up high and gazed up at the hall. Soon, he ran back and forth along its length, caressing the black surface with a wild expression, as if he'd never seen it before.

"Father, the torch! You are very close, be careful!" another of the men shouted.

"I see it! Why didn't I see it before?" The Narim fell to his knees and dropped the torch to the ground. "It stood before me as plain as the mountains and yet I could not see!

Emzara ran after her husband, full of concern. The man and woman holding Sarah released her and ran after Emzara. Sarah dashed to Aizarg and tried to stanch the bleeding with his kaffiya.

"Father, speak to us. You are frightening us," Shem beseeched the Narim.

"After 120 years, this stranger has shown me the very will of God!"

Emzara grabbed his face and shook him hard, tears of fear running down her face. "Tell me, Noah! Tell me God's will!"

"When God commanded us to the mountaintop," he stuttered. "He did so with the promise to deliver us from His judgment when He cleansed the world of the Fallen. I thought that is why He sent us here, so we would be safe from the deluge."

Terror flashed in the old woman's eyes. "We will not be safe up here? He will not deliver us?"

He kissed her hands and held them to his cheek. "Yes, Emzara! Yes! But this isn't merely an ark, a shelter of boards and nails, in which we will hide from the coming storm!"

Emzara shook her head. "I don't understand."

"It is a *vessel*, a mighty vessel God will lift from the mountaintop and carry away." Noah's voice boomed. "He will cover the mountains and drown the world in the doing!"

Emzara, wife of Noah, looked back at the great wooden structure with a blank stare, seeing it anew. The magnitude of the coming cataclysm dawned on her and she began to scream.

Sarah heard everything. The God of the Narim was about to flood the world and even cover her beloved mountains. There would be nowhere to run, nowhere to hide. She now shared Aizarg and Setenay's terrible vision.

Sarah placed her head against Aizarg's chest and cried.

25. Conversations With A Narim

The ark was built long before Noah laid the first chalk line. Its keel set when my mother's kind spawned a race of demigods and its planks were laid when Noah's ancestors were exiled from the Garden.

The story of the ark is the story of three fallen races: the immortal Nephilim and Narim, and the mortal Tall Men. It was for the folly of immortals that the Tall Men would suffer.

The Chronicle of Fu Xi

***

Someone kissed him. More specifically, someone repeatedly licked him, and that someone smelled very bad.

Aizarg cracked open one eye and found himself face-to-face with the goat, who only took a passing fancy with his face before she tried to eat his blanket.

"Jasmine, you infernal beast!" a strange woman's voice scolded. A woman in a gray wool robe appeared at the edge of his vision and struck the goat with a stick. "Off with you!"

The goat bleated a protest before bounding away.

Where am I? Surrounded by darkness, his foggy mind grasped for something familiar.

Sharp pain radiating from his right arm assaulted Aizarg as he reached up to rub his eyes. He winced and opened his eyes again.

Other than the pain in his shoulder, Aizarg reclined comfortably next to a roaring fire. Covered with a thick blanket, a soft straw layer provided a cushion beneath him and his head rested on a rolled blanket.

"Water," Aizarg croaked.

The woman knelt over him with a dripping gourd. She looked familiar, as if he'd seen her in a dream. Perhaps Sarah's age, she possessed a child's large, soulful eyes. She placed her hand behind his head and lifted him slightly. She held the gourd to his lips and he drank greedily.

The cold water sated his thirst and woke his memory. He pushed the gourd away and tried to speak.

"Where is Sarah?"

"You mustn't get up. I don't want you to tear the stitches." The woman slid slightly to the left and nodded in the direction of the fire. There, Sarah and Ezra lay snuggled under a blanket fast asleep.

How did he get here?

An iron tripod stood over the fire. A wonderful aroma floated up from a ceramic pot hanging from its hook.

"I am Zedkat, wife of Shem. I am a healer and tended your wounds."

Aizarg placed his left hand against his forehead and tried to remember what happened as Zedkat continued to talk.

"Please, do not be angry at my husband, he was only trying to protect us." She looked about and then leaned closer to Aizarg, her child-like eyes wide with wonder. She whispered quickly, bouncing from question to question, statement to statement, like a toddler.

"Your daughter said you are not from Hur-ar. Your face was hurt, too. Did someone hit you? I haven't seen anyone from beyond Hur-ar since I married Shem. Father Noah was building the wall back then."

Aizarg opened his mouth several times to answer, but she didn't pause long enough to give him a chance. "Did you see any of the women in Hur-ar? Do they really paint their faces? I can't imagine that. Shem says I am pretty enough without painting my face. What color do you think would look good on me? If I could paint my face one color, it would be rose red, like the sunset over the valley. I like roses, but father won't let us grow them in here. He's says there isn't enough sunlight..."

"Zedkat, that will be enough," a deep, rumbling voice chided from somewhere behind him. Zedkat lowered her head.

Aizarg rolled his head around, searching for the voice.

"Perhaps our guest is hungry. Have you offered him food between your ramblings?" the voice said.

"No, father," she raised her eyes to Aizarg. "My apologies, are you hungry?"

"Yes, I am very hungry."

She turned her back to Aizarg for a few moments and turned around holding a wooden bowl full of something steaming.

From Aizarg's right, a white haired man stepped into the firelight. Wide of chest and full, the giant of a man wore a plain grey robe similar to Zedkat's. Aizarg didn't think the young woman a Narim, but this man might be.

After being shot Aizarg remembered little, but this man's voice sounded familiar.

Zedkat helped Aizarg sit without too much discomfort. The pain in his arm prevented him from holding the bowl, so she used a wooden stick with a flat end to feed him. The simple, yet effective tool intrigued Aizarg.

A journey of wonders, great and small.

Made from some type of crushed grain with generous chunks of tender meat, Aizarg never tasted stew so rich and satisfying (though he would never tell Atamoda that).

Aizarg swallowed as fast as Zedkat spooned it. "Not so fast," she giggled. "I don't want you to get sick. Here, drink some water." Aizarg felt a light wave of nausea as the heavy, rich food hit his empty stomach.

As food and water nourished his aching limbs, memories slowly coalesced in his mind. Soon, everything came back to him.

The man with white hair sat down on a log across the fire from Aizarg. "That is my wife's lamb stew. Fortunately, you choose the Sabbath to steal into our compound and we had plenty of leftovers.

"Zedkat says the arrow passed through without hitting bone, though how, I don't know." He motioned to Aizarg's face. "Your face was in worse shape. According to the young lady, you two had a very difficult journey."

Aizarg couldn't pull his eyes off the white-haired man, even as he resumed eating, albeit slower this time. The more Aizarg looked upon this Narim, the more he doubted him a god. The lines on his face spoke of time's relentless influence.

"You were going to kill us, weren't you?" Aizarg said between bites.

"Yes. Yes, I was," the white-haired man said uncomfortably. "I am sorry, Aizarg of the Lo. God gave my people a law to live by. Sometimes, it can appear harsh, but its harshness doesn't give us license to disobey. However, you taught me an important lesson — justice should never be meted without the council of the heart." He pointed to his chest. "It is here where God's voice can always be heard."

The white-haired man leaned back, picked up a stick and poked the fire.

Aizarg sensed he'd had enough to eat. "Thank you." He held up his hand to Zedkat. "It was delicious."

"I will tell Momma Emzara. She will be pleased." Zedkat bit her lip, as if she were thinking intently about something.

"I don't think she's ever cooked for guests, at least since I've been here."

"Zedkat," the white-haired man said impatiently. "Please bring me the jug from the upper cupboard and then you can go to bed. I will take the air by the fire with our guests."

She gave the white-haired man a mildly disapproving glance, which he ignored, and hurried off.

"Who are you?" Aizarg asked.

"My name is Noah, son of Lamech." He opened his arms expansively. "You are guests in my domain."

Aizarg looked around. To his right, he saw the stone cottage in the firelight. He couldn't see the giant hall to his left, but he felt its looming presence.

The memory suddenly crystalized in Aizarg's mind. "A boat! The great hall is a boat!" Aizarg shouted.

"Shhh! You will wake everyone." Noah looked past Aizarg toward the ark. "Yes, so it is. So it is."

"Why would you build a giant boat on a mountaintop?"

Noah smiled and chuckled softly, "Because God told me to!"

Zedkat stepped back into the firelight and gave Noah a ceramic jug with a long, thin neck. She folded her arms and resumed her disapproving look. "Momma Emzara won't approve."

"Momma won't begrudge an old man something to sooth his achy back." He harrumphed. "Besides, we have guests and I have to convince them we 'Narim...'" he chuckled at the word, "...haven't forgotten the art of hospitality." Noah pulled Zedkat down and kissed her cheek. She glowed under his attention. "Go to bed, my dear."

She kissed Noah on his head and vanished into the cottage.

Aizarg knew these were not gods. *There is love here. He is a family man, obviously the patriarch of his clan.*

Noah didn't drink from the jug, but instead handed it to Aizarg. "Drink this, Aizarg of the Lo. It will take the edge off your pain. Be careful, it bites before it purrs!"

344

Aizarg took the jug with his left hand and sniffed the top. *Odorless.*

Noah grinned and motioned Aizarg to drink.

If he wanted us dead, we would be so already.

Aizarg held his breath and took a healthy swig. He swallowed quickly and almost gagged. His throat burned like fire.

Maybe I was wrong.

The pain quickly subsided as a warm sensation spread throughout his belly. The fire burned warmer, the air smelled sweeter and Aizarg's shoulder felt much better.

"Ah!" Noah grinned. "I see you approve." He reached over and took the jug. Noah took a drink, squinted and shook his head. He exhaled with a generous smile. "One taste is enough to take the edge off the day. Too much, and well, getting up the next morning can be painful."

Aizarg basked in the warmth of the drink's euphoria, his questions and fear momentarily forgotten. He let the flames lull him into a trance and his mind drifted away.

Aizarg never realized such a wonderful feeling could exist. Even Virag's wine did not have this effect.

A short, straight blade with an antler handle appeared in Noah's calloused hand. He picked up a small, fat chunk of green wood and began carving it.

"You've been asleep since sunset. Dawn is still several hours away. Zedkat has been tending you and your family all night." He nodded to Sarah and Ezra. "Zedkat and my other daughters-in-law have not seen the world beyond the wall since they arrived," Noah said without looking up. "They are excited about your arrival...and afraid. Until now, I don't think they understood why God has not blessed their wombs with children."

Noah looked down at Sarah's sleeping form. "You are blessed with a wonderful daughter. She told me much about your journey while you slept. She wouldn't leave your side. When she realized we would not hurt you, she told us of her brother hiding on the ledge."

Noah held the wood at arm's length, as if trying to discern what shape might be hiding inside its raw form, waiting for his knife to free it. He looked up at Aizarg.

"You and your people are safe among us, Aizarg. We will not harm you. You have my word."

Aizarg sensed no ill will or deceit in the Narim's eyes.

"Your daughter says you are a fisherman. She says your people live in huts built over the water," Noah said. "I've seen the sea once, but only as a child as we journeyed north from Havilah. In those days, the Nephilim had yet to teach the craft of boat building to men. I've fished the mountain streams for trout, though."

"The Great Sea is abundant in trout," Aizarg said. "We fish for them with both the net and the spear." Aizarg stared at the fire and spoke of the Lo and their way of life while Noah whittled and listened quietly. Like the fire and the drink, speaking about his people soothed Aizarg's troubled spirit.

Time passed and Aizarg's trance melted away. He looked up and found Noah staring at him, as if taking his measure. Aizarg didn't know why, but he felt a bond with this man, a kindred sadness of the spirit all good fathers share.

"Why did you want to kill us?"

"My God gave us a code, a law to live by. It guides every facet of our lives, from when we rise in the morning, to what we eat, to when and how we pray. Part of that law is that no one may enter the Black Fortress.

"Over the years they've tried to scale the walls and climb the cliffs to enter our compound. In greed they seek the riches of the Narim. It has grown worse with the rise of the cult of Ba'al, the Black Dragon." Noah spit on the ground. "Foul evil has taken root in among the Hur-po, evil bent on destroying my family. I am sorry, Aizarg. I did not see you for what you truly were until it was almost too late."

"I understand, Noah. I would do anything to protect my family as well. There is nothing to forgive."

Noah smiled and Aizarg sensed a weight lift off the great man's shoulders.

"Noah, why did your god tell you to build the boat? I fear for my people. I must know what this means for them."

Noah paused and tapped his finger on his knee. "Why did God tell me to build that boat?" He repeated and then resumed his whittling.

"My God is the Creator of Heaven and Earth, but he has cursed the Earth." Noah said flatly. "He commanded me to build the ark because he will send a deluge..." he momentarily wagged his finger, "...and send it soon, mind you, to cleanse wickedness from the land." Noah stopped whittling and shook his head. "'A deluge.' That is all God saw fit to tell me. I assumed the river would rise and sweep the Hur-po from the valley, and perhaps the Scythians from the steppe. My family and I, along with any men or creatures God so desired, would take shelter high on this ledge, safely deposited in the ark."

Aizarg wasn't sure he grasped what Noah insinuated. "Do you mean you didn't know you were building a boat? How can you build something so grand and not know what it is?"

"Of course I didn't know!" Noah scoffed. "I'm a shepherd and a carpenter, not a boat builder. God said 'build an ark...'" Noah held out his hands as if holding a box. "...A container, a place of safekeeping."

Noah leaned in. "I will tell you, fisherman, how I built this giant ark!" Noah poked the stump with the knife tip, accentuating each syllable. "One piece at a time! God said 'Place a beam here' and I obeyed. God said 'nail a plank here' and I obeyed. Sometimes He showed me a small part of His grand vision and trusted me to make it real. Sometimes He was stubbornly silent.

"Yes, I thought some things about it odd, and like a child, I guessed at His plans. Why did the planks run left to right and not up and down? Why was the internal structure so strong? Why all the pitch? A boat builder?" Noah chuckled. "I am no boat builder, only a servant of God."

He speaks like a patesi-le.

"If he would have told me to build a boat, I would have made my own conclusions, my own plans. Even if I didn't want to, I would have put my vision ahead of His. I would have failed. He led me one step at a time.

"You, Aizarg, were an answered prayer. Through a fisherman's eyes God told me to look up and see His plan!"

A thousand questions bubbled up in Aizarg's mind, but he kept coming back to one. "This deluge you speak of. How and when will it happen? "

"I think it has already begun. From the ramparts I've watched the Hur River swell to three times its width over the last few days."

Aizarg thought of the Black River they crossed two days ago.

"That is only the beginning," Noah continued. "Then the rains will come."

"Rains?" Aizarg asked. "What are 'rains'?"

Noah grunted and considered Aizarg. "Yes, you are of the steppe and might have never seen rain. On this side of the mountains it is rare. It is water that falls from the sky. My people call it the Tears of God. It is common in the lands from where my people hail. It falls from dark clouds. It may fall gently or pound from the heavens with streaks of lightning and claps of thunder."

Aizarg tried to imagine this 'rain.' "I've seen lightning and heard thunder, but rain...," Aizarg shook his head. "What does this mean for my people?"

"It shall rain for forty days and forty nights, this has been promised. Now that I know the hall is actually a boat, it is apparent God will lift it from the mountain. The water will reach the very tops of the mountains and the steppe will become the bottom of a sea."

"Please, you must save my people! The boat will hold all of them. Perhaps that is why it is so big. This must be why I am here. Noah, let me bring my people here, I beg you!"

Noah didn't answer him at first. He took another swig from the jar and whittled in silence.

"Obviously, the ark is intended for many more than just my family. At God's command, we have stored mountains of grain, hay and other food stuffs deep in the mines over the years, untouched by rat or rot." Noah pointed up into the darkness in the general direction of the cave. "There is enough in there to feed all of Hur-ar for weeks.

"Many years ago, God told me to warn the Hur-po of the coming doom. I did so, before I secured the last segment of the wall. They ignored me, too smitten with their earthly pleasures.

"I suspected the time of the deluge was nearing when God commanded me to start moving the food into the ark. That work is almost complete. I hoped God would instruct me to throw open the Black Gates and, once again, beseech the Hur-po to repent. Alas, no such command came. The Hur-po had their chance and let it pass them by. They will perish with their gold."

"Didn't you give them the gold?" Aizarg asked.

Noah stopped whittling and looked straight ahead. "It took many nails to build the ark. Gold is a nuisance; its veins block our way when we dig for iron, tin and copper. The Hur-po traded for gold for generations without falling into corruption. It wasn't until the fall of the Nephilim and the rise of the Black Dragon when lust for the soft metal turned them away from God."

Noah paused and sighed. "I pray for them every day." He returned his attention to Aizarg. "And then you appeared! My heart says 'Yes! Aizarg of the Lo, bring your people here and enter the Ark.' But God is silent on the matter."

"Noah, your god is unknown to me, but I see this great ark and know he is real. I acknowledge the power of your god and will forsake the old gods and follow yours if it will mean salvation for my people," Aizarg said, searching the Narim's eyes for a hopeful sign.

Noah leaned over and placed his hand on Aizarg's knee. "Peace, Aizarg," he said softly. "Do not be afraid. You strike me as a righteous man, though only God can judge a man's heart. You are here for a reason. I see God's hand in this."

Noah touched Aizarg's hair. "Has your hair always been this way?"

"Only recently."

"I used to have the blackest hair you've ever seen!" Noah laughed. "Emzara said it was one of the things she so loved about me. One day God spoke to me in a voice as real as mine sounds to you, though I could not see its source. He commanded me to stay in the Hur Valley, even as my father and my brothers prepared to move our flocks west. On that day, my hair turned white as snow."

Noah pointed to Aizarg. "Pure white hair is the scar left by God's direct touch." Noah gave a short laugh. "God must truly hold special favor for carpenters and fishermen! He is guiding you to an unknown purpose. If that purpose is to join us in the ark, so be it."

A concerned expression crossed Noah's face. "I labored for years under the assumption I was building a shelter to weather the storm high on this mountaintop. I was wrong. I thought all the gated chambers, both great and small, within the ark were for the repentant and their flocks. With your coming, I see through new eyes and I am unsure of God's designs."

Fear festered in the bottom of Aizarg's gut. He wanted Noah to tell him his people would be allowed in the ark.

"Surely, my people will not be forsaken? We are good and simple, never asking for more than our next meal and to raise our families in peace. Will your god judge us with the Hur-po and the bloodthirsty tribes of the g'an?"

Noah handed Aizarg the jug. "You are here, are you not? He has chosen you for a purpose, trust Him." Noah leaned back, as if trying to find the right words.

"I will tell you what I told Sarah while you slept. My wife is a gentle and loving woman. Emzara has patiently endured suffering and trials no woman should ever have to face." He held his arms up to the sky. "I thank God for giving her to me, for she is a better woman than any man deserves." Noah pointed to Aizarg's hair. "Emzara was frightened of you. This has been a difficult life, but one we've grown accustomed to. She knew your arrival meant that this life was coming to an end. Emzara forgot she should trust God and not fear the future. You, Aizarg of the Lo, must also trust God and not fear the future."

It wasn't enough for Aizarg. "Can you ask your god why he brought me here?"

"I will pray about it, though I cannot say how or when He will answer." Noah sighed. "Aizarg, I want to help you, but I need to know of your people and how you came to be here. Sarah told me some, but I want to hear it from you."

***

Aizarg spoke deep into the night about their journey. He told Noah of the Valley of the Beasts, the vanishing fish and the events of the Council of Boats. Noah's expression became graver with each new unfolding of the tale. He asked Aizarg to repeat his tale of the Valley of Beasts several times, asking him many questions regarding the gathering of animals.

Soon, Noah put down his whittling and stood up with hands behind his back. Sometimes he asked Aizarg a question or to expand on some point of his story, but mostly he listened.

After Aizarg finished his account, Noah finally spoke. "The spirit you encountered in the mist was an angel."

"What is an 'angel'?"

"They are powerful servants of God." Noah raised his fingers and nodded knowingly. "Based on what you told me about the ghosts following the spirit, I believe you encountered the Angel of Death, God's agent for bringing the dead to judgment."

"What would this 'Angel of Death' have of me and my people?"

Noah looked Aizarg up and down. "You're not dead, so I think we can eliminate that," he said dryly. "You said the angel brought you a message?"

"The message came from a ghost. The dead followed in this angel's wake like minnows in the shadow of a boat," Aizarg said.

Noah nodded. "Yes, the dead are drawn to this particular angel. It is in this spirit's nature."

"They said I was not to accept strangers in our midst after we crossed back over the Black River," Aizarg continued. "I assume his meaning was during our return journey. For this, he said we would be delivered to a promised land."

"You, Aizarg of the Lo, have made a covenant with God, much as I have. It also means you were meant to return to your people, perhaps to lead them here." Noah shrugged. "Perhaps. I sense in my heart time is short." Noah frowned. "Did the ghost say anything else?"

Aizarg thought for a moment, and then remembered. "Yes, I remember now. Before I blacked out, the angel said something to me. I recall its words clearly. It said 'The doom of the Fallen is at hand.'"

Noah stepped back and sat down, as if the wind had just been knocked out of him. "Once again, my eyes are open and God has shown me His will.

"The land has flooded before. My grandfather told me stories of great walls of frigid water pouring out of the northlands, sweeping away entire villages. These floods were sufficient to destroy the likes of mortal men. What God is about to unleash is a flood to destroy no less than gods! That is why He guided me in constructing the ark."

Noah took a long drink and passed Aizarg the jug. He resumed his whittling. Aizarg saw a shape emerging from the wood in Noah's hands.

Is it a bird or a beast?

"Listen, Aizarg, and understand why God sends this mighty deluge. To know the story of God's judgment you must know the story of my people and how the world came to be."

And Noah began his tale.

***

This is the saga of the Narim, as told to the Uros and then told to me, Fu Xi. While this is also the story of my mother and her kind's fall from Grace, I will dutifully relay Aizarg's words and not my own.

"*After the God of the Narim created the world and put all the living things upon it, He created mortal men and women in the shadow of His image. God bred into their nature the will to cover the earth and subdue it. The Narim called them 'Hollow Men;' formed in flesh, but incomplete in spirit. They were like seeds, ready for planting but not yet fertilized with God's spirit. These common mortals lived short, savage lives and were susceptible to all manner of evil and corruption. The Hollow Men were as children, waiting for the firm hand of their loving maker to guide them.*

"*That hand was provided by the Children of God, a race of powerful angels sent to earth to live among the Hollow Men. These were spiritual entities, which could only exist in the earthly plane by inhabiting the bodies of mortals. As teachers, mentors and protectors, the Children of God were to lead mankind to choose righteousness and forsake evil. To do this, men were given a perfect example by which to strive in their earthly mission.*

"*Those shining examples were the Children of the Garden. In those ancient days, God planted a grove in a sheltered valley, far to the south of the Great Sea where the steppe met the mountains. It was protected from the outside world so that sin and corruption could not enter. In the Grove of God, He created a perfect man and a perfect woman, the forbearers of the Narim. The Children of the Garden were formed in*

God's image both physically and spiritually. Unlike the Hollow Men, they were immortal and innocent and walked with God the way a child walks with their father.

"Of the three races, God most loved the lowly Hollow Men. Born without Grace, common men only had the gift of free will and a yearning to seek out their maker. It is free will that is the wellspring of true, lasting love.

"At a time of God's choosing, the Children of the Garden would emerge and, with the Children of God, lead the Hollow Men on the path to their Creator. Together, the immortals would serve the Hollow Men and fill their spirits with the light of God.

"Alas, the Corruptor came to the Garden and tempted the perfect man and woman. The Black Dragon, the betrayer of God, deceived the Children of the Garden into tasting the fruit of the forbidden tree. Their immortality drained away and they became as Hollow Men. Though exiled from the Garden, the spirit of God still echoed in their souls and they begot a race of long-lived mortals, the lineage of Noah and the Narim. God placed a powerful kerubim, a winged creature wielding a flaming sword, to guard the Valley of the Garden and the Tree of Wisdom. As the Narim fell from Grace, so did the Children of God.

"The Corruptor came to the Children of God and said to them, "Behold, the Emperor of Heaven has failed. Do you not love the Hollow Men? You are the only hope for the race of men. Are not the sons and daughters of men fair? Take them and breed a new race of men, perfect and immortal. This thing you must do if thou truly love them." Though it was forbidden, they loved the daughters and sons of men and spawned a race of powerful demi-gods, heroes of old. The Children of God became drunk on the elixir of the material world and forgot their purpose. In their pride, they established earthly kingdoms. At first, they were content to be called kings, but soon called themselves gods. They possessed the most beautiful of mortal bodies, often not willingly given. They transformed into vain and prideful creatures. They made their immortal offspring princes and enslaved the Hollow Men. The servants of man became its oppressors The Nephilim, the Fallen.

"The kingdoms of the Nephilim built great fleets and armies and set about bringing the world under their heel. Meanwhile, Noah's *ancestors became a race of wanderers, seeking their way to redemption as the Hollow Men drifted in darkness, alone and separated from God.*

"All the while, the Black Dragon strode creation unopposed as the world fell farther into his clutches."

The Chronicle of Fu Xi

***

It wasn't the strong drink that made Aizarg's head swim; the power of Noah's tale and its implications staggered him.

"How old are you?" Aizarg asked as he stared at Noah.

Noah laughed again. "Tomorrow, I will turn six hundred years old! Your arrival was quite the unexpected birthday surprise, I can tell you."

"And yet you Narim are not gods?"

"Absolutely not! There is but one God, all other creatures of earth and heaven are but his servants," Noah said indignantly, as if Aizarg had offended him. To reinforce his point he took the edge of his knife and made a small nick in his thumb. A few drops of blood fell to the ground. "I am a man, every bit as mortal as you. And that word, *Narim...or Narts*...or whatever, they are not our words, mind you! It is what those Hur-po call us; it means 'hero' or 'god.' We are neither. We are the Tribe of Adam, the Children of the Garden."

Noah thumbed over his shoulder at the cottage. "Zedkat was a little girl when her father brought her to me as a betrothal for Shem. That was the last time the Black Gate was fully open to the western sun, almost a hundred years ago." He leaned back and sighed. "And that was the last time I saw another of my people."

"She is almost a hundred summers?" Even after Noah's tale, Aizarg could not believe such a thing. "You are all so old."

"No, my friend, you are so young! I don't live abnormally long; your lives are abnormally short." He stroked his beard thoughtfully. "Though, in recent generations our life spans have noticeably shrunk." His eyes lit up and he reached over

355

and patted Aizarg's knee as if they were old friends. "My grandfather is nearing a thousand years old!" Suddenly, Noah's face grew grim. "He may still be alive, along with many of my tribe who moved on to the west."

He bowed his head and closed his eyes. "Please, dear and wonderful God, protect your devoted servants beyond these walls." He opened his eyes again and looked about until he found his knife and wood and commenced whittling again.

"Anyway, it does not matter how old I am. The days of a man's life are not his own, to sit about and count them like the Hur-po sit about and count their gold. The hours of the day belong to God, spend them to honor Him and you will inherit the treasures of Heaven.

"You and your kind are separated from God at birth. Without His spirit dwelling within, you do not live very long. You are creatures of this world who have no understanding, no inner voice leading you back to your Creator."

Aizarg felt for his li-ge, suddenly uncomfortable and irritated. Noah challenged every tenet of his faith. "My creator is Psatina, the Earth Mother."

Noah appeared frustrated, as if he couldn't find the right words. "Please, I did not mean to offend. Your gods are manifestations of the Nephilim. After they fell, they led the Hollow Men to worship the creation and not the Creator. It is for such crimes that God sends the deluge to wash them away."

"I don't feel any 'hole' in my spirit," Aizarg said.

"Tell me, Lo man, had you ever felt warmth akin to that elixir spread through your body before?" Noah pointed to the jug.

Aizarg shook his head.

"I could have described it to you, but my words couldn't do justice to the feeling. I am as a man with sight trying to describe the world to one born blind. My people have tasted the elixir of God's very presence." He put down his knife and wood. "My people are born with the Creator's spirit dwelling within us. I can hear His voice in my heart. When He chooses, I can hear His voice in my head."

After a long pause Aizarg finally asked, "What is your god called?"

Noah frowned, as if surprised by the question. "That is a question I haven't heard in many, many years. He has no name, at least a name we are worthy of calling him."

"Then how do you worship him?" Aizarg asked, truly intrigued.

Noah leaned in with his hand on his hip. "Do your children call you by name?"

"No," Aizarg shrugged. "That would be disrespectful. They are not my equal."

Noah smiled. "And how do your children honor you?"

Aizarg considered the question for a few moments. "They obey me. They honor and respect me. They show me that they love me."

"Yes!" Noah pointed a finger to the sky. "And so it is with my God. He is our father and to worship Him is to simply be a good child. *That* is how my people worship Him."

Something about that answer angered Aizarg. He thought about his people, and the innocent street children in Hur-ar. Aizarg spoke slowly, measuring his words carefully as not to offend his host. "A good father loves and cares for his children. A good father must forgive. Why should we 'Hollow Men' suffer for the sins of Narim and Nephilim? If your god is so powerful why doesn't he strike down the Black Dragon?"

Noah stopped whittling. His eyes bore deep into Aizarg. For a moment, Aizarg felt a tremendous power channeling through Noah, and he seemed to fall under his spell. "There is no forgiveness without sacrifice, and the price of forgiveness is always blood."

Noah stood and broke the spell. He stretched his back. "Enough talk. There is still enough night to get a good rest. Sleep, Aizarg of the Lo, and I will pray about your people's fate." He brushed the shavings off his robe. "We will speak again at dawn." Noah looked down upon Aizarg and smiled warmly. For a moment, Noah reminded Aizarg of his own father. "You can pray to Him, too, Aizarg."

"How do I pray to a nameless god?" Aizarg asked.

"Open your heart. Speak in truth. Bow in humility. Do these things and He will listen."

"Noah, do you love or fear your god?" Aizarg asked.

Noah touched his heart. "My father once told me love and fear are often one and the same. My God commands me to do both." With that he placed his carving on the stump next to Aizarg.

The fearsome, winged beast with a long, graceful neck reminded Aizarg of the dragon statue in the market.

"What is that?" Aizarg asked.

"It is the kerubim that guards our lost garden paradise, the Place of Perfect Sorrows. It serves as a reminder to my people that we can never go back and the only way home is always forward."

***

Aizarg woke to a cool, gray dawn and the smell of roasting meat. Stiff and sore, he struggled to sit up. His shoulder throbbed and burned with the slightest movement. Sarah and Ezra sat around the rekindled fire as Zedkat tended a spit with a haunch of meat.

"Good morning, Father!" Sarah beamed. She came around the fire and knelt next to Aizarg. She pecked him on the cheek and lightly gave him a hug. "I have so much to tell you!"

"I spoke with Noah while you slept," Aizarg said.

"That's wonderful." Sarah seemed genuinely happy. "Zedkat says they have plenty of room in their enormous boat. We're saved!"

He patted her hand. "We shall see."

Aizarg's mind raced last night before he found sleep. He would have to fetch his people and lead them here across the g'an. Leading hundreds through Scythian territory would be much more challenging that sneaking a handful.

I'll have to cross over the Black River again...twice. How will I get out of the city and bring my people back through its gates? The hurdles were daunting.

Zedkat touched Sarah's shoulder. "Go eat. I must tend to your father."

Zedkat carefully removed the cloth bandages around his shoulder and examined the wound. "The stitches are holding and the bleeding has stopped."

Aizarg examined the wound. A blood-crusted, puckered hole bristled with ends of sinew strings, each tied into a thick knot. The Lo also practiced the craft of stitching wounds and Aizarg knew Zedkat had done an excellent job.

Zedkat cleaned the wound with clear, cool water and then smeared a yellow, odorless balm over it. She applied fresh linen and then tied a sling over Aizarg's shoulder.

"Leave it in the sling. It will heal faster and won't hurt as much."

"Thank you, Zedkat," Aizarg said.

She smiled and blushed. "In about a week you must carefully cut the stitches and pull each out by hand. I will also give you some of the balm to rub on the wound when you change the dressing. Do this each morning. I showed Sarah how to properly dress it when I first treated you."

Aizarg's stomach growled loudly enough for everyone to look up and snicker, especially Ezra. The man vanished with the morning, replaced by a happy, gangly boy reunited with his sister.

Zedkat smiled. "Appetite is a good sign! You are strong and will heal quickly." She fixed him a bowl, which he held in his sore right arm. The Lo considered it taboo to eat with one's left hand, but Zedkat gave him a spoon. Since he never actually touched the food with his left hand, he decided it must be acceptable.

A simple but hearty fare, a haunch of goat meat and a pot with simmering porridge sat to one side of the fire. Zedkat gave him a flat, circular piece of food he recognized as neither meat nor grain.

"It is called bread." Zedkat took one and ripped it in two. "It's best when dipped in the porridge."

Aizarg followed her example, pleased to discover the bread both light and filling.

One more thing I will bring back to my people.

Ezra and Sarah ate and talked quietly, occasionally snickering. Sarah giggled and punched her brother in the shoulder. He feigned pain and then returned the punch. Aizarg couldn't quite put his finger on something about the way they ate and spoke to one another. An air existed about them in the way they ate, their refined mannerism, and the eloquence of their speech. Ezra seemed too well-spoken for a beggar and thief and Sarah underwent a profound change since they entered the valley. He had many questions for her, but they would have to wait.

Aizarg looked up and saw an older woman staring at him in the gray light of dawn. He recognized her face from last night.

"I am Emzara, wife of Noah," she said without smiling, but Aizarg saw tremendous sorrow in her eyes. Aizarg put down his food and struggled to stand. Zedkat and Sarah rushed to his side and helped him.

"I am grateful for the hospitality of the House of Noah," Aizarg said as he motioned to the fire and food. "There is so much food! Your warm generosity is appreciated. I cannot thank you enough." Aizarg bowed slightly to the matron of the Black Fortress.

Emzara reached out a trembling hand toward his wounded shoulder and then pulled back. Aizarg saw black circles under her eyes, even in the dim morning light. Emzara looked as if she'd been crying all night.

She adjusted her hair and smoothed her robe. "You are welcome, Aizarg of the Lo. Breakfast is our biggest meal of the day, so it was easy enough to make a little more. We usually only cook in the morning and then eat what is left throughout the day." She pointed behind Aizarg. "Noah and the men were up before dawn. They are loading the last of the food stored in the mines. Noah is in the ark. After you eat, he requests you join him there."

Aizarg turned and beheld the ark in its full glory, a gray behemoth in the morning fog. When he didn't concentrate on the details and took it all in as a whole, its shape and purpose became apparent.

Emzara turned to Sarah and Ezra. "Would you please help me in the house?"

Ezra bowed low, and in a formal voice said, "Oh, Lady of the Narim. We shall render whatever assistance you may require."

Emzara put her hand on her chest. "Oh, my! Well..." She cleared her throat. "How about you start by simply calling me Momma Emzara." She took their hands and led them to the house. "Zedkat," Emzara called out over her shoulder. "Get to your chores. There is much to do."

"Please, eat as much as you like. Leave your bowl and spoon and I will be along shortly to clean up," Zedkat said to Aizarg and hurried off.

***

The fog lifted quickly as Aizarg stood at the base of the ramp leading to the enormous entrance. It only took a minute to realize the ramp was also the ark's door. Heavy ropes attached to iron eyelets on either side of the ramp were to draw it up against the wall. He marveled at how the ramp, heavily coated in pitch, would seat against the frame with any water pressure.

The weight of the water will press the door against the frame and seal it.

Aizarg slowly stepped up the ramp. His imagination ran wild at what he might see. With each step, he felt a power emanating from the ark, like a hum vibrating through his flesh. Halfway up the ramp, the vibration became a warm sensation, and then elevated to a burning pain shooting from his feet all the way to his head. Aizarg beat a hasty retreat down the ramp, and the burning instantly ceased. He tried again, but met with the same results.

It will not let me enter.

"I prayed, Aizarg, but God saw fit to answer you directly." Noah stood in the entrance, grimly looking down at Aizarg. His robe now replaced by the leather apron and waist wrap. A bronze headband pulled Noah's hair back and a light sheen of sweat covered his face. He gripped a bulky iron hammer in his right hand.

He may not be a god, but looks the role.

"What does this mean?" Aizarg asked, but his heart already knew the answer.

Noah put the hammer down and descended the ramp. "Come."

Aizarg followed him down along the length of the ark until they came to where a heavy coating of fresh pitch covered the gouge made by Shem's arrow. Aizarg's dried blood still streaked the ark's planks.

Noah pointed under the ark. "Is that yours?"

Aizarg bent down and hefted the staff with his left arm. It felt heavier this morning.

"Yes, this is mine. I'd forgotten about it."

Noah snorted a quick laugh. "I wouldn't make that mistake again. Is this your spear that was transformed in the presence of the Angel of Death?"

"It is."

"I found it here this morning when I was patching the gouge. I tried to pick it up, but it burned me." Noah paused, looking intently at Aizarg. "It repelled me much like the ark just repelled you." Noah placed his large, calloused hand tenderly on Aizarg's left shoulder. "Do you understand me, Aizarg?"

"We cannot come with you," Aizarg whispered.

"No. I am sorry. We must all follow the paths God has placed us on."

A faint rumble sounded in the distance, slowly growing louder. It played at the back of Aizarg's consciousness, not quite loud enough to draw his full attention.

"Why were we led here if it wasn't to join you? Why is your god condemning us?" Aizarg tried to control the swirling anger and fear brewing in his heart. "My people cannot survive the coming cataclysm without you."

"Condemn?" Noah pointed to the ark. "This is the manifestation of my people's salvation, inspired by God but built with my hands." He pointed to the staff. "This is the manifestation of *your* salvation, forged by the finger of God himself! God has surely judged your people and found them worthy of a second chance."

The hollow rumbling sound grew louder, the sound of approaching wagon wheels.

Once again, Aizarg felt himself staring into the abyss. "My people will perish," he whispered.

Noah focused beyond the Black Gate. "The Hur-po come to trade. Our time is short." Noah turned back to Aizarg, expression as resolute as stone. "Did or did not God make a covenant with you?"

Aizarg stared at the ground and didn't reply. The flood had already poured into his heart and washed away all his hope.

"Aizarg!" Noah shouted and shook Aizarg. The pain startled Aizarg and he looked into Noah's eyes.

"Did or did not God make a covenant with you?" Noah repeated.

"He did," Aizarg whispered.

"Then honor it!" Noah shouted. "Keep your promise and He will keep his." Noah lowered his voice to a whisper. He leaned in close and grasped the back of Aizarg's head the way a father may when speaking to his son. "Last night God gave me a message for you. He said 'Cut the anchors to this doomed world and let the waters carry you to the Promised Land.' That is not a message given to a condemned people."

Aizarg finally noticed they were not alone. All of Noah's family stood to their left, along with Sarah and Ezra. Sarah and Ezra were dressed in fresh, heavy wool robes. They carried large packs made of oiled wool with heavy stitching.

Ezra appeared stoic, but Sarah cried.

They know we can't go with the Narim.

Shem handed another bag, heavy and packed, to Ezra. "This is your bag, Aizarg. Ezra said he would carry it for you. The bags are filled with several weeks of provisions and a spare set of clothes." Shem smiled sheepishly. "I'm sorry about shooting you last night."

Zedkat spoke quickly as tears welled in her eyes. "Aizarg, There are spare bandages and balm in your pack and...and...I put some loaves of bread in there, too." She turned and buried her head in Shem's chest, trying to stifle her sobs.

"Stop it, child!" Noah chastised her. "They are not condemned, but in God's hands, as are we!"

The rumbling grew louder, echoed off the cliffs, and then ceased.

"Ham...Japheth, prepare to open the inner gate," Noah commanded. The men walked down the slope to the two towers on each side of the gate. The rest of the group followed, with Noah and Aizarg falling to the rear.

The realization of what was about to happen suddenly dawned on Aizarg.

"The Hur...why are you sending us out into their clutches?"

Noah smiled as if he had a secret. "The sun will rise soon. When the outer gate opens, just keep walking until you pass out of the city gates. The Hur-po will not hinder you, I promise."

Aizarg looked up at Noah through the corner of his eye.

A loud, deep bell rang from beyond the wall and reverberated off the cliffs. Ham and Japheth stood in front of two large wheels at the base of each tower. A long loop connected the wheels to the rigging in the towers. The men looked to Noah and waited beside the outer wheels.

Ezra and Sarah held hands and faced the wall.

"Good luck, Aizarg of the Lo," Emzara said and gave Aizarg a light kiss on the cheek. She approached Sarah and Ezra and kissed them lightly, too. The rest of Noah's family stood around their patriarch.

Aizarg clasped Noah's hand. "Thank you, Noah. I do not know what your god has in store for us, but I will keep the covenant and try to find hope."

The patriarch's hands enveloped Aizarg's. "He is *your* God now, Aizarg. Do not forget to pray to him. Prayers and love to God are like fire and ore to the smithy. They are the raw materials with which He forges hope."

Noah turned to his sons and raised his hand. The men grunted and began to turn the wheels. A cheer went up from beyond the wall.

"Ha!" Noah laughed. "The Hur-po think we are trading gold again." He looked at Sarah and Aizarg and laughed louder. "Today, I give them silver! Today, I give them *Narim!*" Noah bellowed.

Aizarg stepped between Sarah and Ezra and held Sarah's hand. The wheels stopped and Japheth and Ham rested, both out of breath. Beyond the inner gate the rumbling briefly resumed.

The bell rang again.

Noah nodded to his sons. The men turned the wheels in the opposite direction until a loud thud echoed off the canyon walls. The men moved to the inner wheels and began to turn them, but with less effort. The inner gate smoothly swung inward, revealing a large holding area between the two gates. Two enormous wagons sat in the holding area, each heaped with bulging sacks.

Aizarg, Sarah and Ezra stepped forward into the holding area.

"Father, what of the wagons?" Shem asked.

"Leave them," Noah said.

Aizarg, Sarah and Ezra took one more look back over their shoulder. Daybreak approached the crest of the mountains beyond the ark. Noah and his family waved once more, dwarfed by the backdrop of the giant ark. Noah nodded and the wheels turned again until the patriarch and his family vanished behind the black gate.

Sarah gave a small sniffle. Aizarg squeezed her hand and led them around the wagons until they faced the outer gate.

A deeper, louder bell sounded from within the compound and the cheers went up again from the outside the wall.

"Be strong, children." Aizarg took a deep breath and placed his hope in the God of the Narim.

My god?

The gate slowly opened inward to reveal a crowd of richly dressed men. Behind them were dozens of nude male slaves, heaving and sweaty with red harness welts across their chests. To either side were warriors and more Hur. All of them leaned around and peered expectantly into the holding area. Cries and gasps suddenly went up. Looks of shock and disbelief rippled through the crowd. A few of the warriors pushed the traders to the side and rushed forward.

"Look at their hair!" a voice shouted. The Hur-po looked at one another with trepidation. "Their hair!" someone else yelled out. "It is as the legends say!" another shouted. Soon, a chorus of shouts cried out, "The Narim! The Narim!"

The sun crested the mountain and Aizarg's staff caught the sunlight. It reflected the streaming rays and scattered them across the crowd in a dazzling spectrum of red and golden rays. The crowd dropped to their knees and averted their eyes.

All three of them looked at one another and then, without a word, strolled through the open path between the prostrate Hur-po.

Like a wildfire, shouts of "The Narim have emerged!" and "The Narim walk among us!" preceded Aizarg and his company as they made their way down the Cliff Road and into the city. The crowds parted and bowed low before them.

On that morning, a fisherman, a slave girl, and a thief passed unmolested through the City of Gold as gods.

***

Noah stood on the roof of the ark and looked over the Black Wall to Hur-ar and beyond. Now that he saw the ark for what it truly was, he examined the Black Wall with fresh eyes. He knew a smaller, simpler wall could keep the Hur-po out. It's true purpose would remain a mystery to be revealed in God's time.

Noah gazed out at the Kupar Bridge.

The river is wider this morning. The bridge looks besieged.

Building the bridge all those years ago started his journey to this moment. Without it they could not have transported all the lumber across the river. But it, too, was more robust than that task demanded. Noah often contemplated why God wanted it to be so big, so strong.

God is preparing to reveal all his purposes.

To the southwest, far across the steppe, Noah spotted what looked like smoke drifting high into the morning sky.

Shem approached Noah and stood by his side. "Is that smoke on the horizon?"

Noah didn't answer him. "Did you do what I asked?"

"Yes, Father. The food is loaded. The mine is empty and the walkway has been destroyed as you commanded. The women have moved our belongings into the ark. Shall we enter the ark and close the door?"

Noah thought about the message God instructed him to tell Aizarg. He only told Aizarg half the message, the other half of the message remained for another to deliver.

The Lo shall not be forgotten.

"Father?" Shem asked. "Are we ready to move into the ark?"

Noah clapped Shem on the shoulder and pointed to the dust cloud. "No, my beloved son. Tell your brothers to standby at the gates and tell your mother to prepare for guests...many, many guests!"

**

For seven days and seven nights the creatures of the land gathered in the Valley of the Beasts. They lay about, slept, and drank from the rapidly swelling stream.

Over those seven days, the stream overflowed its banks and soon ran too swift and deep for the animals to cross. Animals that entered the water were pulled under by a demonic undertow of shadowy hands. By the third day, the marshes were submerged and the river became an extension of the Great Sea. The animals trapped on the west bank perished. The east bank became the new shoreline of the sea and the animals remaining there still were legion.

By the sixth day, many of the weaker animals on the east shore were dead. With the last of their strength, they crawled to the edge of the water and died. Black hands slithered out of the water and pulled their carcasses into the depths.

The surviving beasts waited along the shore of the dark ocean. On the red dawn of the eighth day, they stirred. The larger herd of animals and predators lumbered into a great counter-clockwise circle around a solitary hill between the shore and the eastern ridge. Toward the center of the living circle, smaller animals scurried at a faster pace. Above them, birds soared in the same direction; the larger birds to the outside and the smaller birds in tighter spirals near the center. In the innermost center, the flying insects created a buzzing whirlwind spiraling high in the pale morning sky.

And so the living wheel turned and turned throughout the morning.

26. The Raft

Of the ten Nephilim who walked the earth, only my mother repented, but her forgiveness came with a terrible burden.

She would wield the Offering Blade that cleansed the world with blood and water.

The Chronicle of Fu Xi

***

No man directly witnessed the events in the Valley of the Beasts. Nomads observed the dust cloud from miles away as they fled the rising rivers. Already fearful, they dared not approach the Valley of the Beasts. If they had, they might have glimpsed a human-like form visible in the eye of the cyclone of living flesh.

The angel faded in and out of focus like smoke. Her ghostly limbs blurred and faded away, only to reappear again in a spiraling mist within the maelstrom of animals. Sometimes only her burning eyes were visible, like diamonds forged from blue lighting.

As the sun reached its zenith, she stretched out her arm and pointed northeast. At that moment, from the outskirts of the spinning wheel of beasts two elephants emerged, one a magnificent bull, the other a young female. They trundled up the slopes and disappeared over the eastern ridge. Then two rhinoceroses, a male and female, exited the dust cloud and followed the elephants. One after another, animals peeled away from the edge of the circle and formed a long procession to the east. Sometimes they went in pairs, sometimes in groups of seven.

Over the course of the morning and afternoon animals spun off the living circle like thread from the weaver's wheel. Then, while the sun still had life in the west, hordes of insects and creeping creatures slithered and scuttled away. Finally, the birds and bats went last into the twilight until the procession vanished over the eastern ridge. Yet, most of the animals still marched and soared in the circle. So few departed it did not diminish the clouds of dust.

***

The sun almost crested mid-day when Aizarg, Sarah and Ezra reached the hilltop beyond the bridge. Ghalen and Setenay waited on the crest, as if they knew Aizarg approached.

Aizarg had never been so glad to see Setenay. They embraced and Ghalen slapped his back with a wide grin.

Ghalen considered Ezra. "And who might this be?"

Ezra hung back. Aizarg sensed the boy's uncertainty.

The old patesi-le grabbed the boy's chin and turned his head left and right. At first, Ezra brought his hand up to swat her away, but Sarah cleared her throat and gave him a stern glance.

Setenay poked at his ribs and felt his arms. "He is lean and hungry like a swamp fox, but he has a lion's eyes." She looked at Sarah. "A prince's eyes."

Ezra and Sarah frowned at each other with a surprised expression.

"He is my brother, Setenay," Sarah said.

"I see." She looked at Aizarg. "Your family grows surprisingly fast, Uros."

"There is much I must tell you, Setenay," Aizarg sighed. "We have so little time."

"You have seen our fate. I can see it in your eyes," Setenay said grimly.

"I must tell the men, and then we have to return home as fast as we can."

"What is our fate?" Ghalen asked cautiously.

"The Narim cannot help us. The rest I will save until I can speak to all of you at once. What of the others?"

"Okta, Levidi and Ood-i stumbled into camp this morning, without Ba-lok and with even worse news," Ghalen said.

The news of Ba-lok gave Aizarg a sinking feeling.

"Where are they now? Searching for him, I hope."

"No, Uros." Ghalen looked about, as if trying to find the right words. "They are west, in the low ground from whence we came. We need to leave immediately. I will tell you everything as we walk."

***

They descended back into the canyon and walked west for a short time until they crested a small ridge. Aizarg beheld a grim sight.

The Great Sea has followed us. The deluge has begun.

The water stretched to the horizon, dotted with hundreds of tiny islands that used to be ridges and hill tops. Occasionally, chunks of what looked like jagged islands of snow floated by.

Aizarg could only think of his family and his people.

Levidi, Ood-i and Okta were waiting for them. They were stripped down to their loincloths and busily constructing a raft from the driftwood heaped along the shore.

My men look like respectable Lo again, making a raft by the water's edge.

The men rushed to meet them. They all stood in a circle exchanging hugs and back slaps. Sarah rushed to Ood-i, threw her arms around his neck and kissed him passionately. At first he hesitated, and then abandoned himself to her embrace.

Sarah and Ood-i had promised as part of her adoption to break off their affair. Shocked, Aizarg started to say something, but Setenay grabbed his arm and shook her head.

"Let them be. The sun will soon be hidden from our view, let them enjoy what warmth is left to them."

Levidi squeezed Aizarg so hard his shoulder hurt. "I knew you'd come back!" Levidi looked at his sling. "What happened?"

"All in good time." Aizarg basked in his friend's affection, thankful they were all together again.

But they weren't all together.

"Any signs of Ba-lok?" Aizarg asked.

Okta spoke up. "We searched as far north and south as we could before we encountered the rising water. We even entered the Hur Valley and searched its eastern slopes. I'm sorry, Uros. I called off the search to build the raft.

"The water is getting higher by the hour. We've had to pull the raft back twice to avoid getting swamped." Okta poked the raft with his foot. "The water is wickedly cold, just like the Black River."

"Okta," Aizarg shook his head. "I think this *is* the Black River."

"River or no river, it's water and a welcome sight. This raft will take us home. Anyway, I'm out of mud weed and I don't think I can take another infernal day on dry land!"

Okta is happy. He's making his raft and returning to the water. Even in the face of doom, I find comfort among my people.

Levidi spoke up, "We only have about another hundred or so paces of gentle slope before the water forces us against the ridge. At that point, the raft will get wet, whether we are ready or not."

"Not to worry, it will be finished by nightfall," Okta said confidently. "It only lacks a mast. We've used up all the good, straight wood on the deck. We'll have to scout farther up and down the shore for a good candidate."

"I do not recognize this hardwood," Ghalen said. "It must come from far upstream, far beyond the g'an."

"We found st-strange animals among the timber," Ood-i said

Levidi nodded. "Yes, big hulking monsters like the dead thing we saw several days ago. Some were smaller, with horns sticking out of their heads. All of them were drowned."

Sarah tested the raft with her foot. "Will it take all of us?"

"Easily, young lady," Okta beamed. "I've been making rafts since I was a boy."

"Where did you get the rope to tie it all together?" Sarah asked.

Aizarg studied the different widths of thin, tan strips crudely lashing the logs together. He glanced at his men in their loin cloths and laughed. The men smiled at each other.

"L-Let's just say I'm glad we brought our w-winter clothes!" Ood-i grinned.

"Who is this?" Okta pointed to Ezra.

"He is Sarah's brother. He saved our lives."

Okta eyeballed him, stroked his beard and put one foot up on the raft. "Can you swim?"

Ezra shook his head.

"Can you handle a spear?"

Ezra shook his head.

Okta snorted, "Well, what can you do, boy?"

In a flash, Ezra's knife flew through the air and sank into the raft only inches from Okta's foot.

Okta didn't flinch, but his eyes opened a little wider. "I suppose that's a good start."

Ezra snatched his knife out of the wood, never taking his eyes off Okta.

The men tried not to snicker, until Okta laughed.

"What did you learn in Hur-ar?" Ghalen asked and pointed to Aizarg's shoulder. "And how did you get hurt?"

"Sit down, all of you," Aizarg said. "And I will tell you everything as quickly as I can."

***

The shadows grew long by the time Aizarg finished his tale. Sarah rested her head in Ood-i's lap while Ezra examined Ghalen's sagar. The men held their heads low and remained quiet several minutes after Aizarg finished.

Levidi spoke first. "If the water rises here, it rises at home, too."

They all nodded. Aizarg expected more trepidation from his men. Instead, he saw cautious concern.

"'Rain,' you say?" Okta chewed on the word. "Water from the sky, eh?"

Setenay raised her head to the sky and closed her eyes as if reliving a memory. "I saw rain once, long ago when I was a young mother and never again since."

"It does not matter where the water comes from," Okta continued. "A well-made Lo boat will float forever, even if swamped, *if* it's properly resined. A marsh oak raft will float two months before it waterlogs, longer if the builder took the time to strip and resin the logs."

The men murmured their agreement.

"It seems to me, Uros," Ghalen said. "This is a disaster for the g'an dwellers, but something we might survive. This Narim god, maybe he thought of us before he sent this disaster."

"True." Okta grinned. "A world covered in water? My clan calls that the Mother's Womb, not a curse."

"You are all calmer than I expected," Aizarg said with mild surprise.

Okta leaned in. "Uros, unlike that...that...," he searched for the word, "...'angel' we encountered two days ago, this flood is something we understand. We can grapple with this enemy."

Hope swelled in Aizarg's spirit.

Setenay remained conspicuously silent, arms folded.

"W-we only need to f-find the f-fish, and we can stay on the sea forever," Ood-i said.

"It really doesn't matter," Levidi said. "We are committed to the sea whether we like it or not. Our people back home are probably already afloat. We only have one choice, sail to them and ride this out."

Aizarg stood. "Levidi is right, the only way home is forward. Okta, this is an excellent raft. Let us finish it. Ghalen and Levidi, look for Ba-lok again. Look all night if you must. I can't bear to leave without exhausting all hope. While you are searching, please scour the shore for a suitable mast. Be back by dawn. I want to sail home at first light."

"Uros," Ood-i said. "What w—will we use for a sail?"

"Good question." Aizarg frowned. They'd used all winter clothes for rope.

Sarah stripped off her Narim robe and threw it at Aizarg, leaving her clothed only in her torn dress. Ezra did the same.

"Excellent!" Aizarg pulled his robe out of his bag while Setenay hefted the material and judged its suitability.

"It's a bit thick and heavy, but I suppose it will work. I have enough sinew to stitch them together. Sarah, can you sew?"

"Yes, Setenay."

Ghalen and Levidi had their sagars in hand and their boar spears strapped to their backs.

"We will work upstream first, then swing wide to the east and come back in from the south," Ghalen said. "Expect us at dawn." He turned to go, but Levidi motioned him to wait.

"Boy, what is your name again?" Levidi asked.

"Ezra," he replied.

Levidi pulled his boar spear from his back and tossed it sideways to Ezra, who caught it without dropping it. Even though he tried, the boy could not suppress his smile.

"Come on, we need a strong arm. Don't worry if you don't know how to use a spear, Ghalen doesn't know how to use one either. I've been trying to teach him to throw since we've been on this quest, but he won't listen to me."

"Don't listen to Levidi." Ghalen laughed as they walked away. "I will show you how to throw a spear. Now, about this man we're looking for...keep your ears open, because you'll hear him before you see him...he won't shut up..."

As the sun set, Aizarg leaned on his staff and looked at his people. Sarah sat in the grass, busily cutting the robes into flat material. Okta worked on the raft while Ood-i started a fire from the plentiful drift wood. Aizarg took a cleansing breath and looked out across the water. Strength returned to his spirit.

Setenay stood on the shore and peered into the water, which had crept several feet closer since they'd arrived. She whispered something. He stepped next to her and looked out over the water.

"The current should carry us to the Great Sea. We'll look for signs of the coastline and work our way west toward your arun-ki. We'll collect your people and sail west, gathering the Lo nation as we proceed. We will create a flotilla and ride out the coming flood as one people."

She didn't respond for a few moments.

"In my vision, the God of the Narim spoke to me," Setenay said. Aizarg detected a wheeze in her breathing, as if she wasn't drawing enough breath. "He told me His name."

Aizarg turned, astonished at this revelation.

Setenay looked out over the water somewhere beyond the horizon. "He whispered it, like a soft spring breeze that surprises you with its warmth after a long winter. I found comfort in it.

"When you step on that raft tomorrow, your long journey will just begin, Aizarg. These past few days will be as a passing dream. At the end of that journey you will know God's name and also find comfort. Remember that in the darkness, Uros, and know you are never alone, never forsaken."

A thousand questions flooded Aizarg's mind and he opened his mouth to speak, but something caught the corner of his eye. He thought he saw a dark object, like a darting fish, move through the water in front of Setenay. For a second, he thought he heard hissing, like water drops falling in a hot cooking stone. He peered closer, but saw nothing except a thin crust of ice hugging the water's edge.

Aizarg rubbed his eyes and turned back to Setenay, who stared at him intently. His feelings of unease returned.

Setenay turned back to the camp fire and Sarah. "I have a sail to make."

***

Aizarg's tale of approaching doom haunted Virag with every step. Doubts, as cold and dark as the water encroaching on the grasslands, swirled through the slaver's mind. The look in Aizarg's eyes haunted Virag the most.

Fear and truth.

I should have killed them as they reveled in my yurt. I should have sent runners to Prince Tuma that easy pickings wandered the steppe. He would have rewarded me for the tip.

It did not matter now, as Aizarg and his band of fools were probably already dead somewhere on the steppe. Virag returned his attention to the business at hand. What was important was getting to the cache, one of the slaver's many secret stashes hidden up and down the coast, ahead of the rising water.

Virag followed the two burly Sammujad warriors wielding their swords like machetes, cutting a path through the head-high reeds. This cache originally sat hidden several hundred paces from the shore. Now they slogged through almost knee-deep water.

Clouds of black marsh flies should have assaulted them, but the air was clear. Tadpoles and water bugs should have danced at their feet. Instead, silence dominated a marsh every bit as sterile as the steppe.

The marsh men's arrival at his trading camp heralded the beginning of a string of ill omens. The day after Aizarg's party departed, word reached Virag of a great horde of cursed beasts gathering in the east. Gentle grassland streams suddenly swelled with dark, cold water and swept away all in their path. Soon, they began to consume the marshes. Several nights ago, a thousand stars fell from the sky and then, this morning a great star thundered from the heavens.

The water comes from the land, not the Great Sea. Another half a day and it will cover the reeds and sweep away the cache. I am just in time.

With a muted thud, the lead warrior's sword stuck something solid.

Virag shoved him aside. "You damn fool! If you damaged it I'll run you through myself."

Virag parted the reeds to reveal an enormous tarp of stitched and oiled horse hide concealing his treasure. He held his breath and lifted a corner of the tarp.

It's all here, in perfect condition.

The two Sammujad considered the objects with ignorant disgust.

"The Captain of Hur-ar has paid for these, has he not, master?"

Virag slowly turned and let his eyes sink into the henchmen like a slow, twisting knife. The warrior turned away under the smaller man's burning gaze.

"Will they still work, master?" the other warrior asked.

"Of course. I stored them exactly as the sco-lo-ti Ba-lok advised. Both of you return to camp and bring back everything as I instructed." Virag looked down at the water. "And hurry!"

The two warriors nodded and sloshed off through the marshes, leaving Virag to further examine his treasure.

A good trader always hedges his bets.

27. Dawn's Bitter Duty

The mighty Scythian king, Sosa, spied the young maiden bathing by a stream at the edge of the marsh. Intent on enslaving her, he carried her far across the steppe.

Instead of becoming his slave, she melted his black heart. Stricken with love, he made her his wife over all the maidens of the Scythia. In time, the horse warriors came to revere the wise and beautiful Lo princess, whom they called the Lady of the Water. Soon, she bore Sosa an heir, whom they named Sawseruquo.

Sosa doted on her and gave her all she desired, but sadness still filled her heart. Though she came to love Sosa, The Lady of the Water always pined for the Great Sea.

"What will make you happy? Tell me and I will make it so," Sosa beseeched her.

"Bring me a white marsh flower and plant it in front of our yurt that I may remember the smell of the sea."

He did, but in a day it withered. As the flower died, the Lady of the Water fell ill.

The next day Sosa brought back another flower, more lovely than the first. "This one will thrive and so shall you," he said and planted it outside their yurt.

It, too, withered and died. The Lady hovered on the edge of death.

Desperate, Sosa rode once again to the marsh and found the loveliest flower of all and planted it outside their yurt.

That night, the goddess Psatina scooped up some of the Great Sea in her hand and carried it far into the steppe. The sky grew dark in her shadow. The heavens flashed when the goddess blinked her eyes. The horses fled as ear-splitting booms echoed with her footfalls. The Scythians cowered in their yurts as the goddess opened her hands and showered water over the third flower.

The next morning the flower was alive and in full bloom. So, too, did the Lady's health recover. Sosa knew the Lo goddess had sent him a message. His beautiful flower would die separated from the Great Sea. With a heavy heart he returned The Lady of the Water to the marsh, content he would see his beloved in the eyes of his son, Prince Sawseruquo.

From that day forth a beautiful white flower blossoms alone and unmolested on the barren g'an. The Blossom of Lady Setenay blooms eternally on the steppe, a sign that love can find root far from home, and hope can bloom in the darkest of places. - Conversations with Sana

The Chronicle of Fu Xi

***

In the center of the living circle, the spirit's features sharpened and focused until she crystalized into the shade of her final earthly shell. Black hair piled high on her head and clothed in a white silk robe emblazoned with the form of the golden dragon, the goddess appeared as she had for countless Offering Ceremonies. She unfurled paper fans in each hand and wrapped them around her like folded wings, one below her chin and one behind her back.

Her delicate feet, wrapped in silk slippers, floated a hair's breadth above the ground. Her almond eyes simmered with a blue glow. The spirit could not smell the dust nor feel the chill in the air, but she remembered their physical sensations and mourned her earthly lives with each memory.

She sensed Fu Xi far to the east, climbing the Roof of the World on his gray mare. Her other son dwelt closer, beyond the Great Sea to the southeast.

Untouched by the living cloud of animals, she turned to the west and raised her arms high over her head, fans outstretched.

May this act begin my atonement.

As the last sliver of the red sun vanished into the sea, the age of Narim and Nephilim came to an end. The Angel of Death dropped her arms and the fans closed with thunderous snap.

Every creature in the circle crashed to the dust, from the smallest insect to the mightiest elephant.

Along the Black River, the Valley of the Beasts became the Valley of Death.

***

Okta woke Aizarg before dawn to find the water almost to the fire.

"When I woke the tide was starting to lift one side of the raft," Okta said, chewing a bit of dried fish and handing Aizarg a piece. "I pulled the raft back, but I think the water is rising more rapidly now."

Aizarg's shoulder still throbbed, but felt better than the day before. He shed the sling and slowly ate the fish.

Aizarg opened his mouth to ask where Ood-i and Sarah were when the big man stepped out of the shadows and looked at Aizarg nervously. Ood-i threw more wood on the fire until it blazed enough to cut the pre-dawn chill and provide enough light to pack their belongings.

Winter is coming, perhaps a very long one.

Setenay remained where Aizarg saw her before he fell asleep – sitting by the fire and gazing into the flames. Her rolled bed mat sat next to her unopened pack. She looked exhausted, her wheezing worse.

Aizarg began to worry about her.

"Setenay, did you get any sleep?"

She nodded to a place next to the fire where the new sail was neatly folded. "When I get sewing I lose track of time." Her voice reminded Aizarg of the sound of the wagon wheels crossing the Kupar Bridge, deep, rough and hollow.

The gray false dawn lightened the eastern ridge.

"Where is Sarah?" Aizarg looked about. Setenay didn't respond and looked back into the fire. That's when Sarah stepped out of the shadows, adjusting her dress.

Anger boiled in Aizarg's heart as he realized she came from the same direction Ood-i emerged just moments earlier.

Setenay grabbed his hand and pulled herself up. "I know what you see," she hissed into his ear. "Say nothing!"

"They both took an oath! It will poison the arun-ki."

"The arun-ki is gone!" she shouted. "Look at the water! Our people are most likely afloat and praying for our return. The last thing you need to do is dwell on whether or not two people in love can keep an oath we both *knew* they could not honor."

Okta, Ood-i, and Sarah watched them. Sarah stepped forward, tears in her eyes. "I am sorry, Father. I love him. I cannot deny it, especially now."

Sarah hugged Aizarg and tucked her head into his sore shoulder. "Please don't turn me away, Father," she sobbed.

Aizarg looked at Ood-i. "I love her, Uros," Ood-i said clearly, his expression firm. "We w-will face the deluge alone if we must, but we will never be parted again."

Everyone looked to Aizarg and waited for his reaction.

He sighed and nodded.

What was it Noah said? 'Justice should never be meted without the council of the heart. That is where God's voice can always be heard.'

Aizarg pulled Sarah closer and held her tight. "You are not going to be turned away, daughter. We will find a way."

She wrapped her arms tightly around his neck and sobbed.

Ood-i placed his hand on Aizarg's good shoulder. "Thank you, Uros."

Aizarg thought about Ula and Su-gár. *How will we work this out?*

"Setenay, is there a ceremony or tradition which might be useful to resolve the situation when we return?" Aizarg asked.

Setenay sat back down and rested her head in her hand. "If not, I'm sure Atamoda can make something up." Okta and Ood-i gave Setenay a bewildered look.

Setenay impatiently rolled her eyes and waved her hand dismissively. "Oh, don't look so surprised! The gods know I've conveniently "rediscovered" enough ancient rites in my time. A good patesi-le does what she must to keep peace in the village." Setenay sighed, "It will work itself out. One storm at a time, Uros. One storm at a time."

The real dawn fast approached in a cloudless sky, breathing shapes and color into the gray shadows along the shore.

Okta pointed to the pink line heralding the approaching sun. "Someone approaches over the eastern ridge. It must be Ghalen and Levidi." He bent over and tossed his pack onto the raft. "Perhaps this god of the Narim saw fit to help them find a mast."

"Or my grandson." Setenay shot Okta a stern glance.

"Yes, old mother," Okta corrected himself. "I hope they found Ba-lok."

Sarah looked up at Aizarg through tears of happiness. "Thank you! Thank you, father!"

Aizarg kissed her forehead. "Atamoda and I have much to discuss, but Setenay is right – one storm at a time. You and Ood-i must refrain from...from you know, until Atamoda and I can sit down with Ood-i and Ula and sort this all out."

Sarah searched Aizarg's eyes with a worried expression. "Will Atamoda think less of me? I fear she will not accept me."

"She will see everything I see in you. She will love you." Aizarg grinned. "You have no idea how much she wants a daughter! She loves the boys, but boys can't fill the place in a mother's heart a daughter can."

Sarah almost squealed. "I can't wait to meet them all!"

Aizarg heard a faint *thunk* and Sarah jerked forward in his arms. Her eyes grew wide.

"Father?" she whispered. Her eyes rolled into the back of her head as a trickle of blood ran out of her mouth.

"Sarah!" Aizarg screamed and caught her as she slumped. A dark, red blot rapidly grew between her breasts, a bloody arrow poking out of its center. Aizarg peered over her shoulder and saw a black Scythian arrow shaft between her shoulder blades.

Six dark figures descended from the eastern ridge, silhouetted by daybreak. Two carried bows at the ready, walking side-by-side in the lead. Four followed behind.

"No!" Ood-i snatched his sagar while Okta grabbed his boar spear.

Screaming furiously, Ood-i rushed the Scythians from Aizarg's right as Okta charged from the left. Ood-i reared back, building momentum for his throw.

The Scythian archers released a volley and Ood-i crumpled to the dust, arrows protruding from his chest and neck.

With a grunt, Okta threw his spear. It sailed gracefully toward the Scythian archers. The archers calmly stepped back and the spear sank harmlessly into the ground at their feet.

Aizarg heard the Scythians laugh and realized he had no spear. He looked around for his staff, but it rested against his pack on the other side of the fire.

Setenay rushed to Aizarg as he lowered Sarah to the ground. "Do not lay her fully on the ground, support her!"

Setenay commanded as she snapped off the portion of the arrow protruding from Sarah's back.

Okta didn't slow down. He pulled his knife and charged the archers. They fired again. Okta dodged one arrow, but another found his thigh. He fell, clutching his leg in agony. The archers ignored Okta and closed in on Aizarg.

The Scythians were calm and self-assured. They walked almost shoulder to shoulder, bow-legged from years of living in the saddle. They had the same shaved head and top-knot of the Scythian prince, but their trousers and vests were of plain horse leather.

Now Aizarg got a good look at the four other Scythians behind the bowmen. Two men carried light spears. To their left strode a tall, dark woman dressed similarly to the men. She held a leash tied to a battered and bruised man.

Ba-lok!

The older Scythian on the right had a long scar across his tattooed face, giving his grin an evil twist. "Kill the witch before she curses us. I will slay the man," he said to the younger one, perhaps a few years older than Ezra.

Setenay placed herself between the Scythians and Aizarg. "You are already cursed, children of Sosa!" Setenay pointed an accusing finger at the Scythians. "The rising water will forever seal your kind in an icy tomb."

So this is how it ends. Aizarg held his daughter close and stared defiantly at the Scythians.

As the Scythians notched their bows and began to draw, a sagar sliced out of the sky and impaled both men. It penetrated the older Scythian's neck, almost beheading him, and continued on through the younger man's abdomen. It sank so deep into the ground it held both dead men upright.

Then Aizarg heard a sound that had never been heard before: a Lo war cry.

The two other Scythians turned their head in surprise, just in time for one to see a sagar penetrate his chest.

Ghalen and Levidi charged along the riverbank from the south, with Ezra close behind. The last two Scythians shrieked their own battle cry and rushed them, knife and spear at the ready.

"Father," Sarah whispered and coughed in a series of weak spasms.

"I am here!" Tears streamed down Aizarg's cheeks and fell onto Sarah's bloody chest.

Disoriented, Sarah tried to move her head. "Where is Ood-i? I cannot see him." Aizarg glanced over at Ood-i. One of the arrows had gone halfway through his neck.

Setenay knelt next to Aizarg as the battle raged along the shore.

The remaining Scythian man loosed his light spear at Levidi, who barely dodged it. A few seconds later they clashed. The Scythian jumped and planted both feet into Levidi's chest, hurling him backward. In an instant the Scythian fell upon him, dagger drawn and thirsty for blood. They rolled in the dust, Levidi desperately trying to hold off the horseman's blade.

The tall, lean woman leapt at Ghalen with the nimbleness of a deer. Her black hair flew about like a wild mane as she wielded a long, curved knife against Ghalen's boar spear. She dodged, twirled about, and delivered a solid kick to Ghalen's head. He wiped a spurt of fresh blood off his lip as he stumbled back.

She lunged again. He brought the spear up in both hands to block her assault. Like lightning, she kicked straight out and cleanly snapped the shaft in two.

Dumbfounded, Ghalen held the two broken pieces of his spear. The Scythian woman briefly laughed and fell upon him with renewed fury. Ghalen jabbed the pointed end of the spear at her, but she deflected it with the side of her arm. Before she could pivot, Ghalen swiped the blunt piece across her face. She spun about and crumpled, unconscious.

Ezra joined in Levidi's battle. He jumped on the Scythian's back and succeeded in pulling him away from Levidi, but couldn't get his knife under the man's throat. Levidi pulled himself up, forearms dripping with bloody slash marks. Levidi grit his teeth and punched the Scythian hard across the jaw. The Scythian fell backwards on top of Ezra and didn't move.

Sarah grew pale and cool in Aizarg's arms while Setenay tried to stanch the bleeding with strips ripped from Sarah's dress. Setenay looked up at Aizarg and shook her head.

Aizarg released a long, mournful wail and pressed Sarah close to him.

"No, no, no, no...!" He looked to the heavens. The stars were almost gone as sunlight streamed over the horizon. "If you are a god, *the* God, save her! Where is your mercy?" Aizarg almost spat the last word. "Where is this love Noah spoke of? If you created this world, why is it so flawed that you see fit to destroy it? Why do you bring suffering to those who are innocent?"

Ghalen, Ezra and Levidi approached and stood over them.

"Sarah!" Ezra cried and fell to his knees next to Aizarg. Setenay put her arm around him.

"Father," Sarah whispered and smiled weakly. "You promised to leave your tears in Hur-ar." Her breaths came in sharp, short cuts as her lungs filled with blood. Her eyes glazed over and became distant.

The sun broke over the horizon and a ray of light fell on Sarah's face. Her face suddenly took on new life and she focused beyond Aizarg. A smile touched her blue-tinged lips.

"I see Ood-i!" She held up her hand and reached out. Then her eyes suddenly grew wide. She extended her index finger and rolled her head to the right, to the north. "I see her! She is beautiful! The spirit has come to take me home, just as she promised." Her voice trailed off into a strange, unfamiliar whisper. "The Offering Blade is raised. Dawn's bitter duty is upon her."

The northern sky suddenly flashed.

Aizarg and the rest turned to where Sarah pointed. Setenay stood and faced north, where only a few stars were still visible.

The Heart of the Dragon twinkled and brightened spectacularly. It rivaled the sun and bathed the shore in brilliant white light.

"It has begun," Setenay said grimly. "The God of the Narim has sliced open the sky and will fill the sea with the tears of the dead."

***

The spirit waited in the circle of death throughout the night. Her blazing eyes were the only light except for the stars. The dust still hung in the windless valley as the stars faded in the false dawn. She snapped closed the fan in her right hand, and with an elegant flick of her wrist, transformed it into the Offering Blade. She faced north and pointed to the star called the Heart of the Dragon. With the tip of the blade, she drew a line from the Heart of the Dragon to a point on the southeast horizon.

"Behold, I have cut open the roof of Heaven."

The Angel of Death lowered her arm and leaned her head back. In the sunrise of a new age, she closed her blazing eyes and evaporated like a puff of smoke.

The Heart of the Dragon twinkled, and then gave birth to a ball of fire. Its long, blazing tail lit the entire valley with white light. Like a fiery sword, the giant meteor hurtled across the sky in claps of thunder on the exact arc traced by the angel's dagger until it fell below the southern horizon.

In a blinding flash of light, the Herald of the Cataclysm plunged into a nameless ocean far to the south.

***

The shore fell quiet. Everyone stared at the heavens, where a thick, white trail hung from horizon to horizon like a tear in the fabric of the sky. Dawn gave the cloud a gilded edge.

Setenay didn't look up; her concern remained on the wounded...and the dead.

Ood-i sprawled on his belly, head to the side and eyes wide.

He died before he hit the ground.

Setenay closed his eyes and moved on to Okta. She knelt beside him and examined the wound.

"I am fine! Help me up!" he protested.

"Hush! You will not think you're fine in a few moments. This isn't a simple bone hook, it's a barbed Scythian arrowhead." He winced as she broke off the shaft and pulled a knife from a hidden fold in her dress.

"Open your mouth and bite down on this," she said and held up the broken shaft.

"I'm not going to put a filthy Scythian arrow in my..." She crammed the shaft between his teeth as he protested. Before he could spit it out, she sank her knife into his thigh alongside the arrow head.

Setenay twisted the tip and pried the arrow from Okta's thigh. He bit down hard in agony.

"The Scythian points do as much damage coming out as going in," she said. "Fortunately for you, it wasn't too deep."

She ripped a strip off her dress and bandaged his wound the best she could. Okta stood and winced. "I can walk," he grimaced and limped to where Ghalen tied up the unconscious Scythians.

Setenay stood and saw Levidi cutting Ba-lok's bindings.

Ba-lok's battered and bruised face, one eye swollen shut, testified to his treatment at the hands of the Scythians. Levidi removed Ba-lok's gag and tried to tend to his wounds, even though his own arm bled profusely. Ba-lok slapped Levidi's hand away. "I don't need your help!"

He will be fine, at least on the outside.

Levidi threw his hands up in disgust and went to help the others.

Except for Ba-lok, they gathered around their Uros as he embraced his daughter's body. Unwilling to let go, he rocked her back and forth, his eyes still locked on the northern sky.

Ezra knelt next to Aizarg, sobbing and running his bloody fingers through his sister's white hair.

"She's dead," Setenay whispered, trying to get Aizarg to look at her. "Sarah is with the spirit of the mist. She is with the God of the Narim. The water is rising, Uros. You have a responsibility to the living."

"Uros," Okta gently touched his shoulder. "We must give Sarah and Ood-i to the Great Mother. We must place them into the water."

"No," Setenay said flatly. "The water is cursed and old ways are dead. They are already one with the God of The Narim. Okta, Levidi and Ghalen, do what I say and be quick. There is no time to mourn."

She put her arm around Ezra. "Young man, help us honor your sister."

Ezra wiped his eyes, leaving bloody smears like war paint. "What must I do?"

I must guide them once more.

Setenay looked across the water. The demons were gathering near the shore, bunched up and writhing near the raft.

Only once more...

Over the next few minutes Setenay gave them specific instructions. The men worked quickly, with only the occasional sniffle or sob to break the silence.

Ba-lok didn't help them. He sat on the raft and stared out across the endless expanse of flat, swift water. Only a few hilltops could be seen poking above the water. The edge of the raft lifted slightly in the current.

"Stay out of the water," she called to her grandson, but he didn't respond.

A loud hiss drew everyone's attention. The water reached the camp fire, only a few feet from where Aizarg held Sarah.

It didn't take long for the men to lay down the first layer of rocks. Under Setenay's supervision, Ghalen and Levidi carefully broke off the ends of the arrows in Ood-i's flesh. Together, they picked up his body and laid him out on his back on the right side of the rock bed.

Setenay called to Aizarg, "It is time. Bring Sarah."

Her voice pierced the fog of Aizarg's grief. He looked about as if he were seeing everything for the first time.

"Come, Aizarg. Come and honor your daughter."

Aizarg gently lifted Sarah and carried her to the rock bed. There, he laid her down next to Ood-i.

Setenay signaled the men, and they began to cover the bodies with stones.

"Wait!" Aizarg reached down and joined the lover's hands. "They will never be separated again."

"Lo dogs!" a voice screamed. The Scythians were awake, sitting up with their hands and feet bound. The man sneered through bloody teeth. "You and your witch brought this curse upon us. You drove our horses away! We found your tracks next to those of our horses. We will make you pay under a hail of arrows. Your men will be impaled on our spears and your women and children will be our slaves." He nodded to Ba-lok. "We will use them like we used your sco-lo-ti."

Ba-lok flinched and seemed to shrink down on the raft.

Ghalen snatched his sagar and strode to the Scythian. "I will finish what I started!"

"Stop!" Setenay shouted. "In due time, Ghalen. Let us honor our dead first."

She looked back at Aizarg. He stood over the bodies, gazing down upon them, seemingly oblivious to what transpired around him.

Ghalen turned back and the Scythian man laughed. Ghalen spun around and knocked him out with the end of the sagar. He raised the handle against the woman. "Will you defile our dead with your words, too?"

She offered up her chin defiantly, but her eyes weren't as hard as the man's. "I do not speak with my cousin's tongue," she said. "I will not dishonor your dead, marsh man, but...but..."

"Speak!" Ghalen shouted and reared back the spear handle.

"Why do you bury your dead in a Scythian zhaqa? I thought your kind surrender your dead to the water?"

"The water is cursed," Setenay spoke up. "We honor our dead as we did your dead prince we found several days ago."

Ghalen lowered his spear. "Yes. It was this woman's *mercy*," he pointed to Sarah, "that convinced us to bury your prince. He was dragged to death by his horse. She said he was worthy of mercy. It is only because I honor her spirit that I don't kill you now." Ghalen threw down his spear and walked back to gather stones.

The Scythian woman lowered her chin, her defiance gone.

The zhaqa quickly rose around the bodies, only a few paces from the rapid upslope of the eastern ridge. Okta and Ba-lok moved the raft back several times and loaded it with the rest of the supplies. The water completely submerged the campfire now.

Except for Ba-lok, they surrounded the burial mound.

Aizarg spoke. "I have no words for the sadness that takes my breath."

"There will be more pain...more grieving," Setenay said. "There will also be hope. Let Sarah's spirit light your way through the darkness to come. Let Ood-i's bravery inspire your courage for the trials ahead."

"Uros, the water is almost upon us. We must go," Okta said urgently, but Aizarg didn't respond as he stared at the zhaqa.

Setenay looked at Aizarg and shook her head.

Time is short. Snap out of it!

"Yes, it is time to leave, but one thing remains to be done." Setenay walked to the prisoners and pushed the man with her foot.

"Wake up, *shawa!*" she shouted.

He rolled over with a groan. "How do you know my title, bitch?" he sneered and spat at her.

Setenay whacked him across the face with her stick. "I know everything about you by the lack of beads adorning your cherkesska. You were the page to the prince we buried, were you not?"

He rubbed his cheek. "I was."

"Death or life, shawa. The choice is yours," Setenay said coldly.

"I will die before I submit to the will of marsh men."

Setenay glanced warily at the sky. The cloudy trail high above them wasn't blowing away or dissipating. Instead, it slowly expanded over the sky. Both beautiful and terrifying, golden tendrils of glittering, wavy light danced and streaked beyond the milky veil.

"So be it. Ghalen, Levidi, take him to the edge of the water. Untie him and then throw him in, but do not enter the water yourselves. Drag the woman to the edge, but do not throw her in yet."

"Are you sure?" Ghalen asked.

"Do as I say!"

They dragged the Scythians to the water's edge. The man tried to bite and claw Levidi. The woman resisted, too, but not as much. She seemed more intent on trying to decipher the Lo's intentions.

Setenay walked back to Aizarg, who still stood in a trance by the zhaqa. She slapped him with full force. He staggered back under the old woman's assault. Setenay hit him again and again until he grabbed her wrist.

"Stop!" he shouted.

"Are you through?" she said. "Sarah is dead. You cannot help her now!" She pointed to the sky. "Death is here and will now be your constant companion! The God of the

Narim will only save those who fight for life. Death or life, the choice is yours, Uros of the Lo."

Lucidity returned to Aizarg's face. All eyes were on him. Without a word, he walked to the edge of the water and retrieved his staff before the black fluid covered it.

Aizarg considered the two Scythians. "What of them, Setenay?"

"Throw him in," she commanded.

Ghalen pinned the man's arms behind his back while Levidi cut his bonds. Then, with considerable effort, they tossed in the Scythian.

He bolted upright, shivering in the knee deep water. "A-ahh h-ha!" he laughed through his shivers. "I am wet! Y-you will h-have to do b-better than that, Lo dogs."

Levidi lifted his spear. "Shall I kill him?"

"Hold your spear," Setenay commanded.

The Scythian began to turn blue and shivered uncontrollably as the strange hissing returned and grew louder.

"Something moves in the water!" Okta shouted.

Setenay turned to Okta, surprised. "You can see them?"

"I see them, too," Ghalen said in awe.

The Scythian woman screamed as several pairs of black hands shot out of the water and dug into the man's legs. He screamed, fell face-first into the water and vanished below the surface. The murky water swirled and then lay flat without a ripple, as if it were a heavy blanket. A thin crust of black ice formed with an evil, cracking sound, and then broke apart in the current.

The Scythian woman screamed again.

"What were those, Setenay?" Levidi gasped.

"Water demons!" Okta said. "I've heard of them, but never seen one."

Setenay stood before the Scythian woman. *By the look of the beads on her red cherkesska, she is a princess.* Setenay looked the tall, slender girl up and down. *She has both her breasts and is not yet a woman.* Scythian maidens sliced off one of their breasts during the rights of womanhood to better wield a bow.

She fights like a woman, though. Setenay recognized something familiar in the girl's eyes.

"Death or life?" Setenay asked.

"Do not throw me to the demons!" the terrified girl pleaded.

"Then obey."

"I will obey."

Setenay put her hands on her hips and straightened, looking down on the girl. Then she held out her hand. "A proper Scythian woman carries four daggers. Give me the one called Death."

A quizzical look briefly crossed the Scythian girl's face, and then her eyes narrowed. Slowly, she reached into her cherkesska and withdrew a small, but wickedly crooked knife with an antler handle and handed it hilt-first to Setenay.

"What is your name?" Setenay asked as she turned the black blade in her hands.

"Sana."

"Sana." Setenay chewed on the name. "The dead prince was your brother, wasn't he? You are the granddaughter of mighty King Sosa, daughter of Sawseruquo?"

Sana nodded, mouth agape at the old woman's knowledge of her people. Suddenly, Sana gasped and held her hand to her mouth. "You are the Lady of the Water!"

"The past is dead and the white bloom will soon be washed away," Setenay said, the edge in her voice replaced with weariness. "Sana, Princess of Scythia, your tribe will soon perish. Forsake the name 'Scythian' forever." Setenay turned to Ghalen and handed him the knife. "Never return this knife to her. Never. She has three others hidden on her body, but she will not raise them against you. Place her on the raft."

"Setenay!" Ghalen held up his hands. "She helped kill our friends. This is madness! Let us slay her now. I will kill her mercifully."

Sana trembled, teeth clenched, and glared at Ghalen.

Setenay looked from the Scythian to Ghalen and remembered last night's bittersweet joy. She touched Ghalen's cheek and whispered, "Out of darkness, mercy."

Setenay then spoke again to Sana. "You will obey this man. He is Ghalen of the Turtle Clan and is responsible for you until his patesi-le can figure out what to do with you. Remember, one push and you join the demons."

Ghalen picked her up and dropped her roughly in the middle of the raft.

Through clenched teeth, Sana looked past him to where the water encroached on the bodies of her tribesmen. Her eyes misted, but the black-haired woman did not cry.

She is strong, Setenay thought. *I would only expect as much from my granddaughter.*

Setenay turned to Aizarg. "If men can see the water demons, then the evil spirits have grown powerful indeed. The God of the Narim has unchained them from the icy pit to ensure none survive the deluge. There will be more. They will pour into the seas to feed on the dead and the living. Boats and rafts will not be safe."

"Our people!" Levidi's face paled. "My wife."

Setenay held up her hand. "The spirit in the mist showed me what is to come. She also bestowed a gift, one I already possess, but now a thousand-fold more powerful." She closed her eyes and placed her hands over the orb on Aizarg's staff. The red metal began to glow a ruddy red until heat radiated off its surface. Setenay's hands fell away and she opened her eyes.

It is done. Her breathing became more labored. Dizzy, she almost fell until Aizarg caught her under her arm.

"Aizarg, give your staff to Levidi," she said.

Aizarg did as Setenay commanded. Levidi hefted the staff awkwardly.

"Levidi, step to the edge and stretch the staff over the water."

Everyone now saw the demons writhing under the surface. "There are so many!" Levidi said. He motioned the orb over the water and, instantly the demons streaked away. Thin tendrils of mist danced on the water's surface, as if the water suddenly warmed.

"I think I heard them shriek!" Okta said. To Setenay, the cry shook her soul.

Pay the price, old witch! The demons screamed at her.

"No, they only fled," she said. "They will not approach the staff. Levidi, give the staff back to Aizarg. It is his to carry, but you will wield it on his behalf."

"Why can I not wield it?" Aizarg asked.

"Levidi was chosen to wield it to remind you that the power within the staff comes from the God of the Narim, not you." She turned to Levidi. "Serve your Uros well."

Levidi nodded and gave the staff back to Aizarg.

"The raft floats," Okta said. "We have no mast for our sail."

"The current will carry you to your destiny," Setenay said. "Uros, lead them."

Aizarg nodded. "To the raft, let us save our people."

Okta anchored the raft with a long pole while everyone climbed aboard. Aizarg stepped aboard with Ezra and showed him where to sit. Ghalen and Levidi prepared to shove off.

Setenay came to the side of the raft where Ba-lok sat. He wouldn't look at her.

"All of you abandoned me," he seethed.

"Grandson," she said with resignation and bitter sorrow. "May you become the man your father wanted you to be, the man I know you can be."

Something in her voice seemed to connect with Ba-lok. He gave her an uneasy look. "Grandmother...?"

A rumble echoed to the north as one of the remaining hilltops crumbled and thundered into the water. It spawned a deep wave, which grew as it raced towards them.

Ghalen saw the approaching wave and pushed Levidi onto the raft. He jumped up and held out his arm. "Hurry, Setenay, take my hand."

Setenay stepped back. "Goodbye, Ghalen."

Aizarg turned around. "Setenay, get in the raft!"

"No, Uros. I cannot." She backed up against the zhaqa. "The God of the Narim promised the demons the flesh of all creatures beyond the walls of the ark. They are the vultures and maggots of the coming deluge. There is a price to turn away their claws. The power I placed into the staff did not come without a price."

Aizarg handed his staff to Levidi and lunged toward Setenay. "Get onto the raft!"

One last duty, one last task and I can rest. Setenay spoke the words from her vision, the message from the God of the Narim.

"The Lo will not be forgotten, Aizarg! We will be remembered!"

The heavy, rolling wave swept across the shore and hit the raft, lurching it hard to the right. Aizarg almost spilled over the side before Okta pulled him back.

The wave pushed Setenay over the zhaqa then quickly receded, sweeping the raft away from the shore and downstream.

"Setenay!" Ghalen prepared to dive into the water. Levidi grabbed him and pulled him back. Ghalen fought him, but Aizarg helped Levidi hold him as the raft quickly accelerated downstream.

"Do not jump in!" Levidi screamed. "The demons will rip you to pieces."

A black tide of demons flowed in a wide arc around the raft, giving them a considerable berth and shot toward the shore in front of Setenay like a squirt of ink. She crawled on top of Sarah and Ood-i's burial mound and sat calmly. Ice formed and reformed along the shore, now only inches from the stones. They squirmed over one another in a frenzy to reach the last Isp of the Lo people. Black claws dug into the clay, breaking and reforming the ice in a dark, angry froth.

Setenay crossed her legs and waited for her icy death. She watched the raft float away as the first stones of the zhaqa crumbled into the water.

"Farewell, my fishermen."

***

Ghalen sat cross-legged with his face in his hands, racked with uncontrollable sobs. Levidi put his arm around him, tears filling his eyes. Everyone sat down as close to the middle of the raft as possible except for Okta and Aizarg. Okta stood on the back of the raft, trying to use his pole to keep them straight. Soon the water was too deep.

"We are at the mercy of the current," Okta said through his tears.

Aizarg's tears were spent. He stood at the front and could not bring himself to look back at Setenay. Without Sarah and Setenay, he felt like both his arms had just been severed.

I am alone.

"So be it," Aizarg said at last. "Let the current carry us. We are in the hands of the God of the Narim now."

The shore fell away and disappeared into an endless horizon. The Black River became a sea in its own right, relentlessly hurtling toward the Great Sea beyond the southern horizon.

Will it devour the Great Sea? Will our beloved home become a cold, sterile Black Sea?

"Look!" Ezra pointed up at the thin white veil expanding across the entire sky. Through it, bright sheets of shooting stars streaked from the southern horizon.

Aizarg didn't look, transfixed on the dark wall of clouds boiling up from the south like the coils of a giant black serpent rising from the sea.

Epilogue

As his mother had commanded, Fu Xi rode Huise relentlessly for days until they came to the mountains called The Roof of the World. The gray mare had no more to give. Yet the brave horse, found the strength to go on. Pride and love for her swirled in Fu Xi's heart.

I am killing her, he thought as his tears quickly dried in the dry, thin air. Guilt tore at the god's soul. *This gentle, majestic creature is suffering for me.*

They cleared the alpine trees before dawn and still he gave her no rest. He sensed the doom his mother spoke of approaching like a wolf at their heels. The horses seemed to sense it, too. Salvation meant reaching the top of the narrow pass wedged between two glaciers, still a thousand feet above them.

They trudged up the dry canyon, narrow and steep, toward the bare rock outcropping marking the top of the pass. To the north and south jagged ice covered peaks towered in the starry pre-dawn.

It was difficult to breathe up here, even for a god. Heise, the black stallion, struggled to follow at the end of his tether, though he had no rider and only a light load.

When Fu Xi's gentle chiding and praises no longer stirred the mare forward he lashed her, kicked her sides and drove her at a gallop up the steep mountainside. He could sense her heart on the edge of bursting, but still the god drove her on.

Her hooves slipped and clawed to find traction in the loose gravel and shale. Then, without warning, sweet, gentle Huise had no more to give. She collapsed, throwing Fu Xi forward onto the slope.

Heise stood over the mare, gently nuzzling his companion, trying to get her to rise. The mare's eyes were wide and glazed. Thick, bloody foam bubbled from her snout, mottled gray coat well lathered.

Fu Xi crawled to her and cradled Huise's head in his lap. He ran his hand gently over her neck, trying to impart some comfort to his dying friend. She felt as cold as the icy air at the top of the world.

"I am sorry," he whispered over and over.

The sky suddenly flashed in a brilliant glow. Fu Xi marveled at the tremendous fireball arcing across the western sky to the south. In it he saw the hand of Nuwa.

"It has begun."

A sharp crack issued from above. Fu Xi looked up at the peak in time to see the glaciers on either side of the canyon begin to slowly slide down towards him, as if releasing their grip on the earth at some unheard command.

With nowhere to run, he would be crushed. He stood and snatched Heise's harness to keep the horse from bolting in terror. But Heise stood calmly next to him, as if soothed by an invisible hand in the face of the overwhelming natural violence.

In a matter of seconds, thousands of tons of ice gently slid to either side of Fu Xi and his horses. With very little sound except for the occasional snap or pop, the walls of the ice canyons passed them by with only inches to spare. The glaciers picked up speed and began to crumble in a deafening crescendo, shattering into enormous white boulders tumbling into the valley thousands of feet below. Suddenly, the glaciers on the peaks to his immediate south and north gave way and thundered into the barren valley from whence they rode last night. Avalanches of rock and mud followed the ice, making the valley impassable.

Had Huise collapsed only a few paces down the slope we would be buried below that ice.

Fu Xi looked down at Huise. Her eyes were lifeless, her suffering over. He removed his gear and supplies from her body and loaded them on the black stallion.

He gave her cold flank one more pat. "Thank you."

Looking back to the east and the rising sun, Fu Xi allowed himself a brief thought of Nushen.

"There is no way back. Home is forever gone," he whispered. Heise gave him a gentle nuzzle. Fu Xi rubbed the horse's neck as he turned to consider the barren pass, now devoid of ice. When he crossed over to the west he would enter unknown lands. Somewhere beyond dwelt the man with white hair, the man he must help, and a half-brother he never knew he had.

Fu Xi slowly turned and led his horse up the mountain.

"Come, Heise. The only way back home is forward."

To Be Continued in The Chronicle of Fu Xi Book II: Tears of the Dead.

ABOUT THE AUTHOR

Brian L. Braden is the author of the novelette *Carson's Love*. His articles have been featured in a variety of defense magazines and websites, to include the *Military Times* and *Air Power Journal*. He is a founder and assistant editor of Underground Book Reviews.

Please support indie literature. If you enjoyed this novel, please rate this book on Amazon.

Sneak Peak of *Tears of the Dead*

Prologue: The Lion and the Snake.

"In Hur-ar it was said, the Narim were the gods of the poor, Ba'al god of the rich. But the only true god in Hur-ar was gold." - Conversations with the Uros.

Chronicle of Fu Xi

***

Before the Cataclysm

Head held high, chest puffed with pride, the Lion of Hur-ar marched to glory. The crimson glow silhouetting the mountains announced dawn's imminent arrival, ushering in his ascendency as one of Hur-ar's most powerful men. He only need ensure nothing went wrong during this morning's routine ceremony.

He gazed up at the Black Fortress only a few yards ahead, its darkness untouched by the rose-colored rays chasing the stars from the sky. Bal-eeb, Captain of the Wall, sidestepped to the Cliff Road's edge and inspected the procession as it passed. The ceremonial guard marched by two abreast, sandaled feet crunching the gravel in unison. Eyes locked forward, their misty breath floated on the chilly autumn air. Highly polished bronze chest plates clinked softly against chainmail and provided an eerie music to accompany the trade delegation.

Behind the warriors, six muscled slaves, nude and sweating in the morning chill, struggled under the gilded litter's weight. They bore lounging Norrufi, Supreme Royal Trader and second cousin to the King. Rolls of perfumed fat spilled from underneath an ornate blanket, jiggling in rhythm with the jostling litter. His threadbare beard hung under a perpetually dour expression and did nothing to conceal the eunuch's many chins.

Bal-eeb nodded in deference as the litter passed by, trying not to wrinkle his nose in disgust.

He smells like a woman. Suitable, I suppose, for someone who traded his balls for power.

Men possessing such power and wealth could not be trusted with an heir to challenge the King. Nevertheless, the Supreme Royal Trader held significant influence in court and Bal-eeb suffered the fat fool's insolence. He needed Norrufi's well-placed whispers if he were to depose the Captain of the Palace Guard. The man reclining on the golden litter assured Bal-eeb this morning's duties played no small part in advancing this goal.

In many ways Norrufi's opposite, Bal-eeb stood half a head taller than most men, in the prime of youth and well-muscled. Powerful, wealthy, and brutally ambitious, the city idolized the man they called the Lion of Hur-ar.

The warriors crested the cliff overlooking the city just as dawn's first rays crept over the mountain beyond the Black Gate. They split into two ranks of five and formed a wide opening for Norrufi's litter and the wagons.

"Look sharp, lions of Hur!" Bal-eeb barked.

A simple assignment, yes, but there could be no mistakes this morning.

Three massive ox-drawn wagons, almost too wide to negotiate the narrow Cliff Road, rumbled close behind Norrufi's litter. Goods from Hur-ar's vast trading empire, iron tools and bags stuffed with grain, packed each cart to the breaking point. With mouths foaming and eyes wide in agony, the oxen struggled up the mountain. A small army of slaves, scribes, and functionaries from the royal houses and trading guild, trudged in the caravan's dusty wake. Each man played a small part; from carrying the Supreme Trader's piss pot to interpreting the clay tablets left by the Narim.

Deep in thought, Bal-eeb stroked his curly, coal-black beard. His mind raced beyond this morning's proceedings, to plans and plots laid months, even years, earlier. His mother once instructed him, *Make fear and gold your friends and Ba'al will grant all the desires of your heart.* Like his mother, he knew what he wanted and did what was necessary to take it. Events put in motion by his role in this morning's trading ceremony, might eventually place him on the Throne of Gold, as King of Hur-Ar. Today, he also took an important step in slipping from beneath his mother's long shadow.

*Ashtoreth...*common folk only spoke her name as a curse symbolizing seduction and betrayal. In court it dripped from noble lips, gushing with false reverence and adoration, knowing her spies lurked everywhere. Most in the city simply called her "The Snake".

She confided to Bal-eeb her fondness for the title.

Ashtoreth insinuated herself into the House of the Second Prince of Hur-ar as a lowly Sammujad consort, accompanied by her bastard son on the edge of manhood. She quickly bewitched the prince and, in only a few months, cunningly eliminated her rivals one-by-one to claim the role of First Wife. Ashtoreth and her son banished or slew the children of the deposed First Wife, leaving Bal-eeb to inherit the prince's fortune. After the prince's mysterious death, Ashtoreth reigned as the Court's most ruthless and feared noble.

In spite of her reputation for cruelty, Ashtoreth's beauty and sexual prowess fueled a fierce competition among Hur-ar's nobles to share her bed. Some say she was Ba'al's own concubine, summoned from hell by a rogue temple priest. If hell was a Sammujad village razed to the ground by Scythian raiders, then Bal-eeb would agree. He knew what truly motivated his mother, death and hunger.

Now only Hecktar, First Prince and Captain of the Palace Guard, stood between Ashtoreth's son and the throne.

Ashtoreth arranged every step of his career, including his posting as Captain of the Wall. Bal-eeb vowed to supplant Hecktar by his own hand, without The Snake's gold or influence. The Lion carefully laid his own plans, which didn't include The Snake.

The King grew weary of holing up in the city, waiting for traders to bring the world's wealth to his doorstep. Unchallenged on the vast steppe, the Scythians grew more powerful and arrogant with each spring. The filthy horsemen demanded greater tribute to permit caravans to pass unmolested to Hur-ar. Only the mystique of the Narim and their Black Fortress kept the raiders at bay. However, this state of affairs was about to change.

Three successive Hur kings built a magnificent army, one possessing bows and horses every bit as powerful as Scythia's. The Hur legions would strike swiftly on winter's eve as the horsemen settled in their winter camps. They would torch the horsemen's winter food stocks, driving the haughty barbarians to starvation. With spring, the well fed and rested Hur army need only clean up the mess. With their western flank secure, the Hur armies would sweep from the edge of the northern Icelands, to the Great Sea, to the mountainous southwest. Booty and slaves would flood into the city. Then they would turn south, where the eastern shore of the Great Sea met the mighty Adyghe Mountains. These were the lands of the Thrax, who held the treacherous southern passes. Beyond the Thrax lay Havilah, where traders spoke of abundant gold, summoned from the ground not by Narim, but by men. Havilah, the ultimate prize, could not be seized without first liquidating the Scythian horde.

As the procession began to take their appointed places, he peered over his shoulder at the city far below. Torches twinkled across rooftops and in the streets. Bal-eeb thought of Hecktar asleep in the palace, blissfully unaware a delegation stood before the Black Gates this morning.

A thousand pardons, Norrufi would shrug to Hecktar before the sun set this day. *I'm sure all the required notifications were made. If the Captain of the Palace Guard cannot carry out his required duties, then the Captain of the Wall is obligated to escort the King's trade delegation.*

"Bureaucrats!" Bal-eeb chuckled. "Deadlier than assassins."

He studied the city far below, from the city wall to the base of Cliff Road, a thousand feet immediately below him.

So few of these soft city dwellers have ever ventured beyond the wall.

Bal-eeb secretly ventured far and wide to lay his plans, plots neither his mother, the Commander or the King knew of.

Bal-eeb knew Scythia stretched farther west than anyone in Hur-ar imagined, even the King. The horsemen could summon tens of thousands of kinsmen and roll over Hur's legions. If they ever lost their superstitious fear of the Black Fortress, they could take Hur-ar itself.

But only Bal-eeb knew the horsemen's weakness. Now *his* influence, *his* gold, *his* schemes would ensure his appointment as the campaign's second-in-command, next only to the Commander himself. The Lion, not the Snake, would eliminate Hecktar and seize the throne on his own terms.

The Captain of the Wall gazed into the darkness beyond the city, beyond the steppe.

The Great Sea and its endless marshes...that is the key to defeating Scythia.

Bal-eeb turned and climbed the short distance remaining to the top. There, he took his place and prepared for the trading ceremony.

The slaves deposited the Norrufi's litter softly on the crushed stone before the Black Gate. The wagons rolled between the columns of warriors and halted behind the litter. The entourage split into two halves; free men behind the warriors' right flank, slaves behind the left. The delegation crowded forward on the narrow ledge, avoiding the drop off by several paces.

With the help of his body slave, Norrufi sat up with a huff. Doughy fat spilled over his golden girdle as he adjusted his waist wrap and straightened his tall, conical cap. Despite the cool morning, sweat trickled down his bare chest. It took all of Bal-eeb's guile to mask his disgust.

Breathing heavily, Noruffi waddled up to the massive iron bell, suspended from a heavy kupar frame and secured to the gate with iron spikes. Offerings left by the city's poor; withering bundles of prairie flowers, clay jars of honey, and candles littered the black stained gravel before the Black Gate.

Noruffi took his place next to the bell's rope and peered into the crowd with narrow, pig-like eyes as if looking for someone. A tall, painfully thin man, with an axe-like face pushed through the line of warriors. Bal-eeb bowed slightly as Shellbaz, High Priest of Ba'al, passed by. A bejeweled golden jar in his bony clutches, he stank of sour wine. Beardless, like all of his order, the priest's black kaffiya and open chested robes fluttered behind him. To Bal-eeb, he resembled an emaciated crow.

The Order of Ba'al despised the Narim, constantly seeking to turn the city against the Masters of the Black Fortress. Only the Hur-po's love of the yellow metal spared the mysterious immortals the Black Dragon's wrath. However, during the last king's reign the Priests managed to inject themselves into trading ceremony.

Bal-eeb didn't believe in Ba'al, though his mother did. Bal-eeb believed only in power, gold and himself. However, that didn't stop him from courting the influential High Priest's favor, going so far as mandating his warriors wear the Black Dragon amulet.

Wearing a look of disgust, Shellbaz kicked several of the offerings aside and, in doing so, almost fell over. Steadying himself, he took his place beside the bell, opposite Noruffi. He held the jar high over his head and, with a slurred voice, shouted to the crowd, "Let the power of the god of this world, master of earthly princes and mortal thrones, sanctify these proceedings!"

He tipped the jar and let the crimson fluid pour onto the gravel. Shellbaz's hung-over, bloodshot eyes came alive, a hungry, sexual, grin flashing at the sight of blood. Norrufi stepped back to avoid being splattered. The priest tucked the empty jar back into his robes and nodded to Noruffi. From another fold he produced a bottle of wine and staggered back into the crowd.

Sludgy and full of clots, the blood seeped away from the gate. The Supreme Royal Trader covered his mouth and tried not to gag.

With the exception of the intercession of the priests, the trading ceremony remained unchanged since the Narim sealed themselves behind the Black Gate generations ago. The Supreme Royal Trader would ring the iron bell, and a few moments later, a brass bell answered from within. The outer gate would open, and the teamsters would wheel the wagons into a central holding area. After that, the Supreme Royal Trader rang the outer bell again, and the outer gates closed. A groan would rise beyond the wall as the inner gates opened. The delegation always listened intently as someone, or something, unloaded the wagons. After several minutes, the groan returned and the inner bell rang again. In short order, the outer gates reopened and the goods would be replaced with gold ore and clay tablets bearing magical markings. The markings held the Narim's wishes for the next trade delegation and could only be interpreted by guild scribes.

Norrufi grasped the gray, fraying rope and swung the bell, beginning the ceremony in earnest. Under Norrufi's soft, pudgy hands, it issued a single, dull clunk.

A child could ring the bell louder, Bal-eeb thought, but knew it didn't matter. The Narim always heard.

As he waited for the answer to the call for trade, Bal-eeb's mind drifted to a woman with olive skin and almond eyes uncannily like his mother's. She possessed ambition every bit as naked and ruthless as Ashtoreth's. He could not say he loved this woman, though he'd never loved a woman. She did hold a certain raw allure the pampered creatures in court lacked. This woman held a more important allure than her body. She held the key to defeating the Scythians.

An unexpected western breeze caressed his face. He could almost feel the Great Sea's sultry air and her lithe, sun washed body pressed against his in the tall marsh grass.

Patience, my little Marsh Snake. I will return soon enough.

The breeze shifted again, dry and cold, snapping him back to the moment.

Something is wrong.

The inner bell did not answer. The outer gates remained closed.

Norrufi wiped the sweat from his brow and smiled weakly. "Perhaps the Narim are still asleep." He snatched the rope and yanked with all his considerable bulk. The bell clanged twice, slightly louder this time.

But the inner bell remained silent. The sun shone fully over the mountains. By now the carts should have been in the holding area between the gates.

The Supreme Trader laughed nervously as the warriors began to fidget. The delegates looked at one another, sensing the situation beginning to deteriorate.

No! This can't be happening.

Bal-eeb marched up to the bell.

"Your Excellency, perhaps you are correct, and the Narim slumber. May I assist you?"

The fat man wiped the sweat from his face. "Well...ah,..."

Bal-eeb didn't wait for a response. He grasped the rope with both fists and pulled with all his might. The kupar mounts creaked, and the bell rang so loudly everyone on the cliff covered their ears. It echoed for several seconds off the surrounding mountains before silence returned to the cliff.

The Captain of the Wall and the Supreme Royal Trader stood side-by-side, as the brass bell remained mute.

The Narim never fail to answer a call to trade. Never.

412

The Hur-po would have been less shocked if the sun had failed to rise.

Bal-eeb stepped back and glared up at the Black Gate towering above. The inner bell remained stubbornly mute. A knot formed in his gut as Bal-eeb sensed his plans slipping away.

Singular laughter arose behind the delegation's pale faces. Everyone turned to look at Shellbaz, who stood with his back to the delegation. He held a bottle of wine in one hand, his penis in the other and pissed over the side of the cliff, laughing gleefully as his urine rained down over the City of Gold.

Glossary of Terms and Characters

ai-halah: (eye-HAL-ah) Means "the reed and the wood", traditional Lo music. *Ai* is female vocals, *halah* is male vocals. Sung without instrumental accompaniment.

Adyghe (ad-YAH-gay) Mountains: Meaning unknown. Eastern edge of the known world, home of the Hur-po and the Narim. Never seen by the Lo.

a-g`an: (AYE-gha-ahn) Lo word meaning 'of the steppe' or 'enemy'.

Aizarg: (AYE-zarg) Means "good father." Sco-lo-ti of the Crane Clan and Uros of the Lo Nation, husband of Atamoda, father to Bat-tor and Kol-ok.

Alaya: (ah-LAH-ya) Means "her mother's joy." Wife to Levidi.

arun-ki: (ah-ROON-ki) Means "village upon the womb," a stilted village built off-shore in shallow lagoons.

Aryans: (AYE-rans) One of the three nomadic tribes of the g'an. Almost wiped out by the Scythians, exist now only at the edges of the steppe.

Atamoda: (At-ah-MOH-dah) Means "father's and mother's hope." Patesi-li of the Crane Clan, wife of Aizarg, mother to Ba-tor and Kol-ok.

Atta: (AT-ah) Means "old father." Levidi's grandfather, oldest man in the Crane Clan.

Ba'al: (BAH-awl) A sinister deity called The Black Dragon, worshipped by cult in Hur-ar.

Bal-eeb: (BAHL-eeb) Means (Hur) "sword of Ba'al." Second Prince of Hur-ar, Captain of the City Gate. Son of Ashtoreth.

Ba-lok: (BAY-lok) Means "hand that protects his people." Sco-lo-ti of the Minnow Clan, Second to Aizarg, husband to Kus-ge, son of Aie-lok, grandson of Setenay.

Bat-or: (BAHT-or) Means "eye of his people" or "beloved." Toddler and youngest son of Aizarg and Atamoda, brother to Kol-ok.

Bla-la-te: (blah-LAH-tay) Means "his mother is always watching." Xva's uncle and sco-lo-ti of the Trout Clan.

Carp Clan: Lo village of which Okta rules as the sco-lo-ti, the chieftain.

Crane Clan: Lo village of which Aizarg rules as the sco-lo-ti, the chieftain.

Council of Boats: A gathering of the more than one Lo village or perhaps the entire Lo nation, usually a festive event.

Ezra: (ezz-RAH) Meaning unknown. Sarah's brother. Thief and gang leader of pack of feral children in the slums of Hur-ar.

Fu Xi: (foo-HI or foo-ZI) Immortal demi-god, son of goddess Nuwa, often called the God of Names, or the Wanderer.

Gar Clan: Also known as the Lost Arun-ki. Kus-ge, wife of Ba-lok, hailed from this arun-ki, once the farthest east of all Lo villages. Shortly after Kus-ge departed as Ba-lok's new bride, the villagers vanished without a trace, the arun-ki burned to the water line.

g`an: (gh-AHN) Means "inner lands" or "steppe." Place of enemies. Lo word for the open steppe bordering the marshes north of the Great Sea.

Ghalen: (GAY-lehn) Means "strong stomach" or "fortitude." Younger brother of Masok, sco-lo-ti of the Turtle Clan.

Great Sea: Immense body of fresh water and home to the Lo people. Its northern shore is lined with vast expanses of reed beds, marshes and narrow coastal forests which give way to open steppe.

heli-dar: (hell-EYE-dar) Means "surrounded by death." The gateway to the afterlife. The Lo believe it is far out to sea beyond the reach of any boat.

Heise: (HAY-suh) Fu Xi's black stallion, his name simply means "Black".

Heng: (H-eng) Nuwa's last mortal husband.

Huise: (Hhway-suh) Fu Xi's gray mare, her name simply means "Gray".

Hur-ar: (her-AR) Means (Hur origin) "City of the Yellow Metal," located at the base of the Adyghe Mountains in a deep canyon overlooking the Hur River; also called *Ghund-Ghund*, The Place of Mazes, by the Scythians.

Hur-Po: (her-POWH) Means (Hur origin) "People of the Yellow Metal, those who inhabit Hur-Ar.

Hur River: River running north to south separating the Adyghe Mountains from the open g'an; spanned by the Kupar Bridge.

Ice Men: Savage race living in the far north lands.

Isp: Meaning "lady of the water." Patesi-le selected to serve the Uros.

Kol-ok: (kawl-AWK) Meaning "protects his home." Aizarg's and Atamoda's oldest boy, brother to Bat-or.

köy-lo-hely: (coy-ee-LOW-hell-ee) Meaning "the sacred place where the people gather"; a large wooden platform without a hut at the heart of the Lo community, usually a in the middle of a lagoon encircled by huts.

Kus-ge: (kuss-GEE) Means "leads with fist." Ba-lok's wife, hails from the mysterious Lost Arun-ki, the farthest Lo settlement to the east than vanished years earlier.

Ood-i: (OOWD-eye) Means (Sammujad origin) "works leather." Member of the Crane Clan, husband of Ula, father to Su-gár.

Levidi: (lev-EE-dee) Means (Sammujad origin) "sheltered water." Aizarg's best friend, husband of Alaya.

li-ge: (lie-GHEE) Literal translation "spirit and heart." Lo symbol meaning "balance" or "joining of flesh and spirit."

Lo: (LOW) Means "the people" or "the family." Can also mean "humble." Nation of fishing tribes divided into different clans. They live along the Great Sea's northern shore in stilted villages over the water.

Masok: (MAY-sock) Means "man who walks in front." Sco-lo-ti of the Turtle Clan and Ghalen's older brother.

Narim: (nah-RHEEM) Race of long-lived demi-gods who once walked the g'an, and now only exist in the Black Fortress in the mountains above Hur-ar. Called "Narts" by the Scythians.

Nushen: (NEW-shen) Village of Goddess, an ancient village that has served the goddess Nuwa for ages.

Nuwa: (NEW-ah) She is also called the Queen of the West and the Celestial Queen. A goddess who sired Fu Xi with a human man. She dwells in seclusion in her temple on Tortoise Mountain above the village of Nushen.

Minnow Clan: Lo village ruled by Ba-lok as sco-lo-ti.

Oeto-sy: (oy-TOW-see) The sky god or "father above" of the Lo pantheon. Husband of Psatina, father of Sethagasi.

Okta: (AWK-tah) Means "Blessed male." Leader of the Carp Arun-ki. An older sco-lo-ti, but not yet an elder. Tall, lean and light complexioned like Aizarg, but older, nearing the age of an elder.

patesi-le: (pah-TEH-see-lee) Means "holy woman." A lo shaman, always a woman and the wife of the sco-lo-ti.

Psatina: (sat-EEN-a) The Earth Mother, prime goddess of the Lo pantheon.

sco-lo-ti: (skoh-LOW-tee) Means "leader of the people", village chieftain in peacetime.

sagar: (SAY-garr) Sammujad spears, heavier and longer, made to defend against Scythian horse warriors.

Sammujad: (sam-MOO-jahd) one of the three nomadic tribes inhabiting the g'an. They occupy the fringes of the steppe and rely mostly on trading to survive. They have been pushed back in recent years by the Scythians.

Sarah: Meaning unknown. Former pleasure slave in bondage in Virag's camp. She is originally of the Hur-ar and vows to lead Aizarg's party to the Narim.

Scythians: (sith-EE-ans) Means (Sammujad origin) "the blended ones." Horse warriors who've come to dominate the g'an over the course of several generations, they are the most savage and feared of the three steppe tribes.

Setenay: (set-EN-aye) Means "rose with many thorns." Patesi-li of the Minnow Clan, grandmother to Ba-lok, oldest living member of the Lo people. Called "The Grandmother of the Lo."

Sethagasi: (seth-GOS-ee) The sea goddess of the Lo pantheon, daughter of Psatina and Oeto-sy. Synonymous with Great Sea. Also means "womb."

Summoning of Spears: Ceremony where the Lo choose an Uros to lead them in time of war.

Silt Flats: Place near Crane Clan village with the shallows meet the deep sea and large waves form and the village boys wave ride atop their small reed boats.

Su-gár: (sue-GARR) Means "sunbeam", daughter of Ood-i and Ula.

Tiejiang: (Teh-ZHANG) Blacksmith of Nushen, friend of Fu Xi

Time of the Spear: Lo term for a time of war when an Uros leads all the Lo nation, superseding the power of individual sco-lo-ti.

Tortoise Mountain: Home of the Goddess Nuwa.

Trout Clan: Lo village of which Bla-la-te rules as the sco-lo-ti, the chieftain.

Turtle Clan: Lo village ruled by Masok as sco-lo-ti, also home to his younger brother, Ghalen.

Ula: (OOW-lah) Means (Sammujad origin) "small fish." Wife of Leedi, mother of Su-gár.

Uros: (UR-ows) Means "source of power." War Chieftain of the Lo.

Valley of the Beasts: A valley discovered by Aizarg and Levidi filled with a milling multitude of animals of every sort.

Virag: (veye-RAG) Means (Sammujad origin) "He is black inside." Sammujad Slaver, former owner of Sarah.

Wu:(WOO) A mysterious land far to the east of Cin. Fu Xi thought of this land as the end of the earth..

Xva: (ZEE-vah) Meaning "beloved son." Aizarg's cousin and youngest man in the Crane Clan Nation.